Rapidan

By the same author:

The Man Who Walked Out of the Jungle

Rapidan

Jeff Wallace

2017, Jeff Wallace

Historical fiction / suspense / literary fiction / slavery / U.S. Civil War / Underground Railroad / Virginia

Rapidan / Jeff Wallace

ISBN
978-0-9983291-5-4

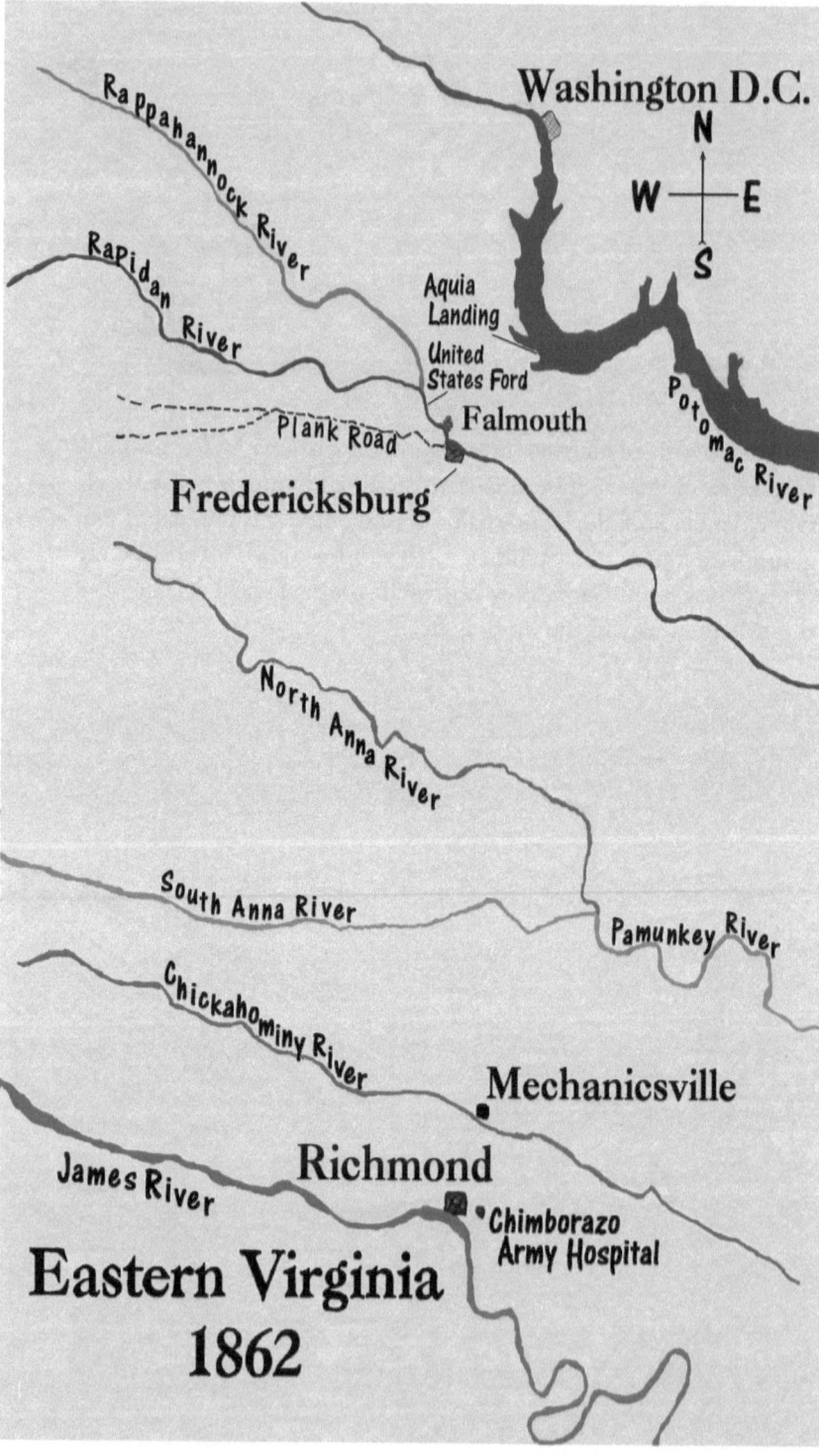

Part I

- 1 -

Anna remembered a day long ago when she'd pulled a cinder sack over her head and emerged with blackened skin. For a while she'd gone about playing she was black and mimicking the voice, provoking the single occasion when her mother ever thumped her. The swinging palm had stung dully through the dress layers. "You must not play this way!"

"Why?"

"You diminish a people who are crushed at no fault of their own—to mock them is a sin. And look at you! What have you done to your hair? You're covered with soot!"

On the night they delivered Captain Holland, Anna from behind the cast-iron gate could make out carriage lanterns far up the Osborne Turnpike below a sky like ashes. The scarcity of candle wax and lamp oil had extinguished other lights; you might as well don a cinder sack on your head as try to see anything.

A sigh gave away Bookman outside the gate. He hunched against the stone wall; she could glimpse only his straw hat brim. "I'll hail 'em," he said. "No need for you to wait out."

She said, "I'm happy to wait for the army."

Bookman caught meanings in inflections. From his youth as a slave came an intuition for the ones who'd owned him. Though he was a freedman now, the habit was permanent. "Be careful what you say 'round these men, Anna."

"I know that."

Gripping the gate, she stretched her arms, arched, let her hair plunge to the bare space between her shoulders. The air seeped like unpicked fruit. Sweat pasted her forearms.

"Things gonna change after tonight," he said.

"We've had it too quiet, you mean?"

"Quiet is precious nowadays."

"Unfair to keep for ourselves?"

"I don't know what's fair or not. Too much of this war not to get some on you."

She liked his idea of the war as something spattered. "I think those who want the war should have it in abundance and leave the rest of us alone."

The coach neared. Extended on poles, the lanterns pitched yellow funnels that crept up her dress. She smelled dust, the wheels' grease, the animals' sweat.

"The Van Meers' house?"

"You've found us," she replied.

"Where's Mr. Van Meer?"

"He'll be back soon. I'm his daughter. You may come in."

Already Bookman had gripped a horse's bridle to lead them through the carriageway. The coach had odd dimensions, long like a hearse, tall like a circus wagon, and the compartments and skinny windows formed jumbled rectangles. Bending forward, the driver unhooked the lantern poles and pivoted them inward so they'd slip through the gate. In the yard he swung them out again ten feet abreast. The swaying lamps cast dizzying shadows. Partly muddied over, the words *Chimborazo Army Hospital* surged and faded.

The two soldiers dismounted. In their tunics and hats, they resembled costumed men in a stage drama who strode with dire purpose and enacted a ceremony too serious for polite chatter. She lit a foyer lantern and led them along the corridor, where one of them paused to measure its width, an action she'd witnessed only once before, during the undertaker's call after her mother died. At the hallway's end, in the rear sitting room converted to a sickroom, the soldiers peered at the walls and ceiling, maybe for cobwebs or other signs of uncleanliness. All day the Van Meers and their freedmen servants had prepared the room. She'd sheeted the bed and laid on their best embroidered quilt. Her father had brought in the bedside table and lamp, adding the last of their lamp oil. Bookman and Sarah had scrubbed from the window tops to the floorboards. "We put in a new screen," she said, tapping with her fingertip to dislodge a moth that clung to the outer cheesecloth. "My father inspected everything."

"Is he a doctor?"

"He's a teacher at the Kingsland School."

The teacher's title seemed to satisfy the soldier. He said, "We'll get the captain settled momentarily. Can you sign?"

"What do you mean?"

"The hospital receipt, to take possession of the patient. We can wait for your father if you'd like."

"I'll sign."

Bookman had been right when he'd said things were going to change after tonight. Theirs was a quiet house; never had soldiers intruded. The soldiers made no regard to suppress their voices; they grunted and strained to maneuver the litter through the hallway. They did display courtesy in unhooking the paintings from the walls, fortunate because, heaving a brass-cornered trunk, they nicked the plaster. Powder silted to the floor.

This past year, to conserve oil, most of the lamps had stayed dark. Now they glowed brightly, lit by the soldiers lest they crash bearing the captain and his accoutrements. The lamps gorged smoke, burning not merely the oil but all that had settled in their basins in the months of disuse: mold, dust, pollen, a driblet of silver polish, the remnants of moths—all became ingredients in the tiny pyres. Eyes stinging, she waited in the foyer while they labored in the sickroom, taking too long, she thought. How could her father have offered their house for a wounded Confederate's convalescence?

The soldiers concluded their noisy business. The one, his beard as fresh as spring grass, slid from his tunic a leather folder he opened to a pinned document, peeled wax paper from an inkpad, and rolled the pen's tip to lift with a flourish. "You can write your name, or just inscribe an X if you can't write."

In a clerk's precise script, the receipt said that she accepted the transfer of John S. Holland, Captain of Cavalry, CSA. Neatly she penned her name, Anna Van Meer, on the first official document she'd ever signed.

"Dr. Slate will visit tomorrow to instruct you in the patient's care."

"What should we do until then?"

"Change the dressin's twice a day. We just did, so they'll last till morning."

"How... serious is his wound?"

"Oh, quite serious. A deep wound is always so, and the captain's 'specially. He took a bullet in his thigh, fractured the femur bone and tore the muscles. A wound such rarely 'scapes amputation."

She sensed that the soldier, his face as soft as hers, craved uttering words so weighty.

3

"So may I meet Captain Holland?"

Not having had anything to say until now, the older one hawed, "You signed for him—he's posted to your house. You can do with him whatever you like!" He hacked donkey sounds that bespoke crude thoughts.

"I see."

The younger one reasserted himself. "If an emergency arises, send for Dr. Slate at the Chimborazo Hospital." He craned out the door until he sighted Bookman. "Your boy'll guide us out?"

"Yes. Good evening."

She waited until doing so would no longer seem impolite and closed the door. Extinguished the hallway lamps, which only spewed more smoke that drifted toward the sickroom. Their guest coughed.

Already the affair had tired her of soldiers, and she thought the tiredness would not soon lapse.

Too much of this war not to get some on you.

Her father would be home soon. He'd inflicted this disquietude— let *him* deal with the captain. She stopped at the foot of the stairs. She shouldn't go to bed before she introduced herself to the convalescent, asked if he were comfortable, and informed him that her father would be home imminently. No Southern woman would fail to perform such a courtesy, and wasn't that the point, so they could play the role of proper Southerners? If the captain wished to sleep, she could douse the lamp. All this seemed correct, yet her legs proved reluctant to move. She attributed her sudden lethargy to the lateness of the hour, the smoke in the air, and the day's profound strangeness.

* * *

A noise clapped her out of sleep. She sat up in bed to see a dust cloud purl past the window, raising a smell like an old log turned over. Felt as if she'd been plucked from another place—a dream vivid and already fleeing, leaving behind her mother's pale outline and the sensation of lost comfort.

The noise again—a single knuckle's peck. Only her father knocked like that.

She said, "What is it?"

The door eased open, and Henry Van Meer leaned past the frame. She made out his buttoned vest and starched collar. Tufts of his hair, more white than gray, leapt like little devil horns. He said, "I did not wake you, I hope."

She fingered her hair from her view. "You did. I was dreaming of mother. I cannot remember more."

He entered and stood at the lower bed corner whose post leaned. By habit, he straightened the stanchion ineffectually. "I'm sorry for disturbing you."

"It's fine."

He smiled. He knew that when his daughter declared that something was fine—in fact when any Southern woman said so—she generally meant the opposite.

He said, "I dream of her too. Her face is an oval facing me. I strain to see her clearly. She looks at me as if through a veil."

"My dreams of her are like that."

"And when she speaks to me, though her voice is audible, I cannot figure what her words mean."

This part did not sound like Anna's dreams. Her mother's words, what she remembered of them, preserved their meanings. "Why do we forget?"

"Our minds are like pitchers of water, and as we age, we must pour out what we've kept from the past to allow room for the fresh. I would rather forget my own name than anything your mother ever said. Nature does not ask my permission. In succumbing, we shouldn't feel we've done less by her."

Another gust rattled the window.

"Just a storm," he said. "Started blowing last night when I came home. You were asleep."

She asked, "How is our guest?"

"I have not seen him this morning. Last night he seemed settled enough. Did you speak to him?"

"Ever so briefly. I would not be surprised if he thinks me a fool of the first order."

Her father cocked his head. "Why do you say so?"

"After the soldiers left, to be polite, I entered his room and told him we were charmed to have a fellow named Holland stay with us, inasmuch as we too are of Dutch ancestry."

"He must have found it a pleasant opener."

"Apparently not. He replied, 'My family are Americans,' as if I had insulted him by suggesting that a man so named could have Dutch blood in his veins. And I thought, is the name even Dutch—what if *Holland* is English? So I said, 'I am an American too, perhaps not from so exclusive a lineage as yourself. And do not all Americans come from somewhere, whether Holland, or England, or Africa?'"

"You said Africa?"

"Are the Negroes not also Americans?"

"I meant…"

"I recognize I should not have reacted defensively. The hour was late, and I was weary. In any event, you will be happy to hear he assigned no significance to my statement or my rhetorical question. He said he hoped I would forgive him for being unpracticed in trivial conversation…"

"He was exhausted, dear. To travel in the hospital coach from Richmond must have taken hours."

"…implying that anything I might say would be so superficial, even the time of a man who fribbles away his day in a sickbed would be dissipated in the engagement."

"He is unaccustomed to social etiquette. I'm sure he has not recently encountered young women of your quality and was at a loss for words. Imagine how awkward for him, to be clasped in a bed, in that strange box, when a young woman suddenly entered. He could not adapt."

"Why should he have to? Who did he expect to see—are only *men* to be found in the houses beyond Richmond?"

"My dear, please."

"That box, what is it for?"

"I don't know. I've never seen the like. We shall learn from Dr. Slate when he arrives."

* * *

Surrounding Holland, the unfamiliar house and its creaks, knocks, and recurrent, bewildering sounds of scratching. At night at the Chimborazo Hospital, orderlies with lanterns had circulated through the wards, and when not walking their rounds, they'd sat alert at their watchposts, their lanterns suspended nearby. Thus everywhere illumination had brushed the planks or ceilings or bed sheets. In this room, only the distant lightning cut breaches in the dark. He did not care for the blackness that sat like a wolf upon his chest.

Dawn improved his perceptions, at least those he could attain from the bed. To his right, the door and sliver of the hallway. When the orderlies had borne him in last night, he'd apprehended a decorous house. The parlor furniture still wore its summer dress—periwinkle-striped gingham covers. Above the foyer, candles in a gilded candelabrum sharpened the ornate white moldings and the hallway's barrel-vaulted ceiling. The orderlies had bumped into the walls again and again, and he'd scolded them to show care.

Along his room's lower side ran a louvered, framed-glass door whose six sections on brass hinges folded like an accordion. Beyond he observed an enclosed courtyard with limewashed walls and a fitted-stone floor. A soil strip edged the patio flagstones, and flowers fronted scrolling vines. A burgundy rosehead bashed against the cheesecloth screen, elucidating the scratching noise.

In his early convalescence, he who for many months had slept no more than five hours a night, rarely in a true bed, sometimes on a moving horse, had luxuriated in the license to doze at will. The original traction mount had required extra space, and he'd enjoyed a modest separation from the other patients, a surrogate for privacy. The comfort soon had vanished. During the Seven Days battles, the wounded had thronged the ward, their wails persisting at all hours amid ceaseless voices, hammering on wood, footsteps on the planks, and rattling wagons. The cacophony had shattered his ability to rest, and the hours accumulated like a greasy dust he grew manic to alleviate. He'd conjured pictures on the wall opposite: the hills at West Point; the Shenandoah's dewy meadows; the Potomac's rapids; his horse, now dead; the faces of his men, some also dead.

Occupying a plateau above the James River on Richmond's eastern outskirts, the Chimborazo Hospital was a complex of wards, support houses, recuperative annexes, and mortuaries that plank walkways connected. By the summer of 1862 the South's largest medical facility, no less did it covet its ward space. Soon after Dr. Slate had removed the traction and substituted the Banderton device in late August, the casualties from Second Manassas had filled every square foot, and the overworked medics had groused that the *infernal box* occupied too much room. Though the complaints hadn't encroached on his privileges—the celebrated Dr. Slate got his way about everything—they had fed Holland's impatience, and he'd seized the chance to move to a private residence for his further convalescence.

The house was cooler than the hospital. Physically he was content. The orderlies had secured the sturdy stand, adjusted the box settings, and fitted the bedpan under him—necessary after the long coach ride. He lay on soft sheets, much in contrast to the ward's rough linens. A quilt covered him. Nonetheless he wondered whether he should have remained at the Chimborazo, where personal modesty served no purpose, and among those whose guts and limbs had been cut through, embarrassment did not exist. In the hospital he'd become accustomed to bedpans, and last night he'd been peeing without much aforethought when Anna had stopped by to introduce herself, causing him to retard his urination abruptly. He'd gone ashen with shame. Fortunately, from her demeanor, she had not detected the sound or scent. Of what she'd said, and he'd said in reply, he had no recollection.

Her father, Henry Van Meer, had come by later and agreeably emptied the bedpan, though the task was obviously beneath him. Holland hoped there was someone else—wasn't there a servant about?—to handle the unpleasant chore henceforth. Above all, he did not wish for Anna to be the one to attend to him. He did not know why he felt this way. Perhaps because she was quite pretty, and obviously he was not on his best display in this posture.

* * *

She dressed and came downstairs to prepare for the doctor to arrive. Their first visitor was not him, rather the traveling white preacher who held services once a month in the upper meadow. The wind blustered, and the preacher asked if he could use the buggy house whose ground floor also served as their stable, and whose upper floor housed the freedmen.

"I forgot he was coming this morning," her father said after he'd ushered the fellow into the buggy house.

She asked, "What's the matter?"

"Dr. Slate is due. Those two will not mix well."

"Why must they mix? The preacher will be with the Negroes."

He shook his head. "I am going to tell him not to come anymore. The sound of his sermons will carry. With an officer convalescing in our house, the preacher's themes shall be inconvenient."

"*Everything* about the officer's presence is inconvenient."

"Dear, I am aware of how you feel, yet we go to this trouble for a reason. To be seen as loyal citizens is useful. The preacher is not the one to help us convey the impression; in fact, he will accomplish precisely the opposite. Why should we set ourselves to a plan, only to permit it to become unraveled?"

How rare, she thought, to witness his patience frayed. Why did he strive to create the illusion they were supporters of the Southern cause? They'd never gone to such lengths before. And how far must they press the charade?

To clear space for the congregation, the blacks had rolled the buggy, wagon, and pushcart outside, and they'd tethered the two horses to the meadow fence. By the kitchen window, Anna listened and occasionally glanced past the curtains. Sounds permeated the wall, and she recognized the black women's murmur like a wheel askew on its axle. She mused at how the blacks in their worship acted differently from the white people. Whereas the latter stood solemn and composed, the former made varieties of noises, from grumbles to exclamations to hoots, and often they erupted spontaneously into song. In the buggy house they sat on plank benches or crates. Here were slaves from the neighboring farms, the faces familiar to her all her life, though she knew none by name. Not as many slaves as in years past, and fewer still were able-bodied men. When the Northern army had invaded in the summer, a preponderance of the white residents had fled, taking along their valuable working slaves.

Carola, Sarah's and Jerome's six-year-old daughter, sported a braided pigtail that swung against her flowered Sunday dress. The dress did not fit her anymore; the fabric was threadbare.

I must buy new cloth.

Not long ago, Anna had taken in mind to teach Carola to read. Jerome had refused, contending that his daughter was too young. In his obstinacy, he seemed to have admonished the girl to stay away from the white woman. Now, at Anna's approach, the girl would dart away.

Against a buggy wheel, legs crossed, leaned Bookman. Five years older than Anna, like a sage half-brother, he was the single male aside from her father with whom she felt wholly comfortable. Of course, she could describe him this way to no one beyond their household. Her father and mother had bought him as a slave boy and immediately freed him, and though educating blacks was illegal, they'd taught and renamed him as a way to declare he was literate. Her oldest memories evoked unwieldy words from his lessons. When he'd stumbled over one, her father would pronounce and define it and instruct him to repeat the syllables. Bookman had filled her ears with his elocution of the incomprehensible—*ameliorate, guarantor, persecute*—and she'd perceived him as so advanced she might emulate but not surpass him. Despite his black skin, she'd not at first connected him to the race society cast as inferior—an attitude universal beyond the house. Her naïveté had ceased on the day her father had driven her and Bookman in the buggy to New Market. Stopping to purchase something, he'd left them alone for a minute, and a white man had come along and ordered Bookman to help him, perhaps to hold a mule. Bookman had refused to step down from the buggy, asserting he was required to stay to protect little Anna.

"Well, aren't you the sassy monkey," the fellow had nipped, and thereupon had cuffed Bookman on the head.   Returning, her father had rebuked the bully, affirming that the boy indeed had been under instructions to stay with Anna, and the man had apologized—to her father, not to Bookman.

In the freedmen's quarters above the buggy house, another measure of intimidation. Jerome, able neither to read nor write, had criticized and ranted at his young brother-in-law. She remembered wondering why her father and mother never had intervened. Over the years, Jerome's railing had abated, though the two men still argued occasionally.

When she dreamt, her mother spoke to her. This occurred almost every night, and her mother's presence usually made sleep a comforting sojourn. Anna did not believe in spirits—dreams simply were stories the sleeping mind invented. She knew this because she dreamt of Bookman too, and in them he was mostly just himself, one of the household's strong hinges and forever good natured. Sometimes she dreamt of him in a way she could reveal to no one, a figure who pressed his muscled skin against hers. She did not dwell on the images or allow them to follow her into her waking hours, yet sometimes they recurred as if of their own accord, one in particular, of his wide right hand on the bare, stretched skin of her ribs, the ebony distinct against the white. Watching him work, she'd discretely studied his hand to discern if it was the same as the one she'd dreamt, and it was.

In the summer after her mother died, her father had taken her and Bookman on a long journey to visit friends who lived near Culpeper Courthouse. They'd come to a promontory above the Rapidan River, and her father had pointed westward at the hazy raised horizon. "The river descends from the Blue Ridge. The mountains run all the way to Pennsylvania."

By the river, the air had cooled deliciously, and her father had relented when she'd begged to swim. Wading into the chill current, she'd shrieked, and she in her slip and Bookman in his pants had splashed and shouted, chasing each other shore to shore in the shallows. They'd stayed in the water until late afternoon, and she'd so delighted in the frolic she hadn't minded the sunburn on her shoulders and neck. In the years afterward, she'd imagined plunging into the Rapidan, wearing her slip and pulling a floated bundle behind on a cord, and Bookman beside her, both of them kicking wide to propel to the opposite shore. How beautiful, to emerge from the water with Bookman, and to follow the Blue Ridge to a free place.

She'd asked him why he hadn't gone north to Pennsylvania or Ohio, states where blacks supposedly were treated as equals. They'd been by the old well—an important place in those days—and she'd lingered while he chopped wood. She enjoyed his company she didn't often have—he roved everywhere performing his chores, took the buggy into town, and might be on the roof one minute and across the turnpike by the riverside the next. Bookman had the latitude to organize his work as he pleased, although, unlike her, he did not possess the option to do nothing. He said, "My sister and brother-in-law don't wanna leave. Carola's too young—no sense taking a child from where she has shelter and supper to somewhere she don't. Who knows how we'd make a livin'?"

"Why not go on your own?"

"We're a family. Ain't me gonna be the one to break it up. Anyway, I'm not so courageous as to set off by myself alone."

"Why do you need courage to go? You have your freedom papers."

He snorted. "Goin' is harder than you think. Stories come back 'bout men who've headed to a northern city, only to find themselves among whites from Europe who work jobs for low wages. Northerners don't need the farming or horse-tending skills we have. A man went there who ran a whole plantation, scores of workers, and he couldn't get work 'cause he couldn't keep up with the boys from Ireland tossin' eighty-pound sacks. And when we *do* get jobs, the whites resent us—they say we're takin' the work that's rightly theirs and money out of their pockets. Soon as blacks intrude on their comfort, they forget about equality."

She said, "If I go, will you go with me?"

He laughed as if this were a jovial game. "You'll have to ask me closer to the time."

The scent of the chopped wood, the light soft, nobody else near. On such occasions, had he touched her, she might have let him. But he never did.

What had started her thinking of all this? Maybe the preacher's sermon full of metaphors. His words to the blacks edged on abolitionism, which was why she listened crouched by the window—he wouldn't have spoken so had whites been present. "In life we are the children of God separated from Him by time, long and gripped with pain, but finite, and at the end, Jesus will be waiting, and He'll reach out his hand and lead you across the River Jordan to the cool shore, where all people are truly equal in God's sight."

Her father touched her on the shoulder. He'd donned the coat that she remembered him wearing alongside her mother, and he fidgeted with a loose button. "Dr. Slate is here. We shall need Bookman and Sarah to assist us."

"They're in the buggy house hearing the sermon. Might they finish?"

"I'm afraid not. Please call them out." His voice creaked, and his brows furrowed. "Now, dear."

* * *

She summoned Sarah and Bookman—to the chagrin of the gathered worshippers—and felt again the disconsolation at her father's introduction of a Confederate officer into their house. His presence was like a noxious smell that rendered her life wretched. Pronouncing her father a fool under her breath, she imposed a polite demeanor before she stepped into the parlor, the house's largest room her mother had called '*le grand salon.*'

Her father said, "Dear, this is Doctor Thomas Slate. Doctor, my daughter Anna."

She extended her hand that Dr. Slate did not kiss, merely shook. Tall, poised, gracious, so unlike last night's soldiers, he ranked as a colonel in the Confederate army, though he wore no uniform or military paraphernalia. A gold watch chain extended from his riding jacket; the heels of his glistening brown boots resonated on the floorboards. The road was dusty, and he must have wiped them fastidiously before entering the house. His dark, combed-back hair topped a broad forehead with no furrow marks, as if he did not worry much. Releasing her hand, he presented her father with a slender cloth sack tied at the top. "Courtesy of the Chimborazo Hospital, to ease the cost of burning your lamps attending to the patient."

Her father loosened the string to uncover a full bottle of lamp oil. "Thank you, we shall make good use."

She'd been prepared to despise the doctor who hallmarked this hateful situation. Her hostility was not taking root. Perhaps it was the politeness he paid to Sarah when she served him tea, looking a bit harried after her abrupt commandeering from the buggy house.

"How thoughtful of you," remarked Slate. "What is your name?"

"Sarah, sir."

"Sarah, thank you kindly."

The white people sat around the low table.

"I will be relieved when this strange weather ends," he said, folding his butterscotch leather riding gloves, first aligning the fingers, an act remarkable for its idiosyncrasy, she thought. Who went to such pains to fold a glove? Perhaps he did so because they were huge, fitting his hands that spanned immensely from the first knuckle to the fourth, without rings. She did not know how to regard him. His confidence and deference were at opposite ends. If his meticulous ways matched with what she thought surgeons were like, his sizable hands did not, though the way he reposed them in his lap did again.

"I rode through tempests of wind and dust. In places the air seemed to rush from an oven, in others from a damp cave. Fortunately, I encountered no delay."

The preacher's sermon thumped through the walls. Slate's expression registered puzzlement.

"We are grateful you could visit so soon," her father hurriedly inserted.

"In truth, I am refreshed to be free of Chimborazo for a few hours. What a restless hive. Early this morning, wagons brought men from a skirmish afar. The deliveries happen frequently, and often the wounded are many."

Her father remarked, "Dr. Slate is among the most accomplished surgeons in the Confederacy."

"Accomplishment through trial and error," Slate said. "and the process is aptly named. From war's harshness, we've developed new methods to save lives. Not even in Europe have physicians attempted to apply innovations on so vast a scale. We've discovered much about how to stop the bleeding. Sadly, the immediate care for the wounded takes place at the site of battle, and often they die from loss of blood. Yet if a man reaches my operating table alive—young Captain Holland is an example—much can be done. I'm immensely pleased at his progress, and I have looked forward to shepherding him to this next phase."

"We find ourselves curious about the box around his leg," said her father.

"Named after Banderton, the inventor. Only a handful exist, and just one at the Chimborazo Hospital, though I have contracted for more. They require exquisite craftsmanship in wood and metal, and certain of the materials are hard to obtain. The filigree screens, for instance, are fashioned in Europe, and we must substitute for them, for the original is no longer available due to the sea blockade."

"The blockade is indeed a nuisance," commented her father. "We used to drink coffee. These days, we get by with the spicebush tea you now sample."

"You were saying about the box," interjected Anna. She'd not spoken until now, and something in her tone, perhaps its intensity, made Slate evaluate her. She did not like for men to study her, yet she thought his gaze bespoke intellectual and not amorous curiosity.

"The purpose is to immobilize the healing bone while permitting free access to the open wound, and to flex the limb to various positions so the muscles do not contract and weaken irreversibly. The therapy is based on theories we are proving in earnest application."

"So the therapy remains unproven?"

He smiled. "You are a keen listener, Anna. John's leg suffered a compound fracture together with a large gunshot wound. Rarely have such cases escaped amputation. His treatment introduced revolutionary techniques, concluding with the use of the extraordinary box. Enough time has passed that I am confident of success, or I would not have allowed him to leave the Chimborazo."

"What about Captain Holland merits special consideration, to be the subject for this care?"

"Another superb question, one that speaks to the dilemmas of medicine. In an ideal world, the best treatments would be available to everyone in need. Sadly, I have never witnessed the ideal. We must attend to thousands of wounded men, some with wounds as grievous as John's, and little time avails to deliberate. He is fortunate—his father is a man of powerful influence in his region of Virginia, a benefactor of the Confederacy and a friend of President Jefferson Davis. John's father managed to convince a district in the western hills against joining the counties that sided with the North. People say he is headed for a post in the national cabinet. I've heard too that President Davis intervened personally in John's case, with those of higher station than mine, of course. The Chimborazo Hospital thus was honored to expend every effort to spare his son's leg."

Anna listened for a hint of irony in this last statement; heard none. "Is his leg spared?"

"I am sanguine, though I cannot reassure you completely. Gangrene is an insidious foe that lurks in the shadows, like an assassin who contrives his moment to kill."

"What if gangrene arises?"

"We would have to take the leg quickly, to save his life."

Appalling, the notion that a man's leg might be amputated within their house. She glanced to her father, anticipating he might have the same reaction. His face remained expressionless.

"Thank you for your candor," she said queasily.

"I do not mean to alarm you—the peak danger has passed. Yet candor *is* important, so you may grasp the principles that underlie the therapy." He positioned his teacup on its saucer. "Shall we call upon our distinguished patient?"

Her father led them through the hallway, past the paintings restored to their places, to the sickroom whose curtains stood open. The daylight made the space feel altogether different from last night. She noted the rich tone of the captain's skin, compared to hers pale in a way people liked to label pure, and she considered toneless. Someone, perhaps Bookman, or the captain himself, had combed his wavy dark hair.

He smiled like a host in his own parlor.

- 2 -

At the Chimborazo, they'd told him he would lose his leg. Certainly he would have, had he been wounded at a place more distant than the highway by Mechanicsville, or with men not skilled to ride fast horses with a wounded man lashed on. Even in the feverish state in which he'd reached the hospital, he preserved the lucidity to comprehend they were preparing to amputate. In the operating ward, the blade's metal glinted before being tucked out of sight. Beneath the ceiling trusses ran rows of windows meant to admit sunlight. Now clouds darkened the sky, and the orderlies hoisted lit lanterns that swung like guttering artillery flares. Panicked shadows undulated on the beams. He vomited past his shoulder, and the liquid spattered on the bare planks. Into view sidled a black woman who mopped the spill.

The news he was Malcolm Holland's son began to circulate, and what would have been the staff physician's perfunctory decision leapt to the hospital's elitemost strata, and to the finest surgeon in Richmond and perhaps all Virginia, Dr. Thomas Slate. In his starched white shirt and burgundy bow tie, the doctor examined the apple-sized hole in the thigh.

"The bullet broke your femur in two places," Slate announced, wiping his hands with which he'd probed the wound, "tearing the skin and muscle on the way out, leaving a formidable hole and much damaged tissue. I suspect that something slowed the bullet that otherwise would have obliterated the bone, as generally occurs when a speeding mass hits the human skeleton."

"It went through my horse first," said Holland.

"Ah. Your poor beast rendered you a true service. The breaks are clean. Nonetheless, with two fractures, combined with the open wound, amputation is recommended."

"May you say what is *not* recommended?"

"Therein is the devil's choice. If I spare your leg, the odds are about thirty percent you will die, even with the best care. If you survive, you'll face a forty-percent peril we shall still be forced to amputate, as wounds like yours may become gangrenous. And, the remaining thirty-percent chance you will recover with your limb mended."

"I choose the leg."

"Said without hesitation. No surprise from a man of youth and vigor. Yet I must caution you to take stock of your situation. If I amputate today, your chances of surviving are double those of the alternative course. You may limp on a wooden prosthetic, but live to see your children and grandchildren."

The words echoed from more than two months ago. Now Dr. Slate entered the room, and trailing came Henry Van Meer, his daughter Anna, and Sarah and Bookman, who looked quite alike—he guessed they were siblings. These four and Slate traced around the bed like a cane, with Slate at the tip and Anna the handle. She was the most distant physically and perhaps mentally; her eyes roved the room's corners.

Slate pressed three fingers against Holland's forehead. "There are physicians who can detect from the complexion when a patient has a fever. I myself haven't mastered the skill, so I must rely on the touch. John, you are not feverish, and considering the stresses of yesterday's journey, that is reassuring."

"Thank you, sir, and generous of you to spend your precious time to travel here."

"I was happy to do so, to see you and to meet these people who have volunteered themselves unselfishly to your care."

"The least we can do," puffed Van Meer.

On Anna's face, Holland caught a shudder that was gone almost before it appeared. He flicked his eyes to the doctor.

Slate must have detected the patient's changed countenance, for his voice fell. "John, I apologize for the entrance just now. I should have met with you privately before initiating this gathering."

"I'm not at all troubled."

"You're certain?"

"Fully."

"So you won't mind if I give our hosts a brief lesson on the box? They need to know—they will be applying the adjustments."

"Of course. Always a pleasure to hear of this device I've grown so fond of."

"I'm sure you have," chuckled Slate, and his voice resumed its full resonance, commencing the lecture Holland had heard more times than he cared to count: "The femur is an amazing bone, the longest in the human body, and extraordinarily strong. Not only does the femur support a person's weight, when he or she strides, it levers the body and thus must withstand longitudinal and lateral stresses. Imagine the handle of a well pump." With his arm, Slate mimicked the levering motion.

"To mend the femur, fractured at two places, we applied a newly devised technique called Buck's Extension, in which we pulled the leg straight by weighted cords. This allowed the femur to set correctly despite the countervailing impulse of the muscles to twist. The traction lasted eight weeks, as meanwhile we endeavored to stave off gangrene. We know that a connection exists between the development of gangrene and the cleanliness, or lack thereof, of the wound and the surrounding skin. As a wound tries to heal, blood and other fluids seep. The tissues around the broken skin are exceedingly vulnerable to infection, and gangrene may begin to feast on healthy flesh, ultimately spreading and killing the victim. We have learned to dress the wound lightly and change the bandages frequently. At the Chimborazo over the past year, we have treated a plethora of open wounds, yielding unparalleled insights."

The doctor sidled to the wooden box with its four lids. "Now we come to the second-phase therapy, in which the bone remains fragile, and we flex the leg to counteract the rigidity the knee and muscles have adopted from their long immobilization in Buck's Extension. We accomplish this via the Banderton box, which as you can see is suspended above the mattress on this sturdy stand. The lids can be opened or closed depending on the leg's configuration—horizontal or flexed. Within are turnbuckles connected to wires that steady the limb from changeable points. The pinions conform, and we regulate the leg's bend according to a timetable. In the first setting, A, B, and C hold the bone in place, and the next, D, E, and F, and so on. The interval permits us to freshen the dressing."

"Indeed brilliant," gabbled Henry Van Meer.

Holland saw vexation cloud Anna's face.

"An innovative feature is this fan, powered by a mainspring that must be rewound at intervals. The air slips through the screens and takes away the toxic odors before they can induce gangrene. The fan's parts can be removed and cleaned—even the fan blade can be immersed in boiling water."

"Why boil them?" asked Van Meer.

"Experience has demonstrated that patients exposed to instruments boiled in fresh water suffer fewer infections. Unclear why this is so; maybe because poisons cannot cling tenaciously to heated surfaces."

"Remarkable."

"Please take a look, keeping alert not to bump the box. Though affixed to the stand, a jolt can unbalance."

The box's lids lay open, and the fan wafted the scent to their nostrils. The visitors peered at the leg Holland himself hadn't seen in full since the box's fitting, and could not see now, reclined as he was. He could anticipate their reactions to a sight that must strike them as grotesque, for invariably they wrinkled their faces.

"The ointment has a familiar smell," her father said.

"Diluted turpentine," explained Slate. "A proven antiseptic."

Underneath a gauze layer, the wound glowed red. "As you can see, a letter indicates each of these turnbuckles. Critical are the sequences and tightness. I implore you to enact precision and to heed the instructions without deviation. This was why, and again I speak candidly, I chose with prudence the family to whom I entrusted the care. They had to be of demonstrable intelligence and diligence. I see I chose well."

"Thank you," said Van Meer.

The sneer quickly vanished from Anna's face.

Not before Holland caught it.

And she caught him staring at her.

* * *

"'My goodness, sir, there are ospreys in the eaves!'"

"'Ospreys! Call for the magistrate!'"

Holland threw back his head and laughed so forcefully she startled and lost her place in the book. The lines' comedy struck her as insipid. His laughter subsided, and the mirthful visage dissolved. His black hair splayed like a spider's legs on the pillow.

She asked, "Are you all right?"

"Yes. I haven't laughed like that for a long time. I am not accustomed."

Her mother had owned a collection of books, old and modern alike, and from these Anna had selected one she guessed an army officer would enjoy, *The Venables of Charleston*. Apparently she'd chosen well, for he seemed delighted, though she found no charm in the characters, boorish scions of the Carolinian aristocracy.

Dr. Slate had exhorted them to read to the convalescent daily as a means to lift his mood. Bookman could read, yet he was not the one to entertain their guest, and the task fell to her. To read aloud was familiar—her mother and she had read Bible verses to each other. Had her mother lived, Anna certainly would have grown up steeped in the scriptures.

When she'd died, her father had severed his religious ties, neither attending church himself nor remonstrating with Anna to do so. He'd offered no explanation—he'd not even raised the subject—and a mystery remained how her mother's beliefs in the abolition of slavery had so transformed him, while her religious passions had taken no root. The Augusta Seminary had required its students to attend Bible studies, and dutifully Anna had done her turns at the podium reading the scriptures and applying the correct emphasis, though she'd credited nothing she intoned. Always she'd sensed hypocrisy in the practice of religion—for instance how those who owned slaves could pretend righteousness. She didn't remember precisely when she had decided she did not believe in God. What was religion's purpose, she'd asked herself, except to tell people what they should think? If God did not exist, to pray to him was folly, a diversion of time and action, imposing the illusion of a dialog. If He *did* exist, what difference whether she believed in Him or not, for wouldn't His goodness surmount all else?

"Anna?"

"Yes?"

"You have stayed silent for a long time. Are you all right?"

She closed the book. "You should rest."

* * *

In the evening when she arrived to read, he held a newspaper. He could read this way, though with difficulty—he could not elevate himself much because the box pinned him, and the lamplight fell tepidly on the page. She might have read the newspapers to him but had decided she would not; she did not care to read the war reportage aloud. He seemed to puzzle at her objection, though he said nothing, merely set aside the Richmond papers her father had purchased in New Market center. Despite the box clasping his leg, the captain appeared adept at shifting to various postures. She understood he did so to avoid bedsores from the sheets' friction—no doubt at the doctor's instructions.

The papers over the past two weeks had reported General Lee's march into Maryland, without saying precisely the location of Lee's army. Then came the news of an epic battle by a town called Sharpsburg—the Northerners called the battle Antietam, after a creek—and thereafter of Lee's re-crossing the Potomac River into Virginia. The articles said Lee had won at Sharpsburg. She'd read of the controversy the general had stirred by taking the war to the North, contradicting the Confederates' rationale that they were fighting purely to protect their homelands from the Yankees.

The front page recounted another story, of an arsenal explosion in Pittsburgh, Pennsylvania. Bursting gunpowder had killed scores of workers, most of them young women whose dexterous fingers were adept at fabricating cartridges. The fire had burned their bodies beyond recognition.

She sat in the straight-backed chair three feet from his bed.

"I do not believe that General Lee carried the day at Sharpsburg," he remarked. "If he had won, why would the army have withdrawn at once into Virginia?"

She was still thinking of the poor Pittsburgh women the gunpowder explosion had killed. She said, "Perhaps the hypocrisy of invading the North began to weigh."

He sighed. "Do not let that sentiment sway you. There is strategic merit in taking the conflict northward. Lee spares Virginia from war on her soil."

"So that's what he's doing."

"Do I detect sarcasm?"

"Do you?"

"And I am reminded I know nothing about you."

"Has my father not told you about us?"

"He has not. He asked how I was feeling, whether I was comfortable, or too hot, on the occasions he stopped by. Perhaps he thought I was too fatigued to be interested."

"Well, you are billeted with the Van Meers, of Dutch ancestry, as I informed you before."

His expression evidenced no recollection.

"I did tell you, but never mind. I am Anna Van Meer, twenty years old, a solitary child. My mother passed away ten years ago. I was educated at the Augusta Female Seminary. My father is a teacher at a school on the Kingsland Road."

"Isn't the Augusta Female Seminary a Presbyterian school?"

Despite its simplicity, the question threw her. "Yes."

"So you are Presbyterian?" He blinked in curiosity.

"Are you?"

"In name only," he said. "I do not attend services. In fact, I do not practice at all."

She stared at him. "I see. Anyway, this house is nine or so miles south of Richmond, on land cupped in birch, maple, and pine, between a creek on the east and the James River on the west, which you can reach by crossing the Osborne Turnpike and over the lower meadow. Our Negroes are paid freedmen, not slaves. Their family of four lives above the buggy house. Sarah and Bookman are the house servants."

"Bookman told me they were not slaves."

"It is an important distinction."

"Do you have a gentleman friend?"

The temperature had stayed dismally hot, and though the screens afforded circulation, she felt herself blush. She was tempted to tell him to mind his business. Instead she answered, "I returned from the Augusta Female Seminary barely three weeks ago. I don't think the gentlemen of this county are aware I am here."

"Three weeks? Are they dullards, the county's gentlemen? Where I live they would have been lined up bearing candies and flowers the very next day."

"The young men are off at the war. And I am not a debutante—my schooling was not to prepare me for the autumn ball!"

"I apologize if I gave offense."

She stood. "Do not concern yourself. You are at a disadvantage, obviously. Still, you are advised not to make this situation more awkward."

"So you will continue to converse with me from time to time?"

"As long as it is not about my personal life."

"I shall think of something else."

She left the room.

* * *

Sweat slicked his skin, and he longed to writhe on the bed the way a dog rolls on the grass. He could not—the box immobilized him. In two hours, six A.M. would arrive, and Bookman would rewind the fan spring, and the whirring blades would pull air against his leg, a minor comfort he looked forward to. The night sweltered. The mainspring handle was on the far side, out of reach. Why had Banderton designed the box so the patient couldn't wind the spring by himself? Apparently the distinguished inventor never had pondered that a patient might not have the benefit of a servant standing by in the middle of the night, or when the fan stopped after 45 minutes.

If he'd gone home, he thought, he'd have had one of the family's slaves outside his door continually.

Over the hours, his awareness of Anna resurged, and he realized he'd been counting the minutes until her promised time to read to him. He'd not planned to ask her whether she had a suitor; the question simply had leapt out. So unlike him, to speak impolitely to a woman. Fortunately she did not seem fragile—though she was quite ready to take offense. The question had flushed her out the way a horse charging across a field chases small animals from their hiding places. Revealed: how the light bronzed her hair; the color of her irises, not a single shade but arrayed in bands, reminding him of water in its various moods; her crispness of diction that emotion honed and her thoughts held aloft, each syllable skipping flawlessly to the next; her hands' repose, her long fingers languid, as when she balanced the book, and then the repose vanished and they became agitated, tapping at what might be an imaginary piano suspended in the air; her flashing expressions, of which she had no apparent consciousness and that survived barely an instant, and afterward her face reverted to its former mien. Among them, her eyes widening in dismay, as when she'd exclaimed, "I am not a debutante!" as if the idea were so preposterous she might have said, "I am not a porcupine!"

He did not wish to dwell on what he'd exposed of himself: past the veneer of charm, an awkward fellow who could not calibrate his manners. He must put on a thoughtful demeanor, show poise and artful timing. Elevate his speech. He was adept at none of these graces.

23

They said an officer's education was the costliest in the world, paid for in men's lives. In an instant he could interpret a rifle's crack, read truth in a dust cloud, redirect his company's march, and pull together a violent charge with life and death tossed like pennies in the air. All the sagacity gained in life's harshest lessons, offering not a word he could say to this young woman.

At least he recognized his shortcomings, and the knowledge spared him from self-pretense. Just as his damaged leg, his immobility, nose and chin too prominent, and teeth slightly askew were facts, so was his deficit of social finesse. Of course she would have noticed immediately. Clothed in the pathetic hospital gown, his leg anchored in the box, he had no refuge from her perceptions.

* * *

"Miss, ladies at the door."

"What do they want?"

"They come callin' on the cap'n."

"Oh, damn." Anna rose from the muslin pad on which she knelt when working in the garden. Pulling scallions had soiled her fingers, and she swished them in a water bowl. The swishing did not dissolve the grit under her nails.

"Gimme your hands, miss."

By the kitchen door, she let Sarah scrub her nails with the soft brush. Sarah had done this for her as a child, and though years had passed since the last time, the familiar tedium weighed. She composed herself and reassumed her stature as an adult, and with chin high she entered the foyer where waited Mrs. Appleton, Mrs. Hawkins, and Mrs. Kern. They'd brought bread rolls and a jar of orange marmalade. Whether the captain liked marmalade she had no idea. She knew him well enough to say he'd be sociable in accepting the gifts.

In the parlor they remarked on the handsome gingham chair covers. "A marvelous deed your father performed, to give your house for a wounded soldier's care," said Mrs. Appleton once they were seated. Sweat beaded her brow, and she fanned herself with one of the paper fans that lay about for guests. "So many wounded boys these days."

"Some are quartered in New Market," added Mrs. Hawkins. "They were wounded at Malvern Hill."

"They're quartered everywhere," rejoined Mrs. Appleton.

"Where did your captain's wound befall him?" asked Mrs. Kern, the eldest.

Anna shook off the impulse to assert that the captain was not *hers*. "I don't know."

Mrs. Kern was about to comment when Mrs. Appleton interjected, "He was shot at the Chickahominy."

How had these women heard about Captain Holland? Anna guessed that her father had disseminated the news through his circle of acquaintances at the school, inviting one and all to visit, leaving her to play host and bellowing the embers of what kept the war going—the public's enthusiasm.

She wiped her forehead and hoped her annoyance had not been evident.

"How you've grown," remarked Mrs. Kern. "You look just like your mother when she was your age. Doesn't she?"

"Her hair is lighter," pronounced Mrs. Hawkins. "And she's taller."

"I don't think she's taller."

"Undeniably she is. Elsa was barely five feet seven. Anna is five feet nine. Stand up, dear."

Anna obeyed. She normally postured herself quite straight and did so now, obviating the corrections these women surely would have prescribed.

"You see?"

"I wonder if Elsa wasn't taller than you remember."

"I stood alongside her on countless occasions."

"If taller, she's not by so much," retorted Mrs. Kern. "You may sit, dear."

Mrs. Appleton accepted a cup of tea Sarah delivered. "Well, perhaps Elsa seemed of greater stature because her personality was so forceful. The church never was the same after she passed."

Mrs. Kern severed the disadvantageous topic. "Anna, do you still speak French?"

"Not recently. At the Augusta Seminary, I tried to brush up by taking a course."

"A shame. Elsa's French was so elegant—what a pleasure to listen to her crisp pronunciation. She spoke to you in French so you could learn."

"Yes, sometimes," affirmed Anna. She squeezed her hands together in her lap.

Mrs. Hawkins said, "Dear, when are you going to introduce us to the captain?"

"Let me see if he's awake." She rose and brushed her dress down. Strode to the hall's end and entered the sickroom (*le petit salon*, formerly) where the drawn curtains shadowed the bedded figure. She eased closer. "Captain Holland?"

"Call me John," he muttered, his voice thick with sleep. "I detect that you have visitors."

"*You* have visitors. Women of the community wish to say hello."

"Send them in."

"I'm going to fold back the curtains. Guard your eyes."

He squinted in the sun's glare off the courtyard's walls. She opened the louvered doors to admit the air and let dissipate the turpentine ointment's odor. By the time she brought in the guests, the air was fresher, if still sultry.

No doubt from his soldierly experience, Holland was immediately alert, courteous, and cheerful. The women asked about his family. Seemed disappointed he was not from a place closer by. They'd not heard of the Hollands, and this gave Anna satisfaction, for she'd not heard of them either, before Dr. Slate mentioned their notoriety. The ladies were curious about the Banderton box, and he explained its workings and how the settings required readjustment several times daily. To her quiet umbrage, he implied she was the one responsible for the settings, though Bookman had done all the work thus far. The box lids were closed, so the woman had to crane close to listen for the fan's soft whirr. "I hear it!" exclaimed Mrs. Hawkins.

Anna doubted this, though she smiled, playacting to their amusement, as her father certainly would have wished her to do.

After the women left, she returned to the sickroom. "If you don't mind, I'll draw the curtains again. They keep the room cooler."

"Very well." He seemed to sense how tedious the visit had been for her.

The masquerade had its limits, she thought. Her father mustn't invite people unless he'd be present to host them—otherwise she would refuse to let them in. No sooner had she resolved so than Sarah reappeared. "Folks at the door again."

"Oh no."

This time, the callers were a reporter from the *Richmond Daily Dispatch* and a photographer with his camera and tripod. The reporter asked to interview the renowned Captain John Holland; the photographer would capture his image for an artist later to convert to a printable sketch.

Would the visits never cease? She considered refusing on the basis she'd received no forewarning. How unfair for this nonsense to consume her day!

In the end, she made no objection and dutifully led them to the sickroom, hearing the camera's tripod bump clumsily against the hallway wall. While he replied to the reporter's questions, she seized the opportunity to slip away. Returned at the photographer's behest to open the louvers to admit sunlight and to vent the room from the smoke his array of candles disgorged. Holland posed perfectly still. (She recalled the procedure from having her own photograph taken last year.) When all was ready, she stood in the doorway facing his profile. He did not smile, yet in the instant before the shutter clicked, he winked at her.

- 3 -

Jerome, Sarah, Bookman, and Carola dwelled in the two rooms above the buggy house. They accessed the space via a staircase that rose nearly vertically. The upper rooms did not adjoin at the level, and the occupants had to step up and down the ten inches between, their thumping footfalls audible as far away as the mainhouse kitchen. Anna had climbed the stairs once, before her mother died, and she remembered the straw mattresses and the scant furniture—a plain table and chairs and shelves. In contrast to the limewashed main house, the buggy house showed brown paint without and within. The color dated from ten years ago, when her mother had hired the painter. Hating the interior darkness, she had commissioned a carpenter to install two windows that faced the upper meadow, and a seamstress to fashion curtains. Through error of measurement or craftsmanship, the windows canted inward at the tops, and when Anna viewed them from the meadow, she thought they resembled eyes tilted in a disapproving expression.

The family had a surname they rarely used—Fournier—their former owner's name. Twenty years ago, no longer in need of so many slaves, he'd sold them to Henry Van Meer. The former master might have profited more had he sold them separately, but he was a man of morality who didn't wish to tear apart the family—the fate slaves dreaded just short of death. He was not so moral as to have set them free, or in earlier years to have overlooked Sarah's quality as a child breeder. She'd borne two boys he'd taken away and sold and who were lost to her thereafter.

Upon purchasing the threesome, Henry Van Meer awarded them their freedom. Legally he had not only to free them, but to petition the Henrico County court that they might remain in Virginia beyond the one year the 1806 Virginia Slave Act afforded for emancipated slaves. Van Meer attested accordingly that they were peaceable, orderly, industrious, and not addicted to drunkenness or other vices. In doing so, he fulfilled a promise to his wife Elsa, who'd refused to live in a house with slaves, and who'd asked him to forsake owning them ever after. The Fourniers worked as house and grounds servants, earning the common wage for freedmen, not much, still better than the nothing slaves garnered.

The money went to Jerome's pocket. Just as Anna always had thought of Bookman as her wise older brother, to her Jerome was a brooding adult.

She was in her room when she heard angry voices behind the house. The volume lessened—the participants apparently had receded toward the creek—still the noise carried. She descended the stairs and crossed into the kitchen, where Sarah chopped greens, ignoring the confrontation beyond.

"Sarah, should I go out there?"

"No, miss." She did not look up from her work.

"The argument disturbs our guest, I'm certain."

"I'm sorry, miss. I'll go talk to 'em."

Leaning over the table, aligning the greens, Sarah did not shift her feet. Whereas a white person affirming *I'll go talk to them* implied immediacy, a black person saying so did not. To the two races, the words harbored different meanings. Anna had believed this since she was little.

Outside, the angry exchange continued. She weighed leaving them alone. Yet Sarah's obduracy chopping the greens vexed her.

"Sarah?"

"Yes, miss?"

"I said this argument is disturbing to our guest. He is convalescing, and his restfulness must be respected."

"Yes, miss." Sarah kept her gaze to the table.

"I'll tell them myself," said Anna. She pushed open the kitchen door and strutted over the wavy dirt yard, sidestepping cut wood, past little Carola who peeked from the buggy house's doorway. At the clearing's edge where the yard melded into the upper meadow, she found the two men. "How rude of you to make so much noise you compel me to come out!"

"We'll go down by the creek," said Jerome. Enormous, the breadth of the man, the thickness of his shoulders.

She said, "I have need of Bookman."

"We'll finish this later," muttered Jerome.

"How dare you utter a threat in my presence!"

"I ain't made no threat, miss. I got my own uses for him, when he ain't busy." He glared at her, then averted his eyes.

She strode without thinking where she was headed, hearing Bookman's footsteps behind, and veered around the buggy house's north end, skirting the main house's adjacent wall, emerging in the yard beyond. In the oval of foundation stones where the old well had stood and grass grew haggardly, she spun to face him. "Don't think I will put up with further insolence from your brother-in-law!"

"We're just talkin,'" said Bookman. "We should have moved away from the house."

"You say he wasn't threatening you?"

"I'm sayin,' we're free men."

"Meaning none of my business?"

"If we're free, we're free to talk, even to argue." His voice stayed irritatingly calm.

"That man does not argue. He dominates."

"Our ways of talkin' are different."

True. When Bookman spoke with the other blacks, he might be using a separate language. She'd been away for a year at the Augusta Seminary. Had she forgotten?

Her anger banged like horse kicks in a stall. "Never again do I wish to hear Jerome's bellicosity. I am the mistress of this house, and I will not be treated less. The insolent way he spoke to me, I am tempted to insist he leave and not set foot on this property again. He can wander the fields, sleep under the trees for all I care!" The venom in her words surprised her and seemed to astonish Bookman too.

Softly he said, "I'll talk to him. Won't happen again."

"How can you promise for him?"

"I can."

"What's happening, Bookman?"

"What do you mean?"

"When I was away at school, I missed being home. And I missed you. Now I feel like I don't know you."

He said nothing. No gesture or expression. Leaving her to wonder if she had any more insight into his thoughts than she had into Jerome's.

"I'll talk to him," Bookman repeated. "What did you need me for?"

"To speak with you. That is all."

He walked off.

* * *

At sunrise, Bookman was at work chopping the tree that had listed badly in the recent winds. Chopping was his specialty, and often she'd watched him work, his sinews glistening in sweat. Sometimes she took the ax herself to hack pieces into kindling. She could balance the ax and swing the handle, even over her head; of course she lacked the power to chop hard.

When she'd reached the age of fifteen, the five years that separated them, which heretofore had notched him at an elevated status, ceased to do so. One day she'd sat by while he broke wood, and their conversation was no longer between a man and a girl, rather between a man and a woman. The realization she'd crossed the boundary came in the wary looks he gave her, as if she'd been transformed into something quite potent.

She said, "I'm of marrying age, aren't I?"

She'd caught him as he hefted the ax, and he let his arms drape loose, cradling the handle in the tips of his long fingers. "Why are you askin' me that?"

"Who else can I ask?"

On such occasions, men said things that either weren't true or were completely pointless, to guard themselves from women. Bookman had paused, seeming to weigh how to answer. Not until later had she understood that what was to be henceforth between them, the way they spoke to each other and the trust she felt, rested on his choice. Maybe he'd sensed so, which was why he took his time to decide.

Sometimes Bookman lapsed into the black voice; at other times he spoke so she could swear he was white: "You're of marryin' age. Child-bearin' age. Plain just lookin' at you. You have breasts and hips, and you're pretty. On top of that, you're clever, and you can run a household." He stared at her directly, without bashfulness.

"I'm not so sure."

"Ain't so much if you *can* be married, but if you should be, or want to be."

"I absolutely don't."

"Good. 'Cause two already have asked."

"What? That cannot be." Surely her father would have told her.

Bookman seemed to read her thoughts. "You didn't need to know. Your father sent them away."

"Who?"

"One was Lyman Hock from down the road. Don't tell your father I told you."

"Hock! He's an *old man!*" Hock, owner of a farm a mile south, paid occasional social visits. On his saggy face and neck, bristly hair poked like scarecrow straw.

"He's forty-two, ain't so old. He gave a regular testimony about himself to your father, so intent was he on earnin' you as his wife. He says he wants sons and you're one who can breed 'em."

"Breed? Why would he say such a thing?" She thought of how she must appear to men. Her breasts were small, her hips narrow for a woman of her height. What suggested her as a breeder?

Bookman said, "He probably meant to be flatterin.'"

"It wasn't."

"Hock's a prosperous man. A respectable suitor. Got land, animals, a few slaves. He says he'll forego a dowry. He knows you'll inherit your father's land. Maybe not before he himself dies, though."

"Did my father tell you that?"

"Not straight out. I know how these things go."

Here was Bookman making marriage calculations, as surely Lyman Hock had done.

"Who was the other one?"

"Justinian Tassell."

She puzzled at the name.

He read her reaction. "Man's a tax collector. Thin. Blotchy skin. Laughs a lot."

"How can someone I can't remember ask for permission to marry me?"

"Your father said the same thing. 'A fool might learn to act the wise man, but the fool's impulse is always on him.'"

She thought Bookman did an uncannily accurate imitation of her father and his oft-spoken adages. She said, "Who I shall marry, and when, and if, is up to me!"

"Don't worry. Your father knows the world has its ways."

"And what about you? What do you think?"

"Ha. Don't matter what I think."

"I want to hear."

"Well, I agree. You should marry who you want, when you want."

The statement's irony shone in his eyes, and she laughed.

He said, "To me, ain't sensible for a man to marry a girl and make her bear children so close to bein' a child herself. I guess Hock and Tassell wanna get there before somebody else does. Plenty of widowers go lookin' for young wives. Figure they'll feel young again."

Never had Bookman spoken to her so, and the significance of her age settled. She contemplated the meaning behind his words: *Get there before somebody else does.*

He said, "They won't be the last. Men will come askin' about you. They got you on their minds."

She helped him collect the chopped wood. Though her arms were thin, her fingers were long, and she could grip the pieces firmly and carry a quite a few. While they stacked the wood, she calculated in her head the stocks and how long they'd last. In years past, her estimates had proven so accurate her father always asked for them as the winter approached.

She thought her skills with numbers were among the reasons he hadn't been willing to see her married off.

For he'd needed her help with an extraordinary activity.

* * *

Holland asked, "Where have you been? I thought I had missed my reading."

"Delayed, not missed. We went to Richmond today." She sat in the chair beside the bed, found her place in the book, and began to read aloud. After a minute, she was able to separate herself from the narrative she could deliver without paying attention. What she couldn't do was lift her eyes from the page and let them wander. Her mind was able to do so for her, and she pictured the streets of Richmond center. This morning, after instructing the driver where to pick them up later, Anna and Sarah had strolled between the soot-smirched facades. Men stared at her. She returned neither glances nor greetings.

They made their way toward the Capitol Heights. A year and a half ago, as a means of enticing Virginia to join the rebellion, the Confederate Congress had declared Richmond the rebellion's capital. If the city had welcomed its newfound role, the cost was crowds, noise, and dust. A lingering euphoria blended with something vague and bitter, like an aftertaste. Less than three months ago, the Northern army under General George McClellan had occupied positions barely five miles from the city. Confederate General Robert E. Lee's victory in the ensuing Seven Days battles had spawned rejoicing, and she expected to see ribbons and banners. None was visible. She did notice ambulance wagons rumbling amid the buggies and cabriolets that clotted the streets. The horses nosed so close to the carriages in front that Anna and Sarah had to squeeze their way between. By the Virginia capitol building toured hundreds of soldiers on furlough. Farm boys gaped at the columned edifice that—as her father pointed out to her every time they visited Richmond—Thomas Jefferson had designed from ancient Roman ruins he'd seen when he was the American ambassador to France. The soldiers ignored the buggy-drivers' yells to move out of the way. Foreigners, a man in a teal silk suit and powdered wig, a woman with a parasol fashioned grotesquely from stretched fox skins—must be heavy, mused Anna—edged around the gawkers. Catholics: For the first time in her life, she witnessed a marching coven of nuns. More determined and disciplined than the soldiers, they marked a steady cadence, their onyx habits hissing like steam. People shuffled warily aside.

From the heights, Anna and Sarah promenaded westward on Main. She scanned the descending sidestreets. Two years ago, she'd strolled here with her father, during what had been sleepier times, to bring shoes to the cobbler her father much admired for his craft. Today the surroundings seemed unfamiliar until a landmark flinted her memory, a bump gravel fillings had smoothed but not eliminated, and she led Sarah along the street that guttered toward the James River. To the sides ran passages, open or gated. In the distance she could see the river and the stacks of the Tredegar Iron Works. The air clung florid, and she wondered if the street had become the place for undertakers who'd done a heady business since the war's onset. Did rows of dead men repose beyond the fences? The flower smell dissipated and another, less ominous, wafted—goats. Someone kept them nearby or had shepherded them through recently. Now the women ambled between plank-sided buildings rising three stories. From the facades protruded rickety porches dangling every sort of object from dead rabbits to bird cages. The balconies suspended garnets with slender ropes for hoisting items from the street. The insides must be cluttered, she thought, and she imagined them spilling out the way she'd once witnessed a strung-up goat disemboweled, the intestines uncoiling.

Two women in fluff-fringed pastel petticoats leaned over a third-story railing and stared at her. The one, her pink toes curled over the ledge, spoke to the other, who giggled. Before Anna could strip her stare away, she fathomed they were prostitutes.

"Hi there," said the one in powder blue. "Lookin' for somebody?" They laughed gleefully.

"Miss Anna? Ain't this the place?" Sarah, who'd been paying attention to where they were going, stood by a shoe-shaped sign painted in red letters: *Jacob's Shoesmithing.*

"Yes, thank you."

"You don't need to be sayin' nothin' to *them*," growled Sarah, glancing toward the balcony. She pushed through the gate. They faced a stone walkway between walls.

Anna remembered the walkway, though not as it was today, for here reclined soldiers waiting for their boots to be mended. The legs stretched to bare feet as rutted as old poplar bark.

"Y'all let the lady through," commanded Sarah.

The dozen-or-so soldiers grunted up from their lethargy, while the women squeezed past their chests in the confined space, emerging onto a patio no less occupied. Cobblers were busy in these foot-weary times, she mused.

A half-door opened in a brick wall. In leather aprons, Jacob and his two assistants plied at footwear. Attached on the doorway's side, a petite wooden tube she recalled from her previous visit, a four-inch cylinder resting at a tilt. All the nearby doors sported one. Her father had explained that the hollow tube contained a tiny scroll with a blessing in Hebrew. The owners of the houses along the alleyway were Jews.

She stood at the window, Sarah behind and partly shielding her from the soldiers' ogles. Festooning the recess, shoes of every color—white, crimson, violet—some so exotic she thought only rich foreigners or stage performers would wear them. Jacob's dark eyes tipped up. His face was misshapen, as if a horse had kicked him in the jaw and the break had healed unevenly. His smile ramped from his cheek on one side to the lower chin on the other. "You are the daughter," he said.

Uncertain if this were a question or statement, she said, "I'm Anna."

"And I am Jacob, as you know." He took her father's boots she'd deposited on the sill and reached into one of them, to divine the condition, she supposed.

She asked, "When will the boots be ready?"

Unable to interpret his shrug, she folded the cloth bag in which she'd carried the boots and began to step away.

"Wait, please." He receded into his shop, brushing behind leather sheets pendant on wires like giant russet leaves, and returned with a pair of women's black shoes. They had thick, medium heels, lovely polished sides, tapered leather ankle straps, and dainty brass buckles. "Try these on," he said.

"Why?"

"Try them," he repeated softly. His smile looked like a bend in the James River.

She did, mindful her actions were in the view of the soldiers behind, and tried to keep her calves from showing as she kicked off her old shoes and buckled on the new. They fit superbly, the ankle straps snug and the leather supple, having been burnished so the edges wouldn't cut the skin.

"They are lovely," she said. "Who are they for?"

"For you."

The money she carried was meant for fabric, not new shoes. "I'm sorry, I cannot afford them."

"They are a gift."

"I cannot accept."

"I give them to you on friendship for your father. You cannot refuse a gift for him, can you?"

She wondered whether her father had left the cobbler a trace of her old shoes—otherwise, how could these fit so precisely? "You surprise me, sir, but agreeably so. Thank you."

"Pass my regards to him."

Her father hadn't spoken of the cobbler as a friend, only as a Jew whose work he admired. She retrieved her old shoes. How luxurious, to stand in the new ones. Turning, she caught the stare of every soldier. Some studied her face, some roved to her shoes, others fixed blatantly on her bosom, the way those in the streets regarded the capitol edifice.

This time the soldiers moved out of the way without Sarah's command.

The women found their way back to the heights. Soon they reached Cary Street. Her heeltaps on the cobblestones pleased her, and she didn't mind the stroll. They came to a crowd facing an open yard, and she beheld an object she'd never before witnessed—an inverted urn, black sides stark against the pale sky, above a suspended basket. She'd read of the famous Confederate balloon lofted during the battles of the Seven Days, its body of colorful dress silk inflated with gas from the Richmond Gas Works ahead on Cary. But today's was not a gas balloon. A burner issued an orange flame and smoke that smelled like the ointment on Holland's leg. The basket strained against the tethering ropes. Voices gabbled. A man shouted, "Let 'er go!" Another said, "They're waitin' for Lee." Someone else remarked that General Lee wasn't in town; General Jackson was the one who'd officiate. He wasn't here either, said another. People craned on tiptoes, perhaps to catch a glimpse of a military luminary or to view the balloon that hovered like a gigantic paint dollop about to fall upward into the heavens. She imagined a spatter against the top of the sky, if such a place existed.

Anna and Sarah skirted the confused scene before any generals arrived. They promenaded into the Shockoe Bottom district, first through the fruit market, a place formerly awash in oranges, pears, apples, melons, and plums mounded in stalls in front of brick facades with maroon doors, an extravaganza of color and the richest scents, today harboring no fruit whatsoever and a different odor—the junk wagon's. Cross-legged on the ground or behind tables, people hawked their finery, especially jewelry. She paused at the table of an older woman who wore a plain dress because she was selling the fancy ones: gowns, shawls, jackets. Fingering through the garments, Anna found one that looked her size, a charcoal jacket with ivory buttons, and she was examining the stitching's firmness when she noticed, against the smoke-grimed bricks beyond, a woman in a gray dress and black stockings visible at her ankles. Slim, perhaps Anna's age, she had straight blond hair to her shoulders, and in her pale fist she clutched an open black umbrella that hid her face except for the instant when she tipped the rim to glance around. Tears ribboned her cheeks. Why did she pose so? Then Anna realized, in this market of used things for sale, the woman was selling *herself*. Unlike the jaunty prostitutes on the balcony, here was a poor woman driven to a terrible expedient.

Anna released the garment. Stepped toward Sarah, who waited behind. Then, bedlam. Through the market, parting the crowd, charged a man wielding a stick he alternately waved at the sky or thumped on the ground. He shouted, "We licked 'em, thank you Jesus!" Bash. Grizzled, wearing a soldier's hat, his linen shirt open at the chest, he seemed to behold wonderments not apparent to anyone else. At first she thought him drunk, then she caught his eyes and interpreted the glowing coals of insanity. When he neared her, his stick-gripping hand fell to his side: "What rings but makes no sound?" he said softly, to her alone.

"Don't get no closer, mister." Sarah tugged at Anna's arm. "Do you *know* that man?"

"No," managed Anna.

Sarah craned behind to be sure he wasn't following and nearly crashed into two men who dodged around. "There go the asylum keepers," she said, "chasin' crazy folks. If they're white."

"What do you mean, if they're white?"

"Crazy black people? Don't put 'em in no asylum. Just shoot 'em dead."

"How awful."

They passed a slave auction, today inactive. Vacant rose the platform where the auctioneers paraded the slaves, turned them to face left, right, backward, so the bidders could view their breadth of shoulder and straightness of spine, and squeeze the women's legs to judge their breeding potential. On the cobblestones beneath, a boy splashed water and knelt to scrub with a brush. "He can scrub till judgment day, and *that* place won't be clean," huffed Sarah.

They arrived at the cloth shop, which seemed sedate and orderly compared to the other Richmond locales. Anna purchased a partial bolt of gray muslin—the white having become too expensive since the embargo—after first ensuring the material showed no rips, pills, or disfigurement. She might have bought less-pricey calico, or even homespun, but earlier in the week, aware she wanted new dress fabric for Sarah's daughter, her father had pressed into her palm a stack of federal coins. "Use this for the cloth," he'd told her.

The amount had astonished her. "Don't we need the money for other things?"

"I sold a parcel of land, one we cannot lease. The buyer gave me more than I expected."

"What land do you mean?"

"Across the river."

"We own land *across* the James?"

"We used to. Please tell no one of this. If people find out I've sold land, they will besiege me with inquiries."

At a veranda, Anna and Sarah drank tea and ate sweetbread while the James murmured by. The autumn leaves wafted. Anna let the tea settle her. Gazed serenely at the water and the cloth they'd purchased, now doubled over to fit in the sack. The fabric's sheen made her want to rub it through her fingers.

What rings but makes no sound? When the madman in the market had spoken to her, she'd been thinking the balloon was like a ringer in the sky's vast bell. People said the insane could read thoughts. Perhaps true, yet not wholly, because she'd been thinking too of the land her father had sold, land no one had mentioned to her before. How strange, that the blurry panorama across the river, which all her life she'd considered exotic and distant, had been theirs.

* * *

"Anna?"

"Yes."

"Are you aware you are repeating the same page you just read?"

"I am? I'm sorry."

"Don't be troubled. In fact the second time is quite rich, because I can anticipate the words and how you will say them."

She thought, she must have done so because she could not distinguish one page of this silly book from the next. "My mind wandered."

"To where?"

"No concern of yours."

"You seem... annoyed."

"You misjudge."

"Oh?"

"You are not perceptive of me, Captain. Let us go no further on the subject."

"Please call me John."

"Very well." She turned the page.

He said, "Your father asked me if I desired for a preacher to stop by, inasmuch as I cannot go to church."

"And?"

39

"I told him I hoped he'd not gone to trouble to arrange a special service, fellow Presbyterian though I am, for I am not religious. And he said neither were the two of you, and you'd not been to church since your mother died."

"True."

"And yet you went to the Augusta Female Seminary, a religious institution."

She stared at him. She did not wish to explain how she'd endured a year of sermons and Bible readings, investing her presence as required, paying scant attention, and during the religious sessions had daydreamed at Staunton's hills the school's windows faced. "The Augusta Seminary accepted me because my mother was prominent in the Presbyterian community. The school's curriculum features proper learning, Captain. I studied literature, mathematics, geometry, and French."

"Ah. *Comment allez-vous aujourd'hui, mademoiselle?*"

His French sounded terrible. "Where did you learn?"

"The obligatory French lessons at West Point."

"That which is forced on us sometimes doesn't settle well."

"Indeed. So it must have proven tiresome, your theological instruction at the female seminary."

She thought she had deflected the topic; he'd circled back. Flipping through the book, having lost her place, accidentally ripping one of the pages, she was of a mind to hurl it at him.

"Were you aware someone was digging outside last night?"

"What?" She felt lightheaded, and the book in her hand seemed to lose its significance.

He said, "Though I have no clock, my intuition for time is intact. Late was the hour, about two in the morning, when I heard a shovel blade ring against a pebble, though faintly, as if the digger were trying to hide the noise. I am familiar with the sound, as on occasion my soldiers dug rifle pits at night, cautiously so as not to alert the enemy to our presence."

"An animal, I think."

"An unusual animal who uses a shovel. A possum, balancing on his tail while he presses the spade with his furry foot?"

"So you have an imagination."

"The both of us, apparently." He flipped his hand. "With our imaginations, we might take a far, exciting journey together and never leave this spot."

She said, "I expect we would go to different places, on our journeys."

"I would go on yours happily, for the excellent company."

"Not likely."

"Why not?"

"You would encumber me, Captain."

"I see."

"Obviously you have remembered nothing from our conversation about the bounds of your inquisitiveness. When will you learn?"

She stood and walked out.

*   *   *

How long ago? Three weeks? Soon after she'd returned from Staunton, her screened window open, she stirred sweating under the gossamer mosquito net. The night noises were familiar—the house's creaks and the river's laps. Then she heard a scrape, and after a minute, a distinct metallic clink. Animals approached the house at night—deer, foxes, and raccoons left tracks, and bats and owls roosted in the trees—yet no animal would make a chime like a gardening till against a stone. Her room's window faced the front, so she padded downstairs to the side room—later Holland's room—and peered out. The silver maple tree blocked her view. Toeing cautiously, she opened the front door. The moon had fallen, and she traced the walkway to the gate and gripped the cast-iron tips, stretching on her tiptoes to crane over.

Muffled in the syrupy air, another metallic scrape from the north side. She opened the gate and stepped soundlessly over the dewy grass, the wetness penetrating between her toes, so quiet she could hear her nightgown swish. Twenty paces and three silhouettes took shape against the loam. From their sizes relative to each other, she guessed that two of them were her father and Bookman. The third figure, taller and thicker than the others, puzzled her. Jerome? No, the figure wasn't *that* big. He posed with one leg thrust out, arms folded. Who stood so? Nobody she could recall. She couldn't even say if he was black or white.

The third man angled toward her.

Silently she backed up, apprehending that her white nightgown rendered her as visible to them as they were to her.

The third man whispered something.

Her father snapped, "Who is there?"

The three turned toward her, and she felt as if she were emblazoned in torchlight. She said, "What are you doing out so late?" From practice she kept her voice low, barely above a whisper.

They occupied the spot where the old well formerly had stood. Inside the long-dry hole, when you displaced an inner dirt layer and a wooden hatch, had nested a recess where two people of ordinary size could squeeze. She'd entered the hideaway herself once, and Bookman at her behest had fitted on the cover and strewn the concealing dirt. In the stifling heat the earth's spices had clotted her nostrils. She knew she could breathe—Bookman had chiseled narrow holes at the stones' base. No less pitch dark, and she thought insects or lizards might have burrowed in. She'd imagined another person pressed within the cramped space. People had hidden here for many hours, willing to suffer any discomfort to escape slavery, while they awaited their journey's next leg. When they'd had no runaways to conceal, Bookman had strewn dirt on the lid and laced pepper on the ground to confuse the hounds the county patrol used to pursue escaped slaves. Fortunately, no searchers or dogs ever had tracked runaways to this place. At the war's onset, her father had instructed Bookman to fill the hole and tear down the well's old parapet. Afterward the ground evinced a scar where the grass refused to grow.

Upon this patch, the three ghostly figures now confronted Anna. Her father said, "Dear, please go back inside."

"What are *you* doing out?" she repeated.

He stepped over, took her upper arm, and swung her gently toward the gate. "Anna, for you to be here is unwise."

She jerked loose from his grip. "Why? What *are* you doing?"

"Nothing that concerns you."

She pressed her lips close to his ear. "You told me you closed the Railroad station when the war started."

"I *did* close it."

Too dark to read his face. Emotion tinged his voice. She hadn't heard him sound so tense since the nights when they'd wended their way by trails they knew well, past markers they could identify in the dark, to a place where other station tenders would meet them to transfer escaped slaves to their safekeeping. Her father always had gone, sometimes with her along, more often with Bookman. The third person had stayed behind as a sentinel ready to sound the danger signal, three spoon taps on an empty jug, given every two minutes until the danger had passed. The nights when they'd guided the runaways had so ridden her with anxiety, the next morning she'd felt her lips bitten and puffy.

When the war began, her father had decided that their Underground Railroad activities had become too dangerous, and he'd shut their station. Or so he'd told her. She'd thereupon agreed, as he'd implored her previously, to pursue her education. A friend of her mother's served on the faculty at the Augusta Female Seminary, and the opportunity had availed for Anna to attend. At the time, the school's location in Staunton town, in the Shenandoah Valley, had seemed safer than the Richmond peninsula.

He leaned to her ear. "The station *is* closed, yet some contacts are preserved, the embers kept burning, while we hope the war shall succeed, and we'll not have to use them." His voice quavered. "Even the Railroad's vestige is perilous, and we must be exceedingly careful. You understand, surely?"

"Of course. Why didn't you tell me? Did you think I wouldn't be interested?"

"What is to tell? No slaves are being moved."

"I can help you."

"There's nothing to help with, dear. In any case, I have explained to you why we're out. Now let me conclude with this fellow and try to quiet his heart from your unexpected appearance."

"I heard digging. Why?"

"Nobody was digging. We were talking, that's all."

"Who is that man?"

"Go inside—please!"

- 4 -

The sound of the ratcheting fan spring wakened him.

"Good mornin,' sir."

"Hello, Bookman."

The freedman was at work changing the dressing. Holland had noticed that when Bookman adjusted the box mechanism, he didn't consult the sequences roster. Apparently he had memorized the changes, or he grasped their logic.

In the post dawn, his features were in shadow. "Sir, do you mind if I open these curtains? I can't see very well in here."

"By all means." While Bookman was tugging back the fabric, Holland remarked, "I understand that Henry Van Meer taught you to read."

"Yes sir. When I was little."

"And what do you read?"

"The Bible, of course. The newspapers. And books he gave me. I finished the books long ago, but I read 'em over and over."

"What is your favorite?"

"*Moby Dick*, sir. I like the seafarin' parts."

"A popular tale."

"Gotta say, my true favorite ain't a book, but a story in a book of stories. *The Murders in the Rue Morgue*, by Edgar Allan Poe."

"Yes, I love that one too."

"Before she died, Anna's mother gave me two of her books she said I should read. *Wuthering Heights* I liked. But *Pride and Prejudice*, well, I *tried* to read. Just couldn't. Why do you think that is, sir?"

"I don't know. Maybe some books are simply a woman's hegemony."

Holland studied Bookman's eyes for puzzlement. Saw none.

Bookman knew the word *hegemony*.

* * *

When Dr. Slate next visited, he brought a three-pound parcel of dried fruits he called *antiscorbutics*: shriveled cherries, apples, and figs. He explained, "They are supplementary, in case you run out of fresh fruits and vegetables, which are the best preventers of scurvy."

She sampled the fruits. Tasty, though their texture was odd, particularly the apples and the figs.

Two days later she entered Holland's room late, having worked for an hour in the garden, washed, and brushed her hair. For breakfast, she'd eaten bread she'd bladed with butter and topped with cinnamon and dried cherries from Slate's parcel, and with a toothpick she'd cleaned her teeth, flashing them in her room's hanging mirror to reveal the clinging grains.

The sickroom's louvers stood open; through the screens a breeze plucked at the tied curtains. They were tattered and needed replacing. She thought of the money she'd paid for the fabric and dressmaker. None remained to commission a curtainmaker.

Bookman already had performed the daily box adjustments and changed the dressing. Uncharacteristically, he'd left the old one like a rat's nest by the door, and she noticed oatmeal-colored blotches, dried putridity from the wound. She thought, Bookman must have lost his concentration; heretofore he had not abandoned a soiled dressing on the floor for her to witness.

She searched for him. Through the kitchen window, she espied Jerome entering the buggy house—his size identified him instantly. In the parlor she found Sarah, who was removing the furniture dust covers to take out and shake. Anna asked, "Have you seen Bookman?"

"No, miss. Not since early this mornin.'"

"If you do see him, I would like to speak to him."

"Yes, miss."

She returned to Holland's room. Decided to leave the bandages on the floor where they lay.

He said, "I was afraid you wouldn't come back."

She dropped in the chair and spread the book in her lap. "Shall we hear more of the Venables?"

"You forgive me for being inquisitive?"

"Forgiveness is not necessary. However, I do have a question for you."

"Wonderful. The chance for recompense."

"How does…" She straightened herself in the seat, mulling whether her question would trespass the bounds of etiquette. "How does a man from a socially prominent family, one with connections and even personal bonds to President Jefferson Davis, end up convalescing here with us?"

"A fair question."

"The western mountains aren't so far you mightn't have traveled home to your family by train or even coach, as you were brought here."

"Dr. Slate preferred to keep me close by, so he could check personally on the therapy's progress."

"So Dr. Slate took the decision."

"In truth there was more. I told him I did not wish to go home."

The shabby curtains cavorted. She said, "I should not have broached what is a personal matter."

"Do not be concerned. There is no rancor between my family and me. They simply find me an oddity, one who prefers the company of horses to people."

She almost laughed. She willed herself to remain composed, lest she seem frivolously insensitive. She knew he found many topics amusing, perhaps not this.

He said, "My older brother Vernon is an attorney and businessman, adept and charming, and especially on occasions when he convinces people to spend their money. My sister Beatrice is the debutante you declared yourself not to be, and she has invested her youth in the perfection of social brilliance, and succeeded, to the extent I can judge. My father is forceful and wields much influence locally. He resembles his admired friend President Davis: reedy, his expression intense, his temper more so, a slaveowner and entrepreneur of businesses, among them a foundry, the names of whose workers—men sheathed in soot and grease—he has not bothered to learn."

If no rancor existed, why did he describe his father in such terms? She asked, "What of your mother?"

"She is dead these many years. You and I have the loss of our mothers in common. I'm told I take after her. I cannot say if this is true; she died when I was three, and we have no portrait."

"Sad to have had no mother in your life. Perhaps what love and loyalty you would have given her, you gave instead to…"

"To what?"

She hesitated. To speak her thought felt awkward. "To horses. You mentioned them."

"Yes. And to the out of doors. My father often hosted guests, and when their voices and cigar smoke filled the house, I crept through the upstairs window onto the portico roof. I dreamt of being atop a moving horse, able to see to the horizon, as far from enclosed spaces as I could get."

Yet here he was, she thought, in such a place. She averted her gaze from the box and his wrecked leg protruding at the knee, the day's setting.

He went on. "My father tried to recast me like a flawed ingot in his foundry. He sought to divert me from what he interpreted as my dissipation, to inspire my interest in important affairs. Failing to achieve this, he campaigned for my appointment to West Point, so at least I might have a profession."

"A grim one."

"I was happy to be gone."

"I see." She flipped the pages to the third chapter, aware he was watching her. She did not look at him because she was unsure how to interpret his self description, which had settled like dense food in her stomach, to be digested slowly. The other cognizance was of the box's dark bulk, from which leaked the turpentine scent, and beneath, a smell she had not detected until this minute, like a wet animal.

"'Jessup Venable's house overlooked the harbor, and he liked to imagine the boats were his own...'" She mouthed the words, giving no attention to what they meant. Flicked from time to time to Holland, who on his pillow seemed perfectly at peace, his focus drifted to the courtyard flowers. *"A relaxed patient is a healing patient,"* Dr. Slate had declared. He'd insisted on rigor and process in all aspects, from the box sequences to the daily readings, imposing discipline on civilians who might not be so inclined. For reasons she could not say, she admired his methodology, though he'd made her a handmaiden to a cause she detested. The war could not be divorced from the things that sustained, and now she was one of them.

"'Flowers and grass at their feet, they stepped along the hill above the bay to behold the ships and sails like so many toys for their pleasure. The pure whiteness of her skin and his weathered face contrasted like milk against coffee. His peppery hair cast a shadow on the golden waves that curved over her neck and halfway down her back, a mane so perfect as to belong to a goddess.' Are you not irked, to hear this?"

"What?"

She stared over the top of the page. "The banality of this prose."

"Banal? Why do you say so?"

"A good narrative is such that you cannot readily anticipate what will happen, yet it feels true to life at the same time. The characters are rich and genuine. These people are flat silhouettes."

"Really?"

"Well, you did say you preferred the company of horses. So perhaps this book is the appropriate one for you. I continue: 'And this perfection proclaimed itself in her eyes, pale blue like the winter sky at morning, with a wisp of the same coolness, not which freezes men, but soothes them…'"

"Anna, please excuse us."

Her father entered. Trailing came Dr. Slate and Bookman, their expressions wooden. A fourth man in a simple gray uniform carried a rectangular wooden case painted white.

She stood. "What's the matter?"

"Dear, you should step out." Her father gripped her upper arm. She pulled away from him.

The man in the gray uniform lowered the case that clunked against the floorboards.

At the bedside, Slate said, "Hello, John."

"Doctor."

"Are you feeling all right?" He unclasped the Banderton box's lids and tipped them open. Wafting came the wet-animal smell she had detected before, now acute—a death odor.

On the white box's edge, lettering she squinted to read: *Field Surgical Kit.*

She gasped.

Her father: "Anna, you should go!"

"No, stay if you can," said Dr. Slate over his shoulder. To her father, "I need her help."

"I will stay," she affirmed.

"Can you steady this pinion? Yes, like so. Bookman, please assist me with these turnbuckles."

She pinched the metal pinion that connected to the track along the interior base, while Slate adjusted the apparatus from the elevated angle to the horizontal. Her sense of touch suddenly had become acute, and she felt the residue of tiny fibers from the padding. Fearing to look at Holland's face, she riveted on the box seam, glancing occasionally to Slate, whose crunched countenance, whether from dismay or concentration, she could not decipher. The doctor held out his palm, and the gray-suited man inserted a pair of angled forceps. Not a word spoken.

"Might those doors be opened all the way?" He referred to the louvers halfway ajar. Her father lifted the floor and center latches and folded the doors against the opposite walls. Removed the framed cheesecloth screens, admitting the hum of bees and the flowers' scent.

"Not bright enough," said Slate. "With all of us gathered, I believe we can transfer the box from the stand onto the mattress and bear the entire bed into the patio's sunshine. Bookman, how are these sideboards affixed?"

"Nailed in tight, sir."

"Good. We have no stairs to cope with, only the modest bump. Everybody take a place. We shall lift an inch or two and move slowly, keeping the bed perfectly level."

With Bookman and the gray-suited fellow, Slate shifted the box to rest wholly on the mattress, pushing the stand aside. Together they lifted and baby-stepped toward the patio. Her place was across from Slate, to Holland's left.

"Anna, the pinion!"

She steadied it. The sun torched her neck, her forearms, her brows' ledge. She breathed the dry air, again cognizant of her senses' uncommon sharpness. In the embrasure hovered a bee she fluttered away. She heard Slate's soft sigh. Her father twisted to free his pant leg caught in the rosebush thorns; he kicked and the stem flailed and the dry burgundy rosehead whacked against the whitewashed wall, fell off, rolled, and bristled in the dirt. The surviving roses expressed a hot perfume.

In the sunlight, Holland squinted.

She asked Bookman, "Can you shade the captain?"

"Not necessary," said Holland, blinking. "I haven't felt the sun for a while. The warmth is pleasant."

She thought, he was on the verge of having his leg amputated, and he remarked on the pleasantness of the sun. Was this courage or self delusion?

Inadvertently her view had slipped onto his thigh, porcine pink with a velveteen texture, grotesquely captivating, like a freak animal a circus exhibited. Captured in the forceps' tips, a snake of gray flesh Slate snipped with scissors and deposited on a petite metal tray of a kind she'd seen in a Richmond jewelry store's window. "If this is the sole culprit," he said softly, "we may be spared a reversal."

"I hope so," said her father. The snake seemed to transfix him.

The forceps probed the margins of broken skin. "To stop the spread, I must debride all traces of the infection from the living tissue. This may hurt, my friend." With cotton at the end of his forceps, he applied a liquid to the cut's edge. "This is nitric acid, to burn away the infection."

Holland winced as Slate applied the acid and scratched and poked with a pointy instrument. "According to the literature, gangrene originates from foul air. I suspect other processes are at play, and medicine does not yet understand. Perhaps worms too minuscule to observe. They devour the flesh if they are allowed to multiply, and the gangrene is their foul residue."

This sounded absurd to her, but she said nothing.

For several minutes Slate continued. Holland lay back, teeth clenched. Another wordless exchange with the assistant, and now Slate held another set of forceps whose ends clutched a clean patch. From a brown bottle, he poured tinny-smelling liquid onto the patch and coated the wound the way a portrait artist painted the background on his canvas, with the same detachment. "I have no proof these worms exist; if they do, this tincture should poison them. I obey my instincts that tell me a leg come so far in healing will struggle to survive."

Her father asked, "How soon will you know?"

"A week. Apply this tincture every six hours, including at night. Change the dressing as frequently. I trust you will be true to the task despite the inconvenience. If the infection does not return by then, we will have crossed the threshold." He turned to Anna. "You are the one I trust to watch over the settings. Check four times a day. Understood?"

His tone sounded scolding. Why did he speak to her this way?

"Anna?"

"Yes, I understand."

They carried the bed inside. Her father redid the louvers and curtains. Slate said something to the gray-garbed assistant, who commenced to refit the metal stand.

She accompanied the doctor to the parlor, where he retrieved his gloves and hat from the chair. Bookman, her father, and the assistant stayed the sickroom.

Slate said, "You were brave to stay."

"I wanted to."

"I sense I have treaded on your feelings today. I did not intend to. Yet too much is at stake to let slip our vigilance."

She wanted to aver he'd spoken harshly indeed. What she said was, "Do not concern yourself with my feelings."

He tugged on his gloves, pulling each tight. "I meant to bring along a present I have for you, and in my haste this morning left behind. I shall remember next time."

He stepped out to where Jerome had the horses ready.

* * *

She lay on her bed. Sweat beaded her skin. The scent of the river's brine and shores redolent with wildflowers flooded her nostrils. She filtered in and out of dreams. In them, she saw the forceps' shiny tips, the swinging rosehead, the box's dark edge, her arms' freckles beneath hair so delicate as to be invisible had the sun's brilliance not revealed.

Rising from the box, stinking like a goat, the gray snippet. She averted her stare, only for the captain's mien to lure back. As her heart careened in terror, his face was like the river on a windless day, a visage of calmness. If fear touched him, it skimmed like a heron's wings over water without ripple. Her panic withdrew. Panic dwelled in the mind, she told herself, and the mind could be managed. She willed her facial muscles placid, her lips closed, chin set, skin smooth and without tension.

On the bed sheet, her legs pedaled. Her toes clutched and splayed like a cat's paws. The wind quieted. The curtains did not stir. In the room, she was the only thing moving.

* * *

She checked the box at six A.M.. She'd meant to rise for the day; instead she went back to bed and slept for four hours in the dusty heat that marked the onset of the harvest season. Descended the stairs into a layer of cooking smoke and the smells of grits and bacon, passed along the hallway to Captain Holland's room. Moved directly to the box.

He had *The Venables* propped on his chest. Apparently he had grown impatient.

Annoyed at herself, she asked, "Does your leg hurt?"

"Sore from the debridement. The term is French, you know."

"Is it?" She moved to the box. "Did Bookman change the dressing?"

"He did, a while ago."

"And he adjusted the box?"

"Yes."

"May I check?"

"I'm confident all is correct."

"So you object?"

"Recall, Anna, that I was present when the doctor instructed you. I know what he said, though he did not ask for my opinion in the matter."

"Nor did he ask for mine." She clicked open the outer lids, spewing the ointment's scent. She turned the buckles and reversed them the same, testing the resistance. The leg was at the proper angle, the gauze white and unstained. She pinched the corner, as Slate had taught her, to reveal the reddened, crab-shaped wound and the tincture's fresh glaze. Pressed her face toward the box and sniffed. Detected the sweaty musk. Pivoted her head toward the lower end. The fan blades puffed against her cheeks.

She closed the outer lids, which bumped on their felt pads, and rewound the fan spring.

"Bookman was quite thorough," he remarked.

"As is his habit."

"Then why not trust him?"

"I do. Perhaps you noticed I was not the one who saved your leg by detecting the infection and alerting my father and the doctor in turn. Nor do I have the slightest familiarity with medical care or any mechanical device. Nonetheless I am the one called upon, presumably because I am *white*. You of course said nothing, because to you this sounded altogether proper."

"He entrusted you because you are a person of responsibility."

"How could he judge anything about me?"

"It is obvious," he said, not lifting his focus from the book page.

"Did he tell you that?"

"No. My observation only."

"An empty compliment. You don't know me."

"Not a compliment. An officer sees these qualities. He *must* see them or else he risks the lives of his soldiers. You can bear more weight than others. A fact, Anna."

He steadied the book on his chest to read.

* * *

Holland disliked a long beard and every few days clipped his to a reasonable neatness. Not so his hair that had erupted into a shaggy mat, the longer strands corkscrewing like errant vines.

Anna brought scissors, towels, and a wooden bowl for the hair clippings.

He asked, "Have you cut hair before?"

"I have. Women's. You will be the first man. I see no difference."

He squirmed.

"Surely, a captain of cavalry is not apprehensive of a haircut?"

"I suppose you can only be an improvement upon my last barber, a sergeant who was not averse to risks, a skilled scout and horseman, yet a perilous choice to trim hair."

"Were there not more fitting choices?"

"He was the one agreeable. You cannot force such a thing on a man."

"You confront the same situation today. Or do you believe a woman's gender forces the chore upon her?"

"I didn't say that."

She laid the towel over his shoulders, which though wide felt bony under her hands. Muscles shrank with disuse—who had taught her that? Probably her father. Oddly at ease touching him, she positioned the towel to its optimum place, snipped the longer locks that sprang loose into her fingertips, and tossed them in the bowl. Scissored three strands in rapid succession and dropped all three; they fell past the towel and skittered on his upper arm. Retrieving them, he reached for the bowl.

"Keep still!"

"Sorry."

As she sifted for locks, a question occurred to her, and she was surprised when the words popped from her mouth: "Do you have much experience with Negroes?"

"Some."

"What do you do with a Negro who threatens those around him and is insolent to whites?"

"Who do you mean?"

"Sarah's husband Jerome, a man of considerable height and breadth. You've not met him—he does not often enter the house. He tends the horses and does other labor. Brute's work."

"Tending horses is *not* brute's work."

"He is a brute nonetheless."

"My father would say a Negro so sturdy is worth two others."

"I do not judge him like a commodity at the slave market."

"Have you spoken to him? Explained your complaint?"

"When I have spoken to him, I've felt only his resistance. He is an angry presence who bites the hand extended to him. I'm of the mind to ask my father to send him away."

"By dismissing the one, you will separate the family."

"Listen to you, who fights to oppress the blacks, and has become the advocate of their family welfare. They're paid freedmen, not slaves. The rest of them can do what they want—remain or leave."

"I'm neither the oppressor nor the advocate. I merely point out that consequences will result. Anyone will tell you the same. In the South we have insights into the Negro race. More than the abolitionists do."

"So you know about the abolitionists. Remarkable."

"I mean, experience teaches."

"So the masters always say, in their rationale to perpetuate control over the Negroes. We *know*, they smugly declare. Their *experience* is of cruel opportunism—an enslaver's argument." As soon as the words quit her lips, she thought, what foolishness to speak this way, as if she were with the women of her poetry circle. *Shut up!*

He seemed unfazed. "True, he would find work—the army hires free blacks to dig entrenchments. Even so, if you separate a family, you will incite rancor. Anyone who knows about Negroes will tell you the same."

"What a mentality you have."

"Do you intend to press me wholly through the bed?"

Steadying his head to shear the strands, she'd been pushing down unintentionally. "I'm sorry."

"That's all right. My neck has grown too long these idle months."

"Long neck or short, you're alive. Be grateful."

*　　*　　*

In the kitchen, Sarah was calling out the window, perhaps to Carola. Bookman had departed the house. Sarah did not observe Anna enter the kitchen.

The welt on Sarah's eye was quite prominent.

"Sarah, who did that to you?"

"I fell against the stairs," she said.

To Anna's recollection, she'd never seen Sarah fall; the woman moved around the house like a cat. "On *our* stairs?"

"The buggy house stairs. Dark as the devil in there."

"Sarah, we both know Jerome hit you."

"You don't know that."

"I intend to speak to him."

"Please let it be, miss."

"Go get him and bring him to me."

"I *fell.*"

"Go get him!"

She waited by the kitchen door for Jerome, who was slow to arrive. With each minute, her temper surged. When finally he showed, he sauntered casually, wiping his hands on a rag. Sarah was nowhere in sight.

He said, "You sent fo' me?"

"I did. If you strike Sarah, or anyone, again, you shall be gone from here at once."

Jerome shifted his feet, looked at the ground, finally at her. When he spoke his tone was oddly without agitation. "I didn't hit her. She fell on the stairs."

"I don't believe you."

He shook his head. "You changed, Miss Anna. You used to be a sweet girl. Then you went 'way to school and came back coldhearted."

"You are *not* the judge of me, Jerome. I'm the judge of you."

"You the judge of me, like you own me. I thought I was free."

"You're an employee on my property, and you will not be allowed to mistreat people."

"Your property? Thought t'was your daddy's." He flapped the rag he'd been using to wipe his hands, his sedate tone edging on mockery.

"Don't banter with me. I've warned you, and I shall give no other warning. If you dare doubt me, I will have you sent away. Just test me!"

Softly he shook the rag, perhaps to loosen dirt. To her the shaking looked like a dismissal, and in his eyes she saw he meant it so.

*   *   *

The garden's autumn vegetables approached ripeness. Measuring seventy yards by fifty, the patch grew scallions, sweet potatoes, tomatoes, cabbage, squash, peas, carrots, and parsley and other herbs. Calculating what the family needed to eat over the next day, Anna harvested, rinsed, and passed them to Sarah. Used the rinse bucket to clean her hands, then to spill onto the plants.

She wanted to stretch her legs.

Strapped on her new shoes. Reluctant to scuff the lustrous leather, she treaded carefully. The upper meadow escalated to a modest ridge she'd often climbed growing up, her favorite spot a clearing from which she no longer could see her house except from the lip, though she'd been able to hear her mother's call. During the summer's campaign, as her father later had described, the ridge had become a lookout and defensive battlement that military engineers had reinforced with scores of logs, using seconded slaves and freedmen for labor. He'd related to her how an engineer had inquired at the house if the army might temporarily hire the freedmen as diggers. One of the soldiers, encountering Bookman, had told him that when the Yankees came across Southern blacks, they sold them to Cuba. "Boy, you'd better grab yourself a pick and help us." Her father had refused to release Bookman or Jerome to work on the battlements.

Turned out that the Confederate congress in Richmond had passed a law requiring freedmen to register, and the legislation gave the government authority to press them into labor, their employers' objections notwithstanding. And so the army had compelled Jerome and Bookman to toil at these and other fortifications until August, when the Yankees departed and the peninsula quieted.

The late afternoon heat lingered, and she mounted the ridge and decided to go higher, to a stone rise that proffered a breeze for those agile to ascend. She tested her soles against the rock. They gripped firm, and she felt the strain in her legs. Recalled Dr. Slate's description of the femur as a lever, and as she climbed she tried to isolate her thigh's movement, and yes, the bone functioned just so, elevating her with each step. Atop the rock she felt the wind toss her hair and skim under her clothes.

To the southwest her father's property stretched past the turnpike to the river. Pines obscured the view north toward Richmond. Southward opened the creek aisled with marshy woods that flooded in certain seasons, especially after heavy rains, and ran for more than a mile to the Kingsland Road and past the farm of Lyman Hock, the widower who'd asked her father for her hand in marriage.

On the eastern horizon she made out the silhouette of Malvern Hill, where rose a vague smoke plume she assumed was from normal activity and not war. Away at the Augusta Seminary, she'd missed the tumult when General McClellan's army had maneuvered toward Richmond last summer. Except for the battle in May when Confederate cannoneers had beaten back Union gunboats at nearby Drewry's Bluff, no Yankees had penetrated this far west on the peninsula—they'd stayed to the center and east. In June came the land battles: Seven Pines, after which the Confederacy had appointed General Robert E. Lee commander of the Army of Northern Virginia; and his ensuing campaign of the Seven Days when he'd chased the Federals through the fields and swamps and cornered them at Malvern Hill. On the grassy mound, the Yankees had lined up cannons and stopped Lee's soldiers. Her father had described how the artillery had boomed for hours, audible here though the battlefield was six miles away. One day on the ground behind the house she'd discovered lead bearings, no doubt from a cannon shot a far distance away, and she wondered if war scraps peppered the entire peninsula.

The invading Yankees had stirred quite a panic—civilians by the thousands had packed their belongings and fled deeper into Virginia by way of Richmond. Her father had described how the evacuees had ridden along the Osborne Turnpike past the Van Meers' land. The wagons rolled in shaggy skeins, possessions dropping from the hasty piles at every shake, slave children jumping off to fetch the fallen items and scrambling back atop as if on a camel's hump. After the campaign ended, McClellan's men stayed at Harrison's Landing on the James until mid-August, when they'd marched southward and boarded ships. The peninsula was free of war—the few Yankees who remained were in Williamsburg and Fort Monroe—and her father had consented to her return.

The white residents who'd fled had returned whooping—the Confederates had chased away Lincoln's army! Some brought their slaves back too. Others had left them with relatives or leased them to the Confederacy, for fear they'd abscond—multitudes of the region's slaves had escaped to refuge at places the Union army occupied, Fort Monroe especially.

By then, Staunton had become quite uncomfortable. To open rooms for folks the fighting had displaced, the Augusta Female Seminary had asked its students to move from their regular boardings. They'd crowded into temporary lodgings, from whose windows they'd watched the soldiers and evacuees rushing about. Rumors and uncertainty had abounded. Plainly the Shenandoah Valley was no safer than the Richmond peninsula. The worst day came when one of the students, walking past a wagon bearing casualties from a battle, had recognized her brother's face among the ashen dead. The poor girl had wailed, inconsolable.

Anna had determined to spend the rest of the war at home. If the Confederates won, she'd leave the South—she'd ask Bookman to go with her. If he wouldn't, she'd go alone. She'd not spend her life in a land that enslaved people. A society that condoned slavery was insane.

There were two types of madness, she thought: the single person who no longer recognized reality, like the fellow she'd seen at the Richmond marketplace waving his stick; and an entire society gone delirious. A person might succumb suddenly, like an apple gone wormy. Society's madness took longer. To accommodate slavery, society must rake together fear, arrogance, hypocrisy, hate, and greed that clung together like a bird's nest, lacking mortar. Like birds, society always had to remake the nest and repeat the falsehoods: Blacks were too irresponsible to be free, too erratic to decide for themselves, too ignorant to vote or govern, too inattentive to educate.

Earlier generations of the Van Meer family had reaped slavery's profits. Their land had required slave labor to be productive, and the family had acquired slaves though purchase or breeding. The bonds the Van Meers had forged with slavery might have proven unbreakable had her father not married a woman who found its every whiff noxious. The daughter of a Presbyterian family of Scottish roots, Elsa harbored not a minute's doubt that slavery must be abolished. To her, the evil was as apparent as the fallen night, and nobody she married or raised could think to the contrary. Soon after their marriage, Henry had inherited his father's property, and he'd freed the slaves and leased out the fields. Later, needing servants, Elsa and Henry had purchased the Fournier family and freed them too.

Elsa was the one who'd brought the preacher to the Van Meer farm. She'd heard of the minister whose messages contrasted with those of ordinary white preachers who exhorted the slaves to remain obedient and docile, claiming God so willed. She'd invited him to the farm and discussed with him the writings of the Northern abolitionists she'd read and admired, like John Greenleaf Whittier and William Lloyd Garrison. Anna recalled the preacher's first Sunday sermon, and he'd continued for years to visit, until her father had abrogated the practice soon after Captain Holland's arrival.

Had her mother lived, surely they'd have gone north and become abolitionists. Instead, her father with Anna's and Bookman's help had opened a station on the Underground Railroad. They'd spirited runaways toward freedom, over the years moving more than thirty slaves, one at a time or in pairs. They'd used codes written on paper scraps they tucked into tree hollows or other hiding places. The Railroad had ignited her passion, and she'd played her role brilliantly, gaining her father's trust and admiration.

When the war began, he'd closed their station. His reason: The conflict added dangers beyond what they could manage. The slave patrols, now part of the Henrico County Home Guard, scouted the roads and manned checkpoints. Though the war's locus had shifted from the peninsula into northern Virginia and recently to Maryland, the countryside remained jittery. Soldiers were posted nearby—an army detachment guarded the bluff on Susan Chaffin's farm up the road. The Railroad's noble enterprise must stay dormant.

In mid-August she'd returned from the seminary, and all had seemed normal—or as normal as a place could be in wartime. Then she'd begun to notice things she could neither explain nor dismiss, manifested in peculiar incidents, like the digging sounds she and Holland had heard on separate nights. Who was the shadowy third figure? Where had her father obtained the money he'd given her? And why did he, who in her memory had not socialized much, regularly stay out late, sometimes not returning until hours after dark?

When in the past she'd climbed this ridge, she'd cried for her mother whose face she could picture against the sky, and whose strength and wisdom she missed. Today she didn't cry. She puzzled at what her father was up to, a secret activity from which she'd been excluded.

Ignore it, she told herself.

She couldn't. Most aggravating was that Bookman played a role in whatever was happening. They crossed paths once or twice daily, and on these occasions he had nothing to say. He replaced the dressings on Holland's leg and adjusted the box. Left the house on chores her father assigned. Took the buggy to New Market center. He neither consulted her nor offered explanations.

How could Bookman have shut her out?

*   *   *

The day after her walk to the ridge, she encountered him at the field's edge below the house. "Someone is digging by the house at night," she told him.

"Digging?"

"Yes, *digging*. The captain told me he heard the sound. I heard the same myself, on the night I found you outside with my father and another man, whose identity I am not trusted to know."

Bookman stayed silent. Dusting off his hands, he wouldn't look at her.

She said, "If the Railroad is running, the captain must not grow suspicious."

"Have you talked to your father?"

"Not yet."

"You should. But there ain't no Railroad. That's God's own truth."

All of her life, if Bookman had evoked God's own truth, she would have believed him without question. Now she no longer did. Truth had been replaced by something opaque, like glass that tumbled around in the river currents to turn cloudy and rounded. Did he not care if she stopped trusting him?

She said, "By not telling me, you are hurting me."

"Tell you what?"

"Who was the man with you and my father that night?"

"Talk to your father."

Her father too had changed. He returned late and adjourned to his bedroom to prepare his lessons and papers, shutting the door behind. Often he ate alone. He'd worked at the school for years, but never before had his work so consumed him.

That evening, observing the candlelight under his door, she knocked. She heard papers rustle, a drawer open and close. When she entered, she perceived the mien of one who braced himself against annoyance. "Yes, dear?"

"I know you're busy. Still I would like to speak to you."

"Of course—you may speak to me at any time. What is the matter?"

She opened her mouth to make one declaration and abruptly made another. "Jerome has become intolerable. You are too busy to notice he abuses Sarah and threatens Bookman. He regards me with ill-disguised contempt."

"What? That can't be true."

"I tell you something and immediately you say it isn't true?"

"Wait, please." He held up his hand, and she noticed ink smears on his fingers. "I spoke hastily. You are right—I don't pay much attention to Jerome. He is simply here, as he has been since soon after you were born. He threatens Bookman, you contend?"

"Yes."

"Bookman has made no complaint to me."

"He would not speak against his family. Neither would Sarah, who wears a bruise above her eye from where Jerome hit her."

He frowned. "Dear, you must be mindful that within families are... *privacies* we are not open to probe, lines we should respect and tolerate, albeit to our discomfort."

"Should we also tolerate his mockery toward me?"

"No. Respect must run both ways. I shall speak to him."

"He is mulish and antagonistic. Speaking to him will have no effect."

"What would you have me do?"

"Dismiss him from our employ. Send him away. Sarah and Carola can stay."

"You're serious?"

"Yes."

"Why do you so desire to have him gone?"

"I cannot be the mistress of this house and not be taken seriously."

He stared at her, and his face passed through a series of expressions, none lasting long enough for her to interpret, although their prevalent theme was reluctance. "What would happen to him, if we sent him away?"

"Certainly a strong Negro can find employment. Everywhere you see freedmen. The army hires many."

"True. Yet even if he obtained work, laborer's wages do not provide for all he would need—shelter, food, and a family to distribute life's tasks. He would not readily gain substitutes. We bear a responsibility for him"

"So he may act toward me as he pleases?"

"Dear, if we sent him away and caused him to be separated him from his family, he would have a terrible grievance against us. He'd be angry and might act in unpredictable ways."

She thought of Sarah's statement in the Richmond market: *"Crazy black people? Don't put 'em in no asylum. Just shoot 'em dead."* A myth? If true for anyone, so for Jerome, whose bulk would cast him as a threat.

"The circumstance is of his own making," she said.

Her father lowered his gaze to his socks where Sarah's darning tracked white against the darker wool. "Anna, never would I wish to think of you as naïve, but perhaps your emotion carries you away. Do you not see how Jerome's proximity to our Railroad station complicates the matter?"

She hadn't considered that. Unlike Bookman, Jerome had not been central to the Railroad's functions—he had not ventured out to receive the escaped slaves from the other station keepers. Still he had accomplished vital work at key moments. She remembered him immersed to his waist in the river shallows, dredging the silt in buckets so the launch could slip easily to shore. He had helped tear down the old well wall, fill the cavity, and smooth the ground.

She said, "How can you say I'm carried away? I am as concentrated as you are."

"Yes, concentrated. You are too young to be *deliberate*."

"What is the difference between concentrated and deliberate? I see none."

"There is a difference, in how far a person can project beyond the immediate and anticipate consequences. The lack is not your fault—deliberateness is a quality that comes to a person with age. We wear two masks, so if the one falls off, the other remains."

"Must you always resort to your silly adages? What does that even mean?"

"It means…"

"You said you closed the station. Is it true?"

"Yes. The peril of those times lingers, and we must comport ourselves accordingly. We must preserve Jerome's willing silence, which is founded in trust and good will."

Her father had introduced the subject himself, and this seemed like the chance to ask him what was going on. For reasons that escaped her, she did not. She turned and left the room.

The door closed softly behind her.

We must preserve Jerome's willing silence…

Heretofore dormant in her thoughts, a notion wriggled under her suppressing efforts—that Jerome, Bookman, Sarah, all of them, knew more about the nocturnal activities than she did.

- 5 -

On a day when her father was not at home, Dr. Slate visited. He brought her the present he'd mentioned, and she unwrapped white tissue to reveal a hand mirror with a lacquered chartreuse frame, the handle shaped like a raindrop.

She asked, "Is this courtesy of the Chimborazo Hospital?"

"My present to you for your steadfast efforts, and those you shall yet exert."

The lamp oil and the antiscorbutics had fitted the Van Meers as hosts for a convalescent soldier. The mirror seemed too personal, meant for her alone. "How can I accept? It must have been expensive."

"I am occasionally the recipient of gifts from those who feel gratitude for one reason or another. The mirror was given to me and frankly does not suit me. Hence, I thought of you."

"Thank you."

Men will come askin' about you. They got you on their minds.

Now she stood alongside Slate as he examined the captain's leg. The box ejected the scent of ointment—no hint of the goat's odor that would have heralded the fresh eruption of gangrene. She was confident Bookman had followed Slate's procedures rigorously, and she'd inspected with equal diligence, though she hadn't done so today, for fault of waking up late.

The room was warm, and her attention had drifted a bit when Slate tapped her on the shoulder. "Observe this," he said. He indicated Holland's thigh where the skin blushed red. The sight reminded her of a fish on display at the market, its head cut off. "May I speak with you for a minute?"

She trailed him to the parlor, out of earshot of the sickroom. He spoke softly: "The turnbuckles were improperly set. I see no harm beyond the bruise on John's leg, yet further injury mustn't recur."

She blinked. "Bookman is capable, intelligent, and diligent in his duties."

"I'm aware you rely on him for the settings. Nonetheless he has made them too tight."

Her anger welled. Slate no doubt assumed Bookman had erred because he was black. In fact, Bookman was more skilled and meticulous than she was. "Was anything wrong with the dressings or the leg's angle?"

"They were correct. The sole fault was with the turnbuckles."

"Show me again."

In the sickroom, Slate demonstrated the box settings, guiding her hand as she turned. Upon hers, his huge hand was like a cottonwood leaf against a holly. "They must be firm, not tight. Preferable a woman applies the settings, because they require sensitivity to the touch—a man may twist past the optimum. When a turnbuckle becomes resistive, the pressure is correct. Always pad the tips with clean cloths. No configuration should endure for more than eight hours."

She practiced under his gaze, repeating the configuration, and he seemed satisfied. In the carriageway, he said, "Please don't take my remarks as a rebuke. The therapy has progressed. Bookman is a heedful assistant, and his mistakes are few." His voice trailed off, and she perceived his tiredness. She thought of the wounded men who crowded the Chimborazo's wards, a thousand Captain Hollands.

He stepped with his one hand on the horse's bridle, the other tucked in his watch pocket. He said, "How pedantic my exhortations must sound—I apologize."

She said, "To speak plainly is better than to be excessively polite and misunderstood."

"Indeed, though hard to strike the precise balance. Like the box settings.

He seemed unsure of himself, and his demeanor had nothing to do with his surgeon's mantle, rather with how he related to her. Aware of this, she made no attempt to make him feel comfortable. When he led his horse under the vine helix, she did not follow.

He turned, "I shall see you in a week, Anna."

"Very well."

"Goodbye then."

He was about to mount the horse when she asked, "How much longer until the captain's leg is healed?"

"Fully? I would suppose seven more weeks before we can take away the box. Thereafter, he must recuperate for at least the same interval, exercising progressively until the leg gains strength. Complete recovery may take a long time. Possibly he always will walk with a limp, however slight."

"He should not return to the war."

"He's an officer. He has no prerogative."

"He could plead he is unfit, because of his leg."

To converse across the yard's span was awkward, and Slate stepped toward her. "Others have done so. I doubt he will submit such a claim."

"Why not?"

"Two types of men come to the Chimborazo. One has had his fill of war, his spirit stripped away, and he will evade the restoration. He may become a hospital rat who purposefully prolongs his convalescence, or desert the army upon his release. The other is the man of duty. I know John well enough to say he is the latter. He will rejoin his unit at the first opportunity."

"What foolish duty compels a man to his own destruction?"

"If you ask people what we fight for, they say for our homeland invaded by the Yankees, or for our way of life President Lincoln strives to take away, or for the cause God has appointed. These are words for speeches. When a soldier witnesses a cannonball cut the man next to him in half, words fail. What endures is the wish to stand by one's friends, a deep and true feeling."

"I see."

"You do not. But it is well, my dear. Enough innocence has been sacrificed; we cannot spare all."

He stepped toward her, and involuntarily she retreated. "Thank you again for the mirror," she said, not knowing what else to say.

He smiled. "You are welcome. I am happy to leave the settings in your hands. And to have seen you today, Anna."

*   *   *

Harvest season in the land of the James. The dawns peeled to crystal skies. Gusts swayed the trees and the fields billowed dust, an oatmeal cloud. People cinched scarves to their faces, sealed windows, stuffed rags in the shutter cracks. Under the sun, the house transformed to an oven, and hands left sweat prints on whatever they touched. Anna lay sedentary on her bed and tasted the grit. The dust sketched lines in the sky. Years ago she'd told her mother they looked like witch scratches. Her mother had said there were no witches; all things were the work of God.

Then her mother had died. Now when Anna noticed the lines in the sky, she told herself there were no witches, or God either. Both were nonexistent.

Holland suffered the heat. Propped on pillows, his shirt's collar and armpits drenched in sweat, he clutched a handkerchief and daubed his face and neck. In the evenings she read to him from the Venables book, for whose characters she'd invented voices: the brittle mother, the selfish sister, the pompous minister, the stumpy-toothed, liquor-steeped sea captain, the lavender-lipped heroine, and the honorable, somewhat vapid protagonist. Into their dialog, Anna interlaced sighs and inflections of irony or cynicism the author could not have intended. Though Holland did not remark on these embellishments, his brow furrowed as he tried to follow characters gone fickle.

She finished the chapter. Closed the book.

He said, "I heard the digging again last night."

"Oh?"

"Often I cannot sleep in the heat. Over these weeks I've become accustomed to your house's creaks and bumps, and I've grown adept at detecting deviations in the sounds. Last night, I so wished I might call to you, to alert you, so you might hear too."

"I heard nothing."

"Well, I hope you will forgive me for mentioning." With the handkerchief he wiped his forehead.

The dust persisted, the worst she'd ever seen, lasting through a fortnight. The heat did not abate. The temperature inside became unbearable. One evening, her father tramped from window to window, throwing them open. "I cannot breathe in here!"

Earlier in the week, he wouldn't have dared to open them. Fortunately, the dust was momentarily in abeyance, and he left them ajar. The breeze spilled in, and the torpor subsided. In Holland's room, Van Meer folded the louvers, set aside the screen, and hefted the chair to the patio where they'd borne the bed on the day Slate had snipped off the gangrenous skin.

Propped up on his pillows, Holland remarked, "Wonderful—the out of doors at last."

"I hope I do not disturb you, Captain. How are you today?"

"I am well, thanks to your daughter's ministrations, and Bookman's. And how are you, sir?"

"Occupied with my lessons. Before the war, I had an assistant, a younger teacher. He joined the army, leaving me behind with no less work."

"I have met teachers in the ranks."

"I would think they'd make peculiar soldiers, some of them."

"I am fortunate to be in the cavalry, where a certain high spirit is indispensable. If a man has the spirit, and can ride and shoot, let him be as peculiar as he wants."

Van Meer laughed. "Perhaps fitting, peculiar men for a peculiar war."

"Indeed."

"What do the soldiers say?"

"In what sense do you mean?"

"How long do they believe the war will last? Surely not much longer."

Holland paused before answering. Conscious how his ill-chosen remarks had given offense to Anna, he hoped to avoid antagonizing her father. "Of course they yearn for a quick end. The war takes its toll."

"The fighting must be terrible."

"Yes sir. And not only the fighting, which is occasional, but the strain and tedium, which are constant. Of men who desert, few are cowards. They simply cannot bear the soldier's life, the marches especially."

"And you? What do you think?"

"The Yankees have not done well against us. Maybe their politicians will lose their stomachs and settle for a truce, so we may negotiate in the way of a democracy."

"Do you doubt we can win by arms?"

"In war, if a commander has the proper instrument, victory becomes a matter of his judgment and timing. General Lee's qualities are impeccable, that is certain. Whether he has the instrument is another question."

"I am surprised to hear you say. Most people express cocksure optimism."

"I do not mean to sound pessimistic."

"Please trust that your remarks will stop with me."

"The truth is, we are outnumbered. Our strategy has been to confuse the Yankees with mock cannons and marches back and forth by a single unit, to raise dust to cause them to think we are myriad. Our soldiers are told to claim likewise, if the Yankees capture them. We make feints on Washington, to create fright and uncertainty, and to divert their attention."

"These tricks fool the Yankees?"

"Until now. Yet each time we encounter them, they seem more formidable, and I cannot help but anticipate they will put themselves in order one of these days."

"Your assessment is thoughtful. And rare to hear."

"I would not share my views with many. Among honorable men, there is candor."

"I am pleased you count me so."

"I do, sir. But you shouldn't lend much weight to my military opinion. I'm merely a junior officer, and I've been out of action for a while."

Van Meer folded his arms. He looked over the courtyard as if noticing for the first time. The honeysuckle had browned, the fragrance vanished. New roses blossomed. Ants made a trail across the flagstones. He said, "My wife and I used to sit on the patio from time to time, and when we did, she would pour a bucket of water on the stones to wash them. She was finicky in that way. We would watch the water separate into patches to shrink and finally to disappear. Sometimes we'd choose two puddles and bet on which one would evaporate first." He chuckled, and the mirth fell away. "I had not thought of that in a long time."

"When did your wife pass?"

"Ten years ago."

"Your memories are clear."

"Not always, but just now, yes." His mien waxed pensive. "You know, whatever goodness I have in me, I owe to my late wife. Anna is much the same as her mother—brilliant and spirited. Also willful."

Holland wanted to ask what Van Meer meant by *willful*. Would the inquiry seem intrusive? He regarded the courtyard roses, thinking what he should say. When he looked up, Van Meer had gone.

* * *

"Who opened these doors?" exclaimed Anna.

"Your father. The room was unbearably hot."

"Does he not comprehend that the box fan pulls the dust onto your wound?"

"Well, he might have, if I had told him."

"Why should you have to tell him—is he not a teacher? A teacher of folly, apparently."

Holland remained quiet while she closed the louvers, came over, and examined the settings. She wrapped her fingers around the turnbuckles, sensing their tension. Checked his leg for dust. Lifted the dressing.

He could feel her fingers moving, her nails' scrape. He coughed awkwardly. "Do you mind if I ask you something?"

"Go ahead."

"Are you well?"

"What?"

"I mean, in good health?"

Her eyelids fluttered. "I believe so. Do I look sickly to you?"

"I'm sorry. I mean no offense. At times you appear troubled."

"I am fine." She closed the box lids. "These patio doors should remain closed in this season. I will remind my father." She turned to leave.

"Please, wait a minute."

She stopped halfway to the door.

"I have thought more about the digging outside. The sounds are subtle. Certainly the digger is wary of being heard."

She stared at the curtains' unraveling hems against the floorboards. "You speak as if this person's existence is proven, and he is not the product of your imagination."

"Surely he is *not* my imagination. The question is, who *is* he?"

"What do you imply?"

"A deserter might be hiding in the woods nearby."

"That's absurd. Why would anyone lurk in the woods and approach the house at night?"

"Well, suppose, during the day, the fellow occults himself, and after dark he emerges to uncover a cache of food a sympathizer has buried for him in a chosen spot. With a small till, the deserter digs up what has been left for him."

"No one from this house would bury food for a deserter."

"I didn't say they would. Those involved merely use the house as a landmark."

"I refuse to credit a theory so preposterous. You heard an animal."

"The metal ring was distinct. I'm familiar with the sound."

"Ah, your keen ears."

"The deserter might be caught. The Home Guard can comb this area or lay in wait for the next time he appears."

The Home Guard? Weren't they the ones who had militarized the slave patrol? She said, "Deserters are put to death if captured."

"A few have been."

"To execute a man who has given service, simply because he's become afraid or embittered or homesick and run away—the only part that makes sense is to have fled from those who would impose such a fate on their fellows."

"Much otherwise inexplicable happens in war. Anyway, deserters can be dangerous."

"Did you mention this to my father?"

"No. Should I?"

"Please do not. He tends to worry, and he has better things to occupy his time."

* * *

In late September, President Lincoln issued the Preliminary Emancipation Proclamation. The Richmond newspapers printed the edict; the editorialists branded it an outrage.

Anna thought, the world at last knew what the war was about. For a week, she said nothing to the captain about the proclamation, though from the papers by his bed, she assumed he'd read of the momentous event.

Normally Sarah brought him his dinner; this evening Anna carried the plate in herself. On the white china, slivers of spiced meat, rice, greens, and dried cherries. She sat, her own plate in her lap, wiped her brow with the napkin, and tipped her fork toward the box. "The doctor says you have seven more weeks. Closer to six now, I suppose, as he said so a week ago."

"I am surprised he did not enunciate the number of days. He tends to speak—to propound—in precise terms. *Medium to high confidence*," he mimicked.

She suppressed a smile. "And afterward, you are to remain convalescent for a similar period until you have recovered the full use of your limb."

"We shall see."

"Are you so eager to restore yourself to the war's insanity?"

"You regard my sentiment as inexplicable. To me, the war is about the soldiers of my company. They are dear to me, in ways more so than my own family."

"Plus, there are horses."

"Though not mine."

"Given to another man?"

"Killed in saving me."

She thought he seemed saddened by the recollection. "I am sorry for your horse."

"He was my mount since the beginning, and I kept him healthy over a year's service with Stuart's cavalry that did not go easy on horses. If not for him, the bullet probably would have cut my leg in half."

They ate in silence, until she said, "Well, are you going to tell me what occurred?"

"I thought you were not enamored with the war."

"Of course I am not *enamored*. I just want to hear what happened to you."

He chewed a sliver of meat, wiped his lips with the napkin. "One June day, we crossed the Chickahominy River below Mechanicsville. By then McClellan had marched his army up the peninsula, and we were wary of Northern pickets. We came upon a farmhouse where enemy soldiers were foraging. We had the advantage of surprise, having spotted their wagon nearby, and as I contemplated what to do, whether to assault the house or to wait until they emerged, I heard a woman scream. Reacting, I charged ahead—a mistake, for in the confines by the house I was unable to maneuver. One of the foragers rushed out and pointed his rifle at me. I can attest that, at two paces from the muzzle, a Sharps .52 caliber is quite intimidating."

He paused, and she wondered if the recollection had so traumatized him that he couldn't recount. She remembered his calmness when the doctor had cut the gangrenous skin off his leg, and she divined he was merely gathering his thoughts, so he might articulate them.

"Mind you, Anna, I can draw and shoot in a blink, yet even as I glimpsed the maw of his barrel, he fired. He was not a seasoned soldier, for he didn't aim as much as he jerked the trigger. The bullet passed through my horse and hit my opposite leg. Probably the first time the fellow had fired his rifle at anyone, and the last, for as my horse and I toppled over, my men shot him dead. The morning sky was brilliant blue, and I remember thinking, what a fine day it might have been."

"Hmm. Were your men hurt?"

"Only my horse."

"And the other foragers?"

"Killed."

"The people in the farmhouse?"

"The three women and five children were unharmed, although who knows what the foragers would have done to them had we not arrived? The women were brave—they fashioned a tourniquet around my leg."

"You witnessed other such incidents?"

"Yes."

She imagined the rifle hammer's snap, the muzzle's flash. She asked, "Can you see a bullet when it comes out of the gun?"

"No."

"So men are struck by surprise?"

"All the time. Though perhaps they might hear something."

"What do they hear?"

"Oh, a strange noise. Imagine you walk in a forest at the base of a cliff. A boulder dislodges from the top and falls straight for your head, crashing through the branches above. Though you hear the clatter, you don't have time to comprehend, or to look up before the rock strikes."

She who loved to stroll in the forest wondered if this disturbing image would linger and make her fearful. "So to this world of tragedy you hope to regress, to be with your dear men?"

"Yes. I think of them often. You cannot conceive of their spirit, their strong hearts. Not only my cavalrymen—all the army is so. They march long distances barefooted, their clothes ragged. They sleep in the mud wrapped in threadbare blankets, yet when the time comes, oh, do they fight!"

"Do you ever ask yourself whether they fight for the right cause?"

"You're serious in your question?"

"Yes. I refer to the proclamation from President Lincoln that frees the slaves, as you've seen in the newspaper."

"That doesn't concern the army. What matters to a soldier is his duty."

"His duty is one thing, but another is what he fights for, to preserve a society that enslaves people under the law's tolerance, which is morally wrong."

"Is this one of the axioms you learned at your female seminary, Anna?"

"It's the *truth*, obvious to anyone."

"If we lose the war, the foragers we killed that day by the Chickahominy will be replaced by a swarm of villains who will devour the South like a pestilence." For a minute he seemed agitated, then his natural calmness settled. "I suppose it is good there are those like you who think with the purity of ideas. If there were not, only the practitioners would abound, and the world would be the lesser."

I too am a practitioner, she thought. Of course she could not tell him this. The discussion already had ventured too far.

*   *   *

Holland angled the folded Richmond newspaper to the light. The page featured portions of Lincoln's proclamation in an editorial titled 'Illegal!':

'Any man who wonders why the South is at war needs merely to read the so-called 'Preliminary Proclamation' Northern President Abraham Lincoln issued on September 22nd of this year. Among other things, Lincoln orders the following: "That on the first day of January in the year of our Lord, one thousand eight hundred and sixty-three, all persons held as slaves within any State, or designated part of a State, the people whereof shall then be in rebellion against the United States shall be then, thenceforward, and forever, free; and the Executive government of the United States, including the military and naval authority thereof, will recognize and maintain the freedom of such persons, and will do no act or acts to suppress such persons, or any of them, in any efforts they may make for their actual freedom."

'Here stands Mr. Lincoln, imposing his will upon the states. Are the states not sovereign, whether in rebellion or not? Apparently he does not think so. To him, they are simply extensions of his dominion, and he shall dictate whatever he pleases.'

So ran the rebellion's classic argument, thought Holland. The states had ratified the U.S. Constitution that gave the Federal government certain specific powers, and all others the states retained. The central government might broaden its powers by amending the Constitution. Lincoln had not done so; instead, early in 1861, he had raised an army to suppress select states. By ignoring the nation's pact, he lent the states not only moral but legal justification to rebel.

A counterargument interposed: What was a nation, if its constituents could secede at their whim? Under such a model, a state could break away and join another nation. What if Georgia and Virginia were to become the principalities of Great Britain's empire and encampments for her army? The U.S. Constitution's preamble stated that its purpose, among others, was to provide for the common defense. And how was defense feasible, if dissatisfied states could disjoin and become threats?

The editorialist went on: *'And what are we to take from Mr. Lincoln's instruction, that no authority shall suppress any efforts slaves may make for their freedom? Has the President not heard of Nat Turner's infamous rebellion, when a mere thirty years ago the slave and his band massacred men, women, and children in the name of their cause? How would Mr. Lincoln react, if the Confederacy were to incite Jews, who are mistreated in the North, and treated fairly in the South, to commit usury, theft, and assassination in the cause to deprive the North of its money, and promised them no consequences whatsoever for these vile crimes? Would not this be the moral equal of the proclamation Lincoln has issued?'*

According to the editorialist, the proclamation's second paragraph exhorted slaves to murder, loot, rape, and rampage. Any outrage whatsoever, if committed in the name of freedom, would incur no consequences, because the dictate absolved the slaves. *'Now the slaves might as well be kings who can do as they please! Rex non potest peccare—the king can do no wrong!'*

The editorialist was getting a bit carried away, thought Holland.

He had heard the argument about Jews and slaves before. Southern society's religious tolerance stood in ironic contrast to its racial class system, whereas the North's puritan religious culture tended to disparage Jews. Thus, the argument went, the abolitionists should mend their own prejudices before they condemned Southern slavery. Was the logic valid? He was uncertain. He was aware that Jews served in senior posts in the Confederacy, even in the Presidential cabinet.

'All persons held as slaves… shall be then, thenceforward, and forever free.' Bold language. He doubted that Lincoln had meant to incite the slaves to violence. The editorialist's allegation bespoke a profound dread

among Southern whites that their chattels would rise in bloody insurrection. Over the years, a few slave rebellions had occurred, among them Nat Turner's 1831 revolt in southeast Virginia. Though rare, the incidents had created onerous institutions in their wake. The slave patrols gave no quarter to disobedience, and the law condoned punishment of any severity to a slave who shook his fist at his master. Slaves and freedmen alike required written passes to travel if not in the company of whites. Powerless, slaves had merely to hint at malevolence, and they could be beaten or killed without legal redress. The slave laws had stood for longer than the country itself. In 1705, the Virginia colony's legislature had passed the Slave Act to codify disparate laws and customs. In 1806, 1819, and 1837, the commonwealth had issued various revisions—for instance the 1819 law that prohibited the schooling of slaves. And lest anyone should think these state laws were remnants of the bygone past, the United States Supreme Court only five years ago had issued a decision in the case of Dred Scott vs. Sandford affirming that slaves were property and had no rights under the law. Holland knew about the legal history from discussions he'd overheard between his attorney brother and his father over the years.

What had Anna said? He had a strong memory for spoken words, and he conjured hers easily: *His duty is one thing, but another is what he fights for, to preserve a society that enslaves people under the law's tolerance, which is morally wrong.* Her statement had spurred him to conclude she understood nothing about what soldiers were fighting for. He'd never met a soldier who thought he was fighting for slavery. The majority of soldiers were from families that owned no slaves, and all would be averse to giving their lives in defense of slavery or on behalf of slaveholders. The enactment of military conscription had ignited widespread rancor at the deferrals granted to landholders who owned twenty or more slaves. Few soldiers would dispute that slavery was a practice discordant with Christianity, and thus fated for extinction in due course. And had not the founding fathers detested slavery? Thomas Jefferson, himself a slaveholder, had considered the institution deplorable—as President in 1807, he'd signed an act forbidding participation in the international slave trade.

No, the fight was not about slavery, but about men's rights to liberate themselves from a central government that imposed its will against their consent. How should responsible citizens react to a president who raised an army against them? Southern soldiers, like Southerners in general, despised the idea of being ruled by Northerners, whom they saw as trespassers on others' rights and insistent to settle immediately the question of slavery, while fully aware the South would suffer the most dire consequences. Did anyone genuinely believe that the slaves were ready for citizenship? Who could imagine the outcome, if the social order were thus upended?

He reread the editorial. In northwestern Virginia where he'd grown up, there were fewer slaves than in other parts of the commonwealth. His father was the region's largest slaveowner. On his father's land, the slaves were not whipped or sexually abused—practices extant among slaveholders elsewhere. His father fed, clothed, and gave the slaves Christian names, and when he spoke of slavery, he painted a soft picture, like a summer evening in the serene shade of loam you witnessed only in the American South. Didn't the Bible mention slaves, describing them as the loyal servants whose masters treated them almost as their own sons and daughters, proving that God allowed slavery in a gentle form? Did masters not fret over their slaves when they were sick, and summon the doctor if necessary? Were the slaves not happier than they would be otherwise?

His father and the other Virginia aristocrats fancied themselves enlightened and empathetic men who kept grateful slaves. John's observations did not bear this out. The slaves were plainly disgruntled. They took subtle measures to resist. When they performed their master's bidding, they often acted slower than they were capable, whereas on their own behalf they moved with alacrity. When they interacted with the whites, they averted their eyes and couched their language to veil their true feelings. Speaking to each other, they adopted a dialect whites could not understand, leastways its nuances and subtleties.

And what of the idea that masters concerned themselves with the slaves' welfare? If this were true, why did they not educate the slaves? Slaveholders abhorred the notion—to teach slaves to read was a whimsical experiment. True, they kept their working slaves healthy, and they summoned a doctor when necessary. When slaves reached an age when they were no longer useful, or suffered prolonged or terminal sickness, the masters commonly disregarded them. Their care fell to the community of slaves within their limited means. No law required that masters show compassion. A greedy one might begrudge a non-working slave the ration and exile him or her beyond the plantation, to die out in the woods.

And gentle slavery? A myth. The slaveowners retained coercion, whether veiled or in plain sight. His father gave money in support of the county's slave patrols whose ruffians scoured the land for runaways and chased them and retrieved them bound belly down on a mule. If a slave ran off and was caught, his master might sell him into the deep South, severing him from his family for the rest of his life.

He remembered an occasion when his father had taken him to the slave quarters. One of the women had given birth to a son. His father carried a yarn blanket he laid on the bed where she reclined holding her baby. "Senna, this is for you and your new son."

The slave mumbled, "Thank you, sir."

On her stoic mien, John contemplated despair. En route to the house, he asked, "Father, who does the baby belong to?"

"He belongs to me, of course."

"Why?"

"I own the mother, ergo I own her offspring. To whom else could he belong?"

Simple economics encouraged his father to foster the natural increase in the slave population. If a slave woman did not produce babies with her husband, another man could be allowed to lay with her. The woman might be asked whom she preferred to impregnate her. Or she might not. Whether to bear children was not her option.

…what you're fighting for, to preserve a society that enslaves people under the law's tolerance, which is morally wrong.

Before he reached the age of twelve, Holland comprehended certain truths about himself. His memory was strong—he could recall what he'd read and heard, and he might recite certain portions perfectly. He had a talent for perceiving things in their genuine way, shorn of embellishment. Undeniably, the arguments for slavery were pretensions. The truth was that wealthy families owned slaves, encouraged them to breed, and used whatever means were required to perpetuate the system. Common white people weren't fond of slavery, which worked to their economic disadvantage, and they cared even less for the rich slaveowner class. Yet they inured themselves to the institution because they feared the social disruption its abrogation would create. To them, slavery was part of the culture, and in its defense they invoked moralistic language and rationalizations.

Now he was at war, if not for slavery, for the society that upheld it.

He set the newspaper on the bed sheet and sank into the pillow. These days he did not dwell on philosophical dilemmas. Nor did he reflect on his family in the western hills. Two years had passed since he'd visited the place, and he'd not seen his father, sister, or brother in the interval. What did they think of him, who had distanced himself? No doubt they held him to be ungrateful and arrogant. Had his role in the war—the cause his father advocated on behalf of President Jefferson Davis—redeemed him in their appraisal? Or simply transformed him into a hypocrite?

The musings brought on a headache. How had he permitted himself to delve into abstractions? He thought, let Anna entertain her fanciful notions. His role in the war was cast, and his soldier's duty was not open to debate.

* * *

Mid-morning came a rider, his horse nosing at the gate. Sarah fetched Anna, who from the doorway shouted, "What do you want?"

"Ma'am, General Fogarty will be here in thirty minutes."

"*Who?*"

"General Fogarty. He commands the Virginia Home Guard."

The Home Guard again? She was reminded of Holland's speculation about a deserter. Of course, no such deserter existed.

She strode to the gate and stared up at the rider. He was perhaps thirteen years of age—his face showed no wisp of beard. His half-gravelly, half-girlish voice cracked at the consonants. Behind his hat, he'd tied his hair in a ribbon as neat as his mother would have done.

She asked, "How is this household the general's business?"

"Are you not servicing the army, by boarding a convalescent officer?"

"Yes, I suppose we are *servicing* the army. Not serving in it. And, to my knowledge, we've not invited any generals to call."

"You have, ma'am. Under the compact of care, the responsible military authority may visit soldiers who convalesce in private homes."

This child could recite regulations like an attorney. More unsettling, beyond parroting the words, he seemed genuinely to grasp the concept of an implied agreement. She perched her fist on her hip. "And what if the timing is not particularly suitable for us?"

"Ma'am, if I can say, you're looking for a hard time. Your place is neat enough, seems your coloreds are keeping after. You've nothing to worry about."

"That's not the point."

"Most folks don't get visited by a general. A special honor, such a call. The general doesn't come by himself, he brings the staff. If he feels he's been paid discourtesy, he might tell the staff to stop by every day, to check on the patient. The real reason would be to drive you crazy. And the staff will do whatever he tells them."

She marveled at how artfully the boy presented his case. "You've been around generals for a time?"

"Enough to see how it works, yes ma'am."

"Well, perhaps I would prefer the daily visits, just so you can announce them."

"Staff comes unannounced, pretty much at any time."

"You are thorough in your advice. We shall host your General Fogarty."

She had no idea what to expect, having not met a person of high military rank, and she was surprised that the general, when he arrived, seemed altogether inoffensive and not even so full of himself as the local county supervisor who, when not playing the pompous politician, tended a stable. A cut shorter than her, the general wore a white shirt with an open neck—he had shed his tunic in the afternoon heat. He took short, dallying steps, which she thought odd for a man of authority. Two staff officers and a sergeant traveled with him, plus the boy messenger, who remained with the sergeant and horses in the front yard while the officers entered the house.

"You are kind to lend your home to the care of a soldier," said General Fogarty in the foyer, his two officers alongside. Evincing none of Dr. Slate's easy grace or garrulousness, he posed like one who'd arrived at the theater and was waiting to be treated to the entertainment.

"Our pleasure to be of help to the military," she said, nearly choking.

"Commendable. Have you met the Holland family?"

"No."

"Malcolm Holland has not visited?"

"No."

"Curious. The roads are open to the west. The railroad too."

She led them to the sickroom and stood by as they filed in. She'd prepared Holland for the general's imminent advent, given him a fresh shirt with a collar, a towel, and wet cloth. He'd combed his hair and daubed the sweat, the house being sultry, the windows closed to keep out the dust.

One of the two accompanying officers introduced himself as the *aide-de-camp*, whose French term she understood, but whose function she did not. He positioned himself at the general's elbow. Next to her waited the other officer, who sported the brightest red hair she'd ever witnessed on an adult. Captain's rank adorned his hat, which he spun loosely in his hands. Leaning toward her, he asked softly, "Where's your father?"

"At his work. Do you know him?"

"No. I have heard of him."

Very odd, she thought. "And you are?"

"Thad Swan." He flashed straight teeth. The teeth, shock of red hair, and twirling hat left an impish impression. His gray eyes occupied recesses that made him look like he'd been sick. She'd read sickness was common among soldiers.

She asked, "What is your role on the general's staff, Captain?"

"Responsibilities as assigned. One day this, one that."

"Is today a *this* day, or a *that*?"

He laughed. "So far this. Too early to say it will not become eventually the other."

"I see." She observed his smile, less a crescent than a wave, like a tree branch that had striven upward and gravity impeded to grow horizontal, and must inevitably break from its weight. A crooked smile did not mean a crooked man, she thought. Yet his expression seemed evasive.

"Captain Holland appears remarkably well. He's progressed far in his special therapy."

"You are well informed."

"Dr. Slate calls often?"

"Weekly, though the ride from the Chimborazo Hospital takes two hours."

"How well I know that ride. Luckily I have merely visited the Chimborazo, not stayed there."

"Luckily."

"You say the distinguished Malcolm Holland has not come to see his son?"

Why had he asked the question *twice?* "No."

"Other visitors?"

"No."

"Requests to visit?"

"Why are you asking? Do you think we would have turned them away?"

"Of course not. Simply my job to inquire—I do the same with all the families who care for our wounded."

"I'm sorry," she said, though she was not sorry. She sensed his questions had an underlying purpose.

"Ha, ha!" Something Holland said had amused the general, who glanced over his shoulder. "How do you put up with this one for a guest, Anna?"

"He's normally well mannered, sir," she replied, stepping forward, relieved to break off the conversation with Swan.

"That may be a masquerade."

"Well, I am forewarned."

"Do remain wary indeed."

She was about to invite Fogarty to a drink of squeezed lemon water when the aide-de-camp spoke at his ear. She interpreted that the fellow kept track of the general's timetable, and his time must be running short.

In the yard, the three mounted. The general and aide passed through the gate. Turning back, Captain Swan smiled at her. *"Bon après-midi, mademoiselle,"* he said.

Why would he speak to her in French?

Lean and straight he sat, the sunlight torching his red hair. Obviously quick-witted, but to what end? She should nickname him. What nickname meant one who would not hesitate to use his cleverness to the disadvantage of others? She could think of none.

* * *

The book rested in her lap. The Venables tale had come to an end, having lasted too long, as tedious things often did. The dust season had ended too, and the louvered doors hung open. A breeze curled in, and she wanted to drowse in the chair. She felt she could, even in the captain's view. To be stared at by him no longer annoyed her; his eyes had grown as familiar to her as Bookman's. Now they looked tired, as if the visit had drained him.

She asked him, "What was the joke you told the general?"

"It was not at your expense."

"So tell me."

"A soldier's joke."

"John, I wish to hear."

Until now she had not called him by his given name, and she was pleased he gave no reaction. His coiffing before the general's visit had disintegrated to a melee, and a lock drooped between his eyes. He said, "I told him how one evening toward the end of my stay at the Chimborazo Hospital, as I lay in my bed covered by the sheets, for the air was a bit chilly, I was approached by a cleaning woman—a Negress new to the ward. She noticed the box, whose lids were closed just then. 'What that big box for?'" he quoted, mimicking the black voice.

Her mother's: *You diminish a people who are crushed at no fault of their own—to mock them is a sin.* Anna thought, she should tell him of the wrongness of mimicking blacks. No—her exchange with him over the Preliminary Emancipation Proclamation had breached enough discretion.

He went on. "'Oh, that's a special healing box.' She asked, 'What the box do?' 'Well, it heals what you put in.' 'How come the rest of the soldiers with broke legs don't got a box?' And I answered, 'Who said it's my leg that's inside?'"

Anna kept his gaze, alert for gloating. She saw none. "I am surprised you would tell a coarse joke."

"The trick is to choose the proper company and time."

"You managed to do so with the general."

"There is judgment in your tone, Anna."

"I don't judge such crudities. They are trivial."

"You find them distasteful, though."

"The joke is not one my father would have told."

"My father would have, to entertain his guests between sips of liquor. On such occasions, he is invariably the one who holds forth while everyone else listens—his great talent. Perhaps I have learned more from him than I thought." He seemed to sink into the pillow like a stone dropped into a pond.

"Why hasn't he visited you?"

"He may think I do not wish to see him. He would be correct in the assumption."

"You don't desire to see your own father?"

"What a gaggle the occasion would be. Men like the general would arrange to attend, strutting like peacocks with their feathers open. People from the newspapers. Platitudes and speeches whose predictable lines would trail off to applause. And for this I would be the centerpiece. No, let him stay away."

She wanted to ask him about Captain Swan—what were Holland's impressions of the man? His eyes had fallen shut. She watched his face within the pillow cavern, the way certain shadows collided. The house was quiet except for the occasional creak, and she ruminated how he must perceive everything beyond the room through sounds: footfalls on boards, the tin roof's jangle as a branch scraped; the dry petals skittering on the patio.

A shovel's pings nocturnal.

- 6 -

Holland's conversations with Bookman continued. He asked the freedman about his time as a slave.

"I don't remember so well, sir. I was only five years old when Henry bought us from old Fournier. Seems like bein' a slave got in my blood, though."

"How do you mean?"

"Oh, the way I see the world. I got a certain caution in me. And anger too."

"You don't seem angry."

"I don't let folks notice. But sometimes I feel like a snake's venom's runnin' through me. I look at the world and see terrible things. Every black family I ever met has been torn apart at one time or another. Lots don't know their father or remember their mother. How can a man witness such and not feel anger?"

"Slavery will end one day."

"Yeah. I hear that." Suddenly he laughed, a rich, resonating sound. "Bookman, when you laugh, I don't know whether you're laughing in agreement, or sarcasm, or something else."

"I'm not sure I know either." He rewound the box spring a few turns. "Sir, do you mind if I ask you a question?"

"Please do."

"I mean no offense."

"I assure you, none will be taken."

"Do you think Negroes are people?"

"Yes, of course."

"All right. So, I read a lot. Henry buys newspapers and pamphlets and some books, and seems like every one of 'em gets to me sooner or later. I read about the great men of history—presidents, kings, inventors—and I can't help but notice they're all *white*. And I suppose white people notice too, and they say to themselves, look, all of history's great people are white, and none of 'em are black, and it means we're superior to blacks. Do they say that, sir?"

"I have not heard them say, but I don't doubt some do."

"I bet not a single white person asks himself or herself, if there *was* a great black man, how would anyone *know*, 'cause he's a slave, and nobody ever wrote no history about a slave. And if no history of blacks is written, ain't it the same as sayin' they're not people?"

"Some might so interpret."

"And how does a black man, whose life leaves no imprint, and no one will remember him, or his family, or any other black person he ever knew, not think of himself the same way?"

"Wrongful, what you describe."

"You think?"

"I do."

"Then why do you wear that gray uniform?"

"Yes, there is a contradiction. Keep in mind that soldiers are not asked to judge the merits of society's dilemmas. What matters to a soldier is his duty, and to obey his orders, even if he doesn't agree."

"Is that so?"

"You are not a soldier, Bookman, so I wouldn't expect you to understand."

Bookman laughed.

*   *   *

She who had loved coffee since her first taste as a child now found herself stranded in a land without. Where initially the embargo had inconvenienced them in minor ways, in recent months the federal sea patrols had closed off the imports of coffee beans and other craved commodities. Whatever small amounts slipped through and were not supplied to the army sold from under the counter, exorbitantly priced.

Now here was a bag, intoxicatingly aromatic, weighing at least two pounds. "It's worth a fortune! Did Dr. Slate give it to us?"

"No," whispered her father. "Say nothing. I'll hide it, and we'll take out the beans we need at any one time."

"Where did you get it?"

He had just returned from Richmond, and he wore boots freshly soled. Clean white stitches traced the edges.

"Did the cobbler Jacob give it to you?"

"I ask you not to speculate."

"He gave me new shoes, remember? And he charged me nothing for them—he said they were a present for you."

"Well, he's an eccentric fellow. A Jew."

"An unusual Jew," she said, "who gives away his expensive wares."

"You know nothing of Jews, dear. Do not assume."

"I will do better than you at hiding it," she said. "I'm always at home, and I'm quite familiar with the hideaways in this house."

"I trust you are, dear. Yet let me be the keeper of this. I have a place."

She stared at him. "If you trust me, why can't you tell me all?"

"All?"

"You wish to shield me, I understand. Please reconsider. I want you to tell me what you and Bookman and that other man were doing out in the middle of the night."

"Too much for you, to let the matter rest?"

"Was I of no help to you in running our Railroad station?"

"You were more than helpful. You were essential. And if the Railroad reopens, you shall be again."

"If not the Railroad, what are you doing?"

"Nothing you should fret over."

"It must be dangerous."

"No. All the same, discretion remains our friend for as long as the war lasts."

"Discretion does not mean you should keep me ignorant."

"Dear, you are never so. You are wiser than me in your way. Please let me assure you there is nothing to worry about."

"Are you assuring me just to fend me off, or do you speak sincerely?"

"I do. And I'd like you to accept it that way."

What had the captain said to her? *He entrusted you because you are a person of responsibility.* If so obvious to Holland, why not to her father?

"Very well. Are you having coffee?"

"Yes, I would love some."

* * *

Bald drifts under a zinc sky, the greens hazy, the air tainted as if with yeast, the James River low on banks lathed in mud, border between mud and water obscure. You saw herons in the mornings; they vanished with the crowning sun. In the center stream, barges called *bateaux*, pole men on deck, bore tobacco and other goods from the west. Blacks did the crew work, a drowning profession. The floating bodies drew gawkers on the shore, children who dashed to a certain distance and no closer. Victims had beached on their property. The last time, Jerome had spotted the naked figure in the shallows. He'd bundled him in an old horse blanket and hefted him in his huge arms to a straw patch. Her father had notified the authorities; no one came. When flies had mounded the shroud, Jerome buried the corpse at the edge of the leased fields, the place for slaves' graves.

Today, on her way to the river, she noticed Jerome at work beside the house. He did not look at her. Her father would not get rid of him, she knew. Perhaps Jerome did not. She remembered how he'd shaken the rag at her, the subtle insolence.

Let him wonder.

The path was not much used these days. Unkempt grass licked at her ankles. She'd not been to the riverside since before she'd gone away to the Augusta Seminary. As a girl she'd come here often to view the expanse and to shout to the boatmen and hear their voices across the red glaze. Where are you from? Where are you headed? Wilmington, she'd heard. Maryland. One from Alabama. Another from Trinidad, wherever that was.

During the time when they'd operated their station on the Underground Railroad, they'd brought the runaways here at night, to be borne off aboard a launch. Often she'd been the one with the lantern, the glow marking the landing place until the dark boat materialized from the river's matte and slipped soundlessly to shore. Those aboard were from the crew of a schooner whose captain was in league with abolitionists. Anchored at a distance, the vessel dispatched the launch on a precise timetable. The oarsmen loaded the runaways under night's cover and rowed them to the sailing vessel. If the authorities boarded, the runaways would masquerade as crew. As soon as they left southern waters toward a northern port, they'd be safe.

They'd faced the greatest danger when they moved the escaped slaves from the hiding place within the old well and across the Osborne Turnpike to the river's edge. The slave patrol roved everywhere, scouring private lands at their whim. To have been discovered in the open would have meant their arrest along with the runaways. They'd listened for hoof claps. Bookman had perspicacious hearing—at a distance he could distinguish sounds ambiguous to others, for instance between constructive and destructive hammer blows—and he'd taught her a northbound rider's tempo sounded different from one heading south. The northbound riders came slower, because they journeyed toward Richmond at night, a long way. Retrogressing from Richmond, the southbound horsemen pressed insistently, their ride's end near. Horses at a full gallop invariably augured danger.

She smelled the brine and imagined she was in that time again. Conjured the boat's bow nuzzling to the mud, the sweat odor, the oars' glint. The tension had gripped her like the pressure points in Holland's box, lasting until the launch with the escaped slaves aboard receded downriver.

Over the months something had changed in her. Her schooling at the Augusta Seminary may have brought on the shift, or maybe the experience had joined one already underway before she'd left home. Always she'd felt secure in her acumen and articulateness, yet she recognized that much of what had passed for confidence had been a plucky imitation of her mother. Now her sense of herself ran true, and she felt equipped to act on her own. She could stand her ground in a debate, reason her way to sound conclusions, and make decisions without becoming flustered. And if people or events occasionally irritated her, her composure soon returned. Her father saw how capable she was. He grinned when she argued a point; always respected her opinion. In the time of the Railroad, he'd trusted her with vital tasks. Deferred to her in giving instructions to the freedmen. Not often did he assert his will over hers.

She recalled only two exceptions.

One was his decision not to send Jerome away.

The other was to exclude her from what he was doing, the secret activity he denied existed.

What if their Underground Railroad station still operated? Always clandestine, perhaps the enterprise had become more so. To spirit escaped slaves to freedom was criminal; done in wartime, it was treasonous, a capital offense. She could comprehend why her father may have wished to separate her from the peril. Nonetheless she felt betrayed.

She pried a flat stone out of the clay. Flicked it to the river. Watched the skip marks spread until no trace remained.

What should she do?

She came up with four choices.

One, to reenroll at the Augusta Female Seminary. Her father would consent, with enthusiasm. He'd encouraged her to finish her education and become a teacher, though she guessed his real purpose had been to send her away. And if Staunton was caught up in the war, as it regularly seemed to be, a day would come when the Northern army's campaign against Richmond would resume, and the Shenandoah Valley would be no *less* safe than here.

If the war had not intruded, she might have abided the seminary—she could get along nicely enough with the religious women; her mother's friends had been so. But the other students had wrapped their religious fervor around the Southern cause, and this had proven insufferable to her. Of her true opinions she could reveal nothing, lest she draw unwanted attention and endanger those who'd participated in the Railroad. So she'd pretended to be a vacuous person of no political stance whatsoever, and the playacting had run contrary to her character. If she returned to the seminary, could she tolerate muffling herself again?

Her second choice was to stay home and forget the Railroad. Pretend she didn't care. Regard the relinquishment as she'd suggested that Captain Holland treat his own absence from the war—a permanent separation. Immersed in her chores, tending to the garden, supervising the household, she would stay busy. Eventually suitors would call on her, and she would become a man's wife, her fate borne on the currents like everyone else's. What was wrong with that? What would keep her from reconciling herself to the ordinary life that might descend on her like the boulder pitching from a clifftop through the trees?

Third choice: She could leave and go north. If Bookman wouldn't go with her, she'd proceed anyway. Not difficult for a woman to cross the lines. Of course, she had no resources to pay her way. She pictured the blond woman who'd stood under the umbrella in the Richmond market, selling herself in desperation, perhaps to feed her children. No, thought Anna—that wouldn't happen to her—she'd seek out the abolitionists, tell them her story, and surely they'd help her. She'd find sustenance. Live in a women's boarding house.

Fourth choice: She could confront her father again, resolutely.

Nearly dark when she retraced her steps. The path branched, one way accompanying the river, the other threading between trees toward the house. She could remember when this stretch had been lined with painted stones from the time before she was born, when the Van Meer family had kept slaves. All her life, her father had leased out the fields, and another man's slaves worked here in the growing season. She'd see them approach the house and speak to the freedmen blacks, and occasionally she'd caught the banter between them. She'd sensed a reluctance among the freedmen to vaunt their situation, lest the truth sow rancor between those whom society had divided into classes—one of slaves, the other of men free but otherwise not readily discernible from slaves. *Question: Who your master? Answer? Master of this place the Van Meer family.* Between blacks, the truth dissembled.

As between her father and her.

In their time as station keepers on the Underground Railroad, she'd asked him about the morality of leasing their land to slaveholders. His lips had twisted, as when he found a piece of grit in his food. He'd said he'd thought about the quandary himself, and like all moral dilemmas, this one presented a stubborn knot to untangle. "Legally a man may free his slaves, as I have done. And under the law he has the right to lease his land solely to people who use freedmen for labor. Yet what happens when, in exercising the right, he must refuse the ones who have been his clients these many years? They will make him the target of their rancor. Call him to court. Though he will have the law on his side, people will interpret him as selfish and willing to harm their interests for the sake of a principle. Feeling spurned, they'll brand him an abolitionist or a traitor. The man who garbs himself only in the law finds thin cloth."

Why must he continually produce these annoying adages? She'd said, "We help slaves to go free, while we take money from men who use slaves on our land, so people will not think poorly of us."

"You speak with sarcasm. Still, you rightly express the contradiction. Everything comes at a cost, and for us the cost may be to wear hypocrisy's lint on our sleeves. The alternative is to let our land sit idle and earn no money. Aside from bearing us into financial distress, doing so would raise the eyebrows of our neighbors, who would judge us either fools or, cognizant we are not, something worse. We cannot ignore what they think of us."

"Mother ignored them."

"She never had to consider the Railroad. Discretion must guide all we do. Our choices are to achieve what good we can secretly, or to be cast into the light and be unable to help anyone."

"Perhaps there are other choices."

"My dear, if you discover them, please tell me."

She'd not raised the subject again, but he had, soon after she'd come home from the female seminary. They'd been in the family's fenced cemetery in the upper meadow. Her mother's grave was by the southeast corner, and they'd washed the stone and plucked the weeds—chores they performed every year. "Do you remember how you scolded me about the hypocrisy of leasing our lands to slaveholders?"

"Not a scolding, father."

"You did, in your way. I've thought on the matter, and you were correct. We should not be doing so. I shall stop when the proper moment arrives."

"I am glad."

"Just because people are suspicious does not mean we cannot try to do what is right. We may not succeed. Good is not always the outcome of good intentions."

"Shouldn't it be?"

"If deeds were like bricks that stacked and held together like a wall, yes. But human society is not built like a wall."

"More like a nest."

He'd laughed, his eyes wrinkling, and he'd stepped over and kissed her on the forehead. "Yes, and like a nest, the twigs interlace, some strong and others brittle, and the strong twigs might not hold if the majority are rotten."

"Which makes society evil."

"Society is the aggregate of people, who mostly are flawed. But do not despair. For the contrast shows us what is good. Bravery can be known only in its distinction to cowardice, truth in juxtaposition to falsehood, and honor as it shines above dishonor."

"You are full of wisdom today, father." She'd not concealed her mockery, which was playful and not mean spirited.

His eyes had shed their twinkle. "Any wisdom I may possess I learned from your mother. And in truth I am not much like her. I am not religious. Even as a boy, I could not believe, and I never took the idea seriously enough to fear God. But there are other powers."

"What do you mean, *powers*?"

"Perhaps it is not the right word. I mean, phenomena whose influence is powerful, like randomness and coincidence."

"Strange worries to harbor."

"During the battle of Malvern Hill, a man on his farm at New Market was walking with his dog, and suddenly the animal fell dead. A rifle ball from the battle had flown a long way, and plummeting to earth, it struck the poor creature. Might as easily have killed the farmer. This is randomness, and we are all at its mercy."

"The same with sickness."

"Correct. I'll give you another example. As you know, I had Bookman and Jerome tear down the old well wall. My intention was merely to make us safer. Since then, half a dozen people have remarked on its absence. Even our local slave-patrol man Hoskins mentioned it."

Hoskins was the leader of the local slave patrol. He featured scraggly gray whiskers and sun-coppered skin, could neither read nor write, and in his conversations with fellow whites stammered awkwardly. To the slaves he was altogether different—a vigilant and wrathful personage who led mules with captured men or women tied on. When they'd hidden escaped slaves and brought them at night from the well cavity to the river to board the launch, she'd pictured Hoskins as the menace.

Her father had dusted his hands together. "I suppose folks were so used to seeing the well wall when they rode by, the absence startled them. Only then did I grasp that I should have left it alone, just filled in the hiding place and not done anything obvious. I didn't comprehend until too late that the community regards change, even the most innocuous, with suspicion."

"How can we protect against such a thing?"

"By showing a blank mien, never acting in a way to set us apart from our everyday patterns. Thus, no explanations needed."

She'd taken him to mean he'd continue to lease the lands for a time. Nonetheless she'd been happy he'd reconsidered the subject.

She'd not anticipated he'd turn the blank mien against her.

* * *

Having checked the box settings, she sat in the chair, in her lap a small pile of books. She said, "With the Venables done, we must find another book."

"I think I agree with your verdict of the Venables. A shallow tale. Even so, I enjoyed hearing you read it."

"If you like, we can continue with one of these from my mother's collection." She'd dusted the old volumes whose crevices harbored mottles. On the violet bindings, embossed gilded letters. The topmost surfaced in her oldest memories—she recalled sitting cross-legged on the floor, cradling the book in her lap, to read at her mother's feet.

"Those are your mother's. What of *your* books?"

"I don't think you would like what I read."

"Why do you assume so?"

"Just my expectation."

"You have voiced what you don't like. Why not tell me what you do?"

"My prerogative. Or do you continue to insist upon intrusion as a privilege of your convalescence?"

"I regret if I imparted the impression." He turned toward the courtyard's wilting sunlight. "So, your mother's books…"

Anna felt the volumes' weight. Ran her fingers over the cracked gilding.

Abruptly she left the room, brushing past Sarah in the hallway, to the stairs, which she took quickly, her dress hiked, to her room and special hiding place, found her notebook, and retraced her steps. When she reached the sickroom, Sarah was on her knees on the floor, where with a hand broom she whisked below the louvers, collecting grit, a chore she performed every day. Sweat carved a glistening rivulet in the dust on her face.

"Sarah, can you leave that for the time being?"

"Yes, miss." She pushed to her feet, and Anna closed the door behind her.

In the chair again, she said, "I brought a book of mine."

"Wonderful."

"I apologize for being curt."

"You simply expressed yourself, as is your right."

"There are ways to say things; I might have chosen better."

"Spare not another thought."

"Then let us begin. I hope you won't mind if I don't hand the book to you. The margins are full of my scribbling that would embarrass me to confide."

"I much prefer to hear you read."

"*This is a book of poems by... what is his name?... Gibraltar Nash.* Have you heard of him?"

"No."

"He is obscure, yet he enjoyed a certain following at the Augusta Female Seminary. Here is one:

"Themselves

Disconsolate hour of laughter severed
The old partnership dissolved
The orphans go forth
Packs on their backs
Crossing waters
Gray and wide
Shine in their eyes
Wind in their ears
Land nears.

Disquieted, the spirit of equus
Vanish pretense
Splash the youths to sand
Enter cacophony
Volleys and killing
Pockets of crumbs spilling
Amid mocking crows, filling
Behold the great villains
Themselves."

She looked up. "What do you think?"

"An anti-war poem."

"You have a quick ear."

"If you've ever witnessed hard-tack crumbs dribbling from a dead man's pocket, you will not forget the sight. The author seems to have experienced war."

"I don't think so. It is his imagination."

95

"How do you know?"

"Mr. Nash visited the Augusta Seminary a month or so before I returned home. He read to us from his collection."

"Plainly the poem moved you. You read it spiritedly."

"Well, I think it says much, in a handful of lines."

"Yes. And I especially like the first one, the severing of the disconsolate hour of laughter, the uneasiness people felt in the months after the war began."

"Yes, it did feel that way," she said.

"I wonder, is the author a Northerner?"

"No. Why would you think so?"

"The Northern army traveled on boats along the coast and the Chesapeake. The boats transported tens of thousands of men to the Carolinas and to the Virginia shores. Our soldiers sometimes went by water too, though in fewer numbers. I was aboard once when the barge drifted into the estuary where the water roughened, and wind-blown waves sprayed over our heads. The horses were badly shaken. 'Disquieted, the spirit of equus.'"

"You comprehended that in an instant. You are clever."

"Read me another, please."

"Another, let's see…" She fussed with the pages.

"Don't Think

Don't think
If you survive this madness true
Tower upright through
Fields where the balls hit
Others, not you
Living you shan't face the pit
Of judgment.

Where those you enslaved have inscribed your name
And those you raped have imprinted your face for fame
Those you sold have put a price on your head
Those you hung for running away shall hang you, till dead
A thousand blades await you, sir
In quarters more hellish than the fire."

He scratched his chin. "A bit stern."

"Oh? Do you not hear more?"

"The voice of a fanatic. No wonder this Nash fellow is obscure. I'm astounded the author of such a poem was permitted to lecture at a Southern school during wartime."

"So the country should be even *less* free?"

"I didn't say that."

"You implied."

"May I see that volume?"

"I told you, the pages contain my personal notes."

"Let me at least see the cover."

She held it up.

"Blank. Probably so it might circulate without being seized as contraband."

"What a ridiculous thing to say."

"You don't agree with the war, do you?"

"Of course not."

"Plainly."

"Not plain enough. I hope the North wins!"

Her statement visibly shocked him. Apparently unable to reply, he pivoted his gaze to the box.

She should shut up, she thought, even as she surrendered to her impulse. "How can you defend a society that upholds slavery? It runs against every tenet of the nation that calls itself a democracy. You lead men who give their lives for a shameful purpose."

"They don't fight for slavery, for God's sake."

"For what then? For their dear commonwealth of Virginia? The right to self govern? To keep the land free of those molesting Yankees and the arrogant President Lincoln?"

"I'm a soldier, Anna."

"A soldier of a bad cause!"

A click at the door. In the frame stood Sarah, who closed her mouth that had dropped open. She stepped quickly inside, fetched the whisk broom she'd left on the floor, and pulled the door shut.

"I'm sorry." Anna pressed her palms against her forehead. "What a careless outburst."

His fingertips at their full extension touched her forearm. His hand hovered until it succumbed to gravity. "Why are you concerned? You can say anything you want, state your opinion as freely as you like. You needn't fear."

I fear *you*, she thought. "Gracious of you to say. Yet you are here as our guest, and you cannot get up and walk out when offensive words are spoken. Your family would be appalled."

"I would not share our private conversation with them."

"In any event, I've failed in my responsibility, inasmuch as I have incompatible views, to have aggrieved you so."

He stared in puzzlement. Good, she thought. Let him wonder. Think her silly and tempestuous of mood.

And he would be correct. What else would you call a woman who couldn't control her tongue?

*　　*　　*

Holland had dropped into one of his afternoon naps, his head turned to the side, his mouth open, the sheets twined loosely between his fingers. Standing by the bed, she was tempted to brush away the hair threading over his forehead. The urge to touch him was powerful. Why? She knew she wanted to talk to him, to say ordinary things and smooth over the awkwardness from her outburst last evening. But why to touch him?

Perhaps she simply did not like hair out of place.

"Miss?"

She jumped, startled.

Sarah stared at her from the doorway. "A delivery wagon's at the gate."

"Open for them. I'll be there momentarily."

Sarah left. Without touching his skin, Anna plucked the hair from his forehead and trailed it to the top.

Wondered if she still wanted to touch him. Couldn't tell.

The Confederate mail wagon had rolled through the carriageway. The driver, a lumbering fellow missing an arm above the elbow, hefted a carton wrapped in burlap and twine to deposit on the wagon's fold-down gate. "Came to the Chimborazo Hospital for J. Holland and t'was forwarded here."

"I see," said Anna.

"The twine's specially knotted, so you can be sure nobody's invaded between the time t'was sent and got to the destination."

"What's to keep someone from cutting the original twine and replacing it with another?"

"How can they do that when 'tis in my custody?"

"Then why tie it to begin with?"

The question seemed to nettle him. "Y'hanker I split 'er?"

"What?"

He shook his head as if he deemed her witless. "Should I open the crate?"

"Please do."

"They fashion these crates from wet pine. Drive the nails in, and the wood hangs on with the devil's own grip." He took a hatchet and slashed the sharp edge against the twine, which curled away. Whacked at the lid, which resisted, and banged again, splinters flying, making her think he must have lost his other arm to the dangerous practice of opening crates. A dozen strikes later, the boards yawned to reveal two lesser boxes nested amid bright straw. In crimson foil, bound in alabaster silk ribbon, they seemed like enormous ruby jewels. She said, "How lovely."

"They don't come no prettier. Expensive to wrap cartons so fancy. Must be for you."

"I don't think so."

He squinted at his delivery bill. "You ain't J. Holland?"

"No. J. Holland is an army captain convalescing here. He is sleeping at the moment. I can bring them to him."

For the second time, she signed a ledger taking possession of something of Holland's, first the man himself, and now these spectacularly papered gifts. She picked them up; the larger was quite heavy. Listed too were two letters the fellow handed her, in identical envelopes, though penned, to her judgment, in different hands.

"How long have the box and these letters lingered at the Chimborazo Hospital?"

"Can't say. Coulda' been a day or weeks till they got 'round to forwarding the mail."

She carried them to his room and stacked them on the chair she positioned center of the floor.

An hour later she returned to find him awake, arms crossed, pique woven in his expression.

"So how are you, John?"

"Say no more. I'll not parley with one who would taunt me."

"Well, you were asleep. I could not very well slide them under your pillow."

"I think you are well acquainted with the limits of my reach."

"As if you could not have devised a way to snare them over to yourself."

"Dear Anna, the only thing more humiliating than being unable to reach a present is to strain after one."

"Surely you were savoring the moment to come." She picked them up from the chair. "So which first, the lighter or the heavier?"

"The lighter."

"There are these two letters also."

He glanced at the envelopes and set them on the opposite corner of the mattress. With his fingertips, he peeled away the silk ribbon of the smaller box, unfurling the paper. "In the field, I would tear this open, having no use for elegant paper or ribbon." He made a motion to crumple them.

"Don't you dare!" She snatched the wrappings and commenced to fold them carefully in her lap.

"Of course, the idea is hypothetical, inasmuch as in the field I never received such gifts." He opened the plain carton of white paperboard, extracted a tussle of tissue paper, of which she took possession, and displayed in his fingers a brass-framed glass object resembling a miniature dome. "Why would he send me such a thing?"

"Who?"

"My father. He sent me a *toy*."

"It is not a toy. Look, the device magnifies whatever lies beneath. I know women who habitually use one to read."

He said, "I can read well enough without."

"Oh? Imagine yourself on your horse, studying your map after a long ride, squinting to glean the tiny letters with your weary eyes, and on that occasion, wouldn't you be gratified to retrieve this from your pocket?"

He glared at her. "You may have hit upon the singular circumstance of its utility." He laid the magnifier aside and reached out for the other, which she balanced on his palm. He said, "You're right, heavy."

This time he uncovered a case of polished mahogany that cast a rare sheen. Mahogany was expensive, and she could see the wood was genuine. Cradling the case on the sheets, he flipped the two brass catches.

"Hmm," she intoned.

"Well, this makes up for the magnifier." In a bed of maroon velvet rested a revolver of compact size. Engraved in its ivory handgrips, a man on horseback. The midnight-blue frame glistened, and even with no knowledge of guns, she apprehended the elegant workmanship. The compartments enclosed a gunpowder flask, bullets, percussion caps, a rod, cotton wads, and a sized leather holster with flap—all the killer's bric-a-brac.

"Are you going to open the letters?"

"I think later." His attention did not waver from the revolver. "What a prize."

"You seem quite pleased."

"Yes, I think I am."

She picked up the second set of wrappings and left to put them away. At the door she looked back. He was turning the revolver this way and that to see how it caught the light and twirling around his finger by the trigger guard.

And he'd called the *magnifier* a toy.

* * *

Curtains. The curtainmaker brought samples: two of flowers, two of trees, a pond, doves, robins, and horses. In the parlor, the woman and her young assistant laid out their wares for display, draping them over the chairs.

Anna, helped by Sarah, opened the samples to hold by the window. She would have rejected the horses outright, had she not guessed that Holland might like the pattern.

A week ago, when she'd mentioned to her father that the curtains in the guest room were tattered, he'd given her money for new ones.

"This money is likewise from the sale of the land across the river?"

"Yes."

"The land you never mentioned to me before?"

"Anna, it is not a great sum."

"We don't *have* much money. Why don't we save it?"

"Henceforth, we will. For now you should use this for the curtains. They will be a pleasant enrichment for our guest, don't you think?"

Not persuaded, she took the money anyway. Posted a letter to the curtainmaker, the same woman her mother had used, proposing today's showing.

The seamstress was tall with bowl-cut straight hair and man-sized hands that must have complicated her ability to ply her craft. She posed with feet together, arms sketching an X at the waist, shoulders drawn rigidly. Why did she display her wares in this dour stance? To convey her earnestness? Why would she *be* here, if she wasn't earnest?

The woman spoke in a stentorian tone. "You can try a set for a few days. I'll pin them to size. If you're satisfied, I'll tailor them. If you're not, you can return them, or try another."

"What do you think, Sarah?"

"I think they're all good, miss."

"The horseman pattern?"

"The captain'll like 'em."

"I believe you're right."

The seamstress stared at Anna for what seemed like an interminable interval. She said, "Who do you refer to?"

"We are hosting a convalescing officer wounded in the fighting. The curtains are for his room."

Another prolonged stare. "To recognize your service to the country, I'll give you a discount of 20 percent on the horse pattern." Punctuating the offer, she thrust out her chin.

"How generous. Thank you." Why did the woman act so strangely? Anna examined the patterns again. Maybe the horseman pattern did not sell as well as the others. The outer edges were discolored. Well, those probably would be trimmed in the tailoring. And she could put away the money saved.

The seamstress declared, "My two brothers are with Stonewall Jackson in the Shenandoah. And Lily's father is with General A.P. Hill. We cannot do enough for those men."

Anna turned to Lily, who appeared to be fourteen years old. "Have you heard from your father?"

"No, ma'am. He'll come home soon, though, when we whip the Yankees." She glanced to her mistress to certify she'd spoken correctly. Reaped no acknowledgement, as far as Anna could tell.

"Will we disturb the captain in measuring for these?"

"I don't think so. Let me tell him you're coming in."

Two days later, the seamstress brought the finished curtains and affixed them to the rod. They were handsome indeed, more so than Anna had expected. As she'd hoped, no traces remained of the discolored edges. She found herself drawn to the room just to admire them.

In the late afternoon, she did so again. Holland slept in his normal pose, the sheets clutched to his chin. She checked the box settings and the gauze on his leg. All was well. The draft through the open window fluttered the curtains, making the horses look like they were galloping. In the courtyard, the leaves bristled. Suddenly they erupted furiously, and the curtains leapt, and she jumped to avoid them. A plethora of smells—of forest, smoke, soil, water—exploded in. A whirling dust devil had enveloped their house and dipped its tail into the courtyard like a scorpion stinging them with its woodsy scent.

Sarah appeared in the doorway. "'Bout knocked me off my feet," she said. "Blew the trimmin's all over."

Anna glanced at Holland, who had not stirred.

"He sleeps the sleep of the good hearted," remarked Sarah, who flapped the curtains to hang evenly, then left. Anna was about to follow when she noticed on the floor the envelopes that had accompanied the presents from his father. They must have blown out from wherever he'd set them. The open flaps beckoned. Watching his immobile eyelids, she retrieved the envelopes, lowered herself to the chair, and slid out the letter from the first. On crisp vellum, the pen lines ran in neat blue script:

My dear son,

I pray you are well and comfortable. Dr. Slate's letters appraising your convalescence are never without their cautions—'provided this and that,' etc.—yet if I interpret him correctly, you are safe from the gangrene that so terrified us in the early course of your recovery.

I am a poor chooser of gifts, even so I think you will like the pistol, a Colt Model 1849 pocket revolver of .36 caliber, specially crafted as a cavalryman's sidearm, the grips sized to your hand I recall is similar to mine. The small cylinder holds only five shots, a minor disadvantage your good aim should easily compensate for.

Nature's normal course is for sons to perceive themselves as ever advancing on their fathers—in stature, strength, intellect, acumen, and experience—until they overtake them in every meaningful way, and indeed leave them behind like static posts on a road. Fathers interpret this process differently. They consider themselves not static at all, but still progressing, gaining in wisdom what they have lost over the years in physical prowess. Sons are not inclined to credit this much, as it is subtle, while the signs of decline are manifest. Thus even the best and most loving of fathers might become an afterthought to their sons.

I know I was neither the best father nor observably loving. I am a man who spoke of obligation yet who acted selfishly. My mistakes have built one upon the other, to where they cannot be unbuilt. My behavior over the years has done little to slow my descent in your esteem, and any feelings you may have for me must be hoisted from deep in your heart. Of course you owe me nothing, and I merit nothing. Even so, I believe I have changed for the better, and I dare to hope your kindness shall spare me a harsh judgment, and we shall be friends someday.

My wishes are for your health and safety. I am at your service to do whatever I can, whether to travel, lend my voice to push a matter through the bureaucracy, or speak to anyone, at any time.

Your father

Restoring the letter in the envelope, she thought it must be harder to be a son than a daughter. What weighty sentiments! Well, John's father at least had done nicely in his gifts for his son, the revolver especially.

She opened the other envelope, took out the single handwritten page.

John,

I regret to inform you our father passed away two days ago while on the road to Harrisonburg. He was not sick, yet he had worn tired from much travel and from exhorting people to donate money for the Confederacy. At his age, the strain was too much for his heart. We buried him beside our mother on the hillock, a peaceful spot as you remember, shaded and protected from the wind.

Vernon and I do not know where to find you—when have we, for these many months?—so we shall send this letter to the Chimborazo Hospital in Richmond hoping to reach you. We are saddened you could not have been home to have seen our father during his final year. All in all he seemed happy. He spoke often of you.

His last will gives you one-third of everything. Though you have been away and have taken no part in our family affairs—and you shouldn't doubt how demanding these have been—Vernon and I do not begrudge you your share. Please come home when you are healed to travel, and we will speak of such matters—though you may find them tedious. Until then, Please be well and safe.

Beatrice

Anna replaced the letter, set both envelopes on the bedspread. Retreated from the room full of softly galloping horses.

* * *

She entered with a book, descended onto the chair, and smoothed her dress. She had decided she could not pretend she hadn't read the letters. To her surprise, the determination came to her at once, without ambiguity.

She said, "I am very sorry your father passed away."

He nodded as if he already knew she'd read the letters. "As I told you, we were not very close."

"I'm sure he would have been pleased you received his presents."

"The true present he gave me was this." He gestured toward the Banderton box. "Had he passed away before I was wounded, I doubt the same deliberations would have occurred, and the doctors on duty would have cut off my leg, according to their procedures. I would not have come to Dr. Slate's cognizance or been the subject for his extraordinary care."

"It is good you feel gratitude."

"Toward Slate, yes. For my father, in truth I don't feel anything."

"I think you do, in your heart."

Her statement astonished her. What was wrong with her these days? The words that popped out of her mouth abandoned all discretion. She was fortunate he seemed impervious to offense. His sole reaction was to glance at the book in her lap, one of her mother's.

"Am I not to be treated again to Gibraltar Nash?"

She said, "I thought you detested him."

"Not at all. In fact I rather enjoyed your defense of the poet's right to a contrary opinion."

"Whether contrary or not depends on your vantage point."

"Quite so."

For a minute she sat pondering. Went upstairs, retrieved the book from her hiding place, and returned. Under the sun-beaten roof, the cover had warmed, and the pages seemed to turn of their own alacrity.

"Here is a poem not as provocative as the last one you heard:

"Lightning's Zealot

I, thy zealot
In thy brief flashes survey
The reality that ordinary lights deny
Which the world cloaks in a lie
And thy vivid wand doth electrify.

Thou, the sky's wandering Israelite
The horizon's masterful firebug
Tempest's fellow rogue
Friend to the thunder demagogue
While I earthbound must lag.

Impassioned disciple I
Scan the heavens for thy rarity
Await thy dazzling display
To reveal with thy ardency
A triumphant epiphany."

"You know," he said, "the first night I spent here, when the lamp was extinguished, I could see nothing, except when distant lightning flashed. The poem is reminiscent."

"What do you think it means?"

"I'm not sure. What reality does he refer to? What epiphany? Ah—wait—there must be a theme. The light that ends slavery. Such is the way to read the abolitionist poet."

"You think so?"

"How else, if he is true to his identity?"

"Perhaps you are right. Here is another:

"My River

> For every deed and gain
> Let no strength be kept at bay
> Life does not collect like grain
> Its warmth may not survive the day.
>
> My river, once so wide
> With current and force to thrill
> Now lay rocky and dry
> A line of dust, ephemeral.
>
> You whose flow my heart upheld
> By absence, you fade too
> My thirst cannot be filled
> By ancient smiles or love true.
>
> Dear river of my heart
> I wait all my days
> Again to behold your face
> For time to bear me, never to part
> To your loving embrace."

He said, "Sentimental. I'm surprised Nash has it in him."

"Poets are not poets unless they surprise us a little."

"Does the last stanza have a separate pattern than the others?"

"Yes, a different rhyme scheme and an extra line. What does your acute ear interpret?"

"The poem is about loss. And hope at the end. But perhaps the break in pattern means hope is likewise broken."

She peered at him. "I did not perceive that, until this minute when you mentioned."

"So Gibraltar Nash is versatile. Which doesn't make him less of a fanatic."

*   *   *

"Hello John."

Henry Van Meer entered the room. He stood awkwardly, fingering the chair where Anna usually sat. "Anna told me your father had passed away. I was saddened to hear."

"Yes. I was informed by letter, which was delayed."

Van Meer frowned. "Inexcusable that your mail should languish. I shall complain to Dr. Slate."

"Please do not trouble yourself, sir. There is no remedy for the mail."

Van Meer's white hair jutted above his glasses, the wire frames crooked as though his forehead's weight had warped them. His coat showed much wear around the sleeves—the elbows were threadbare, and the lining puffed out at the wrist above his fingers tapping the chair. The Van Meers must be poorer than they seemed, thought Holland, yet they had spent their resources upon him, even to the extravagance of replacing the room's curtains.

Van Meer said, "I must apologize for not mustering more time to converse with you. I sense I have abandoned you somewhat."

"No one could feel less abandoned, sir. Bookman attends to me and the box, Sarah feeds me, and Anna reads me novels and poems. If the convalescents at Chimborazo knew how I am lavished with attention, they would be envious indeed."

Holland did not commonly speak in platitudes, and Van Meer was familiar with the regimen of his care, yet the sentiments seemed to becalm him. Edging around the chair, he sat, reposing his hands in his lap, and the tension in his shoulders visibly eased.

Holland said, "You appear fatigued, sir."

"I am. As with the mail, there is no remedy for a long day. Men are not undone by great burdens but by minutiae that accumulate bit by bit. The trick is to separate the ones to attend from those that can be ignored, for much that at first seems important may be trivial, and vice versa. The sifting process is what matters."

"Spoken with wisdom, sir. As an officer I learned that my task was above all to be thorough. Lives are lost on the cusp of details. Of

109

course, it proves impossible to mind all things, or to lend each the proper consideration."

"There is no higher aspiration than thoroughness." Van Meer's torso swelled, and his mouth forced itself into a grin. "When you are better and can walk, I would like to show you the grounds. I lease the fields to others, though I may discontinue the practice, as complications result."

"More minutiae?"

Van Meer laughed. "How true."

"I much look forward to my tour."

The older man rose, niggling the chair to its former place.

Holland said, "Thank you and your family for your generosity in hosting me. Do not doubt how well you have done, or how grateful I am and always shall be."

Van Meer beamed. "John, you are truly welcome."

- 7 -

The sun had dipped; amber infused the treetops. On the riverside path, she reached the top and crossed the road. Opened the footgate and passed through. No one around—the freedmen must have gone inside the buggy house to eat. She decided to circumambulate the house to check the grounds. The slats and shutters needed paint, but nobody was painting these days—the supplies had grown scarce. Captain Holland's window revealed the backs of the horse-pattern curtains, the glass mirroring the spot where the old well had stood. As she traversed the patchy grass, her toe cut into the soil. She lurched, righted herself, and kept going toward the buggy house.

She halted and retraced her steps.

Within the halo of foundation stones, a beak-shaped notch. She sank to a squat. Tucked her dress's hem to rest across her feet. Dabbed her fingertips over the earth as if absentmindedly tapping piano keys. Mixed sensations erupted: the pine scent; a hint of dew; the dirt's soft texture. The grass grew in isolated tufts amid soil freshly tilled. They'd ripped down the parapet and filled in the hole over a year ago—the intervening seasons should have settled the ground.

She began to scoop the dirt. Her hand plunged in easily and came out full, like sifting through a box of beads. Repositioned herself to keep the house's corner in her peripheral vision. Soon the illumination fled, and she could see what she was doing only because the soil she scooped was lighter than the surrounding. She made no sound. A bat fluttered; the treetops swayed. By the hole, she erected a pyramid eight inches high.

*   *   *

She pulled the room's door until the latch clicked. The door had no lock; she was nonetheless confident no one would enter before knocking and gaining her permission.

111

In the back corner, a small hatch led to a crawl space under the roof. The hatch was painted blue, and she called it the blue corner. The border showed nails hammered flush. Years ago, she discovered that the nails, driven at an angle, pulled loose if she tugged while pressing gently against the hatch face. The blue corner preserved the hardbound notebook she'd brought to Holland's bedside. She'd told him it was a volume authored by the poet Gibraltar Nash.

No such person existed.

Why had she lied? She thought it must relate to the reason she kept her notebook in the blue corner, a space accessible to her alone. Whether the hideaway genuinely accentuated her privacy was doubtful. In practice nobody paid attention to her papers—her father rarely stopped by except to say goodnight; Sarah who came in to make her bed couldn't read; and Bookman never entered. Yet so personal was her poetry to her, she felt compelled to hide it. The practice liberated her to pen her ideas without constraint.

The nails loosened, she removed the hatch door that measured twelve by sixteen inches. Reached in, brought her notebook to the bed, and laid it alongside the object she'd unearthed—an oilcloth with the dimensions and color of a discarded cigar butt. Unrolling the cloth yielded a folded paper she now opened.

L N B C N L M M B R R N D N F H F N V R W T R R C F B
S D D R D C R M N R T D S F T S T R V S V H T H R H T G S T
T T N L M C F S N F S N Y D W C R Y N L L T T M R R S S K S
H T Y N Y N M H R T T N Y F G L C M T R P N T B S S S N T
S T R T D B T S S H N D L N N Y T H N C D H S S T G P G N
H H R X R Y S T S M L P C S S H R F D S S P S R R T N F S T R
R D B C M N D S R N T S M M Y N S H R S

One hundred ninety-six letters, none a proper vowel. With her pencil, she copied them in precise order in her notebook.

She concentrated on her next actions, for she must not make a mistake. In the Railroad days, to hide a message required precision; to conceal it imperfectly or to dally in the placement could bring catastrophe. She restored her notebook within the blue corner, sealed the hatch door, and meticulously re-rolled the paper in the oilcloth.

*   *   *

"Miss?" A tap at the door.

She'd fallen into a slumber on her bed. Frantically she groped for the oilcloth roll, until she remembered she'd reburied it outside. Mumbled, "What, Sarah?"

"A man's 'round in the yard."

She sat up and blinked groggily. "Dr. Slate?"

"No, miss. An army man."

"Did he ring the bell? Or knock?"

"No. He's just standin' by the steps."

She straightened her dress. Stroked the brush through her hair. Glanced out her window; the caller was not within her angle of view. Had the boy messenger who'd announced General Fogarty's visit returned? No—the boy would not have hesitated to make his presence known.

Against the porch pillar, balanced on his right leg, his left boot tucked behind the opposite knee, skinning an apple with a folding knife, posed Captain Swan. The banister evidenced a powdering—he must have tapped the dust off his hat that now rested alongside. His hair flowed as red as the peel corkscrewing from the apple. "Well, hello," he crooned. "I was going to knock as soon as I finished my snack."

"I'm sure we can offer you more than that."

"How generous of you. But please don't trouble yourself—I'm content with my apple while I admire your archway." He waved the bitten fruit at the iron bridge above the carriage gate, a decoration that had perched there all her life and every so often had to be shorn of vines and repainted, lest rust consume the delicate metalwork. Around the curved beams traced a coil narrow crossmembers held in place. Her father had told her the coil represented a vine, which seemed to her extraneous, as real vines grew in abundance. Before he'd died, her grandfather had commissioned the arch, and she judged it a silly affectation that confirmed that the man had possessed more money than sense. He'd added other frivolous features: the rarely used courtyard and pillared porticoes front and back that chipped in the weather and consumed buckets of paint. Her father depicted him as an alcoholic who'd spat invective at relatives and slaves alike, and as a wastrel who'd squandered their wealth, which was why they had so little now, and why their house harbored no alcohol whatsoever.

"Please come in."

"Are you sure? I hate to intrude."

From one who'd taken the liberty to dawdle on her porch without knocking, the statement struck her as insincere. She ushered him to the parlor. "You stopped by to see Captain Holland?"

"Well, yes. I was riding by, and I reflected that I *should* stop to see him, to fill my quota and perhaps spare you another sojourn by the general."

She wondered how he knew of her resistance to the general's visit. The boy messenger must have said something.

"And how are you, Anna?" He leaned his forearm on the chair.

Sarah bustled along the hallway toward the stairs. Anna called out, "Sarah, wait. Can we fetch the captain tea and bread, please?"

"Bread's gone, miss."

"Gone? Where?"

"We ate it."

"Oh."

"I can bake some."

"Do you have time?" Anna asked Swan.

"Don't bother with the bread. I'll gladly have tea." When Sarah left, he said, "Your Negroes are freedmen?"

"Yes."

"I have heard people say freedmen are more reliable than slaves. What do you think?"

"They are reliable. I cannot compare them, as in my lifetime we've never had slaves."

"By circumstance, or intent?"

She caught herself, conscious that Swan was not Holland, to whom she seemingly could express any thought, no matter how contrary, and reap no consequence. She said, "I am not the one to ask."

After escorting Swan to see him, she excused herself and went to the kitchen to help Sarah prepare the tea. She should start dough for bread. Then she saw how little flour they had and thought of the soaring price. Harked to the new curtains in the sickroom. Meant to delight their guest, the curtains now seemed to trumpet money whose origins could not be explained.

What if Swan, eternally curious, noticed them and asked?

Reveal nothing.

She brought the tea on a tray. "Shall I join you, or leave you to speak in private?"

"Do join us, please," said Holland.

Swan flashed his undulating smile. He held the tea cup close to his face, and behind the rising steam, his gaze toured the room, settling on the curtains.

"Nice and hot," Holland remarked.

Swan's eyes mirrored the dark liquid. "Well, John, what have you been up to?"

"No coincidence I am in the same posture as when you last encountered me."

A newspaper lay on the bed. "So you read, which makes profitable use of your abundant time. Anything of interest today?"

"A further account of Stuart's ride around the Yankees in Maryland," said Holland. "Wonderful reading."

Four weeks after the Sharpsburg battle, General J.E.B. Stuart's cavalry had ridden around the entire Union army, repeating his celebrated feat from last summer on the Richmond peninsula. Normally Anna lent no attention to the war's details, yet Stuart's legendary circumnavigations of the Northern army had flooded the headlines.

"Other news?" Swan asked.

"A sad story of the death of General Lee's daughter, from typhoid fever."

"Not even the great are spared," commented Swan. A silence followed, during which the three contemplated their tea. Suddenly Swan's head bobbed, fluttering red. "Anna, may I inquire, how much of this land around is yours?"

"I don't really know the acreage," she answered.

"I mean roughly. Does your property stretch to the river?"

"Yes."

"There's a wooded streamed to the east. Does your land extend that far?"

"Yes."

"And to the south?"

"Honestly I have no idea."

"How about across the river?"

Why would he ask? Had her father been telling other people the same story as he'd told her? She said, "I should know more about our property. I'm not very well informed, am I?"

Holland's eyes narrowed.

Swan chuckled.

She asked, "Are you out to buy land?"

"Not for myself. The army must requisition land for official use, and my business as a staff officer is to be always cognizant of opportunities. Plus there are maps to update. John certainly can relate the constant chore of maps."

"Maps always must be renewed," he acknowledged.

"I hope you don't mind my questions," said Swan.

"No."

"Then perhaps you can tell me, as you travel south along the Osborne Turnpike you notice to the east a shack, though whether a habitation or simply a shed, too distant for me to say. I wonder if the structure is on your property."

She shrugged. "I am not aware of the shack you describe. Our fields are leased. Maybe the workers built a shelter."

Swan smiled his crooked smile. "I find it endearing—don't you too, John?—that Anna knows so little of her own land."

"I hadn't thought about it."

Swan said, "Indeed the absence of curiosity seems infectious."

The men laughed.

"Not what you would expect," he added, "in a teacher's house."

She willed herself not to respond.

Holland said, "I must admit, I am equally in the dark as to how much land my family owns. I have no notion whatsoever of our boundaries—the topic does not interest me."

"A carefree mind must be the purview of the genuine aristocrat," remarked Swan playfully. "When someday I own a vast stretch, I shall yearn to be oblivious of the details."

Later, after Swan departed, she settled on the chair beside Holland's bed. Her irritation had diminished to a vague neuralgia. She asked, "What did you and Swan talk about before I came in?"

"He expressed his regrets about my father."

"So he knew that too."

"What do you mean?"

"Just that... his inquisitiveness nettles me." She tipped her shoulders into a shrug, a gesture rare for her but for some reason she found herself repeating today. *Don't be careless!*

He said, "The discussion was superficial. He is not one with whom I'd share confidences."

"I am glad to hear."

"He also asked about your father and the freedmen."

"And about me too, I suppose."

"He asked how much time you spent away from the house."

"What did you say?"

"That you were home all the time, except for the occasion when you went to Richmond. He seemed intrigued, but when he saw I knew no further, he desisted."

"Why does he ask these questions?"

"Perhaps officers on a general's staff are held to recite the salient and the trivial alike. I've not served in such a capacity, nor do I aspire to."

"I don't like him."

"When he remarked about the absence of curiosity in a teacher's house, you looked like you wanted to hit him."

"So apparent?"

"Yes. Just as it's obvious you're not the type of person who is ignorant about her family's property."

"Perhaps I do not like when people pry."

"I think we may confidently assert that."

*   *   *

In the time when they'd operated their station on the Underground Railroad, Anna had prepared coded messages by arranging letters into a square and scrambling them via a pattern of folds and scissor cuts. The practice had demanded concentration, patience, dexterity, and hours of work. When she'd had to step away for other chores, she'd rolled the papers in a cylinder, tied on a string, and lowered them into her bed's hollow post. The upper stanchion—the one her father straightened every time he entered her room—could be removed. The connecting peg had worn, and the top tended to cant from the vertical.

She hadn't worked with the codes for over a year, and the procedures once so familiar had fallen into the cobwebs of her mind. With concentration, she dredged them out. To create a coded message, first she'd written the plain text, applying as much brevity as possible, using no numerals—numbers must be written out in letters. Removed the vowels and the spaces between words. Counted the remaining letters. To the sum, she'd added dummy letters to raise the total as necessary so she could form the square of an *even* number, each side measuring the square root. Her common way had been to fold the square left to right along the vertical center line, then top to bottom, and cut vertically to sever the rightmost column, producing a stack of four groups. From the stack she'd snipped letters top to bottom, yielding single letters in a stack of four (some face down) to be rewritten in order. Vital to proceed precisely, for a mistake obliterated the undertaking. If she'd changed the fold or cut sequence—bottom to top or right to left; she might even fold the square into thirds, although to do so she needed a square root divisible by three—always the recipient must know her modus. In the exchange of messages, they'd confirmed their readiness to receive more runaway slaves, and learned when they must collect them and bring them to the riverbank for their onward journey.

She examined the code again:

L N B C N L M M B R R N D N F H F N V R W T R R C F B
S D D R D C R M N R T D S F T S T R V S V H T H R H T G S T
T T N L M C F S N F S N Y D W C R Y N L L T T M R R S S K S
H T Y N Y N M H R T T N Y F G L C M T R P N T B S S S N T S
T R T D B T S S H N D L N N Y T H N C D H S S T G P G N H
H R X R Y S T S M L P C S S H R F D S S P S R R T N F S T R R
D B C M N D S R N T S M M Y N S H R S

One hundred ninety-six was the square of 14. Divided by four it equaled 49, a whole number, signifying that the codemaker likely had folded the original square into fours. To decode it, she must work in reverse. She didn't know the codemaker's method, so she must guess, hoping the pattern was the same as they'd used in the Railroad days. On a blank page in her notebook, she drew a hash of 14 vertical and horizontal lines. Began with the first four letters, LNBC. Dropped L into the far right column beneath the blank grid's horizontal centerline. N segued in the same line in the leftmost column, B into the space directly above N, and C into the space above L. The second four letters, NLMM, populated clockwise outside the first four. When the far right and far left columns filled, the inward columns proceeded accordingly. The author of the message probably had added dummy letters; she couldn't determine how many, or whether at the beginning or the end, until she finished. In their Railroad codes, they'd used M's for dummy letters; M was common and blended easily. If a series of M's showed at the end, she would have reproduced what the codemaker had started with.

She filled the grid.

No dummy letters collected.

Which didn't necessarily mean she was wrong. A shrewd codemaker might use random dummy letters, although the recipient should know what to expect, otherwise the result would be confusing. She filled in vowels. No meaning emerged. Here and there she conceived a word. Nothing that made sense when combined with the rest.

The person who'd prepared this code must have used a different order of folds and cuts.

Or this was another type of code entirely, produced via a separate formula.

Her failed efforts had used two notebook sheets. She ripped them out. Should she tear out the letters she'd copied from the original? Was the message one her father had received, or his meant for someone else? Or a notation he kept for his own reasons? Uncertain of the significance, she could not calculate the risk. The letters vexed her, and she wanted to have another try at them at a time when her patience returned.

She left the message, closed the notebook, and restored it to her hiding place.

Downstairs she squeezed the torn-out pages into a ball she tossed among the coals in the cooking fireplace. In the time of the Railroad, she'd done the same with the code clippings, and to reenact this final step felt familiar. The coals glowed softly. The heat shriveled the paper, and the edges sprouted exotic flames: vermilion, absinthe, palatinate. She blew and the fire gave a kitten's roar. At last she tapped the ball with the poker and spread the ashes.

* * *

The harvest over, the fields no longer dispensed dust. Cold crept from the western mountains, and the River James ushered a woodlands scent. Frost sugared the mornings. In the pleasant afternoons, the Van Meers opened the windows to vent the house. They donned shawls and sweaters. To Holland's bed they assigned the thickest comforter stuffed with down feathers, a treasure that had belonged to Anna's mother. He covered himself with the comforter only at night, after they'd let the fire go out, lest he sweat profusely beneath.

In late October, a storm rammed the peninsula. A strange, sweet odor of fruit foreshadowed its arrival. When Anna opened the door, she witnessed the sky sullen and leaves scampering in whirls that might have been playful on another occasion. Today they were the ticket hawkers from hell's traveling show. Shortly thereafter hell debuted in person, to an applause of hailstones hurling first from the southeast, then from the southwest, then from no determinable origin. On the roof, a maniacal drumming ensued.

Through the kitchen window she observed Jerome clutching something to his breast—two chickens. The wind buffeted, and he lost his grip on one. Flailing after, he dropped the second, both fowls vanishing in a horizontal trajectory. Point-tipped planks of the fence that separated the yard from the fields stripped loose and speared against him. Her hands flew to her mouth, and she thought she must go out to help him. But what would the wind do to her, insubstantial as she was, if not snatch her away like another chicken? Jerome struggled, pitting his bulk against the mighty storm, and in that instant she was sorry for having asked her father to send him away, and for her coldness toward him. At last he regained his gait toward the buggy house, where the door opened to let him in.

The house groaned. Her ears popped. Until now, she hadn't considered that a storm might destroy their home that had stood intact these many years. She'd heard tales of fantastic storms, always assuming they were embellishments. Now they emerged from legend and introduced themselves in the flesh. In the space across which Jerome had fought his way a minute ago, the rollcart flipped over. A board skittered away. Overhead, a sound like a dropped vase shattering. Milky plaster dribbled from the ceiling seam, vomited down the wall, and frothed over the floor.

She leapt back. "Sarah, come to the kitchen!"

Sarah did not appear. She must be in the buggy house, unable to hear the shouts.

Moving to the foyer, through the fogged windows Anna perceived her father and Bookman trying to nail the shutters. With each blow, the glass rapped—same as when a misguided bird flew into the pane. Her father stepped rearward to examine his work, and immediately the wind dashed him off his feet. Bookman helped him, and they lurched to keep their balance until, drenched, they resumed hammering. In the streaky rainscape, difficult to say which was which.

The front door blew open; rain immediately doused the floor. The yard was a pool, the boundaries stretching to the gate where she discerned, to her astonishment, the silhouettes of a man, a woman, and children. Beyond the iron spikes they cringed, their hair and coattails streaming. "Can you shelter us?" shouted the man. He bellowed at the top of his voice, yet she barely heard him.

Within an hour, they'd havened two white families, foot travelers who'd been making their ill-timed way along the Osborne Turnpike when the storm ambushed them. The families shivered under blankets on the floor by the fireplace. They gave shelter too to a family of blacks who stayed in the buggy house huddled around the wood stove.

Having nailed the shutters and sheltered the travelers, her father and Bookman shifted their attention to the damaged roof above the kitchen. They entered through the hatch door in the wall opposite the stairtop. (The hatch opened in the same roof line as her blue corner, whose contents she'd temporarily relocated under her bed, so if the roof were torn away, her notebook would not sail off with the shingles.) She crouched by the opening, ready to fetch things if needed, facing a roof cavity the size of a watermelon that the rain sprayed through, wetting her ten feet away. Impossible to repair the fissure in this weather, so her father and Bookman set to spreading a tarp beneath, raising ridges at the margins except for the one that trailed between the roof and outer wall. The process required Bookman to lean precariously into the void to nail the spillway's lower edge while her father held firm to his legs. Onto the tarp they spread grease whose unpleasant odor vented to her. Soon water panned the slickened surface, and she could hear the flow and splash. The men squatted, evaluating their accomplishment. Then they laughed, and her father grasped Bookman at the shoulders in triumph. She thought, here was a father with his son.

Through the breach, the rain's torrent momentarily subsided, and she glimpsed a strange obliquity in the matte. A pattern took shape, and she gasped at a sailing ship's masts, not vertical as they should be, but at a severe slant, at least three, indicating a substantial craft. Horrifying, to think men might still be aboard. The James was navigable to Richmond for seagoing frigates, yet since the blockade's imposition, she'd not noticed such a vessel this far upriver. Must have been berthed and broken loose, to be borne helplessly along.

When her father emerged, she asked him, "Can the river flood us?"

"I don't believe so. We are on a knoll, and the water never has risen to this height. Others are not so fortunate. I am worried for our neighbor, Lyman Hock."

"Why should he be flooded and not us?"

"His property slopes toward the river. Though he has a barn and a root cellar safe on the upper part, his house sits just above the water. His late wife admired the view, and he indulged her." He shook his head at the testament to human folly. "The last time the water threatened, he swore he would re-site the house to higher ground. He did not—the commonest mistake, to forget the menace once it leaves your doorstep."

She recalled Bookman's revelation of how Hock had pressed for her hand in marriage. She imagined herself with Hock, her tummy bulging with her third or fourth child, while the James River slopped at her feet.

Her father said, "The swelling river is unpredictable, as are the creeks. In barely an hour, a humble stream may surge into a torrent too powerful to cross. He who ventures out risks being swept away. Anyway, Hock's responsibility is to recognize the danger and to ask for assistance."

* * *

Eager to lend their hands, the guests helped. There was much to do. The men took turns dashing to fetch fallen branches to break up for firewood. The women converged in the kitchen with Sarah to chop vegetables for soup. Twice Anna went out to examine the garden and to fetch vegetables washed from the ground or off their stems. She return soaked, her hair wildly disarrayed and the skin of her feet wrinkled. Upstairs she changed clothes and picked the grit and leaf shards that speckled her legs to the knees. Of Captain Holland she saw nothing, only the lampglow in his room. She trusted Bookman and Sarah to tend to him.

In the evening the storm diminished. The oilcloth's installation had halted the cataract down the kitchen wall. The house no longer groaned, and the shutters ceased to rattle. They opened the doors to admit fresh air. The shelterers and their children righted the overturned rollcart. Scavenged more wood, raising an impressive woodpile in the buggy house. From the fence that overlooked the road and mist-laced lower meadow, she heard the river's roar.

In that hour, who should arrive but Lyman Hock, sopped and grizzled. He wore a buckskin coat, below which mud caked his trousers to the groin, exuding a marshy odor. Pulled off his hat to display gray strands slicking his reddened pate. They gave him tea and bread, and while chewing he explained the predicament: The river already lapped at his house's joists; soon the current would push it off the foundation posts. The only way to save the house, he contended, was to anchor it to sturdy trees until the water receded.

He asked her father to help.

"You would need long ropes," said her father.

"I have 'em, hemp lines eighty foot, made for ships' masts."

Anna visualized the drifting ship she'd sighted through the roof hole, and she wondered for an instant if Hock had harvested the poor vessel's ropes.

"I bought 'em years ago and meant to use 'em to move the house to higher ground. Then my wife died and I fell in the doldrums. Never restored my intentions." He looked at his shoes, chagrined at himself.

"Is the road open?"

"Not for wagons. The creek's raised up, and she's gushin' mighty over the road. We stretched a line you can hang onto. I got my old nigger waitin' on the other side to guard the rope. I don't think 'twill get no worse."

The creek he referred to was the one that ran behind the Van Meers' property. Normally the modest stream sluiced under the Kingsland Road by a rock tunnel, to empty into a woodsy basin by the James. As a girl she'd played in the creek, descending the steep bank to jump barefoot over the smooth stones and catch frogs and salamanders. There were snakes too, and reportedly wild boars, though she'd not observed the latter. In winter, the creek bed became a bog from which forlorn trees poked.

Hock asked her father, "Can I speak to you in private?"

They withdrew to the porch. Anna and Bookman waited in the kitchen. Soon her father came back—he had left Hock in the parlor with the shelterers. She said, "Surely you're not going with him. Can't he find somebody else?"

"He is a strange fellow. He leases his lands as we do, and he's kept only three slaves—an old man and a couple of young girls—to help with the house chores. His house is now an island. He said he beat the old slave to force him into the water to tie on the rope, but the slave refused—he was more afraid of the water than of his master." He frowned. "Why did Hock tell me that?"

"You have no obligation to help such a man. Let his house float away. Let him drown."

"I cannot afford to be labeled the one who will not come to his neighbor's aid."

"Even a wicked one?"

"The community does not see him that way. To them, he is simply a man in need. Anyway, I do not believe the danger is excessive. I'm a fair swimmer. Bookman, you must decide for yourself."

"I can swim," said Bookman.

She glared at him. "You are used to paddling in the shallows. These are flood currents."

"If your father goes, I'm goin.'"

"You would defy my wishes to help a man who considers you of no more worth than a mule?"

"Anna!" snapped her father.

"Ain't Hock I'm doin' it for," Bookman told her calmly.

She did not break eye contact with him. "Damn your excessive loyalty."

Her father rested his hand on her shoulder. "Calm yourself. You have no right to speak to him so."

"You know as well as I do that *he* will be the one in the water, and whom the current sweeps away."

"You're correct that a flooded river is treacherous. We will decide what to do when we observe the true situation, and no sooner. We will not take foolish risks. I promise, I will not ask Bookman to do anything unsafe."

A minute later, her father declared the same to Hock.

"That's fair. I know he's a free man." Hock didn't look at Bookman, whom he spoke of as if he wasn't there.

Anna's rage surged like the river current. She pictured Bookman receding into the deep like the woebegone ship. She forced the terrible image out of her mind.

Tugging on his coat, Bookman said, "Don't worry."

"Cling *tight* to the line."

"I tended to the captain this morning. I don't think I'll be back tonight, so Sarah'll help you with changin' the dressings."

"I am well practiced," she replied.

Their eyes met again, and she felt the old kinship. Gripped his arm to bid him safekeeping. Wanted so much to embrace him, but didn't.

The shelterers watched.

- 8 -

When at nine P.M. she entered Holland's room, he leaned on pillows, fiddling with something in his fingers. She strode to the box, examined his leg, and tested the turnbuckles, confident that Bookman's settings were perfect. She would change them later this evening.

Rags hung on the chair to dry. She asked him, "Did the rain get in?"

"Yes, by the window. Open just a crack, yet the water deluged as if through a broken dike. I shouted, and Sarah came and mopped the spill."

"I did not hear you shout. I must have been tending to our guests."

"Your father introduced several of them to me."

"Did he?" She wondered where she'd been when this had happened.

"Yes. They were very kind. And grateful for the help you afforded them."

"What is that you are holding?"

"A present for you." He extended his hand and let drop into hers a pod on which he had inked eye dots. "A cocoon necklace," he announced.

"I see."

He laughed. "It's a *joke*. Our friend here blew in with the storm, and I thought I'd try my hand at decorating him."

Threads delicately attached the cocoon to the cord. "Where did you learn to make such a thing?"

"Indians live in the hills not far from my family home. They craft whatnots from the wild to sell or trade."

"You dotted on the eyes?"

"Yes."

"Perhaps you are part Indian."

He said nothing.

"Are you insulted I would suggest?"

"Not a real possibility. But no, I am not."

"I'm pleased to hear."

His eyes seemed oddly gleeful. For the first time she noticed their yellow tint. Without asking, she placed her fingers against his forehead. Felt the skin burning with fever.

In the shadows outside his door, she occupied the one spot where she might command a moment's privacy. Murmurs emanated. Gusts and drips. Voices from the parlor. The wall showed the scrapes from early in his stay. She thought, could the timing be worse, with her father out, and the peninsula's roads mired and probably impassible after the storm?

Why should she allow the burden to weigh upon her? Either he would live, or he wouldn't.

He entrusted you because you are a person of responsibility.

She had not asked for the burden—Slate had levied it upon her as if she were one of his soldiers in red sashes. And what had she accomplished, except to oversee a procedure already devised? She was not qualified to treat a severe fever.

Her legs nearly buckled under her. She breathed, struggling to enjoin calm.

You can bear more weight than others. A fact, Anna.

Straightening, she clenched her fists, lifted her chin, and strode into the parlor where the shelterers clustered in front of the fireplace mantle draped with clothes and socks. The fire crackled, the drying clothes hissed. The faces turned toward her.

To the woman who looked most formidable, a mother whose poise had stayed intact even as she'd trudged in drenched to the bone, she said, "Daphne, I need your help."

Daphne became nurse, Anna doctor, as Holland descended below the rim of awareness. On his forehead and neck they laid damp cloths to siphon the heat. "I've not felt a fever so scorching as this," said Daphne, her fingers pressed against his neck. His eyelids were fractionally open, and he dribbled from the corner of his mouth.

"What do you give your children for fever?"

"They've never had fevers so high. Only my cousin, who did not survive."

"I do not wish to hear about your cousin—tell me what you give the children!"

"Ginger root mixed with cinnamon, boiled in water."

Sarah made the broth. Fortunately they had ginger and a twig of cinnamon she shaved with a knife. Daphne's palms cradled his neck as Anna poured the warm spoonfuls into his mouth. He was completely unconscious now, not even groaning. The spooned liquid slopped down his chin. An hour produced no change—his forehead felt like a fire burned within.

Should she chase after her father? Surely he would be better versed in remedies. The wind had calmed, and the rain pattered weakly. By now the party would have traversed the bloated creek, each gripping the rope to breast the current while the others spoke encouragement. Would they retract the rope? Regardless, she dared not attempt to cross alone.

Sarah came in. "I can fetch Arthur, miss."

Arthur was an old slave who worked at the inn north on the Osborne Turnpike. "Why?"

"He knows more about sick people than anyone else 'round here."

Anna found this hard to believe. Nonetheless something positive to try. The alternative was to sit passively while the fever stole Holland's life. "All right. Go get him."

Not far to the inn, yet Sarah lagged on the return because Arthur did not walk as much as shuffled with what Anna thought must be discomfort. His legs were the most bowed she'd ever witnessed, like half-folded insect legs beneath his torso. The angles at which his feet met the ground had eroded his shoe's heels into wedges.

Sarah said, "The inn lady say we gotta pay fifty cents for Arthur. Pay him first, or he gotta go back."

Annoyed, Anna gave him the coins.

"Bad time to be sick," rasped Arthur. His teeth were as brown as his skin, and folds surrounded his eyes.

"Do you know how to cure a fever?"

"Cure? Not sure about that." His attention riveted on the box. "Well, betcha' that's a leg-mending box."

"It's a scientific invention."

"Always figured there'd be such a thing."

He must think the box possessed some fantastic capability—just stick in a leg to be healed and magic did the rest, she surmised.

One of the lids was open, and fingering a turnbuckle, Arthur commented, "I guess you tighten these so you can keep the press on the leg and change the dressin' too. That's clever."

"Can you look at the captain? He is unconscious, and his fever is terribly high."

Arthur laid his hand on Holland's forehead, sniffed at his mouth. "He smell like ginger root and cinnamon."

"A broth I give my children for fever," Daphne said.

"Ginger don't hurt. Don't always help neither." Atop the box, he set a pouch he unrolled to extract a pinch of dried herbs. Tapped the cluster in Anna's open palm. "Steep this in two cups of boiled water till red, then spoon in his mouth. Hold his head up while he swallows. If you have to, you can steep the same leaves again, just one more time. Lay the cool rag on his forehead, freshen every ten-fifteen minutes. His fever'll come down in a while."

"What is this?"

"Chokey leaf. From the marsh. Shows in July, and hard to find."

She'd never heard of chokey leaf. Another name for spicebush? She sniffed the leaves; not spicebush. The thought occurred that the herb might be a poison this gnarled fellow dispensed. She studied his muddy irises within the skin folds. "Can this hurt him?"

"You wise to ask. Don't eat the leaves—they make your tummy ache. Everything in the forest can hurt you, if you ain't heedful what you doin.'"

They saw Arthur to the door, where he assumed his slow shuffle toward the inn. In the kitchen, she asked Sarah, "Do you know about chokey leaves?"

"No, miss. Ain't heard of 'em."

"Damn it!"

Sarah stared at her.

Breathing through her teeth, Anna willed herself to be calm. "Do you trust this man?"

"Oh yeah, miss. I trust him. So do everybody."

By *everybody* she meant of course the blacks. Who'd ever heard of a slave doctoring to grown whites? What if the chokey-leaf remedy did nothing for white people? Her reason said this was irrational, yet a voice in her head whispered that Holland's body would reject black medicine.

"The water's hot, miss."

The leaves scratched against her palm. Reluctantly she tipped them into the silver tea ball Sarah dunked in the pot.

*   *   *

Deep night, the house quiet. Sarah had retired to the quarters above the buggy house, and Daphne and her children slumbered in the front room in the heat of blue flames that licked the fireplace logs. Holland lay motionless, his forehead warm but not like before.

She sat on the chair she'd pulled to the bed. Pressed her fingers against his neck, feeling the pulsing artery. At the top of his chest, which lofted and ebbed in rhythmic peace, she felt his heart. Stretched her index finger to his open lips. His exhalations bore the musky chokey-leaf odor that had no parallel in her memory and she now associated with his sleeping breath. Flitting again to his neck, she twirled the black strands above his ear. Sniffed the hair. Another musky smell—the man himself.

Some chokey tea remained. She lifted his head and opened his mouth to spoon in. Felt his tongue's roughness. Rested her elbows on the mattress, her head settling against his, their hair intertwining. She concentrated on the spot where their skin met; contentment seemed to flow from the tiny connection. And something else.

The glow that came to her when she wrote poems.

One began to take form.

*   *   *

At eleven the next morning, her father and Bookman returned. The sun commenced to dry the land, giving rise to brilliant fields of vapor so bright she could not look for longer than an instant. For their help, Hock had given them a bushel of vegetables and a goat, and bearing these they'd headed home, splashing through the creek whose waters had receded to shin depth. Sarah cooked the goat after Jerome killed the poor thing with a hammer, the resounding whack shuddering the women. The shelterers mixed in the work, chopping potatoes and carrots. Anna suggested they gift Arthur a pouch of vegetables, and Sarah assembled them and sent Carola to deliver. "Give 'em to Arthur, *not* to the inn lady," Sarah instructed.

The meal prepared, they carried their plates into Holland's room. The black and white families crowded the space and recounted storm tales and heard about the rescue of Hock's house from the swollen river. Her father laughed as she'd rarely heard him do. "Step to the front, Bookman," he said, "and tell everyone of your feat."

Bookman pushed through the guests to the bed corner. He spoke in a low voice, and the room quieted. Sopped from wading the swollen creek, the party had reached Hock's farm, and even in the obscurity they'd seen that the James was about to devour the home that rose on a protruding bunt. The river had jumped the curve and severed the house from the mainland, the current coursing around the foundation posts and gurgling under the floor joists. Sixty feet inland, where the ground rose, they'd gaped at the widened span strewn with flotsam: barrels, a wagon, an overturned canal barge, and countless branches adrift.

Rope tied to his chest, clutching a hay bale for floatage, Bookman had eased into the water. Van Meer and Hock had fed out the rope until the current stole him. Careening at an alarming velocity, he'd brushed over a submerged thorn bush that scraped him like a witch's claw until he washed onto the porch. With a chisel Hock had told him where to find, he'd pried up a board to expose the side joist that ran the structure's length. Lashed and knotted tight the rope. Signaled to Hock and Van Meer, who'd pulled it taut and hitched the end to a stout tree, the line angling from house to shore.

"I hear Hock shoutin,' 'Crawl up the rope!' I go shimmyin' on top at first, and I flip upside down, and my backside's hangin' in the water about to drag me off. At last I reach the end and expect to see Hock take the second rope himself. He says, 'tie on, boy.' He's sendin' me *twice!*"

"Father, why did you let him?"

"Bookman is telling things a bit more dramatically than they happened."

"You think gettin' dragged by that river wasn't dramatic?"

"I offered to go myself, but Bookman insisted. Four times he went altogether."

"You are fearless," she told Bookman.

"Hock's the one shoulda been out there."

"What about his slaves?"

Bookman's face flattened. "They weren't much able."

About to relinquish the stage, Bookman felt a grip on his forearm. Holland was looking up from his propped pillows. "What you did was brave," he said.

Bookman grinned in acknowledgement. And for the first time in Holland's presence, Anna smiled.

After dinner, in the peace of the drying yard, Bookman and Anna stood together by the front gate, and he told her a different tale. "When we got there, straight off Hock set to cussin' the slaves he left behind, two girls 'bout twelve years old. He screamed awful names—bitch and whore—at *children!*"

"Why?"

"He told 'em to stay in the house while he went for help, while the water around was risin.' I guess they got so scared they figured they better get out before the flood stranded 'em."

"Why did he demand they stay in the house?"

"He told 'em their weight would help hold the place down. Those skinny girls were just *ballast* to him, like sacks of sand. I looked in their eyes, and I *knew* he's been using 'em for his whim and pleasure."

"That's why we ran the Railroad station, to get them free."

"We got a few. The rest are still here."

She didn't know what to say. They stayed at the gate, savoring that they could linger and not be pummeled by rain and wind. A tranquil breeze toyed with her hair.

"Bookman, would you tell me something?"

"What?"

"Is the Railroad working?"

"You asked me before, and I told you no."

"I know what you said. I'm asking again."

He huffed. "I can't tell you about other stations, because I don't know. Ours is closed. Been so since the war began."

"So what's my father doing?"

"You need to ask him."

"I did, and he wouldn't say."

Bookman was silent.

"Who except you will tell me?"

"Anna, you know I care about you a lot, and always have, but of your father's business, I can't say nothin.'"

* * *

Dr. Slate's next visit occurred on the last day of October, a warm Friday. Holland's window was open, and a breeze wafted in. Slate listened to the fever account—the long night of care, the cold cloths laid on the patient's forehead, the chokey tea—that to her sounded like a tale of long ago. Slate said, "I have not heard of chokey leaves. Many herbs possess healing properties. The leaf of the yarrow plant, for instance, can stop bleeding when rubbed on a wound. Negroes and Indians use remedies formal medicine has not studied. Perhaps administering the chokey broth benefited John. Likewise, he may have emerged naturally."

"I remember nothing of the slave doctor," said Holland. "Whether he saved my life or not, I'd like to thank him."

"I shall invite him for your next visit," said Anna.

On this cheery prospect, Slate left, and Anna told Sarah to pass the invitation to Arthur.

November opened warm under cadet-blue skies. In the afternoons the low sun cast a golden track on the river, and she imagined a bridge where, if she were she to cross, her feet would submerge in the radiance. Wednesday morning quite by surprise she glanced out her bedroom window and spotted Slate's horse in the yard. Recalling the doctor's unexpected arrival to treat the gangrene, she hurriedly descended and stepped out. He stood at roadside conversing with someone. He must have ridden into the yard—the carriage gate yawned—hitched his horse, and retreated on foot. Ambling toward him, she noticed he spoke to a young horseman in black uniform. The fellow had taken off his hat to reveal long hair the same wheaten shade as hers.

The rider spied her. "Sir?"

Slate, his back to the house, spun. "Anna, I hope I did not inconvenience you by appearing unscheduled. This is Lieutenant Alex Poole, a doctor on my staff. We rode together and will continue shortly to Petersburg on hospital business."

She thought, to reach Petersburg from Richmond, travelers generally rode due south over the Mayo's Bridge. Or they might take the railroad that connected the towns. Less efficiently, they could follow the Osborne Turnpike and cross the James by the Cox Ferry to Chesterfield County. This seemed to be their route today. But why?

Lieutenant Poole appeared quite young. He smiled uncertainly, snapping his eyes between her and Slate. Assuming they wished to converse in private, she retreated and called to Sarah, who was behind the house hanging clothes, to prepare tea for the doctor and his companion. By the time she returned, Slate was at the door, alone.

She asked, "Where is your colleague?"

"I apologize for the fractured introduction. Alex was worried you'd think him impolite, so he did not come in."

"Why should he think that? Ask him to join us."

"Please let him be. I myself can stay just a few minutes."

Through the window she observed the lieutenant by his horse. "He appears too young to be an officer."

"He is your age, and soon he is to be the surgeon of a naval steamer. I have his services for barely a month longer. When he takes his post, he will be responsible for the health of eighty souls, and he will perform under fire, if necessary."

"How preposterous."

"I cannot disagree. The cruel way of things these days. And he is better trained than most."

Slate accepted a cup of tea from Sarah. He seemed strangely ill at ease. If Holland's condition had not changed, why was the doctor here? She was going to ask him when he spoke.

"Often I have told you how I enjoy my visits—the peace of the ride, the satisfaction at John's progress, and especially the pleasure of your company and your father's. I confess that today does not bear the same sentiments."

"What's wrong?"

"I prefer to inform you and John together."

Holland was awake. The doctor stepped at once to the box, examined the dressing, and prodded the leg.

"You are back sooner than usual," remarked Holland. "Not that I'm any less happy to see you."

"The progress is good, and you are on the verge of being rid of the box that will require only three weeks longer."

Anna and Holland stared expectantly.

"I stopped by to tell you that a new policy has arisen in the housing of convalescent soldiers. I have been ordered, to my dismay, to restore you to the Chimborazo."

Anna folded her arms. "Is it not unwise to move him?"

"Indeed. At this stage of his convalescence, I cannot conceive of an action more counterproductive. If we wait three weeks, he can travel comfortably with the box removed. Then I will be confident we have tested the procedure through a sound course, without disruption."

"Then why obey?"

"The army has its protocols. I objected for the reasons stated, and my appeal was summarily denied. I elevated my protest to Doctor McCaw, the hospital's chief administrator, but he declined to intervene. I thereupon asked permission to see Dr. Samuel Moore, the Surgeon General, and I'm awaiting the response. Moore is a difficult personage, and I cannot predict if I will gain an audience with him, or how he'll react if I do."

"When will you know?"

"Within a day or so."

Slate's uncharacteristic vagueness troubled her. Holland said nothing. Because he kept his soldier's demeanor, she restrained from expressing her own acidic opinion. She stepped to the horse-pattern curtains she'd grown so accustomed to and adjusted them half open. She remembered how in the early days she had resented his presence, and until this minute she'd not taken stock of how radically her outlook had changed. Eight weeks ago, she would have cheered to see him gone. Now, informed that an administrative coda would accomplish exactly this, she felt as much turmoil as if the army were evicting her or a member of her household. The shift in her feelings had no equivalent in her life.

Slate went on. "The new policy is unfathomable. Had it originated from the War Department in Richmond, my protests might have had a better chance. But the order seems to have emanated from the Virginia Home Guard, for which each county has parochial rules."

She said, "General Fogarty visited recently. He seemed like a reasonable man."

"Perhaps I should approach him directly. Until now, the orders have come via a captain, a red-haired fellow."

"My goodness—you refer to Captain Swan."

"That's him. He said I must move you within four days. He levied the directive as if he expected me to comply with no regard for the medical consequences. The military officialdom often is frustrating. Here it exceeds all I have thus far encountered."

"Swan stopped by here too," she said. "He mentioned nothing about the transfer."

"How very strange."

"What if you simply ignored him? You don't fall under his authority, and certainly we do not either. By the time they decide what to do, John's leg will be healed."

Slate tapped his chin. "Not a bad idea. I cannot envision they would oust him by force. They are bureaucratic, and everything they do requires authorization. I can devise any number of tactics to slow them down."

"Let them chase each other around with their pens." she said.

Holland spoke. "With proper respect, Doctor, do you expect me to go along with such a scheme?"

"You will be following your therapy."

"In this district, I fall under the local commander's authority. If he orders me to go, I must obey."

"And how will you do so, with this around your leg?" She rapped her knuckles on the box.

"You would imprison me, Anna?"

She felt herself blush.

Slate huffed. "I suggest we allow this matter to play out through my appeals to Surgeon General Moore and General Fogarty. I assume you have no objection, John, if I present my objections, in my capacity as the case physician, as is warranted under military procedure."

"I am agreeable to that."

"Let us be prepared in any event. If my entreaty fails, and the Home Guard insists upon the displacement, we will have to move you Monday—no, make it Wednesday, a week from today. I shall stand on Wednesday at the earliest."

"I am ready," said Holland.

I am not, thought Anna.

*　*　*

After she'd escorted Slate out, she stormed into the sickroom. "What is wrong with you?"

"What do you mean?"

"Dr. Slate is trying to help you, and you dismissed his efforts."

"I have a duty to follow orders."

"Does your duty require you to abandon your therapy? You were honorably wounded, grievously so. Let yourself recuperate."

"What else do you think I have been doing?"

"How can you wish to go back?"

"No doubt plenty have seized the excuse not to. As long as I can ride, I'll rejoin my men."

She sighed. "That is what Dr. Slate predicted you would say."

"I'm sure he expressed the sentiment more eloquently."

"I'm appalled, by you and the ones who denied his petition to let you stay for this short time longer."

"Their attitude does not surprise me. The army construes appeals to orders as distasteful and customarily denies them."

"Why?"

"What if all orders were met with appeals?"

"So you agree with these orders?"

"Irrelevant. Discipline follows the principle that men do as they're commanded. All but the most compelling exceptions must be disallowed. A soldier's personal feelings are unimportant."

"Unimportant though they may be, what are yours?"

He reached and touched the back of her hand. "Calm yourself," he said.

She repeated, "What are yours?"

"To stay."

* * *

The confirmation came by messenger, in a folded letter bearing the district commander's wax seal and one handwritten line: 'Captain John S. Holland will relocate by military wagon at 9 A.M. Wednesday, November 12th, to the Chimborazo Army Hospital.'

She arranged his few belongings: his nightshirts; the lustrous mahogany box with the pistol; his magnifier; the letters from his father and sister. They fit neatly with his uniforms, never unpacked, in the brass-cornered trunk. She busied herself absently around the house, avoiding his room that seemed dangerous to her, a setting where she might erupt in tears.

To show Holland the grounds, Bookman, Jerome, and her father hoisted him along the hallway and outside to the rollcart. Jerome balanced the heavy box and Bookman stabilized the cart while they centered the patient and with pillows propped him nearly to a sitting position. Henry Van Meer seemed to enjoy his role narrating the tour; he pointed out the meadows, garden, and other features. For the last stop at riverside, Henry had to excuse himself—he had an appointment elsewhere—and Bookman, Anna alongside, guided the rollcart through the carriage gate, across the turnpike, and down the river pathway.

Swollen from the rains, the surface frothed. The James regularly ate chunks of the Van Meers' land. She'd witnessed them taken, calf-sized pieces a hissing hypotenuse cleaved while the grass around bent in fearful obeisance. Today Anna treaded the flattened strands while Bookman wheeled the trolley. When he'd made sure it sat level, he wandered off at a distance. The wind writhed down his collar and ballooned his shirt.

Holland said, "How far can you throw?" The river's gray reflection had washed the earthen tint from his eyes.

"You brought your pistol?"

"I thought I would practice on a moving target." He flicked the pistol barrel at a yard-length stick in the grass. She'd skipped countless stones in the James, and she obliged him. The stick sailed far, tumbling to plop in the river's sweep.

"Primo!" He snapped five shots at the lithe distortion racing by, and one of them might have hit—she saw brown specks in the spray. The booms echoed like dull drumbeats, the last one melding with the rattle of his reloading. His quick-moving hands fumbled something in the grass. She picked up a bullet.

She watched the wind toss his hair. Weighed the bullet in her fingertips. Tasted brine on her lips. "You must be eager for Dr. Slate to divest you of the box. You'll have to endure only two weeks more."

"I believe your count is accurate."

"A shame you could not have stayed to finish your therapy. I would have liked to see you walk."

"That would have been my wish too."

She wanted to touch him. Instead, she scolded him. "You should be happy Dr. Slate does not judge you a muttonhead."

"Why?"

"The way you insisted upon mindless obedience to the army's senseless orders."

"Whether the orders were senseless or not, I *am* bound. We are all bound."

"I am not," she said. "What I do is of my own will."

He wore no hat, and the hair she'd once trimmed had grown out; the locks played wildly. He said, "I am grateful for what you have done. For every minute you spent with me."

"Consider it my duty."

"How can I? You said you are not bound."

"Not to the army. To... my family."

"Well, I'll have to get you a better present than the cocoon."

"Don't. A confident man gives one gift, not two."

He huffed.

She said, "I'm surprised you remember, as you were in a feverish state at the time."

The tour concluded. Bookman muscled the rollcart toward the house. The path bent gently uphill. The sun's last sliver disappeared, and the land succumbed. She heard Bookman's breathing quicken. In the clotting twilight, his head swayed.

Part II

- 9 -

Rain and sleet. All night, the Federal soldiers slogged on mired roads, their boots churning so much mud they had to lift their legs high, compounding their fatigue. When men fell, they wore the smelly muck head to toe.

With dawn, they heard a drumbeat, then a flute. Ahead they noticed a platform on which a uniformed drummer, flutist, and lieutenant posed. Smiling fixedly, the officer rendered a crisp salute. The men did not know what to make of this greeting, but they guessed their long march was almost over. Beyond the platform spread a sloping meadow, and here the soldiers formed droopy ranks, staring at the shimmering Cedar Run Creek swollen to twice its normal width. The order followed to stand at rest, and they leaned unsteadily on their rifles. A fellow toppled over, and exhausted laughter spilled rank to rank.

One of them yelled, "Sir, is this our bivouac?"

Their commander answered, "No, but it is close by."

Colonel William Schilling, West Point class of 1854, coaxed his horse to the water, aloof from the ranks so the men would not perceive his distress. Clutching the pommel, he dismounted. The night in the saddle had cribbed his thighs to bleeding. Mud smeared his uniform, and he longed to throw it to the washmen in camp.

The Army of the Potomac had lingered for weeks in Maryland, licking its wounds from the battle called Antietam Creek, a single day so saturated in death that to have survived had enclosed him in a strange waking dream. Seven weeks later, scars still peppered his face from a fence post a shell fragment had blown apart. The concussion may have saved his life, for he'd been unconscious and supine on the ground when the fusillades mauled his regiment.

In the battle's aftermath, the army had assigned him to Major General George McClellan's staff to organize unit drills. The commanding general liked to parade his soldiers, and meanwhile Lee's

Confederates had escaped ever deeper into Virginia. In McClellan's mind, to chase the Rebel army required his own to achieve perfect preparedness beforehand. He envisioned a Napoleonic set-piece battle to etch his name in glory. Antietam's chaotic carnage should have taught him better, but the general had observed the fight—those parts he'd witnessed at all—from a point so distant that the clashes had taken on the spectacle of a magic-lantern projection on a screen.

The army finally had marched, and Schilling had found himself in command of this understrength regiment of replacements who hadn't fired their new rifles, even in practice. Before Antietam he might have disparaged their innocence; now he envied it. His soldiers had soon learned that to serve in the infantry meant sore feet and legs. They'd forded the Potomac River below Harper's Ferry, keeping the Blue Ridge on their right, and columned southwest into the Virginia piedmont past the towns of Leesburg and Middleburg. Lee's Confederates had followed the mountain range's far side, leaving the near one reasonably secure, if not particularly friendly. Now Schilling was within a half-day of his destination, on a road between maple trees last night's sleet had shorn bare. All that held him was a convoy of supply wagons dispatched from Fairfax. He had received orders to escort them the remainder of the way.

The wagons were overdue.

He loosened the reins and let his horse graze. Squinted at his pocket watch. Considered reclining in the grass and closing his eyes. If he did, every man in the regiment would do the same. On occasion, he had roused dead-tired soldiers to their feet, and few orders could incite equal rancor. So he drifted with the horse, his ears straining for the sounds of wagon wheels above the Cedar Creek's sibilance.

From the meadow a man approached. Even at a distance you could tell he was an officer—no enlisted soldier would stride so stiffly. Schilling recognized him as the quartermaster lieutenant who had greeted them when they'd marched in. His stainless blues had eluded last night's rains, and perhaps his pristine aspect explained why he veered so widely around the ranks of mud-flecked soldiers, as if he anticipated their sneers. He reached the river's edge and saluted. "Good morning, sir!"

Patiently Schilling touched his hat brim.

"The quartermaster sends his invitation for you to join him for breakfast in the officer's mess."

Breakfast in the officer's mess? Schilling glanced at his own filthy uniform, picturing how his trousers would leave blood stains on the chair seat. "I regret I'm not fit to sit at a table this morning."

"You're certain, sir?"

"Please pass along my gratitude all the same."

"Very well."

Schilling said, "As long as you're here, I'd like to ask for your opinion on a subject."

"Of course, sir."

"The wagons we are waiting for—will they arrive soon?"

"Yesterday the convoy reached Haymarket. Of its current whereabouts, we've heard nothing."

"Haymarket is ten miles away."

"Well, they could show in a few minutes, or an hour. Or many hours. This is my appraisal from copious experience with convoys."

"I see. And what is the remedy, when the convoy's arrival is as unpredictable as the clouds on the mountain?" Schilling, from New Hampshire, had grown up within sight of the White Mountains.

The lieutenant blinked. "Sir?"

"For instance, might we sleep here? Build fires to dry out?"

"This is a transfer point, not a bivouac site. Your camp is at Warrenton."

"I'm aware of that. But my men have been on their legs for the last twenty hours in filthy weather. Look at them. They can barely stand, and they are sopped to the bone."

"I'm sorry, sir. These are policies." Already rigid in his formality, the lieutenant drew himself more upright still. "If you wish, sir, I'll be happy to pass your request to the quartermaster."

Schilling suffocated his ire. To scold this young fellow gained nothing. The true adversary was the lateness of the march. Just as the interminably procrastinating General McClellan had allowed Lee to escape, he had let slip October's fair weather and dry roads. Now the roads were bad; wagon wheels gouged ruts so deep the axles struck.

Schilling said, "Please do deliver my request."

The lieutenant took his leave, veering around the troops.

Schilling gazed at the creek, the water coursing past, each ripple a wink of irony—*hurry up and wait!*

His men had not experienced battle. At least they knew the army.

Holland tried to sleep.

In the silent hospital ward, not even footsteps kept him company. The quiet reminded him of his first night at the Van Meers' house.

He groaned. What had he done, to insist on obedience, preventing Dr. Slate from applying his physician's wiles on his behalf? In Anna's presence, he might have taken his first steps; walked with her on the flattened grass by the river; conversed with her; listened to her voice that had become so familiar. Why had he preempted his own happiness?

He regarded the box's dun obelisk. The fan had stopped. Slate had instructed the orderly to rewind the mainspring; apparently the fellow had forgotten. Not that it mattered—he certainly wasn't sweating. The ward's heating stove went cold at night, and through the open box lids, the frigid air bit his skin.

In two weeks, more or less, he'd be done with the infernal encasement, and he'd walk out of here.

As soon as he could ride, he would visit her.

Barely twenty-four hours after his arrival, already he was mad with boredom. The orders had scheduled him to travel on Wednesday, but the weather had interfered—an unseasonal snow had mired the roads and delayed his departure until Friday. Over the many ruts, the journey by hospital coach had taken twice its normal time. He'd hardly noticed; his thoughts had stayed fixed on the woman who'd become his friend across these nine weeks, and whose absence he felt more keenly than anything in his life heretofore.

The sentiment would dissolve over time, he told himself. His attention would turn to practical concerns. Unfortunately, the ward offered a short supply of these. Nobody to talk to, no diversion whatsoever other than to contemplate the architectural features. The Chimborazo's standard wards were 80-foot-long oblong boxes of plain construction—a pinewood frame and tented roof. Unskilled laborers had erected over one hundred in a few months, nailing on the slats from deconstructed barns and whitewashing them. This structure, not yet complete, had abandoned the pattern. The wings joined to form an L, and the roof rose to a widow's walk with inset windows. Mortise and tenon joints fitted the roof trusses to the lateral beams, their wooden pegs stronger than nails. To built this way required workmanship and time. Perhaps the hospital's carpenters had run out of tasks to stay busy. Neither painted nor outfitted with beds, except for his, the ward hosted him as its exclusive patient. Somebody had swept the floors, sketching sawdust skeins.

On the floor reposed his luggage trunk, the lid ajar, the brass clasps undone, his clothes distended, as if they'd been rooted through. Had the trunk popped open in the journey? Or had someone culled though his belongings for items to steal, like his boots, service belt, and pistol? He thought of the orderly, a cockeyed, limping fellow.

The hours lapsed. He conjured Anna's face in the truss shadows. His frosty breath ascended, not surviving to reach the beams. Closing his eyes, he craved for sleep and for the time to skip past its excruciating tedium. He must ask for a book or newspaper, he told himself, and the thought filled him with sadness, because Anna no longer would be reading to him.

The late afternoon brought the sharp tap of boots. Not the orderly, nor any black—Holland believed that blacks had a distinct cadence in their walk—rather one who strode imperiously, probably an officer. Not Slate—he knew the doctor's step too well. The steps neared, resounding on the plank walkway, and now the fellow paused before he advanced. Breaching the periphery of his vision, a red mane.

"Hello, Holland."

"Swan?"

"I can tell by your expression you're pleased to see me."

"Surprised. I thought your accountability for me had ended. But perhaps you're here just to say hello."

"I'm sorry you had to be pulled from your snug place of convalescence and made to endure a journey in the cold. I can assure you there were compelling reasons for your displacement."

"I never doubted." He thought, gracious of Swan to stop by to apologize for the dislocation. He must have misjudged the man.

Swan said, "It speaks well of you, that you see things in a positive light."

"Why dwell upon the negative?"

"Indeed. I suspect you are in high spirits too because the day is near when you are to be loose of the dreadful obelisk around your leg."

"Yes. I admit, I have been looking forward."

"What a world. A leg-healing device so fantastic, yet real, contrived from men's ingenuity."

"Certainly real."

Swan chuckled. "To the one who wears it like a coffin, eh?" He took a step and his angle to the lantern changed, and so did everything else about him. Shedding its lighthearted cast, his gaze grew penetrating, and his backslapping manner extinguished as if someone had doused him with a bucket of water. "John, I am present on official business. I must reveal myself to you, and I hope you'll not take offense. You see, the office I portrayed myself to occupy was a guise."

Holland felt his leg tighten. The sensation arose from time to time, especially when the weather shifted, leaving him to hypothesize that newly healed flesh possessed an extrasensory quality. "A *guise*, you say?"

"To hide my true purpose, I had to pretend to be an ordinary staff officer under General Fogarty's command. The fact is, I report directly to the War Department in Richmond. The time for obfuscation has run its course."

What a strange fellow, thought Holland. The discomfort in his leg broadened to his full body, and he recalled a soldier he'd once witnessed whose rash covered every inch of his skin and prevented him from wearing clothes or riding, and he'd marched almost naked alongside his horse. The image made Holland cringe.

"You are perplexed," remarked Swan. "Understandably so." He reached into his pocket and pulled out a sheet of paper, folded but wrinkled in a way that said someone once had crumpled it. "I'd like to show you this, and I want you to give it back after you've read."

"Fine."

"I want you to *promise* you'll hand it back."

"Of course. Why wouldn't I?"

"I would rather hear you promise."

"You have my word. Why should I care one way or the other?"

"Just bear in mind." He proffered the paper, which Holland unfolded to a hand-penned poem:

To My Provocateur

These days I long after the lowering sun
Nothing do I fear more than a gun
The spray its bullet makes
As another evening breaks
In the war of secession

The fading echo of its percussion.

Eyes on a cocoon, a necklace, a joke
Not something understood by folk
In this room no offense stays
No judgment weighs
Or rigid moray grips
To quiet my heart's tremulous leaps.

But discretion I must embrace
Against my desire to cup your face
I wear a mask, with a mask o'er
Remove one, but not the other
A blank mien, my lips sealed
I die before my love for you can be revealed.

I hope to see you at the last
When under the sun's smile this mess will have passed
Then you will gaze upon the land
Held in freedom's gentle hand
And dissolved shall be remorse
Peace the fond companion yours.

Swan said, "Let me have it, please."

Holland did not give it back. He glared at Swan. "Where did you get this?"

With a forced smile, Swan leaned over and plucked the paper upward from the top. Holland stared at his hands holding nothing.

Swan said, "You know who wrote it."

"Why in your possession?"

"Why indeed. The provocateur of the title is you, correct?"

Under the red hair, Swan's eyes were those of a feeding animal.

"Explain yourself!" demanded Holland.

"Your tone and expression cause me to think you are caught unawares. Yet you did care for her, didn't you?"

"What's that any of your business?"

"You know, they kept you as a *show*."

"What?"

"A means to display their patriotic fervor. Did you not sense the farce? Or will you say you were confined to your room, where nothing was asked, and nothing revealed?"

"What are you talking about?"

The upright man restored the paper to his pocket. "We'll converse again soon."

Holland yelled after the receding footsteps: "Where the hell did you get that poem?"

Without turning around, Swan called, "Don't upset yourself; I shall see you in due course."

* * *

Holland shouted for the orderly, the limping fellow whose lazy right eye wandered to the side. When the man appeared, Holland asked, "Why is no one about?"

"Sir?"

"Where are the other orderlies?"

"This wing ain't build yet, sir. Got only one patient—you."

"Fetch me Dr. Slate."

"Yes sir."

Fifteen minutes later, he tracked Slate's distinct footfalls.

"Hello, John." The doctor's tone rang odd, as if he braced himself for confrontation.

"Tell me what is going on."

"I'm afraid I'm not free to speak."

"You're not *free to speak?*" In Holland's memory, never had his words choked out so. Without thinking, he brought his hand to his throat.

"Sadly, I am not," said Slate.

"If you were not already aware, Doctor, I am your indebted friend. I daresay you can trust me."

Slate scrutinized the floorboards, one to the other, as if counting them. "John, please do not press me on this."

"I *do* press you, sir. You must not leave me in this maddening perplexity."

The doctor gazed around the ward. They were alone—he must have asked the orderly to wait outside. "In truth, I know very little."

"What *do* you know?"

"A veil of secrecy has been lowered. I have been directed to disclose nothing to you. I beg you to preserve my confidence."

"Of course."

Slate pressed the flats of his hands against his head, as if to restrain himself by physical force.

"You have my solemn promise," Holland reaffirmed.

"The order to displace you was a ploy to get you away from the Van Meers' house. I did not learn until after you had been moved. The army—Swan's men—today arrested Anna and her father for treason. Swan believes they were running a spy ring. Others allegedly were involved: the freedmen who worked for the Van Meers, and a Richmond cobbler. Swan said they passed messages concealed within shoes."

"My God."

"At Captain Swan's insistence, you have been housed in this unfinished ward separated from the main facility. I could not refuse on a medical basis—your therapy is far along, and the building has a roof, glass windows, and a coal stove. Swan has directed that you shall not enter into contact with anyone other than him, me, and the one orderly. If not for my unique expertise with the box therapy, I would have been excluded from you as well."

"So Swan was the one who went through my trunk?"

"He dumped it on the walkway and searched through your clothes. He even rapped against the sides in hunt of secret hiding places."

"I suppose I should count myself lucky the bastard didn't put me in chains."

"He would have posted a guard, had I not assured him no one else would know of your whereabouts or approach you. The ward is aloof from the main grounds. Only the carpenters come around. He consented, yet he made plain that I too am not free of his suspicions, as I was the one who posted you to the Van Meers' house to convalesce. My choice was for suitability alone. Swan remains unconvinced, and at his order you and I are to be quarantined until he is satisfied he has smothered the ring of spies."

"Quarantined?"

"He mandates that I stay on the hospital's grounds."

"Who the hell is this man?"

"A captain in rank, yet he cites the War Department's mantle and comports himself in a manner suggesting his authority is above dispute."

"Well, *I* dispute it. What mantle allows him to treat fellow officers so discourteously?"

"As I said, he intended for you to be kept oblivious, so do not let on."

"What about Anna?"

"I know simply what I told you."

"Can you find out what has happened to her?"

Slate sighed. "I do not think so. The only one who can shed light is Swan, and he reveals nothing."

"So she is entirely at his mercy." Once again, he found himself choking out his words. He lay silently for a minute, then jerked furiously from side to side, rattling the box that trapped him. "Damn this confinement!"

"Settle down!" Slate pushed against Holland's chest until he reclined, heaving for breath. Opening the box lids, the doctor readjusted the apparatus, his mien as flat as the wood. "You *must* remain calm, or you will injure yourself, and this unique experiment will have gone for naught."

"I'm sorry."

Slate lifted his fingers gently, as if from an object in delicate balance. "Regrettable indeed that your therapy coincided with this strange occurrence. I advise you not to make it your personal burden. You were merely a guest in their house."

"I was there long too long to be a guest. I am their friend, and I am stricken with worry for them."

"You would be wise not to utter the sentiment to Swan. You will beckon his suspicions."

Holland thought of the poem. It painted him and Anna as lovers. Swan's suspicions already were forged.

* * *

Dawn in the ward. Corporeal things disentangled from the shadows. By the door, the orderly occupied his stool. The bucket water had frozen and trapped the ladle in the ice. He fingered the ladle's handle; it didn't move.

Holland meandered between wakefulness and sleep. *Gibraltar Nash. A ridiculous name. You had me, Anna. I should have known. You read from a book, nothing on the cover, full of your marginal scribbling, so you said.* He pictured her eyes the shade of pebbles beneath the water. Spoke to her willowy ghost beside him in a ghost chair. *"You are clever, dear, provoking of thought. Where did you hear of soldiers on boats?"*

"Well, all my life I've lived on the river."

"Ah, it seems obvious now."

She smiled.

"Bring me more poems by the brilliant Gibraltar Nash, autographed by the poet."

"If I can read them to you."

"I much prefer that you do."

The box fan stopped; the ghost vanished. He could not hold her mentally any more than he could physically. He struggled to summon her again. The trees swished in the bitterness. He smelled the fresh-cut pine boards. Visualized the curtains tossing in his room. Sarah whisking his floor.

Anna, where are you?

In her presence, his mind had come alive again. Without his being aware, wrapped in the demands of soldiering, his thoughts had grown constricted, drying like puddles on the summer patio. He had forgotten how he'd dwelled on ideas. Slavery was one. As a boy, he had decided he would take no part, and his thinking had been original and true, like hers. In the lapse, he'd acted out a role whose consequences he'd not pondered. Why not? Had he been too busy, or merely reluctant to grapple with themes that would have inconvenienced him? Or, despite his detachment from his family, had he yearned for their approval? Wasn't that why people behaved as they did, so they could reap the esteem of their family and community? Just because a man developed original convictions at one stage of his life did not mean he would follow through—the urge to conform, to join the mainstream, was too powerful. The beams overhead seemed to drift among the shadows.

"…meticulously obeyed," the doctor was saying. His voice jarred Holland out of slumber. Slate was lecturing the orderly, who looked like he understood only a small percentage of what the doctor was telling him.

Slate stepped to the bedside. "Sorry, I had to instruct that fellow. The fan spring was left unwound all night."

"Not all night. It stopped at dawn."

Slate glanced at his watch. "Hours passed nonetheless. Inexcusable."

"Is it really so important anymore?"

"Attention to detail is always important." Slate opened the box lids and immediately began fiddling with the turnbuckles. He reset the leg at a higher bend. "True, we are close to removing the box. I would rather tolerate it a bit longer than chance too soon."

"You are not the one who tolerates it."

Finished, Slate closed the lids. "Breakfast will be by momentarily, though no doubt cold by the time he brings it from the kitchen."

"I'm not hungry."

"You're not going to fail me as a patient, are you?"

"Not by choice."

"Umm. You are in the doldrums. Unsurprising. Procedures must take their course regardless."

"You speak to me like I'm a fool."

"A terribly unappreciative thing to say."

"I do apologize."

Slate could not have failed to hear the sarcasm. He rubbed the bridge of his nose. "I will not bore you with counsel except this—you *must* adhere to your course of treatment! Do not passively succumb to melancholy. Do not waste the care given you."

"All right. You have counseled me."

Slate stood for a moment. Finally he walked away.

- 10 -

The soldiers called their bivouac site the Gaul Camp, or so Schilling initially comprehended. Soon he realized they meant the *Gall* Camp, so nicknamed because their footsteps churned the ground into a greenish muck. The tents lay far from the designated latrines, and the soldiers urinated and defecated by the nearby creek that fouled in the runoff.

The morning after the regiment arrived, the order came to assemble for a parade, provoking groans of dismay. Mud still smirched the men's uniforms—the quartermasters had not had time to issue fresh. What was happening? He learned that the army was staging a farewell for General McClellan, whom President Lincoln had relieved of command. Nobody seemed to know more.

At the parade field, Schilling observed McClellan atop his spirited black charger. The new commander, Major General Ambrose E. Burnside, followed behind. Burnside had fought at Antietam, and Schilling had seen him in conference with McClellan. Many of the formations cheered for the departing general, affectionately nicknamed 'Little Mac.' Schilling's own soldiers, who had fought under neither McClellan nor Burnside, did not cheer, and he made no effort to rouse them. As far as he was concerned, the affairs of generals were none of his business.

The next morning he allowed them to sleep late. After they exchanged their filthy uniforms for clean, he inaugurated drills, their purpose to instill obedience without hesitation. No spare ammunition availed for marksmanship practice, so he formed lines and conducted dry fires. The rifle hammers clicked like cicadas; the exercise engaged no enthusiasm. He forced their attention, pacing the line, critiquing their grips and the stocks' pressure in their shoulders, judging their firmness in their knuckles' whiteness. "Some of you have never fired a rifle." His voice carried to all three hundred gathered in a semi-circle. "When you do for the first time, the kick and percussion will startle you. You must suppress your nervousness, lean into the stock, and keep the barrel level and your finger steady in the pull. No man develops these skills except through practice. So let us practice again."

In the afternoon, he rode with his executive officer into Warrenton center, a town he'd heard was full of rebel sympathizers, though none was apparent today. Instead, along the main street, sutler wagons peddled sweets and pastries at exorbitant prices, and men from other units lined up to buy. He thought, why should soldiers spend their meager pay thus? Why were the rations the army fed them not ample and nourishing? Upon his return, he assembled his officers and ordered that no passes be issued for Warrenton. Instead, each company should form a squad to hunt game for the cooks to prepare. The nearby woods surrendered scant wildlife. One of the squads fetched a calf he suspected had originated from a farm. He'd noticed other units looting crops and animals from the local population.

Here was the dilemma: to exert strict control and halt illegal confiscations, leaving his men to the bad army rations and the sutlers' profiteering, or to acquiesce and let them eat heartily.

A commander must take account of his priorities, he reminded himself.

He did nothing, and his soldiers feasted on beef.

*　*　*

Holland guessed his ward must be downwind from the rest, for smoke from the coal stoves penetrated, and when he stretched his fingertips to the box top, they came away sooty. Now amid the acrid coal odor he recognized the vague scent of distilling molasses. His family had bottled the brown syrup in autumn, soon after the sugar cane harvest, and his earliest memory was of riding the nag that plodded in a circle to turn the cane press. His father had set him on the animal, and round and round he'd ridden, while the slaves who'd cut the cane, fed the cuts into the crusher, and skimmed the distilling pans had smiled indulgently.

The orderly brought breakfast. The fellow did not smile. He limped with excruciatingly short, slow steps, as if the notion of dropping the plate terrified him. The meal featured bright yellow eggs, fresh apple pieces, and a slice of buttered bread. In September, Slate had told him, more than 300 patients, decrying the poor-quality hospital food, had signed a petition delivered to the Confederate congress, producing improvements.

Holland left the plate untouched. Eventually the orderly took it away, retreating at the same snail's pace. "Eat it yourself, if you want," Holland yelled at the man's back.

In the morning, a cacophony outside—banging hammers and snoring saws. Brooms thrashed, spewing sawdust. Shouted words he could not distinguish. Wood powder itched his nostrils. He pulled a sheet over his face and lay like a corpse.

Later the carpentry noises ceased; the rain must have scattered the workmen. The steady drumming on the roof evoked a momentary peace where he was able to picture Anna. He studied her chin's sharpness, her lips' subtle cant. He began to drift, and she arrived to sit by the bed in her flowered dress. She held a book whose cover he could not see.

"Hello, dear," he said softly.

"Hello, John," said Swan, standing by the box.

Holland blinked. He'd floated unawares into a dream. "You come and go like a wraith, Swan."

"I hope the time is convenient."

"I don't think so."

"Oh?" Haloed in red hair, his eyes resembled jab wounds from a saber. "You lay in your bed like an emperor in his hubris. You hail from an esteemed family, yet one whose patriarch has passed and his influence ebbed. Are you still special?"

"I never was."

"You have said it," snipped Swan.

"What do you want?"

"Unanswered questions surround you. If not for deference to your doctor's wishes, you would be under guard. Nobody would overrule me, I assure you." Swan's expression had a feral quality.

"Do post a guard, by all means. If you could send a decent conversationalist, I would be grateful."

"Well, you are shackled enough for the time being." Swan drummed the fingertips of his right hand on the box, while with his left he held up a fabric pouch. "Recognize this, by any chance?"

"No."

"Hidden under a loose floorboard in the Van Meers' house. Two pounds of coffee beans, of rich quality by the smell. Coffee is nearly impossible to find these days, especially in this amount. People pour water over burnt corn or rye and bravely say it substitutes. The few supplies of genuine coffee that slip past the Yankee blockade go to our deserving soldiers. Somehow the Van Meers managed to acquire two pounds. Did they serve you coffee, John?"

"They served me tea, from leaves that can be picked readily in the forest. And people commonly hoard commodities—I'll bet many families have coffee beans tucked away."

Swan smiled tolerantly. "They have used up their hoards long ago. You are out of touch with ordinary people."

Holland did not reply.

"Coffee was not all the Van Meers hid under their floorboards. We discovered too a cache of silver coins totaling more than five hundred dollars."

"From their leased lands, probably."

"Leases are paid in cash in the early spring, before planting. This is November. An extravagant quantity for a modest family, don't you agree?"

"Perhaps." He visualized Henry Van Meer's mottled coat.

"Did anyone mention a plentitude of money to you?"

"No."

"Discovered too was a sizeable bag of pepper. No family would need this much. Pepper can be spread on the ground to confuse hounds."

"Most people sprinkle it on their food."

"And they do not hide it under their floors."

No reply.

"Where do you suppose the Van Meers acquired these treasures?"

"Maybe from Dr. Slate. He gave them presents."

Holland immediately regretted his words and was relieved when Swan seemed to find them of no interest. "I don't think so," said Swan. "He gave them other things—a bottle of lamp oil, dried fruits, and a fancy hand mirror for Anna. He was taken with her, don't you agree?"

"No."

Swan slashed his fingers over his chin. "Anna kept certain papers in her room, behind a hatch crafted to appear nailed shut. I showed you one of them yesterday, a poem, you will recall."

"Yes."

"Do you know what else did she keep among her papers?"

"I saw none of them."

"None, in two months?"

"She read to me from books that had belonged to her mother. I observed nothing else."

"From this woman so fond of you?"

"I did not know she was fond of me."

"'*I die before my love for you can be revealed*,'" quoted Swan. Again he drummed fingers on the box top.

"What does it matter to you?"

"Perhaps you will agree, nothing should enrage a soldier more than to discover, as he suffers pain and discomfort for his country, risks his life and the lives of the men around him for his sacred duty, there are those on his own side who secretly help the enemy. Does the betrayal not disturb you?"

"By the scenario you describe."

From his tunic, Swan removed a small ochre envelope, opened the flap to produce a rectangle of paper torn off at the bottom. He did not hand the paper across, rather pinched the corner in his thumb and index finger, close to Holland's face, so he could examine.

"Look familiar?"

"No."

"What do you perceive?"

"A collection of letters."

Swan restored the paper to the envelope. "A message enciphered in a spy's secret code. The letters, which are consonants only, number one hundred and ninety-six, a perfect square. The codemaker folds the square in a certain fashion, then cuts with scissors by a sequence, to rearrange the letters. Sly, yet not so difficult for a patient professional to disentangle. We have cracked this code. Do you want to know what the message says?"

"Not pertinent to me."

"We found it written in Anna's notebook, hidden in her bedroom's wall."

Silence.

"What do you conclude of a woman who inscribed a secret code in her papers? Is this not damning evidence?"

Holland regarded the eyes that bored into his. No hint of the thoughts behind. He recalled Slate's remark: *The only one who can shed light is Swan, and he reveals nothing.*

"She is in trouble, your friend Anna. Of course she protests her innocence. So does everyone, guilty or not. We *hang* spies."

"She is innocent."

"Your logic eludes me. Please elaborate."

Holland said nothing.

"In fact, I need you to tell me all you know about her. If you tell me, and more importantly, if I believe you, I will take what you say into account to help save her from the gallows."

"She is innocent," he repeated. The words sounded empty.

"You must *convince* me. I am not swayed by your assertion you were unaware of her feelings for you. Plainly a bond of affection prevailed, and you recognized it."

"If there was a bond, it was unspoken."

"So, we are making progress. Such sentiments forge trust between people. I think she trusted you beyond what was safe for her. You see, for most people, love is a charming gift. For her, it was a weakness."

Never before had Holland felt terrified of another person. Swan's gaze seemed to sear into his mind.

Swan said, "Do you think you can answer my questions, immediately and without deliberating? It is the one way I'll be certain you are telling me the truth."

"All right."

"Did she show you papers of any kind?"

"No. You already asked."

"Did she allude to espionage, on her part or another's?"

"No."

"Where did she go when she left the house?"

"She rarely left."

"Yet she *did* leave."

"I was not told of her whereabouts all the time, nor did I ask."

"Did she mention messages in shoes sent off to be repaired?"

"No."

"Did she travel to Richmond?"

"Once, if I recall."

"What did she do there?"

"She bought fabric. We did not speak of it in detail."

"Did she meet anyone?"

"I don't think so."

"Of whom did she speak—friends, acquaintances?"

Holland paused.

Swan shouted, "I told you not to deliberate! Answer at once!"

"No one."

"Did you become aware of strange or unexplained occurrences during your stay?"

He remembered the digging in the yard. Their conversations on the subject. The recollection slapped him. "No."

"You hesitated."

"I wanted to be certain."

"Why should you be otherwise?"

"I was in my room. What happened beyond was a mystery to me."

"To whom did she write letters or notes?"

"I don't know."

"Who were her friends or acquaintances?"

"You asked me that *twice*."

Swan shook his head. "How can I believe you if you won't speak candidly?"

"I am being candid."

"If everything was a mystery to you, how can you vouch for her?"

"I spent time with her and witnessed her character. She is a good person."

"In other words, you trusted her, and she trusted you."

"Yes."

"So tell me what she trusted you with. With whom did she associate, beyond her family and the Negro servants?"

"I don't know."

"Where did she go when she left the house?"

"You asked me that too."

"I'm asking *again*."

"I don't know."

"Did she mention friends or acquaintances outside the family?"

Gibraltar Nash, Holland thought. A poet who did not exist. "No one," he said.

Swan was staring at him. "You are condemning her, you realize."

"How can I condemn her by not knowing?"

"Do you still not wish to hear what the code means?"

"She is not a spy!"

"From the quaver in your voice, you must feel it in your heart, you pitiful, naïve fellow. You were tricked! Played for the fool. The collection of letters, when decoded and expanded with vowels, says as follows: 'After the Sharpsburg battle, the Army of Northern Virginia counts only seventy thousand men and is far outnumbered by the Federal army. The Southern Command takes great pains to rebuild its strength and conceal its inferiority of numbers and exercises ruses and feints to mislead you. With a forceful press, you can overwhelm them and capture Richmond.' They meant to pass the message to the Yankees, and they surely would have done so, had we not intervened in time. As a soldier, you should be grateful the intelligence was not delivered to the other side."

"Of course."

"What do you surmise from this written in Anna's personal notebook?"

He couldn't speak.

"What else can it signify, except that she was *involved*? So stop telling me she is innocent! Tell me what she *did*!"

"I don't know, damn you!"

"Not me, sir. By your words, *you* damn *her*."

"No."

"Your conversations were intimate. She trusted you, and now you must tell me what she trusted you to hear. Who were the people she dealt with beyond the household?"

"Three women visited early in my stay. They arrived together, to pay their patriotic respects. And on the same day, a reporter and photographer stopped by from the *Richmond Daily Dispatch*."

"What were the women's names?"

"I don't remember."

"Go on."

"Families sheltered on the day of the storm. I did not learn their names."

"Where were they from?"

"I don't know."

"Who else?"

"A seamstress of curtains. She made new ones for my room. A stout woman with bowl-cut hair. Her assistant was a shy young girl."

Swan seemed altogether disinterested in the curtainmaker. Perhaps he'd known about her already, thought Holland. He recalled Anna's mention of how she'd contacted the seamstress by mail.

Had Swan been intercepting the Van Meers' letters?

"Who else?" demanded Swan.

"A Negro healer tended to me when I had a fever. I did not see him—I was unconscious."

"Dr. Slate approved of this medicine man?"

"It happened during the storm. Slate was far away."

"Who else?"

"They are the ones I recall."

"Where did Anna go when she left the house?"

"I don't know."

"Who were the people she was in touch with?"

"You keep asking me the same questions!"

Swan glared. "You are *not* telling me the truth! You are withholding important information, indulging your fondness for her and neglecting your soldierly duty. Between your misguided loyalties and protestations of her innocence, the only time I will be certain of anything is when I see her hanged."

Holland thought, Swan wanted her dead. The man's intention was to prove her guilt, not her innocence.

Swan shook his head. "You are a disgrace. Precious time and money have gone to care for you, to repair your leg in this unique device, because someone deemed you worthy, while men who performed their duty died or had their limbs cut away. What have you done to repay what was lavished upon you?" He seized the bag of coffee from the box. "I'm going to give this to the soldiers of our army who deserve it. What are *you* going to give them?"

Holland sank into his pillow. Involuntarily, a moan escaped his lips.

Swan stared. His expression had flattened like a drained water blister. "Do not feel so morose, John. For if it were not bitter, how could you learn from it?"

Leaving, his heels clacked.

The anguish pulsed so acutely that Holland writhed, turning his head side to side. The phrase reechoed: *The only time I will be certain of anything is when I see her hanged.'*

* * *

On the stool he'd fetched from the carpenters, Slate leaned forward, elbows on the box. "I do not believe that Anna was a spy.

The allegation is preposterous. How could she have lived a secret life beneath the one we saw? If I know anything about people, I'm certain she was not disingenuous."

"You spoke of her in the past tense," said Holland.

"Did I? Not by intention."

Holland observed that Slate's expression shifted like the turning of the seasons, through worry, doubt, indignation, and fear. *Both of us are afraid.* How readily the accusing finger intimidated good men.

"She is a person of virtue, which is immediately obvious," added Slate, correcting his tense.

Nothing was obvious about her, mused Holland. She'd been evasive about the digging. When he'd speculated a deserter might be lurking nearby, she'd called him absurd. She'd been cognizant of the digging and probably of much more. She had the capacity for deceit in abundance.

"A military tribunal will not overlook her fine character," Slate added. "They will refuse to condemn her."

"The evidence condemns her. Swan found a code written in her notebook, hidden someplace in her room."

"I'm sure it is a misunderstanding she can explain."

Not a misunderstanding, Holland thought. He wanted to tell Slate of his insights about Anna. He caught himself. What would the Doctor think? What did *he himself* think? Swan had discovered the code in the same book from which she'd read, the one *she'd refused to hand him.*

Slate stared at him. What had his expression signaled in the last minute of his ruminations?

"Do not despair," said Slate. "Her authenticity will be manifest to one and all. As will her innocence."

"Anything she says will serve to convict her father. And all we tell Swan will accomplish the same, inimical to them."

Slate fingered his moustache. "Perhaps that is why she is not cooperating with him."

Anna must be immensely strong, Holland ruminated, to have frustrated Swan. For two days she'd been in his custody, and apparently she'd divulged nothing. Yet if Swan could intimidate him and Slate, imagine what he could do to her. He could imprison her; threaten her or her father or the freedmen with hanging or mistreatment. Force her to reveal all she knew. Who wouldn't buckle under such pressure?

He thought of Swan's haughty pivot when he'd marched out, his heels clapping on the planks.

How could anyone stop him from conquering her?

$$*\quad*\quad*$$

"Sir?"

A tap on his shoulder. He jolted awake.

The orderly's face hovered shadow-like against the ceiling. "Sir, you thrashin' awful, shakin' that box to fright."

Holland's leg felt pinched—he must have disarranged the box's pressure points. "This ward needs more lanterns. I can hardly see you."

"Guess this ward ain't ready, sir. Got just the one weak lantern. No candles neither."

"Is there water?"

"Pail by the door. Water's dirty, though. The boy's s'posed to bring a fresh one. He ain't."

"Can you shout to the yonder ward to bring some?"

"Won't hear me callin' 'cross the way. They won't come unless I ring the fire bell. Yep, that'll bring 'em."

"Please don't."

"Wasn't 'bout to."

"You cannot simply walk there and fetch me a cup?"

"I ain't quittin' my place of duty at night, sir. Daytime, yeah, but not at night. They arrest you for that. They strict."

"Very well."

The orderly retreated. In the dark, Holland heard the syncopated footfalls. Must be midnight, or a bit earlier. The interminable night lay ahead. He sunk into his pillow, cognizant of his mouth's dryness, and he imagined a soothing drink of water. How could a hospital ward have no fresh water for its patients? Slate must have assumed someone would take care of the logistical trivia—provisioning wards was not his responsibility—that in the way of things not looked after had gone undone.

Barely could he gather the spit to swallow.

He pictured Anna bringing him water.

How well had he truly known her? The bastard Swan had smashed his conceptions. A nefarious patina overlay all that had seemed ordinary and charming.

No!—he mustn't allow his memories to be poisoned.

While he'd slept, she'd read the letters from his family. He'd given her intrusion no thought, until now.

Over the two months of his convalescence, the most memorable moments had been in her company. But there had been relatively few of these. He'd spent much of his day alone. Bookman had handled the quotidian regime of his care. Now he recalled his many conversations with the adept freedman who read insatiably, and of whom he'd become quite fond, more so than he'd credited. Where was Bookman now? No doubt in Swan's custody. Yet Swan had asked not a single question about him. Perhaps the arrogant Confederate assumed Bookman simply wasn't very interesting. How wrong, the misimpression. Holland wasn't about to correct it.

Swan had not asked about Henry Van Meer either.

So ordinary, Holland's conversations with Van Meer. What had they spoken about? Whether he wished for a preacher to visit. His impressions of the war. The mail. *Anna is much the same as her mother—brilliant and spirited. Also willful.*

He remembered the women's call. The delivery of his father's presents. The house full of shelterers on the day of the storm. The newspaper reporter's interview. Anna in the doorway while the photographer lit a bevy of candles and cautioned him not to move.

Had the newspaper published the article? If so, he'd overlooked it. They all had.

Or had Swan imposed his hidden hand?

Leaves rustled outside. He remembered how he'd crawled onto the flat porch roof of his father's cigar-smoke-filled house, to behold the stars in the autumn night sky. Now he strained to isolate the swishing oak leaves, their distinct shapes. He could not. How odd, the commonest sight he'd witnessed growing up, and his mind withheld the image. Neither could he beckon his father's face. He could hear the man's baritone voice, see his neatly combed hair, even make out the texture of his wool smoking jacket. Of the face, nothing.

To his relief, he reproduced Anna's at once, in such striking clarity that she might be physically present by his bed. In her blouse with black-threaded cuffs and collar, she sat in repose. Her lips and jaw were at rest while her eyes in their watery color skipped this way and that. Her fingers occasionally bloomed outward, her sole demonstrativeness—she relied on her words to convey her thoughts, and he heard them crisply. Perhaps later he would try to summon her in one of her agitated states. Yes, he looked forward to doing so—certainly his cache of memories could duplicate her in any of her moods.

How long would the pictures of her stay vivid? He tried to invoke Henry Van Meer, to cast his face onto the matte opposite, the way he had projected his memories in his tedious initial convalescence, and for an instant he saw the man's humble smile under the scruff of gray hair.

The effigy melted in favor of Swan holding the coffee bag.

Of all the images he *didn't* want to see. He shook his head, but the visage wouldn't go away. Swan pervaded his thoughts the way a putrid smell obliterates others. How calculatedly he had posed, hand on the box like a stage actor, hefting the coffee bag he had carried along as a prop. Holland felt a queasy admiration for the man so wily he'd presented the bag like evidence in a court, his pocket harboring the code he thereupon flourished as conclusive proof. He'd brought not one but two dramatic displays.

Two.

As if from a distant corner, Anna's voice: *A confident man gives one gift, not two.*

All of Swan's questions had been about Anna.

With whom did she associate? Where did she go when she left the house?

The ward's silence honed the phrase, asked persistently: *Where did she go?*

The singular purpose of Swan's questions had been to discover where she'd gone.

Why would he ask that?

Unless he didn't know.

Because he didn't have her.

And couldn't find her.

- 11 -

Hissing sand. Chill dampness and mildew. The roughness of the wool blanket she'd pulled around herself, the edges unraveling. Darkness surrounded.

The grains rained. Where was the noise coming from?

Her hair had fallen over her face. She clawed away the snags. Longing for a hairbrush, she grunted to her feet, rising gingerly, and fortunately so, for her head bumped a protruding ceiling joist. Stooping, she shuffled on an earthen floor, sensing moisture through the soles of her shoes.

He hid me here.

A root cellar barely larger than a horse stall. Two vertical beams and the distended ceiling joists further constricted the space. Vacant except for her.

The damp floor smelled rotten. Not wishing to lay down, she had slept crouched, her back to the wall, elbows wrapped around her bent legs. She'd been able to rest in this awkward posture because she'd been thoroughly worn out from the day before. A day of terror and exertions. She fended off the horrible visions.

Now she oriented herself to the trickling sand. Caught a pinpoint of illumination. Groped toward the tiny glow, unsure how far away, and immediately touched a metal surface burred and dented. Light seeped through a pinhole. She fingered the tiny crater. Here was an iron plate someone had punched a nail through.

At the plate's border, faint scraping noises. Grains trickled at her feet. With her fingers she traced the outlines extending to the ceiling, about eighteen inches side to side, twelve top to bottom. A hatch. Did it open to load things into this dank cellar? She probed for a clasp or hinges. Stone and mortar surrounded. Pressed her eye to the hole. Dimly outlined, a black girl's face.

"Hello," said Anna.

The scraping stopped.

"Hello," she repeated.

A rustle of cloth. Receding footfalls.

The girl had run away.

Through the nail hole, Anna's predominant view was of grass. The plate's bottom must be flush with the ground. Fifty yards hence rose a windowless, yellowed wall under a roof and gutter whose top opening she could make out. She overlooked the roof, which meant she stood on higher ground. Like a crack in a window pane, a thin line bisected her vista, perhaps an illusion the aperture created or a hair strand that dangled into her close view. Fingering away her hair, she blew into the hole. The line was still there, and the more she stared, the more tangible it seemed.

The light intensified, revealing the line's texture. Must be one of the ropes her father and Bookman had affixed on the day of the storm, to save Hock's house from being swept away.

Her father and Bookman.

She struggled to push away the images.

A shadow crossed her view. In the grainy ambiance she gleaned a frail figure under close-cut hair. The girl did not so much walk as slink between the house and Anna's vantage point, stopping, crouching, and in a cat's dash reaching the plate. Anna intoned, "Who is there?"

No answer. A scrape at the metal. Sand trickled.

"What are you doing?" asked Anna.

No response. The sunrise at the girl's back cast her face in shadow. Through the hole, Anna strained to make out an expression.

How strange. Never in her life could she have imagined waking to find herself hidden in a root cellar behind Lyman Hock's house, relying on *him*, of all people, to protect her. What was today? Sunday? How long—only two days?—since she'd watched the hospital coach take Captain Holland away?

After he'd departed, she'd busied herself with chores. Cleaned his room, restoring things as before. Reluctantly she'd tied back the horse-pattern curtains. When she'd finished, the sense of his presence lingered. She'd strung his necklace around her neck, pressing the queer, furry cocoon under her blouse. When occasionally it had fallen out, the dotted eyes seemed to stare at her. "John," she'd whispered, "I miss you every minute."

The idea had not come to her until the following afternoon. The weather had stayed cold and wet, the mist shrouding the horses and wagons that plied their muddy way toward Richmond on the turnpike. *I must visit him at the hospital!* Why hadn't she thought of this before? Wasn't the Chimborazo only nine miles up the road? Surely callers were allowed. Slate would not object. The plan had sparked excitement and restored her exuberance.

Misgivings. When yesterday they'd loaded him into the hospital carriage, the urge to embrace him almost had overwhelmed her. Afterward she'd gone to her room and erupted in tears. If saying goodbye had so disconcerted her, what would happen after she visited him? Soon he would rejoin his unit and resume his role the war, perhaps to be killed. She'd thought of the magnifier she'd packed in his trunk—would visiting him only serve to magnify her suffering?

Something else too. The reason she'd not thought about visiting him was that he'd not invited her. What would it signal, to go uninvited?

Why had he not invited her?

Because I hid myself from him.

Disoriented, she'd slumped on the stairs. She must think what to do! Her emotions had tumbled like loose objects in a jolting wagon bed.

She'd ascended to her room, closed the door, unsealed the blue corner, taken out her notebook, and opened to the poem she'd penned on the evening before his departure. Roved over the lines to the third stanza:

> But discretion I must embrace
> Against my desire to cup your face
> I wear a mask, with a mask o'er
> Remove one, but not the other
> A blank mien, my lips sealed
> I die before my love for you can be revealed.

She might have shown him the poem, or copied the lines in a letter to hand to him as he left. Thus she would have disclosed her feelings. She'd not imagined how she'd grieve afterward, not to have done so. Not to have done *anything*. She'd let him go with a nothing more than a smile and a goodbye. Furious at herself, she'd ripped out and crumpled the page. Immediately regretted having done so. *No, this is not how you act! You are not impulsive—you shall be deliberate in your actions!* The first, to smooth and restore the torn-out page between the others.

She'd returned the book to the blue corner. To clear her mind, she would walk. Strapping on her shoes from the Richmond cobbler, she'd opened the front door to test the air. Damp, chilly, but not bitter. Donned a skirt with a thick, warm underskirt; buttoned on a long-sleeved blouse. Not expecting to be gone long, she'd taken only her wool shawl she wrapped around her torso.

Soon she'd reached the serpentine path by the deserted earthworks. Despite the snow and rain, the ground hadn't been slippery, and her tread had stayed firm. On the ridge, the sky had presented an artist's pallet of pink-fringed clouds. How fortunate, that her feelings had prompted her to walk, or she'd have missed this rare scene. Toeing the rocks, avoiding the slick spots, she'd arrived at the highest point, normally a windy place, today calm, and the silence had settled her. She would visit him, she'd promised herself, and henceforth she'd not fret at the awkwardness of lacking an invitation. For she knew him, didn't she? A man who relished the company of horses would scoff at the formality. True, she had preserved a certain aloofness from him, even scolded him for his inquisitiveness, yet he'd seen her every day for two months, and her presence always had gladdened him. He would be overjoyed to see her, she knew as certainly as she knew anything, and her visit would be a wonderful gift to him. Whatever else happened, they were friends.

Shouts from below. Tumults on the road happened commonly— maybe wares had dropped from a wagon, or a wheel had slipped into a rut, or a party of riders had passed by shouting to each other. She peered. Though the storm had stripped most of the branches, enough leaves had survived to block her view.

Another shout. She'd ignored it, unwilling to relinquish the spectacular sky.

Was she needed at the house?

Well, she'd be by soon enough.

* * *

Abruptly Holland sat up. The box creaked.

"Y'all right, sir?"

"Get Dr. Slate."

"I can't leave my post at night…"

"Go! I give you an order. I take responsibility." The captain thrashed wildly, rattling the box around his leg. "*Go now, damn you!*"

The orderly clumped away.

God, that man would take an eternity to reach Slate.

In the lapse, Holland went a fair ways toward working his leg out of the box. By shifting his weight to and fro, he was able to rock the contraption, gingerly at first, then precariously, until the pinions within loosened. If it tipped off the stand and crashed to the floor, his leg would dislodge. Or so he calculated. The wood was strong, yet the latticework within seemed delicate, and the jolt might dismantle it. He must roll out of bed precisely when the box tipped, or the pinions would cut his leg.

Which might fracture again.

"Stop that!" cried Slate. He rushed to the bedside, and the lantern he carried swung erratically, spraying wild shapes on the walls and ceiling. Pressed his abdomen against the box to hold. "Confound it, John, I told you to control yourself!"

Through gritted teeth, Holland hissed, "Get me free of this thing!"

The jangling lantern alternately shaped and lost the orderly whose askew eyes roved disconcertingly in different directions.

"You can step out," said Holland, voice compressed. "Fetch some water!"

"Sir?"

"Leave us!" the captain said.

"I…"

"Get the hell out!"

"Please, calm yourself," urged the doctor. To the orderly, "Yes, you may go. I'll attend to him. Head to the yonder ward, and I'll stop by later. Everything will be fine."

Flinging glances over his shoulder, the orderly tapped away.

"Remove it," said Holland.

"I will not. What foolishness has come over you?"

"Swan doesn't have Anna. He doesn't know where she is."

"Nonsense. He has her in his custody."

"How do you know?"

"He told me."

"He is a liar! If he had her, he would not have needed to interrogate me with the same questions again and again, not about what she *did*, but where she might have *gone*. She is in hiding, I'm sure of this in my heart, and perhaps I can get to her before he does."

"You are conjecturing."

"Why would Swan ask these questions, if he had Anna?"

"What if they simply are his regimen?"

"Not him—he acts with cunning design."

"You draw premature conclusions."

"Every minute I'm here reduces my chances."

Slate tapped his fingers on the box. He was not an experimental surgeon because he lacked an open mind. Holland's argument sounded logical. Nonetheless it stood on assumptions Slate could not evaluate. Holland was a cavalryman who regularly gathered observations to inform military decisions, and he had intuited that Anna was at large and in great danger. In this realm, wasn't he the best qualified to say?

"Even if you are right," said Slate, "what can you do?"

"Get her to safety."

"What place is safe from a man like Swan?"

"I don't know. I will find a way."

Slate began to pace the floor, his expression squeezed, and the lantern he'd rested on the box cast him as a roving phantom. He said, "If you proceed, Swan will arrest you. To leave here is contrary to orders, as you who profess to be so attentive to them must realize."

"Orders from Swan? I cannot abide his orders."

"This is reckless. I can play no part."

"Then I will get myself out."

"They will arrest the *both* of us!"

"Tell them I escaped during the night. The orderly will confirm your story. He'll testify to my maniacal fit."

"Swan won't believe it."

"He will *hang* her!"

Fumbling in his pocket, the doctor retrieved his schedule of rounds. The paper crackled like an eggshell underfoot.

"Doctor, time is *burning*."

Slate nodded almost imperceptibly, as if acknowledging that the decision already had moved beyond his power to restrain. He stepped to the box and seized the lantern. With practiced ease he spun the turnbuckles, loosened the pinions, and plucked the dressings from the leg. There were aspects of the box's construction Holland had not comprehended. Slate worked through a series of pegs and latches, tapping and tugging with his right hand, while with his left he worked the lantern overhead like a signalman on a rail line. One by one, the box's innards clanked to the floor. Holland was relieved he hadn't managed to tip the contraption over, for his leg would not have survived intact.

In five minutes the apparatus lay in pieces. His leg was free. Yet he could barely move. He flexed the muscles, and pain sliced through like a sword.

"Only the smallest efforts at first, John."

Slate helped him to his feet, delicately released him to stand alone. "Shift your weight gently to your right leg."

He did. The pain intensified.

"You will need time to regain your strength."

"Time is what I don't have. I need a horse."

"I cannot recommend you ride so soon."

"I shall ride anyway."

Slate sighed. "I suppose you should take mine."

"Report him stolen."

* * *

In the ward across the way, the orderly Silas waited, as Dr. Slate had instructed. Soon the tiredness overcame him, and he let himself slide down the interior wall to rest his bottom on the planks, until in the darkness he no longer resembled a man, merely something tossed aside. His wool shirt—a Confederate army garment dyed a shade of apple russet—didn't keep him warm, and he shivered until the ward's orderly brought him a blanket. Shrouded, he slept.

The ward slumbered too. At dawn, a creaking wagon wakened him. Gingerly he budged his ankle he'd crushed falling out of a tree he'd climbed for his master, and whose bone had healed wrong. Pushing to his feet, he waited until the aching subsided. Limped to the door and out to the stoop. The dawn blushed orange. His skin, cold and stiff, preserved the lines the wall boards had impressed while he'd slept. Reaching around, he fingered the ridges, and they reminded him of the scars from a whipping laid upon him years ago for sassing a white man. Folks who'd looked at his back said they couldn't see the welts. He still felt them, though.

How long had he slept? He wasn't at his post. The army was unforgiving about some offenses, and quitting a duty post at night was one. Men who did so got arrested. If they deserted and got caught, the army might even shoot them. Of course he was no deserter—the doctor had *ordered* him to leave his post. Where was Dr. Slate? The doctor was supposed to have come back and told him what to do.

He hobbled unsteadily. The doctor's quarters were a fair distance off. A fresh pang of anxiety—maybe Slate *had* come by looking for him and *hadn't* noticed him sleeping in the darkness. Figured he'd run away!

Across the plateau he limped, his pace pressured, his ankle tormenting. Folks got lost at the Chimborazo; the grounds were enormous, the buildings a maze. He knew his way—he'd helped build this place in the autumn of 1861, and he remembered when the wards had been bare frames, scores of men hammering on the re-used slats they'd pulled from mounds hauled in on wagons. In the piles had lurked wasp nests, and the insects had swarmed when the men pulled out the boards, and they'd hammered with one hand and swished away wasps with the other.

Edging the paths, he sighted the temporary quarters, a row of limewashed cottages constructed at the same time as the central wards. The staff doctors lived off post, many in boarding houses on Broad Street to the west; only the duty surgeons stayed overnight. For some reason, Dr. Slate had slept at the hospital these three nights since the patient with the box had arrived—he'd instructed Silas where to reach him in case of trouble.

He limped up the steps to the cottage porch and knocked. No sound from within. He tapped again.

A sleepy groan. "What?"

"Doctor, I'm Silas, the orderly…"

"Who?"

"Silas, sir. The orderly from the new ward with the cap'n and the box on his leg."

"What's the matter?"

"Nothin,' sir. I been waitin' all night for you to send me back to the ward. Been sittin' in the ward yonder like you said."

"Very well."

Very well? What did that mean? "Sir, you told me to stay there and I did."

"And so?"

Silas wagged his head in frustration. "Should I head to the ward, sir? Is the patient all right?"

"Yes, of course. No need to hurry. I was with him myself for a while. He is fine, I'm sure. Get yourself breakfast first, and the patient's plate for him, and head to the ward."

Silas ambled toward the plateau's southern edge. He smelled the aroma from Chimborazo's kitchens. Meals for thousands each day. At one corner opened the food line for the blacks—he could see them gathered. The worry that had afflicted him began to melt, and as he neared the line, the scent of fresh bread enveloped him. Not often were Chimborazo's blacks permitted wheat bread—most times they got only cornmeal bread—so today was special. Made him feel like singing. Of course nobody was allowed to sing on the hospital grounds—the noise might disturb the wounded soldiers. After the experience last night, he apprehended how patients could go crazy with what had befallen them, the horrors they'd witnessed and the pain they'd suffered. He thought of the captain yelling *'Go now, damn you!'* after he'd tried to thrash loose of the evil-looking box. No telling how a man like him might react to singing.

Silas was a slave whose master, a mill owner, had leased him to the hospital, and this made for a curious situation. At the hospital, the leased slaves worked alongside the freedmen and were indistinguishable to the hospital staff. His job title was Hospital Orderly, Level 1. He was proud of the title, which was the same for the freedmen who'd been free all their lives and dwelled in Richmond. From the hospital he received a wage, less than what the freedmen got, money still. The slaves at Chimborazo, unlike other slaves, followed the military regulations. The rules both threatened and protected them. Threatened, because a man must not fail his duties, lest he be punished or sent back to his master; protected, because the hospital was not a slaveholder who at his whim would sell the slaves for profit. Nothing whimsical about the Chimborazo; the hospital worked by rules, and the whites, even the officers, heeded them. Though he was a slave, the regulations created a firm place for him to stand. He did not know what name to give the idea all men should be governed by the same rules, only that the way seemed right.

He walked with his head turned slightly, focusing through his left eye. For as long as he could remember, he'd suffered a wandering right eye. The lazy eye hadn't prevented him from learning to read—an old slave woman had taught him the letters in the months when his ankle was mending—yet the split gaze distracted folks who didn't know him and even some who did, and caused them to falsely think he wasn't paying attention, and more than once had reaped him a cussing from his master.

Because he could read and knew the Bible, the slaves at Chimborazo held him to be sage. They'd asked him about their strange circumstance—favorable or unfavorable? "Oh, we good for the time," he'd told them.

"For what time?"

"The time we here at the hospital. Don't think this is gonna last forever, naw. We go back to the masters one day, 'lessen the Confederates lose the war."

"They win or lose, Silas?"

"I know what I pray for."

Working for the army meant he had to listen to the officers' speeches. The officers held that the South was defending its honor against the North, a menace and a defiler of what was decent. They said too that the South was winning the war. Not all the wounded soldiers had much to say. Those who did declared the same sentiments as the officers. The blacks at the Chimborazo cared for the soldiers and listened to their tales of battle and horsemanship and courage. Hard not to feel pride and to want to be part. From the stories you couldn't help but believe the South would win, and if it held true, seemed prudent to have helped the victors and to have earned their gratitude. Yet constant were the reminders of a slave's life. Even the best-treated slaves were not free. Silas knew that God did not condone slavery, and if God did not, then He did not hold with the Confederacy. All his life Silas had been able to recognize God's will. Others acknowledged this gift in him. *It is written in the prophets, And they shall be all taught of God.* Silas knew the Confederacy must end, but when it would happen, he didn't.

The kitchen woman smiled widely. "Silas, you here early today. Not like *you* to be early."

"I must'a smelled that bread so fresh, praise the Lord."

"Take two, we got plenty."

"Oh yeah," he said, accepting the flat loaves almost too hot to hold, sliding one into his shirt. He took a plate of eggs, grits, and beans and ate standing. Steam from the food wafted.

"Sit yo'self down, Silas," said one of the blacks.

"Ain't got time," he replied.

"Takes you all day to walk here. You sure as hell can spare the time."

He didn't like cuss words, but he said nothing. He wasn't a preacher to tell others how they should speak. He was done anyway. Returned his wooden plate branded C.H., same as the patients ate from. Now he asked for the patient's plate and a water bottle. Balancing these in one hand, the other free, he limped toward the ward under construction. Plucked the second bread loaf from his shirt. The night's shadows clung, and he calculated his footfalls as he lifted the loaf that hovered like the moon's pale disk, the fragrance rushing up his nose. Crossed the empty ground, fringing the woods. Downed the loaf and fingered his teeth clean.

God had spiced his life with small pleasures, and in this moment he was as happy as any white man. He was confident of where he was, what he would do today, and that he'd not go hungry. He savored the blissful moments and knew to enjoy them in isolation and not hope they'd last. Over the hours, his thoughts always would turn toward the rage he'd felt all his life. Try as he might, he'd never been able to liberate himself from murderous thoughts, and these were dangerous, for they could be read on his face. So, best he could, he smothered them. God knew his heart, and Jesus who had suffered understood hardship. Let the Lord rectify the agony of men enslaved. The Lord would resolve things, in His time.

Or He won't, and I'll die a slave. Quickly he crushed the thought, lest it embitter his day from the onset.

He was within one hundred yards of the unfinished ward when he heard hoof beats. Had the doctor decided to ride over here? He saw that the horseman wasn't Slate. Someone else, fellow on a gray horse, his form obscure in the half light, except for one feature: the red hair that flared as if from its own luminosity. Silas recognized the officer who'd been by a couple times already to talk to the patient, and on both occasions he'd told Silas to wait outside.

The officer trotted to the new ward, dismounted, hitched his horse, and strode toward the doorway.

Silas's worries resurged. What if the patient told the officer he'd been abandoned through the night? His footfalls adopted a hurried beat, and he gulped from the strain. Heart rapping, steadying the plate, he shuffled to the doorway through which the red-haired officer had passed. *Act like you went off to fetch breakfast, just like every day.*

The officer had halted just past the doorway. Silas clumped in and managed to whisper "Sir" before his throat seized up.

The patient's bed lay empty, the wooden box scattered in pieces.

On the floor, white dressings all trailed out.

The red-haired officer's mouth fell open.

Silas thought, they'll blame *me*.

He felt no panic, only a sensation like memory, like he'd been in this moment before. How strange. Then it came to him. No, he hadn't been here, but *they* had been. The Disciples, on the morning of the Resurrection. What they'd seen at that dawn so long ago, when they'd hurried to Jesus's tomb and beheld the immense stone rolled back, and within the vacant space, the wisps of burial cloth. *Then cometh Simon Peter following him, and went into the sepulcher, and seeth the linen clothes lie.*

The Disciples had stood dumbfounded.

Like us, thought Silas.

Couldn't say a word.

- 12 -

She wrapped her arms around herself. Leaned against the wall. More scrapes and hisses. In the beam of light through the nail hole tossed dust motes, and on them she projected yesterday's clouds and the russet trees. She'd stood on the ridge rocks, and a poem had begun to dance in her head, the words taking shape on their own—she could not force a poem. She'd gazed at the sky's subtle beauty. Felt the cool air against her skin, the lightest flutter of her hair.

From the road below, another shout. Seemed the commotion wouldn't pass of its own accord.

She tried to corral the poem. Slow to coalesce, her poetry moments were quick to flee, and this one did.

Arms outstretched for balance, she toed toward the path.

From which emerged Sarah.

Something odd in her expression. Skin pulled back in what resembled a smile, but wasn't. The climb had left her panting, and she struggled to speak: "Miss… you gotta… My God, they beatin' 'em to death!"

"Sarah, what's the matter?"

"They hurt his head—they hit him with a gun!"

Anna stepped toward the plateau's edge. Below she saw her house, and at once Sarah gripped her upper arm—never had Sarah clutched her so fiercely. She strained against the tugs, and on the road a scene opened like a painting: horses and soldiers, and on the ground her father on his knees, and Bookman and Jerome prone, their faces in the dirt. As she watched, one of the soldiers put his foot on Bookman's back. Why? Because he was trying to stand up.

What outrage was this?

Sarah yanked her so hard she fell over, and now the woman dragged her by the arm.

"Sarah, stop!"

"You gotta run fast as you can. They're askin' 'bout you. They're sayin,' 'Where's Anna,' and I ran 'round back before they saw me. They're gonna come lookin' soon." Sarah's eyes were wild, yet behind their hysteria, Anna perceived the woman's fierce will. "You go *that* way, down into the creek toward old Hock's, and hide yourself."

"Sarah…"

"You don't got time to talk, you gotta go *now!*"

Turning, Anna stepped off.

"Ain't no time for walkin' neither," yelled Sarah. "Girl, you run!"

Sarah had seen Anna run, as a child and as an adult to chase a chicken. Impossible not to obey Sarah's command, and she dashed downhill toward the creek. Glancing behind, saw Sarah slumped to her knees, sobbing.

Anna could not comprehend.

She scampered down the hillside, hiking her dress so her legs could move freely, until she reached the sunken woods whose marshy floor preserved pools in gnarled patterns. Dodging them, alternately running and walking, on her right she sighted the house's roof two hundred yards off. She didn't think anyone could see her here, even so she moved warily. When she'd gone well past, she picked up her pace, splashing ahead. Wondered how far the sounds would carry.

Astride the stream, the marsh pools deepened. Her shoes were getting wet. Pulling them off, she buckled the straps together, clutching them while she pulled her skirt to her thighs. Waded into the ice-cold water. Muffled a shriek.

No dry path ahead.

At a distance behind, dogs barked.

Would the soldiers go to the trouble to pursue her with hounds? Even if they did, they couldn't track her along the creek. No, they'd keep to the roads and fields, as they'd done in the time of the Railroad. The dogs hadn't detected the runaways' scent. She and Bookman had spread pepper around the hiding place and paths.

Where she could, she stayed in the shallows. Waded cautiously, so as not to trip, until protruding branches forced her toward the stream's center. She had to drop her skirt to cling precariously to the branch tips. The farther out she went, the more the current snatched at her, and she lost her grip and pitched, her head dunking under. Taste of leaves and dirt. Borne a dozen feet, she regained her legs. Snorted the water out of her nose. Her dress drooled. She balanced herself on a wagon wheel someone had discarded down the cleft. The wheel had settled upright between stones, and the oddity seemed to suit this place where she found herself a fugitive so close to home.

More than a decade had passed since she'd ventured so far along the creek. Her mother, like all adults, had dreaded marshy places for the sicknesses thought to pervade, and she'd forbidden her daughter to venture beyond earshot. Anna had done so anyway. She remembered a place where the creek's floor lifted into an oblong island. Recalled too the tongue-lashing she'd reaped for her late return.

At dusk the air bled all warmth, and only her energetic strides kept her from freezing. She made out the island and splashed onto the mound so much smaller than in her memory, the prominent feature a raised slab barely ample for her to sit upon. The creek rushed past. She was a mile from her house, she guessed, and some distance— unsure how far—from the road. Nobody could see her here. She pulled off her sopped dress and underclothes, wrung out the water as best as she could, and hung them on a branch with her shawl. Naked on the slab, she nonetheless felt warmer free of the drenched clothes. Rested her forehead on her arms and let the moisture peel from her skin. When she lifted her head, the light had vanished. The temperature would drop. At least she'd be dry, except for her hair. She touched her hanging dress. Still sopped.

In the trees swam visions of her father, Bookman and Jerome on the ground, and Sarah crying on the ridge top. What strength Sarah must have needed, to have witnessed her husband and brother arrested, and to have climbed the slope to warn her. *Girl, you run!*

The wind whistled. She hugged herself to dispel the shivering she wasn't certain had to do with the cold. What had happened? Why had soldiers raided the house? *My God, they beatin' 'em to death!* Had the army ferreted out the Van Meers' role in the Underground Railroad? More than a year had passed since they'd harbored an escaped slave. Should she go back and confront the soldiers? Demand an explanation? But what of the code she'd unearthed, and the activity outside late at night? She must think before she acted. Yes, she must reflect, as her father would have done.

She pictured him kneeling in the road.

Undeniably frozen, longing for a blanket and fireplace, she sobbed. Her thoughts seemed aimless, and she wondered if deep thinking wasn't the purview of those who felt no physical distress. To isolate the mind from the body's pains required discipline. Hadn't Holland separated his mind from the discomforts of the saddle? As compact as she could make herself for warmth, limbs compressed, face in the nook of her elbow, hair like a veil, she tried to calculate what she should do, go back or flee.

Dropped into sleep.

When she woke, the cold bit so sharp her nose stung. She could see her breath against the gray matte. Her shivering had wakened her. Toes and fingers stiff; her body shook.

She pictured Jerome shaking the dirty rag.

Her fingertips brushed the cord around her neck. The cocoon was gone. Must have disintegrated when she'd plunged into the water.

Standing, she teetered—her legs below the knees had numbed. She kicked to restore the blood flow. Her hanging clothes felt as wet as they'd been before. No choice, she tugged them on, keening through clenched teeth when the icy fabric dragged over her skin. Driest was her knitted wool shawl she wrapped around her shoulders. Forced herself to move, flapping her arms like a bird. She'd heard of people caught outside, wet and shivering, unable to get warm, who curled up and died. How close was she to that stage?

She must find help.

Clutching her shoes, she treaded into the stream. It flowed to the Kingsland Road. How far? She seemed unable to steady herself. If the way had been dry, her movement might have restored warmth. Now the opposite—her wet skirt and blouse stole the heat her body churned. The shawl hardly helped. Should she climb out of the creek to the adjoining field? Swan had mentioned a shack—was it nearby? Stepping toward the high bank, her leg plunged into a hole, and she pitched headlong into the water. A squawk like a cowbird's call escaped her mouth. She pushed upright. Water cascaded, and her legs kicked eruptions.

Suddenly the splashing ceased. Her feet touched gravel. The creek washed lightly over the roadway. She scraped the dripping hair from her face. Stepped like she was performing an Indian dance, her streaming clothes leaving a snail's trail. Tried to stand motionless and listen. Her shivering wouldn't let her. Needed a fire. Could she build one? No kindling and no flint. She must ask someone for coals. Sooner or later a wagon would happen along, and surely they'd have blankets and a coal pan aboard.

She plopped eastward. No wagons appeared. Too late at night.

To her right receded a trail. She veered in, treaded one hundred yards, scanning for a house or a slave hut where they'd have a fire. Trees and bushes. No habitations. Through the trees, a shimmery gray. The river?

She stepped into a rut, stumbled, righted herself. Reached a simple gate closed and tied with a lanyard she undid. Tugged, and to her surprise the gate didn't swing but fell with a loud thump at her feet. She strode over. A sheen ahead through the trees. Yes, the river.

"Who's there?"   A man's gruff voice.

She opened her mouth. No sound came out.

"Answer, damn you, or I'll shoot!"

Her lips twitched, and she choked out, "Anna Van Meer."

A figure stepped onto the path, lowering the double-barreled shotgun he'd been aiming in her direction.

She shambled forward. "Mr. Hock? Is that y-y-you?"

No answer.

"I need…"

Without a word, he gripped her roughly by the arm and pulled her along. His fingers felt rough but warm. *He's not trying to hurt me.* Turning off the trail and crossing grass, they reached a building that in the obscurity looked like a springhouse. A stairway sank to a lower level.

"You'll h-h-help me?"

He led her down the steps and through a doorway into a clammy space. "Stay quiet," he said. "I'll be back straightaway."

He returned with a candle, two loaves, dry clothes, a blanket, and a wooden cup of water. He lit the wick whose yellow glow barely reached the rough walls. "Here's flatbread and water. You keep real quiet, and I'll be by in the morning." In the candlelight his eyes blazoned emotion, maybe fear.

Not fear. Something else.

He left. The door creaked, the handle clattered.

Shielding the tiny flame to keep from blowing out—he'd left her no matches—she moved to the door and tried the handle. Locked from the outside. Changed into the dry clothes—a dress and a slip, both too big, yet thick and dry. Soon they blunted her shivering. She tossed her leaf-flecked, drenched clothes into a corner—didn't think she'd wear them again—and knotted her wool shawl over her shoulders. Bit into the flatbread and drank the water. The shaking abated, and her presence of mind crept back.

She faced two immediate problems. One, the soldiers who had arrested her father and the freedmen were hunting for her. Two, she was being sheltered by Lyman Hock, whom she didn't trust and in fact loathed. He'd *locked* her in here. Why? Perhaps for her own safety—a woman shivering out of her mind ought not to be given free reign. She should be grateful to him, she thought.

She recalled his leer in the flicker. Remembered the soldiers' gawks in the tailor's yard, their open-mouthed stares at her bosom.

Show him no submission.

Crumbs dropped from the bread onto her shawl; she'd have eaten them but couldn't find them in the dimness. Outside, crickets chirped. Leaves rustled.

The candle flame extinguished.

* * *

For the first time in three months, he dressed. From his trunk he unfolded trousers he donned painfully and with Slate's assistance. Pulled on his tunic that felt too big. Strapped on his leather belt, fastening the holster that had come with the new revolver. Fitted the gun still loaded from the evening Anna and Bookman had taken him to the river's edge. The trunk surrendered a tight-lidded tin cigar box, and he stuffed in the powder flask, wads, percussion caps, and extra bullets. Pressed on his hat that grated his head after the long interval without.

In the trunk he noticed the magnifier Anna had packed for him. Anything left behind, Swan surely would confiscate. He slipped it into his tunic pocket.

To shuffle the three hundred yards from the ward to the stable took half an hour. So tight was his leg, the muscles so clenched from their prolonged inertia, that he gripped Slate's shoulder the whole way. The leg felt altogether foreign, as did everything previously so familiar—the tunic's rub on his shoulders, the boots' grip on his calves, the gun handle against his side. Slate said, "Be grateful your leg was flexed in the box, or you wouldn't be able to walk at all."

In the unlit stable, Slate saddled his horse and tied on a blanket, canteen, and pouch. Shaking the canteen, he remarked, "Full, though the water is probably stale." The excitement must have winded him, for he spoke in bursts. "I regret I have no money on me. In the pouch are a few dollars. Not enough to get you far."

With Slate's help, he mounted the horse. The pain was acute; he bit teeth on teeth not to yelp. The night sky, mural of the waning moon, stars, and blowing clouds, cast a changing ambiance. Of the doctor, he could make out only a silhouette. "I hope to pay back your help someday. I'm afraid nothing I can do will suffice."

"I'm your friend," replied Slate. "You owe me nothing. Yet I would welcome your promise to take care of my horse, who is intelligent and trustworthy."

"An intelligent horse? Well, I've not ridden one of those. I give you my word, which you may wish to keep to yourself when you tell them I stole him."

"Yes, I must rehearse my tale." Slate took the reins and led him to the path. "John, I know you've set your mind. I must beg you to pause and reconsider—you've taken no irreversible step thus far."

"How could I live with myself if I did not try to help her?"

"You are certain doing this will help, and not bring ruin on the both of you?"

Courteous of Slate not to mention that the ruin might encompass him as well. "What can I tell you?"

"You must be careful with your leg. The pain should dull after a while. Don't mistake the numbness for healing. You must resume a proper therapy as soon as possible. My orders are that you should stand for one hour cumulatively each day and walk no more than half, touching a chair or wall for balance. Do so for the first week, and for each after, double the times."

"And riding?"

"None whatsoever, for four weeks."

"Your prescription is duly heard."

Slate stepped back. "Follow this gulch that grafts onto a road. Stay left until you pass the entry to the canal boat landing. The road spreads into a chickenfoot of three. The center way will lead you to a church a mile along. The highway coming in is yours—the Osborne Turnpike. Travel south nine miles and look to the east side for the homestead with the distinctive arch over the carriageway gate. I predict the horse will take the turns on his own, for he knows the way."

"So intelligent is he," inserted Holland. In the dark, Slate couldn't have detected the smile.

"I will say no more except to wish you speed and luck."

"I am forever grateful, sir."

Holland set out at a walk. The moonlight was intermittent, and to trot along the rutted road would have risked injuring the horse. To his left, the Chimborazo's compound glowed; lanterns illuminated the limewashed rows. Descending by the gulch path, he encountered buildings half built and then abandoned, their bare planks lapping the studs. The ravine separated the hospital grounds from Richmond. He'd heard of this place, initially conceived as a sweet glen where wounded men might shed their weariness beside a cool stream. The notion had evaporated when the prolific mosquitoes feasted on staff and wounded alike, welting their skin and driving them flailing up the slopes. They'd tried burning the vegetation along the stream's banks, and a scorched strip bordered ground strewn with broken bottles. The brush had refilled in thorns, and the buildings—the handful finished—had become forlorn storehouses.

A solitary sentry stepped onto the trail. "Halt!"

No sooner had Holland reined the horse than the sentry backed away. "Sorry, sir. Please proceed."

The sentries who manned the Chimborazo's entryways served two purposes: They protected the hospital's valuable supplies from theft, and they enforced the pass regulations. Soldiers departing the hospital must display a written pass. Officers, trusted, were exempt. By leaving tonight without permission, Holland had breached a trust that might never be restored. He imagined his cavalrymen averting their eyes from him, the officer who had brought disgrace on himself.

He shook away the thought. To find Anna, he must commit to the singular purpose. He continued downhill, skirting a meadow where the hospital's cow herd slept amid the trees. At the river flats, he submerged in thick fog. Leaned to spot the roadway's border he caught one minute and lost the next. Slowed the horse to a gentle walk, grateful that the animal had not gone skittish, as he'd witnessed with other horses ridden in fog. Ahead he discerned nothing. Fog so dense would obscure the canal boat turn and the chickenfoot convergence Slate had described. Ten minutes into his journey, already he was at a standstill.

Voices. The canal delivered food and other supplies to the hospital. Were the hospital's canal boats manned at night? He rode up behind two blacks walking in the fog. "Can you tell me where to find the intersection to the main road?"

One pointed a gaff pole so long the tip submerged in the mist. "Ahead 'bout seventy yards, sir. You can follow us, we goin' by."

He followed the men whose heads, shoulders, and protruding gaff poles swam in the puffs, disappearing at places. Hard to concentrate; his leg hurt fiercely. Slate had predicted that numbness would set in, but the pain seemed to have sharpened rather than subsided. Fortunately the horse, perhaps better sighted, picked up on the task and plodded confidently ahead.

Momentarily the men stopped. "We here, sir."

"I'm told to take the center path."

A hand reached out and gripped the horse's bridle. You might be wary to try this with a mean cavalry mount. Slate's horse did not mind. The fellow led him a hundred paces forward, and the fog dissipated to reveal the road's outline. "You on the middle way, sir. You see the side?"

"I do. Thank you for your kindness."

"Have a safe journey, Cap'n."

- 13 -

On November 15th, Colonel Schilling's regiment columned southward from the Warrenton camp. In contrast to the march from Maryland in which he'd been one of the last, today he was among the first. The sky spat rain amid patchy mist. At elevated spots he looked back to an endless procession following, thousands whose boots churned the mud, while the wagon and artillery wheels milled ever-deepening ruts.

Weather or no, he thanked God he was moving. The camp had grown insufferable. When not engaged in tedious drills, the men had huddled in their tents, the poor rations having robbed their alacrity. Obviously the food provisioners were cheating the army. Infuriated, he'd complained to the brigade commander, a proficient officer who'd promised to convey the matter up the chain of command. The problem, the brigadier had confided, was how to hold accountable the shadowy exploiters who held the food contracts. A remedy would require interventions far above the Army of the Potomac, from powerful men such as Army Quartermaster General Montgomery Meigs and Secretary of War Edwin Stanton.

Shilling took this to mean he should not expect improvements any time soon.

Before setting out, he'd gathered his soldiers to announce their mission: Seize Fredericksburg on the Rappahannock River, thrust toward Richmond, and capture the Confederate capital before year's end. Toward the lofty goal, his soldiers kept a brisk pace. Twelve miles along, they traversed ground strewn with broken rifle stocks, discarded bandages, crushed ammunition boxes, and the clumps of burned horse carcasses. Cannonballs had struck trees, sundering even the thickest oaks. The sad remnants harked to the clashes preceding Second Bull Run, where General Lee had thoroughly trounced General Pope's Union army. Retreating eastward toward Washington, the soldiers had learned that Pope had been removed from command and the popular McClellan was leading them. They'd cheered.

Now McClellan was gone, and Burnside was marching them toward another fight.

The column paralleled the Rappahannock, too far away to see. They skirted bare fields that poor farmers tended. On the march's first night, Schilling encamped on a shorn wheat field close to a shack where a white child clutched a chicken. The colonel put out orders to confiscate nothing from the people. The forage parties cut logs and built fires, and the men ate hard tack.

At dawn, the movement recommenced. The rain had stopped, and he hoped for sun. He didn't worry about the Rebels—hundreds of cavalrymen protected the flanks, their hooves' constant thunder reassuring. As in all long marches, the pace varied, leaving the rearward men to lurch, speeding one minute, plodding the next—the hateful accordion effect.

In the mid-afternoon, he spotted horsemen halted by the roadside ahead. Nearing, he recognized the brigade commander. The officer returned his salute. "Good morning, Schilling. I have a task for you, a formidable one for an untested and understrength regiment. How is your confidence?"

"What's the task, sir?"

The brigade commander turned to his staff officers alongside. "What did I tell you? No cocksure declarations from Schilling—he wants the details first, and rightly so."

Schilling brought his horse close while the brigadier unrolled a map. "Today Rebel cavalry attacked our New York cavalry along the Rappahannock by the United States Ford. The Rebels rode from Falmouth on this side and struck from the flank." He traced his finger along the wavy river between Falmouth town and the U.S. Ford. "You shall march to the high ground above the ford and set up a blocking position. The captain of the new cavalry screen will meet you at the site. When I can, I will arrange for another regiment to replace yours, and you'll join us at Fredericksburg."

Schilling saluted.

He led his regiment to the intersection with the U.S. Ford Road, turning opposite a house the map labeled 'Hamet.' Captain Oulette, the screen commander, awaited him at a point overlooking the Rappahannock. Oulette did not resemble a cavalry officer—he was older than Schilling and sat bulky in the saddle—nonetheless his flinty gaze cast him as a seasoned soldier. Together they toured the ground that draped to the water's edge. The road contoured the bank, curved abruptly, and ascended along ruts.

Schilling surveyed the rushing river. "How deep?"

"Four to five feet at the ford," said Oulette. "Tricky to cross in the swell, yet rare is the obstacle that will deter the Reb cavalry."

"Have you seen any?"

"No."

"Do you think you can keep them from riding up on my flanks?"

"I'll try. Trouble is, they know the ground and the river. They might attack before I spot them."

"With luck, we can fortify this position before they know we're here."

Oulette tilted his head. "That'd be a novelty."

Schilling defended a crescent centered on the road. The bend afforded visibility to the west and south. Across the Rappahannock rose an open field and a structure he could not identify. Thickly forested hills beyond might hide men and horses. No Confederate pickets yet. At its closest, the riverside was one hundred yards away, the ford seventy yards wide. For his headquarters, he occupied a barn whose upper siding showed holes from old gunfire.

If the Rebs took to sharpshooting, they were in distant range.

Schilling brought his officers to a vantage point. "The river protects the army's flank. What protects us is this choice terrain that conforms to the river's bend overlooking descending ground. Our fields of fire are strong. Our flanks, however, are supported only by cavalry. We must attend to our flanks with extraordinary care."

An officer asked, "Will we have cannons?"

"The artillery is on the move toward Fredericksburg." He knew that cannons positioned at a forward salient would only entice the Rebels to ride up and take them. All he said was, "The brigade commander decides where the guns shall be placed."

"Let them dare to come across," said a lieutenant.

The officer who spoke had never seen a battle, and Schilling took a breath before he answered. "We must be vigilant. Riders will charge up and shoot a man in the face, and before anyone can raise a rifle they will dash away, horsemen so quick and skilled as you can scarcely imagine. At night we shall advance pickets. One company shall man the line at all times, and at the sight of rebel cavalry, two shall form, with one in reserve. The enemy may ride forays. The first time they do, I want to make them pay. Drill your men diligently, so they will be ready when the hour comes. I shall hold you responsible."

Every officer endeavors to prepare his soldiers, and he wonders how war will manifest itself to them, and when. At dusk came the regiment's first action, producing confusion, shouts, and scuffles. No one spotted the shooters. A white mist billowed, and the soldiers stared over their rifles. Time stretched, and their eyes, wide and stinging in the excitement, drooped in the failing light.

* * *

The sand's trickle became a cataract. A slit opened, and peering through, she observed not one girl, but two. Side by side they knelt, faces blank. They scraped with sticks. They could not see her, though obviously they knew she was here. Her questions to them yielded no replies.

She'd consumed the flatbread and water. In the corner, she carved out a shallow hole in the earthen floor, squatted, and urinated. Like a cat, covered the spot with dirt. Initially the scent permeated acridly. Diffused so she no longer could detect. She returned to the plate. The sand hissed.

The digging ceased and the girls vanished.

A rattle at the door. She stepped in front, the blanket over her shoulders, while the latch jiggled open. The glare hurt her eyes, and she squinted at Hock's hulking silhouette. He reached out, touching her hip. Tipped his head forward. "What's that cord 'round your neck?" Lifted his fingers to the necklace that once had suspended the cocoon.

"You may *not* touch me," she declared, not raising her voice, rather intoning in the way of a schoolteacher to a child who'd misbehaved.

His hand fell away.

She beamed her disdain. Stretched to her full height to display her Southern woman's authority. "I would like hot tea. And more bread."

He rubbed his chin.

"And another blanket."

"I say what you get and what you don't," he growled, yet uncertainty fettered the words. He departed, pulling the door behind. The latch convulsed.

Had she spoken too sharply, or not sharply enough? For half an hour she deliberated, until he returned with a teapot, cup, blanket, and bread. He brought too an empty bushel basket and upended it on the floor. "Go on, sit."

She did not sit.

He poured tea into the cup he extended to her. "I'll bring more food soon. Meat too." He sniffed. "Smells bad. Stayed damp after the storm. Ain't had time to dry."

"I see." She looked away, not deigning to regard the man who had dared to touch her without her permission.

He stood as if he intended to say further but didn't know what. His head's angle caused the neck's loose flesh to bulge grotesquely.

She caught his leer.

He wants to lay down with me.

Get there before somebody else does.

Her tone with him had been correct, she decided. "I do not feel comfortable in this place."

His expression shifted, squaring doubt against what she guessed was lust. "They're huntin' you. This morning, soldiers asked if I'd seen you. I said no, ain't had no sign. I lied for you."

She did not wish to sound indebted to him. Her upbringing plucked the words out of her mouth. "Thank you."

"Now I'm in trouble for helping you."

"So I should leave, I think."

"Here's the safest place. No tellin' when someone might ride by. If they see you, they'll go and inform the army."

"Why do you lock the door?"

"Do you want the niggers comin' in and gettin' a look at you, and tellin' the other niggers? Why, everyone in Henrico County will know you're here."

She did not reply.

"Maybe at nightfall, you can come to the house."

He retrieved the China tea pot that bore a blue flower pattern. Must have belonged to his late wife. She pondered what she might say to protect herself from him. Perhaps that her cousin or uncle knew where she was hiding and would be coming for her. Seemed the statement would sound exactly like the invention it was, proclaiming her helplessness. Or she could insist straight out she wanted to leave. Maybe he'd let her; even give her a blanket and a loaf of bread to take.

Yet she thought he was telling the truth about the army out searching for her, and if she left, she'd be on the run in the woods and fields. They might have dogs, and a man on horseback could chase her down in seconds. The nights were cold; she remembered her uncontrollable shivering. No money. What could she do, except return to her house and hope the army hadn't posted guards?

Hock left. The locks clinked, conjuring an image from years ago, when she'd seen a slave wagon go by, the men chained together. When they'd moved their arms, the chains had clinked. She'd not imagined how being shackled must feel, until now.

Everything comes at a cost, and for us the cost may be to wear hypocrisy's lint on our sleeves.

The cost was more than her father had imagined. For Hock's leer bespoke an urge he meant to satisfy. He would embolden himself with liquor and try again to touch her. Next time, he'd not withdraw his hand so readily.

*   *   *

The horse Slate had said knew the way knew only *part*. At the church, the animal veered onto the wrong road—apparently he thought he was going somewhere else, not to Anna's. Holland spun him onto the Osborne Turnpike.

So much for the intelligent horse.

In his haste to leave, he'd learned very little about Slate's horse, not even his name. Swinging his bridle hand in tune with the animal's rhythm, he was pleased he responded to the lightest variations, requiring no pressure on the bit. Stride wide and natural; head level. No hint the unfamiliar rider spooked him. The stable hands must take him out for exercise, thought Holland.

Fog lingered in patches. The nearby river's scent evoked the Van Meers' house. Soon he'd be there—on his legs! How soon would he see Anna? He did not expect her to be at home. He would ask Sarah—perhaps she'd confide to him what apparently she'd not done to Swan. Or lead him to her. The thought invigorated him.

He remembered everything Anna had said to him, even her scolding that he followed a wrongful cause. What skulking spy would have declared such sentiments to a Confederate officer? Yet recounted in front of a tribunal, her audacious statements would serve to incriminate her. Her poetry bespoke abolitionist themes. *I hope the North wins!* He imagined Swan presenting the evidence in his rehearsed way. She'd have no chance.

Which was why he'd ridden here, he reminded himself.

He passed deserted fortifications. Behind the mounds, some of the log buttresses had collapsed. Muddy water filled the trenches. The prior spring, as McClellan's sizeable army approached Richmond, the city's women had sewn thousands of sandbags for the defenses. Then, to everyone's astonishment, General Lee had attacked first, maneuvering his forces brilliantly and driving the Federals away. Who could doubt that the South had better leaders and soldiers?

And a just cause. Until now, Holland had believed so.

In the saddle for two hours, his leg ached. The Van Meer farm must be near. How vexing, that he'd not paid better attention to the surroundings or timings during the coach ride or his tour to the riverside where he'd practiced shooting the revolver. Had he ridden past and not recognized the house in the dark? The facade was white, he recalled. So were the other houses. No familiar landmark.

He would have to ask someone. Folks would think him impolite to ride up at dawn to inquire about the Van Meer home. Should he wait? A triangle of clouds, the base tepidly illuminated, hovered to the east. The road's clay blushed red, and the light seemed to usher new misgivings. He had taken a strange diversion and pursued it with each hoofbeat. Would his determination survive the day? If he found Anna, could he help her? What consequences would doing so entail? *My mistakes have built one upon the other, to where they cannot be unbuilt.* What would he do if he couldn't find her? What choice would he have, except to return to the hospital and face whatever punishment befitted an officer who ran off without permission, stole a horse, and brought it back. An officer who no longer could be trusted. He pictured himself full of apologies to Swan. Forced the hateful image from his mind. "I shall keep to my course for the time being," he told himself. "I will not lose heart. Not yet."

Ahead he made out a traveler, the first he'd seen, bumping toward him atop a wagon whose horse plopped languidly. Wrapped in a blanket, the driver dozed, oblivious to the dawn, trusting his horse to guide along the road. Holland let him pass.

A second wagon. The driver was awake and knew the Van Meer property. Leaning forward on the bench, blond brows crushed in a V, he sized up Holland. "They're 'bout half a mile on your left. Watch for an iron arch clutched in vines above the carriage gate."

"Thank you."

"Maybe a fracas there."

"How so?"

"Couldn't make out much in the dark, but the place looked queer to me."

Holland pondered this.

The driver asked, "You ride from Richmond?"

"Yes."

"Out all night?"

"The better part."

"Well, if the Van Meers aren't home, you'll find an inn off the road just northward. Got food, and water and feed for your horse."

"Obliged."

"You're ridin' a bit tilted. You hurt?"

"I've been sick."

"You show the countenance, if you don't mind me sayin.' They put you back to duty too soon." The man fished in his shirt pocket, trailed out a jerky strip he tapped against his leg to shake off the lint, and extended to Holland. "This'll help till you get to the Van Meers.' Salt beef. An ounce sustains me for hours."

The fellow tipped his hat and flicked the reins.

Holland passed a road to the right. More empty battlements. A sign read 'Chaffin.' The road must lead to Chaffin's Bluff, one of the celebrated artillery promontories that guarded the James River. Was the bluff manned? No soldiers in view.

Five minutes later, he spotted the inn the wagoneer had mentioned, set back, a gray obelisk against gray trees, the chimney issuing gray smoke. From the grounds plinked string music so subtle he wasn't sure he heard or imagined.

Pressing the balls of his feet in the stirrups, he picked up a trot. Caught the rhythm and the breeze hit him in the face. Pulled the air into his lungs. At a bend he saw a silver strip in the distance. The river.

Opposite, a house's silhouette. And a carriage gate, vines threading the cast-iron arch. Yes, he remembered—he'd viewed the arch from the rollcart Bookman had pushed to the river's edge.

The house's windows gaped like skull sockets.

From floor to roof, someone had knocked off the siding, hammered through the plaster, and shattered the panes. The front door was a maw, and glass fragments speckled the plaster dust like ice crystals on snow. In the front courtyard, where less than three days ago they'd painstakingly loaded him and the box into the hospital coach, rose a hillock of debris: furniture and paintings slashed open; shards of lamps, cups, and plates like morsels a monstrous mouth had chewed and spit out. For a few seconds, he thought a terrible storm must have blown through.

The trees and fences were intact.

A human storm had struck this house.

Frozen, he stared at the wreckage. Pulled in his first breath. Easing forward, he recognized the hollow shell that once had been his room. They'd ripped up the floorboards, exposing the ground beneath. Everywhere lay splintered planks. A rattle. In what had been the foyer, a beam from the second floor tumbled and whacked the staircase. Dust billowed, and woodchips pattered like seeds. The horse stepped along, and Holland saw that the enclosed courtyard no longer was enclosed. On the stone patio, a strip from the familiar embroidered quilt. The buggy house's upper story where the blacks had lived no longer existed. The vertical studs ended in nothing, like fingers pleading skyward. Below, in random rectangles, books ripped apart at the bindings.

Bookman's books.

He steered the horse between shoveled holes, each about a foot deep. Amid these lay the side-turned buggy, the fabric roof torn away.

Behind the ruins, a young soldier poked with his rifle's bayonet. He uncovered an object he picked up, brought to a pyramid of shards he'd built on the ground, and tossed to chink. Noticing Holland, he straightened and gave a competent rifle salute. "Morning, sir. Did you bring my relief?"

"No."

"'Cause I been here for near two days. They said they'd dispatch a detail to relieve me, but they ain't. All I've had to eat is damned hard tack, and that's gone."

"Were you present when this happened?"

The sentry stared at the destruction. "By the time I got here, they was 'bout done, a dozen men with hammers rippin' the place apart.

They worked through the night. Posted three of us as guards to chase away looters. The other two they pulled off and left me behind."

"Where are the residents?"

The sentry squinted. "Sir?"

"The people who lived here."

The guard shook his head, as if the officer he'd expected to know what was going on knew less than he did. "Well, I can't say where they went, except for those two." The guard indicated with his bayonet.

Holland rode forward a horse length to see, hanging by the neck from the shade tree, the bodies of Bookman and Jerome.

"Dear God almighty."

"I know, sir. A damn shame. Niggers or no niggers, nobody should be strung up for so long a time. I keep throwin' rocks to chase off the crows. Can't do nothin' 'bout the flies though. Lucky ain't been warm, or they'd be stinkin' awful."

Holland stared. The sight's horror ran through his chest like a saber. He forced his voice: "Is anyone else here, dead or alive?"

"No sir. I been all through the mess."

"How did this happen?"

"Hell, sir, ain't you heard? Here was a nest of spies."

Holland struggled to suppress his rage. "I mean, how did these men come to be hung like this, with no trial?"

The sentry seemed to stiffen at the accusation in Holland's tone. "Sir, I didn't witness the event. One of the soldiers in the first detail said the niggers talked back. They said they didn't have to obey no orders 'cause they were free men, not slaves. So the sergeant told 'em, 'you niggers ain't free, can't you see you're under arrest?' And the niggers said, 'Go to hell, we're free men, same as you.' So the sergeant said, 'I don't have to take defiance from such as you,' and he strung the two from the tree."

Murdered them, thought Holland. "Why didn't somebody lower them down?"

"Well sir, the officer said leave 'em."

The officer. Swan. The killings probably had not been part of his plan, but once done, he'd left the bodies hanging, no doubt to strike terror among the local blacks and anyone who might harbor sympathy for the Van Meer family.

"What about the Van Meers? The people who owned this house."

"Sir, I don't know nothin' about those folks. Seems like you're familiar with 'em, though."

"Yes."

"You're from hereabouts?"

"I've been here before." He met the soldier's gaze, saw neither suspicion nor wariness, merely the numbing tedium of those who stand guard.

The corpses' smell promulgated. With no knife to cut the rope, he rode to the tree, leaned over, and plied at the knot in a swarm of flies. The single line suspended both men. Apparently someone had looped the rope around their necks as they'd stood together, tossed the other end over a branch, then hoisted them by horse-pull. The hitch was tight, and he fought with his fingers to untie.

"Sir, let me try."

With his bayonet's tip, the sentry dug into the knot and levered until he was able to slide through the loose end. The rope whirred, and the bodies crashed to earth.

Bookman's neck was a foot long. Birds had plucked out one of his eyes. His tongue, half severed by teeth, poked out of the corner of his mouth.

"I'm sorry they did this to you," Holland said softly. "Thank you for the care and kindness, friend."

Hearing this, the sentry glared for a moment. He came up with a cloth among the house belongings and covered the dead. Under the plaster whitening, Holland recognized one of the horse-pattern curtains from his room. He asked, "The rest of the family of Negroes—a mother and her young daughter—what happened to them?"

"I sure can't say, sir. Seems like you knew these folks well."

"Yes."

"Mind if I tell the sergeant t'was you who took down the hanged?"

"Tell him what you wish."

"Your name, sir?"

"John Holland, Captain of Cavalry."

"That's if the son of a bitch ever comes back with my relief. You're not goin' by the 2nd Regiment, are you by chance?"

"No. I'm going the other way."

The soldier watched the horseman pivot, head to the road, and turn north. The hoofbeats faded. Alone again, he prodded the ruins, stepping over the boards, plaster, and glass. Poked a ceramic teapot. Added shards to his mound.

- 14 -

At dawn, Schilling walked the line behind the soldiers who by his orders were at their posts, rifles ready. Yesterday they had erected a parapet of dirt and logs. The officers saluted as he visited their companies. He confirmed that weapons were primed and everyone had their boots laced, uniforms buttoned, straps done, and powder dry. From several soldiers he took rifles to check they were clean, hammers at half cock, and percussion caps in the striker wells. He said something to each man, usually just a word of encouragement, occasionally a conversation: "What do you concentrate on, Barker, as you attend to your position on the line?"

"Sir, I peer real careful in case a Rebel will light a pipe, or the sun flashes off a bayonet, and I can take aim."

"Good. Of course, do not fire until ordered."

"No sir."

"Another thing. Listen keenly, for sounds may carry far. A man coughs or drops a ramrod and it pings on a stone. The resonance may alert you to an attack about to happen. Do not allow yourself be surprised, and you shall remain steady in combat."

He studied the soldier's eyes for comprehension. Saw none. Of course not.

Schilling climbed onto the parapet, a risk he wouldn't have taken had the haze not puffed like yeasted bread. Tilted his ear to catch the rhythm of hooves—cavalry riding to flank him—or clinks telltale of movement. Heard a boot's scrape, a muffled cough, and sniffs—all from his own men.

In truth, today did not seem propitious for the Rebels to attack. Visibility was poor, and the overnight drizzle had mired the fields and roads. Cavalry detested ground on which horses lost their footing. Of course, the general who gave the order to attack might not be cognizant of the soil's condition—he might have chosen this place by tapping his index finger on a map, and so the Rebels might assault despite the disadvantages. In war, rationality did not always hold sway. A general might even win who dared defy the logic, as Confederate General Lee had done in his campaign of the Seven Days.

He gave the order to permit small campfires. The soldiers were damp and needed to dry their things, and this was proper as long as no more than half receded from the line at any one time. The fires ignited quickly—the soldiers had been waiting for the order and had the kindling ready. One of the lieutenants brought him a steaming cup. "Sir, may I offer you this coffee courtesy of First Company?"

"Thank you, Martin. How are your men?"

"They are well, sir. Anxious to see action."

"Something will happen, you may be certain."

"I hope so, sir. The men know we are close to the Rebs. They long to join a battle, to get up and march out yonder."

The mist made pillows on the water. On the far side, the field stretched half a mile, and anyone crossing it would be exposed to massed rifle fire, as at Antietam. Schilling earnestly hoped he wouldn't receive an order to lead his regiment across the field, yet he had to choose his words carefully, in case the order came. "Good that the men desire to see action. There is no way to prepare their minds for the shock of their first battle, which nothing but experience can describe. But we can practice, and so imprint the actions they should take under fire."

"Yes sir."

"Today we continue to strengthen the line. Tomorrow, if we're still here, we shall commence drills. The coffee is strong and hot— please pass my thanks."

"I will, sir."

* * *

The digging resumed. The enlarged slit accommodated light that outlined the floor and walls and a mound of sand. Hock might notice, and she kicked the accumulation to spread evenly. Through the fissure she regarded the girls, bone thin, their fingernails gritted and broken. She'd given up questioning them—they said nothing back or even acknowledged they'd heard.

When the gap elongated to three inches, the digging stopped. An object poked through the slit, fish-tailing until enough protruded to grip and with gentle tugs she extracted. The light fell on a folded paper. Opened—to her astonishment—to a printed likeness of her, and a text:

WANTED BY THE AUTHORITIES!
ANNA VAN MEER

Anna Van Meer, woman of twenty years of age, is wanted for felony crimes. The lawful authorities will pay a reward of $500 in specie money for information leading to her capture. Anyone spotting her should contact an officer of the Army or the Home Guard or the County Marshal.

An artist had drawn the poster sketch from a photograph taken more than a year ago, in the time before she'd gone away to the Augusta Seminary, in a Richmond studio where she'd posed motionless while oil lamps ribboned smoke to the open windows. Mirrors had magnified the incandescence. Her father had brought her to the new and popular studio as a present for her birthday. Three times the daguerreotyper had clicked his camera before the result satisfied him. Her father had hung the framed picture in the upstairs hallway.

Now the authorities had distributed her likeness on a wanted poster.

She'd seen similar tacked on road posts, always of escaped slaves.

She refolded the paper to hide behind one of the ceiling beams. Through the nail hole, she observed the girls immobile. She said, "Where did you find the poster?"

No answer. Could they not speak? They knelt as if in expectation. She did not wish for them to go away.

An idea came to her. "Do you wish me to tell you a story?"

She peered through the slit. One of them ticked her head.

Perhaps Mrs. Hock had told them stories, or read to them, probably from the Bible, as Anna's mother had done with her. Who read to them now? Or told them stories? Her sadness for them pressed on her.

"All right. Let me think." She culled her memories for the stories her mother or the Augusta Seminary women had told. Ghost stories were popular, but she did not wish to speak of ghosts. She recalled a fable she and Bookman had listened to together at her mother's feet. "There once was a young girl named Tess," she began. "Tess loved music. She loved to play…" She'd been about to say *her piano*, the story's centerpiece. Did the slave girls know what a piano was? Could they conceive of a girl who owned one?

She would have to improvise.

"…to sing songs. Yes, she loved the songs she invented in her head."

The girls seemed to be listening.

"Tess sang delightful melodies, and she had a wonderful voice. She owned no musical instruments because she was poor. Yes, her father had died, leaving her mother and her in poverty. The only one who had money was Tess's stepfather, a selfish tyrant who kept every penny for himself. And he was cruel. He forbad her to sing or to make noise within his earshot, for he hated to be disturbed."

She paused. Did they understand what a *stepfather* was? What was their knowledge of families? What had been the manner of their upbringing? Through the slit she peered. They seemed to be paying attention.

"All day long, the stepfather sat at his table, counting his money and grumbling to himself. He was terribly ugly. Maybe this was why he felt so much anger toward his wife's daughter, for Tess was very beautiful. So ferocious was his temper that the women stayed well away from him when he was counting his money."

The slave girls knelt motionless.

In the original tale, the mean stepfather demolished Tess's piano. The clever house mice gathered the pieces and assembled them for her in the attic, where she played in secret. Should Anna insert an attic in her story? The slave girls might not comprehend. She groped for a suitable idea. "Tess took to strolling by herself in the forest, and here she could sing to her heart's content. She sang beautifully, and her songs carried on the wind. Her lovely voice attracted the woodland animals—the birds and eagles in the branches, the deer and foxes, and even the wolves and bears her enchanting melodies had made peaceable.

"One day, her stepfather looked up from his money. Perhaps the amount he counted was less than he desired, for in his foulest mood he banged his fist on the table and shouted, 'I am hungry. I wish to eat *plums*—bring me plums for my dinner.' The mother told him, 'We have no plums.' The stepfather commanded, 'Send Tess to the market to buy them!'"

In the original version, the stepfather demanded pudding. Anna doubted that the slave girls had tasted pudding; probably they had tasted plums. She reproduced the voices—the stepfather's growl, the mother's sweet, tremulous aria—keeping the volume modest so Hock wouldn't hear.

"'Where is Tess?' roared the stepfather. The mother guessed Tess had traipsed into the forest to sing, but fearful of him, she replied she didn't know. The stepfather began to search the house, the yard, and the stable, and not finding Tess, he took to the forest path, his fury mounting. For truly he was a man of rage and hate."

A rustle beyond. The girls were gone.

$$* \quad * \quad *$$

From the Van Meers' house, Holland trotted north. Visible for the first time, the surrounding lands. The road diverged from the river, and he noticed to the east unmanned military revetments. A road sign: *New Market, Three Miles.* Perhaps Anna had fled there.

A wagon rattled by. The driver remarked, "Get better, son." The comment, and that from the man who'd given him the jerky, caused him to think he must look sickly. What if an officer happened along and asked him if he needed help? He didn't have an explanation for his presence. Unfamiliar with this region, if he offered an obvious lie, he might find himself at gunpoint.

By now the hospital would have taken note of his absence. How long before Swan would hear, guess his destination, and ride after him?

A half mile by, he came to a footpath shooting off to the right amid high weeds. The James River was close to the west. What was to the east? Letting the horse take his own pace, he rode in, scanning for anyone near. Reached a gray-planked shack, the door open. A young black boy crouched in the shade.

"What's along this path?" Holland asked.

The boy leapt to his feet, staring fearfully.

"I asked, where does this path go?"

The boy took a step backward, turned, and ran.

Do I look that bad?

The path narrowed, and the scrub brush crisped against the horse's legs. He crested a low ridge to a line of trees tracing a stream between buckskin-tinted meadows and a few sedentary cows. At the stream he let the horse drink. The water trickled, smelling sweet and brackish at the same time. The hooves sank in skeins of silt, and the air exuded brine, as if the salty James had seeped into the fresh flow. Or maybe he smelled the river a ways off.

His leg ached. Should he dismount? He slumped against the horse's neck. The pose was uncomfortable, but despite this he soon lapsed out of consciousness. The horse wandered, his hooves splashing. Branches clawed over Holland's back, and he dreamed he was in his bed at the Van Meers' house. Familiar sounds comforted, and Anna appeared and pressed her hand against his forehead. "You must rest," she said. For some reason she kept her hand on his head.

A gunshot wakened him. He jolted upright. Another percussion far off. A hunter? Was it morning or afternoon? He sensed the warmth of Anna's hand—must have been the horse's neck. All around, fields he didn't recognize. Now came the terrible image of Bookman and Jerome hanging in the tree. He closed his eyes until it went away.

He felt unwell. How long had he been in the saddle? Too many hours. Rode to a tree and tethered the reins, and dismounting he couldn't hold his balance and fell, fortunately on his left side. Hiked himself by the tree. His bad leg wouldn't bear weight, and certainly he wouldn't be able to remove the heavy saddle. Instead he loosened the belly strap and slid the rig to the croup, watching the horse in the event this peculiar displacement spooked the animal. Took off the saddle blanket to shake out.

A cavalryman attends first to his horse. Lameness in the field endangered horse and rider alike, and to shoot an animal who has become a steady friend, and through agility and endurance done true service, imparted dread. He slipped off the bridle and removed the bit to make the grazing easier. Washed the metal bit in the stream. He'd ridden him enough to judge him comfortably gaited and absent temperamental flaws—at least thus far observed. In the dark, he hadn't had the chance to inspect the animal. Now he perceived a colt over fifteen hands tall and somewhat fat, though his form was in proportion—none of the imbalances that would prematurely tire him and render him unfit for the stresses and deprivations cavalry mounts must suffer. His back straight, cinnamon coat shiny. Hooves well shod.

No abrasions. Balanced his weight comfortably on his forelegs. Eyesight seemed sharp. Ears perked, he breathed softly. Holland checked his teeth by gripping the lower lip and opening the mouth. The horse did not resist. The teeth showed him to be four years old. "You are a gentle one," said Holland aloud. "Perhaps too gentle. Have you been run all night? Or ridden in the foul weather?"

He smoothed the hair and replaced the saddle blanket. Refit the rig and tightened the cincha. Now the challenge to remount. He limped to a fallen tree and stepped up. The problem, to swing his bad leg over. Took a dozen attempts and much wincing. At last, saddled atop, he waited for the pain to subside.

Where should he ride?

No idea.

His predicament slapped him. He roamed an unfamiliar land with no map and no one he could ask for help. The woman he sought might have fled in any direction, to any distance, and he had no notion whatsoever which way he should go. What chance did he have to find her, if Swan and his soldiers hadn't? She might be reasonably close, and still he could ride these lands for days without encountering her. He did not have days. Before this one ended, Swan would spread the word, and everyone would be watching for the rider who'd fled the sickbed prematurely and without permission.

Slate had told him right—to leave the hospital had been reckless. He'd trusted his talents to devise a plan on the move, as if this were an extension of his cavalry missions. In his convalescence, his skills had atrophied. He commanded neither men nor authority.

He muttered, "Anna, I'm sorry."

Better he returned to the hospital on his own, before Swan pursued and arrested him. No doubt he'd face an angry interrogation and remain under guard for a time. He wasn't afraid.

Fear had not brought him here.

A girl with wheaten hair, who wrote poems and hated slavery, cared for him and perhaps loved him, though she'd not told him so. She loved him though she thought his cause was evil.

In the swishing branches, he could reproduce her face easily.

Not the woman herself.

"Anna, where did you go?"

Nothing stirred the bait lines in his mind.

Defeated, he rode toward the Osborne Turnpike.

* * *

Through the slit, she stared at the yellowed wall and the long ropes Bookman and her father had used to anchor the house to trees. Time snared her in its tempo, and she saw the grass sway and birds and branches flutter. The ropes undulated lazily. When she withdrew from the plate, time separated from her, and the darkness seemed eternal.

The light dimmed. The November day was short. Why hadn't she asked Hock for more candles and matches? She would have to remember to do so when he came back.

Maybe at nightfall, you can come to the house.

What would he ask of her, in return for comfort?

She dragged the inverted bushel basket to the corner, sat atop, and tried to configure herself. The basket's wire mesh and spindly panels sagged, producing imbalance. To lay on the damp floor revolted her. Adjusting the basket, she struck a compromise she could tolerate for a while.

She pictured her father on the ground by Bookman and Jerome, the soldier stepping on Bookman's back, forcing his face against the gravel, treating a free man as a slave. She thought of the coded message she'd unearthed. Her father had told her he feared coincidence, and she wondered if that was what had undone him. Why had he lied to her? To keep her away from what he'd been doing, to protect her and as much himself? *Never would I wish to think of you as naïve, but perhaps your emotion carries you away.* Better to have been witting, she thought, so she could have been ready. He'd left her as unprepared as a person could be. She'd had no plan at all.

Would Holland hear about what had happened? For some reason she wanted him to find out, to know everything. She could not say how he'd take the news. *John, I have no regrets. My duty was not to the South. If you want to hold it against me, go ahead.*

She did not think he would hold it against her. His acute ear for what was hidden in poems would not miss what was in her heart.

She tugged the blanket around herself.

- 15 -

Emerging from the brambly path, he let the horse turn northward on the road. *You'll know your way home all right.* In two hours, he'd reach the Chimborazo's grounds.

He halted in the roadway. His mind tumbled. Was there *nothing* he could do? He yearned to believe that initiative and agility yielded results. Action bested inaction—how a cavalry officer viewed the world.

What action could he take? Motion in which direction?

No answers.

He flicked the reins, resumed the gait. The nausea he'd felt at the creek still clung. When had he last eaten? Foolishly he'd turned away the hospital meals, and if he didn't eat, he'd faint from horseback, no doubt to reinjure his leg in the fall. Perhaps he could stop at a farmhouse and ask for food, offer to pay with the money Slate had left in the saddlebag.

To the left twanged a stringed instrument, the faint notes he'd heard this morning. Here was the trail to the inn, and steering the horse along, he came to an old slave on a three-legged stool, bare feet on the pine needles, in his lap a banjo with a wavy, rough-carved neck. Spotting Holland, he ceased plucking. "Hello, Cap'n. Didn't I see you go by early this morning?"

"You're pretty watchful, old fellow."

"Why you ridin' up and down the road? You lost?"

"Trying to rejoin my unit. I'm not sure where they are."

"Ain't up here, naw." The subtle mockery you sometimes heard from blacks talking to befuddled whites. How a banjo-plucking slave could savor a fleeting superiority over a disoriented white officer.

Holland asked, "You sit here all day?"

"I do. Start a bit past dawn. Wait to hear folks come by on the road, and I play. They hear the music and wander curious up the path. Once they see what's makin' the tune, they notice the inn and think they oughta rest for awhile." He showed the three teeth left in his mouth.

How might he phrase a question about Anna to sound offhand? No point in dissembling. "Have you heard of Anna Van Meer?"

"Young woman who live down the road?"

"That's her."

"Well, sir, I don't know her very well. Years ago, I was workin' on a farm, and my master asked Anna's daddy to pull a bad tooth outta my mouth, and little Anna held a towel for me."

"Did you by chance notice her go by a day or two ago?"

"No sir. Ain't seen her in a spell." He plucked at the strings. "You must be with the ones asked 'bout her already."

"Soldiers?"

"Yup. Coupla days ago. Them you lost from?" The mocking tone again, light as silk.

"The inn serves food?"

The three-toothed grin. "They feed you nice."

"Thank you."

"You too, Cap'n."

By the inn a slave boy held the horse while Holland dismounted clinging to the neck. Sat at a porch table. How foolish, not to have eaten yesterday. Now the inn's slave girl served him grits and fried potatoes. Toast with sugared butter. Mint tea. The slave boy fed and watered the horse.

The steaming tea soothed him, and his head took to drooping. His chin slumped to his chest, and he dreamt he lay in his bed at the Van Meers' house, and Anna was near; he could hear her voice.

The fork slipped from his fingers and clattered on the plate, jarring him awake.

Is this the dream I will have for the rest of my life?

Why had he thought he could find her? No longer was he the cavalryman who could ride all night and be razor sharp at daybreak. Weeks awaited before he could regain his former strength. Flaccid in body and mind, he was accustomed to lazing in bed and sleeping whenever he liked. A diminished man.

He'd say so in his defense, when Swan interrogated him.

Under the table, his leg had stiffened. Barely could bend the knee, and when he tried, he might have jabbed the fork into his thigh.

Gnashing his teeth, he thought, what if he couldn't get back on the horse?

What did it matter? Able to ride or not, he'd failed. They'd arrest Anna and hang her. For as long as he lived, he'd push away the dreams of her, obliterate the memories, shroud them the way the dead are covered in sweet flowers. His life stretched desolate.

A white woman who'd stood by while the slave girl had served him the food now reappeared. She wore a half-curious, half-snarly expression. "You look like you been through hell, Captain."

"Who hasn't, these days?"

"Other fellows from your outfit comin' this way?"

"No."

"Didn't think so."

What did she mean by that? She'd tied back her graying hair that seemed to tug her skin the way leather is stretched around a mold. A high collar fenced her scrawny neck. He sensed she was the kind of person who craved disdaining the weak. He considered asking her about Anna. Bad idea, he decided.

"Far yet to ride?"

"Some hours."

"I can put together a pouch of food for you: fresh bread, apple and honey, and a piece of jerky. Cost you six bits."

"Sure, why not."

She returned with a burlap parcel cinched in twine. "Thank you," he said. He started to rise, grimaced at the leg frozen once more.

She said, "If you can spare the time and a little money, I got a nigger who's gifted at makin' people feel better. He can take a look at that leg. Old as Methuselah he is, but people say he's got the touch. Can't testify myself, as I use a genuine doctor. Take you to the nigger, if you'd like."

He considered this. The fellow might at least help him remount. "How much?"

"Six bits for the breakfast and horse feed, fifty for the nigger, and six bits for the food. Two dollars altogether, but for you bein' a soldier, only a dollar and six bits."

"Bring over the pouch buckled on the saddle."

The woman fetched the leather pouch. "That's a right elegant saddle," she commented. "When did the army start givin' out fancy tackle?"

Of course she knew better. The army issued simple, utilitarian saddles. Officers with rigs like Slate's—burnished leather with felt undersides—bought their own (horses too), and the quality pointed to wealth. No doubt she wished she could retract the discount and charge him the two dollars full. Her attention stayed on the pouch. Slate had left him about five dollars in coins. He relinquished a dollar and seventy-five cents into her outstretched palm. She stared at the money, as if by doing so she could multiply the amount. To the slave girl: "Missie, help this fella to the shed."

"Yes'm."

The inn woman glared at him. Seemed about to speak, then spun on her heel.

* * *

She awakened cramped, face on the blanket at her knees. How long had she slept? Seeking a comfortable pose, she'd pulled the upturned basket to the corner, managing to wedge herself awkwardly, shoulder against the masonry, feet braced on the basket's edge. Sleeping this way had stiffened her joints. Dizzily she uncoiled and groped her way to the metal plate. Through the slit, frail daylight.

A dry swish announced the girls. Had they stuffed straw in the slit's depression to prevent Hock from noticing? She heard their breaths puff.

"Hello, girls."

The straw, or whatever, rustled again.

"Shall I resume our story?"

Through the nail hole, she saw them lean close.

"Where were we? The gruff stepfather? Yes. Across the forest floor he trampled, seeking his stepdaughter, shouting her name: 'Tess! Tess!' These were not loving calls, but angry and threatening. Not only did he resent Tess's beauty, he hated her freedom to walk as she pleased into the forest, and he meant to put an end to it.

"Soon he heard the echoes of her song that filled the trees like a pure breeze. Whereas her music tamed the wild animals, the melody took no root in his barren heart. He rushed toward the sound, his anger mounting with each step, and when he reached her, he shouted, 'How dare you sing! I forbad you to sing!' Fearfully she stepped back, not soon enough to avoid the hand he slapped harshly across her face."

In the original story, the stepfather found Tess in the attic, struck her, and set to destroy the reconstructed piano. While he bashed furiously at the instrument, the clever house mice tripped him, and he plunged out the window to his death. The neat denouement would not work in the forest. Should she introduce a nearby cliff? And what about the forest animals? She'd forgotten to make them clever—they were mere listeners. She puzzled for a minute. "The stepfather groped to seize her from where she'd fallen, and just as his grip was about to close, she rolled sideways. At once she leapt to her feet. The evil man lunged for her, but the sudden move unbalanced him, and in the instant he needed to recover, she dashed away. Into the deep forest she ran, his chasing footsteps close behind. Tess was fleet afoot, but her stepfather had powerful legs, and certainly he would catch her!

"It was then she noticed a fox running ahead. And alongside the fox, a rabbit. And next to this, a woodchuck. They were leading her. But where? Very quick these animals were, and she barely could keep up. And now more animals appeared. Deer and wolves and bears on the ground, birds and eagles and owls above, even insects, all converged. In amazement she watched them begin to circle her, and around they spun, lifting dust and pine needles in a cloud that became a whirlwind, and the evil stepfather no longer could see her—he couldn't see anything! When the tempest finally subsided and the animals dispersed, no trace of Tess remained. Where had she gone?"

A rustle. Beyond the grate, the girls had vanished. Behind her, the latch jangled.

Anna stepped toward the door that yawned open.

*   *   *

The inn's slave girl became a crutch he leaned upon. When they reached the wooden shed, he said, "Thank you."

She curtsied, no doubt as the dour woman had taught her, though the woman probably hadn't taught her to roll her eyes in annoyed accompaniment, which somewhat altered the curtsy's effect.

In the shed, an ancient slave sat on a stool amid side-turned crates that formed shelves, each bearing a pot with a labeled plant.

"I haven't seen a fuller collection of medicinal plants," remarked Holland.

"Sit down on the box, Cap'n." Voice like dry leaves tossing over grass.

With difficulty, Holland lowered himself. Kept his hurt leg straight. "I doubt there is anything you can do for me," he said.

"I doubt so too." The slave contemplated the cavalryman's stretched leg. "What's the matter is you on a horse before your broke leg's rightly healed. You ridin' weeks too soon." He canted his head as if to say, what's wrong with you, to be doing that?

"You are perceptive," said Holland.

"You don't remember me."

"No. Should I?"

The old slave shrugged. "You was the one wearin' the healin' box 'round your leg at the Van Meer house in the time of the big rain. Miss Sarah fetched me when you was fev'ry, and I gave 'em chokey leaves to make tea for you. You came through after."

"You're Arthur."

"Yes sir."

"They told me about you. I have no memory of what happened."

"Like I said, you was fev'ry at the time."

They sat in silence. Holland pondered whether he should ask Arthur to help him mount the horse so he could get started back to the Chimborazo. Arthur stuffed grains into a corn-cob pipe. Eventually the slave said, "You already paid her, huh? That's how she does, you pay up front, before folks see me, and sometimes I can help 'em, and sometimes I can't, but she don't never give the money back."

"Don't be concerned."

"I ain't. You didn't pay *me*, did you?"

Mockery in Arthur's tone. The inn's slaves were a caustic bunch, thought Holland. Did they sneer at all white people? He'd heard that, since the war's onset, in the absence of the white men who'd gone to the army, slaves had become sassy. These at the inn seemed to bear it out.

She don't never give the money back.

Money. His mind roved to Swan's claim about finding a sizeable amount beneath the Van Meers' floorboards. Had Anna taken some beforehand? If so, she might pay people to help her. Smugglers, gypsies, people at the fringes of society, took risks for payment. Where could he find them?

Arthur had lit the pipe and was staring at him, perhaps wondering why he was still here.

"Arthur, are you aware the Van Meers had trouble recently?"

"Umm."

"I'm a friend of Anna's."

"A friend, are you sir?"

"Yes."

"Well, I ain't a friend myself. I do feel for 'em. Nobody told me what they done wrong. Couldn't be so bad." The old slave's gaze flicked over Holland's shoulder to the inn's doorway through which the tight-haired mistress had passed. Whatever Arthur might be implying was as clouded as his eyes.

"Arthur, by chance would you know of anyone who could say where she went?"

"Why do you ask me that?"

"I'm here to help her."

"Help her?" The question danced like a water spider on a ripple.

Holland's decision to seek Anna had been rash. For the last hour he'd regretted doing so. Now, staring at Arthur, he must either act so again, or give up and return to the hospital. He didn't know the man. Could he trust him?

No choice.

He leaned forward, spoke in a whisper. "They are chasing me. The same ones who arrested Henry Van Meer, tore apart the house, and hung Bookman and Jerome from a tree."

"Umm. Seen that, have you?"

"I lowered them at dawn this morning."

Arthur's chin floated up. "So they're layin' on the ground." His tone ran bitter, like the juice of a Clementine picked too early.

"I covered them with a curtain from the house."

The old slave's eyes scraped to the side. In the distance, the banjo twangs tailed off. Someone must have ridden by on the road.

"Arthur, please believe me. An officer questioned me at the hospital about Anna. He said he had her in custody. He asked me questions—who were her friends? Where were the places she went? He repeated the questions, and I thought, why would he ask me so insistently, unless she'd gotten away?"

From the inn tapped footsteps. Arthur said. "I better examine your leg after all."

"Where is she?"

"I don't know." Arthur pressed his fingers against Holland's thigh. "The muscles are tight as that fella's banjo strings."

"Did Sarah talk to you? Or to anyone?"

"You think so?"

"I hope she did."

Arthur lightly kneaded the leg muscle, no doubt to convince the inn's mistress he was practicing his doctoring skills. He said, "Black folks 'round here are fearful. Soldiers killed two men, no trial or judge, just the whim of the ones who fancied to hang 'em from a tree, and a minute later they were dead. You look like a soldier to me."

"I'm sorry, Arthur."

"You *sorry*?"

"What else can I say?"

"You can stick that pistol to your head and blow out your brains, for all I care about you bein' sorry."

Never had a slave spoken to him so. Shocking. But why should it surprise him? Had he thought slaves felt differently about Confederate soldiers? About white people in general? The rationality didn't make the sentiment easier to take. No man wants to be hated. Easier to hate back, than to understand.

He should leave now, he thought. Instead he said, "You helped me once. Pulled me out of a fever."

"Umm."

"Will you trust me?"

"Can't."

"Arthur, I don't know which way to ride, north or south. I have no notion which way she ran."

The old man gazed at the center of Holland's tunic and the brass buttons pinching the gray wool.

"There's no one else I can ask."

"White people come here when they're sick, and they pay the lady, and sometimes they don't say nothin' to me. Shames 'em, I suppose, to be helped by a black man. Everyone's 'bout the same, though, in sickness and what gets 'em well again."

"We're hypocrites, if that's what you mean. True. I've always known, but I didn't do anything. Maybe I will now. I want to."

Arthur prodded the leg.

"Please tell me what you know."

"People say things. I don't much recall who said 'em."

"I don't need to hear who told you."

"Folks say, when the army men came to the Van Meer house, young Miss Anna was on the hill behind, where she likes to walk, and when she saw what was happenin,' she ran to the creek, and nobody's seen her since."

"Which way do folks *think* she went?"

"Don't suppose they could say. That way's south. Cold at night, and couldn't be long before she went lookin' for somebody to hide her."

"Who might?"

"No tellin.' Ways down's a farm. Hock's farm. Old Hock, he was friends with the Van Meers. Or so folks say."

"Where are Sarah and her daughter?"

Arthur didn't answer.

Footsteps, and the mistress occupied the doorway. "You feelin' better?"

"Yes I am, thank you."

"I told you he's a healin' nigger."

Holland struggled to rise, and the slave gripped his arm to help. "Arthur, I think I might require assistance getting on my horse. I'd be grateful if you could do me the last favor."

*　*　*

On the hillside above the Rappahannock, the rain had abated, though the soldiers were soaked. Schilling sipped coffee from his metal cup and studied his position, at least the part he could see. The hovering mist permitted him to stand upright at the forward edge.

Across the river, the Rebels had posted pickets who'd taken a few shots. Hard to hit a man at nearly half a mile. Not so far that a .58-inch lead ball wouldn't do harm at trajectory's end. One soldier had been struck. The bullet had severed his arm at the elbow, and his screams had echoed until the medics bore him by wagon toward the main road and the medical station. A man lost. And something in return: The bright blood and cleaved arm had produced a visceral impression on the soldiers who'd witnessed. Apprehending for the first time the effects of rifle fire, they became exacting in their movements and acutely observant of the land opposite from which bullets could materialize like murderous bees.

This morning, to his surprise, a supply wagon delivered the powder and ammunition he'd requested to practice marksmanship. He marched his soldiers back from the line, one company at a time, for the quarter-mile's march to a field where his sergeants had rigged linen targets on a taut rope. He addressed the ranks. "No man will rejoin his fellows on the line if he cannot hit his target at one hundred yards. The cloth is roughly the size of the man who will advance at you. If you cannot see the target, or lack the strength or heart to hold the rifle steady, you'll not be effective in combat. Those who cannot shoot will do other work, whether to load wagons or wash the kitchen pots or uniforms. I have no wish to humiliate anyone; it is a matter of practicality. A soldier must take his marksmanship in earnest and treat accuracy as a prized accomplishment. If we uphold this ethic, our fields of fire will be formidable, and the Rebels will not break us. And for the best marksmen among you, a special honor. I shall select one man from each company to form a squad of sharpshooters, and we shall repay the Rebs for their sniping."

From the ranks, a few whoops of approval. Most stayed nervously quiet.

Gunsmoke skeined over the wet ground. Behind the kneeling shooters, he watched. When they walked forward to check their targets, he commended those who'd hit the centers. "Excellent," he told Grunwald, a gangly Vermont boy who cradled his rifle in hands like giant sycamore leaves. His five shots clustered within the breadth of a silver dollar. "You must have grown up with your own rifle."

"I did, sir."

"I've met no one, even at West Point, who can shoot better than this. First Sergeant, bring the men around to see Grunwald's target, so they can witness what is possible from their fellow soldier. And note him as the first man selected to our squad of sharpshooters."

"Thank you, sir," said the boy.

"You have a good German name."

And eyes like telescopes, thought Schilling.

- 16 -

Hock had left her alone for more than twelve hours, and she hoped this meant he'd come to accept he had no right to touch her, and when he returned, he'd apologize and commit to his neighborly duty and recall his gratitude to the Van Meer family.

He entered wearing no shirt, a blanket draped loosely over his shoulders. Underneath bulged his belly huge and white. Sleep had mussed his hair, and his brambly brows looked like baby porcupines clinging to his face.

She stepped backward.

"I brought you bread." He slurred the words. A dainty towel swathed the bread loaf he placed on the floor. Straightening, he threw wide his hands holding the blanket tips, spreading them like wings, and advanced toward her.

"Stop!" she commanded.

He did not. Apparently he intended to enshroud her in the blanket against his half-nakedness. Tracing a circle, he followed her. His foot encountered the loaf, which skittered.

"Stop, please!" she screeched.

Above corpulent cheeks, his eyes shone like pennies set on sourdough mounds. Flailing, he tried to flip the blanket around her, and the moving fabric fanned his body's tang and the liquor on his breath.

She lurched forward and drilled both sets of her knuckles into his eyes.

"Awww! You bitch!"

She dashed to a vertical beam. Maybe she could use the beam to block him. But for how long?

Hock breathed through clenched teeth. "You ungrateful whore, you hurt my eyes!"

"Don't you *ever* touch me!"

He mumbled something that sounded threatening.

219

"I wish to leave!" she yelled. Her voice cracked.

"I should tie you at roadside for the soldiers to find."

"Gladly, to be out of this place and away from you!"

"Just wait and see if the soldiers don't drag you off by the hair into the woods." He stepped forward menacingly.

She raised her hands, nails out like claws. Bared her teeth and snarled like a cornered raccoon.

Amazingly, her display stopped him. He wiped the blanket's corner against his face. In the doorway's ambiance, his reddened eyes glared. "That special, smart nigger of yours, they hung him from a tree. His neck's stretched long as my arm."

He departed, slamming the door behind. The latch clinked.

She found the bread covered with dirt. Shook out the dainty towel and brushed off the loaf. Sat on the basket and gushed tears for Bookman, her true and lifelong friend, hung from a tree.

At the metal plate, the girls came back. She toed to the wall. Hair against the metal, she leaned for a long time, her tears plopping on her forearms.

Silence outside. Her knees shook, and she braced so she wouldn't collapse. Through the dug slit, she peered at the girls whose presence comforted her.

A whisper. They must wish for her to finish the story.

"All right," she choked, barely able to speak. "The animal whirlwind had borne Tess to a safe distance. The birds flew off, and the animals receded, and she was left alone."

The tears wouldn't stop. They streamed down her cheeks.

"Her mother had become terribly worried, and she decided to seek her daughter. Soon she spotted the stepfather who returned along the forest path cursing and mumbling to himself, and she hid until he went by. She called for Tess, and after what seemed like a long while, she found her and comforted her. Still they dreaded the stepfather. What could they do? They were deep in the woods, without food. Certainly the villain would renew his chase, and next time he'd be even more wrathful."

Anna rested her forehead on the plate. *You must compose yourself!*

"Just as they were about to despair, Tess again noticed the fox, the rabbit, and the woodchuck. 'Who are these creatures?' her mother asked. 'They are my friends,' said Tess. 'They saved me.' And the good threesome led Tess and her mother away on a far journey. Everywhere they traveled, the forest animals brought them berries and fruits to eat, until at last they reached the land of their dreams, where peace and music abided forever."

Another whisper.

She pressed her mouth to the slit. "Girls, if you can dig the hole any bigger, I beg you to get me out of here!"

*   *   *

He reached the banjo player just as a column of soldiers galloped past southward on the Osborne Turnpike. Military horsemen normally didn't ride so fast on a public road—too dangerous with the other traffic. Meant the riders had urgent business. The banjo player didn't pluck a note—these fellows weren't about to stop at the inn. Dust cottoned the path and turned the air momentarily ochre, the color of cemetery stones.

Holland had come within a razor's breadth of being captured.

The banjo player looked up. "They yours, Cap'n?"

"No, I think not, I'm going the other way."

He entered the receding dust and trotted north on the turnpike. The searchers would learn from the sentry that he'd been at the Van Meers' house and had ridden north. They'd question everyone along the way. At the inn, they'd inquire about a rider with a bad right leg, and the woman would identify him. They'd ask which way he'd gone, and the banjo player would tell them he'd headed north.

When certain he was out of sight, he cut eastward. Planned to ride well afield of the road and circle south. The cloudy sky cast no shadows, and he wended among the screening trees. The sparse leaves allowed him to see out; no one could glimpse him except as an obstructed silhouette. Weaving through, he came to a wide expanse of red dirt. Here labored six slaves. What were they doing in the field so late in the season? He deliberated whether to venture out or wait until they left. Discerned no way to cross without being spotted and reported as a lone rider on private land.

He decided to wait. Backed the horse into the brush.

At a trot, he might have reached Hock's farm in fifteen minutes.

*   *   *

Mortar encased the metal plate. The girls scraped with sticks they clutched in bony fingers. Sand trickled. When the hole expanded to the width of her forearm, they pushed in a stick, and she plied it until it snapped. "I need another stick," she told her helpers. In a minute, another fell through.

She panted. The hole widened almost imperceptibly. The girls were not diggers, neither was she, and none had the strength or proper tools to chisel mortar.

The enlarged cavity permitted her to view her rescuers directly. Gaunt ebony faces dusty under rough-shorn hair. Smudged, threadbare dresses. Hock mistreated them, she thought, and did nothing for their well being. They could not read or, as far as she knew, speak. She decided, if she got away, she would go north by any route she could, join the Northern cause in whatever role she might be useful, to defeat the power that Southern society gave to men like Hock.

All her life she'd considered herself a resistor of slavery, yet like her father, she'd been more often a bystander. Her part in defying the institution had been to assist their Underground Railroad station. She'd done another part to sustain slavery, by benefiting from the leased lands where slaves worked. They employed a black family in a status almost indistinguishable from slaves. Though the freedmen were paid, and they might leave if they chose, they possessed neither voices nor rights.

She looked through the hole at the girls, and one of them saw her and smiled shyly.

I will save them, Anna said to herself.

First they must save me.

*   *   *

In the wooded patch, the horse grazed. Holland kept vigil through the pine boughs. The black men were sticks against the red field; he was a shadow amid shadows. They could not see him. Nobody approached. He would have heard them at a distance crunching through the undergrowth.

He ate the food parcel—the apple, flatbread, and strip of jerky. Tossed the apple core into the bushes and pushed the paper wrap into the crack of a broken branch. In the afternoon he heard dogs. Were they tracking him with hounds? He thought, unless they gained his scent, they had no means to differentiate his trail from others. What if Swan had brought a piece of his clothing from the hospital? Might work with a fresh trail, but unless they spotted him and locked on his, the hounds gave them scant advantage. Which was why he waited behind the trees, enduring the sedentary hours, while the black men toiled.

His leg ached. He might dismount, but when he'd done so before unassisted, he'd needed ten tries and the footstool of a fallen tree to remount. The movement might give away his hideout. He was lucky to have this isolated patch with ample grazing; it would not withstand scrutiny. He had no idea when soldiers might approach and leave him no option except to gallop away, and he didn't wish to be caught unprepared.

How much saddle would the horse bear? Cavalry mounts could endure long rides, heavy loads, and short rations, and still maneuver and charge. The noise of cannons and gunfire did not deter them. What about *this* horse? He had done well so far, though plainly he was not accustomed to a cavalry horse's existence.

Holland's mind roved. He shuddered at the vision of Bookman and Jerome hanging in a tree. When he'd lowered them to the ground, he'd felled something more—the notion the war was not about slavery. Bookman and Jerome were dead because they'd been treated like slaves. Men with no rights. *His duty is one thing, but another is what he fights for, to preserve a society that enslaves people under the law's tolerance, which is morally wrong.*

Whatever else Anna might have lied about, this part was true.

Which raised a question or two. If the fight *was* about slavery, how to explain why so many common men who owned no slaves, and who by and large detested the class of wealthy slaveowners, had joined? Did the men so relish their supremacy over blacks, and fear the latter's equality, they were willing to die to preserve the social order?

Impossible. He knew them.

Or he knew *some* of them. The cavalrymen. A class of horsemen. They brought their own horses they could afford to take to war.

What about the rest, who'd joined or been conscripted into the Confederate foot soldiery? They came mostly from the poor. Possessed neither land nor animals. Labored as sharecroppers or in industries, foundries like the one his father owned. The slave economy had pushed wages so low the workers barely earned enough to eat.

Still they were Southerners. Tough and gritty. Nobody was going to take away their pride, least of all the Yankees.

Least of all the blacks.

Were the Confederates fighting for sheer arrogance?

He pushed the disturbing notion out of his head.

In his tunic pocket reposed the magnifier. Now he removed it. *Imagine yourself on your horse, studying your map after a long ride, squinting to glean the tiny letters with your weary eyes, and on that occasion, wouldn't you be gratified to retrieve this from your pocket?*

He was not gratified. With such a device, a man could see too much.

He tossed it in the bushes.

*　*　*

Frantically she scraped. The dirt spilled, and the hole grew incrementally, big enough now so she might stretch her entire arm through. If Hock came in, he couldn't fail to notice the cavity. She needed three more hours. *Three hours, and I will be through and running.*

She heard shouts. Hock's voice, the words indistinct. The girls had stopped digging. Through the hole she saw no one. Had he spotted them crouched at the wall?

Stick in hand, she moved to the door. Could she strike him? She must lurk behind the door and pummel him when she stepped in. Assuming she could, what would happen? Would he fall to the ground impaired? Or would her bashing cause him no grievous injury, merely enrage him and incite him to retaliate? Her legs and arms felt like their sole purpose was to constrict her movement. Perhaps she was not the kind of person who could attack another with premeditation. Which meant all she could do against Hock was flail against his aggression, and if it did not deter him, she would be defenseless, not just for today, for all days, and he might rape her as often as he itched to, for as long as she survived.

She did not think she could endure that. She would have to kill herself.

Could she? With a blade she might slash her wrists.

She had no blade. Or anything sharp.

At the wall, she dug. The mortar grains fell like snow.

*   *   *

The slaves stayed in the field until sunset. Shouldering their shovels and hoes, they drifted like twigs in a slow stream, clustered together to talk or have each other's company. He eased the horse forward and scanned the now-deserted field. The daylight spilled and a reddish tint oozed from broken clouds. He cantered, reins gathered, and the ground swept under and the chill air streamed, and flooding back came the excitement of the saddle, once his everyday companion. At last, his skills had aligned with his task.

The field ended. More battlements. Those he'd noticed today had been deserted, and he assumed these were too. He overlooked a log precipice. How close was the road? He tracked the crest until he hit upon a path and descended. To his left and front, an open field. To his right, a treeline running south.

Lanterns in the distance, maybe a mile away. Either they were not moving, or they were moving directly toward him. He trotted toward the treeline. A powerful smell enveloped—the marsh scent a soldier recognizes at once.

Over the war's nineteen months to date, twice as many soldiers had died from disease as from battle. Common wisdom held that marshes exhaled *miasmas,* or foul airs—origins of sickness. People fancied that cavalryman were immune to the dread discomforts the infantry suffered—dampness, filth, and the infestations of lice, ticks, and worms. In truth, the cavalry suffered as much as the foot soldiers. Ride a horse through a marsh and you will find yourself as wet and fouled as your mount. Holland had traversed marshes, dousing his boots, trousers, and equipment in filth, swatting away the mosquitoes that swarmed over man and horse alike, watching for snakes, leading his horse so he would not break a leg on a sunken stump. Hoped that what lay before him was not a fearsome bog like the White Oak Swamp, where the deep pools could not be distinguished from the shallow. Not all marshes were formidable, he reminded himself.

He pressed ahead until the horse's neck and chest penetrated the brush. The animal halted. Holland gently squeezed with his knees, angled forward against the neck. The horse remained frozen. Nothing visible past the vegetation. He flicked the reins; no response. Only heedless riders kicked a horse's sides. He wore no spurs, so steadily he pressured his heels against the flanks. The move would have jolted other mounts into a gallop.

Slate's didn't budge.

Gently he tugged the reins until he pivoted, and now he perceived what had been in the horse's view. Inches beyond the hooves, the ground plunged twelve feet into blackness. The drop might have appeared infinite if not for winks off the water's surface. Had the animal lurched ahead, they would have tumbled head over heels.

"You *are* intelligent," he said aloud. "I stand corrected."

He gazed along the treeline. Picked up a walk toward the lanterns far ahead. Had Swan posted a checkpoint on the road? What if horsemen or dismounted soldiers patrolled the open spaces? He'd be trapped, just as he'd been in the thicket facing the field of working slaves. "Good that I set off without thinking of these possibilities," he told the horse. "Or surely we wouldn't be here."

Along the woodline he scanned for a place to enter. Repeatedly nudged to precipices. At last he arrived at an opening where a path dropped gently. He brushed the reins and descended into the streambed.

The rain commenced in silver lancets.

*   *   *

Hock did not return to tie her at the roadside. She didn't believe he'd carry out the threat—he'd foreclosed the choice when he'd waited too long, lied to the soldiers, and attempted to take advantage of her. What would he do instead? Keep her locked up. Use her for whatever coarse pleasure he could. Then kill her. Claim he'd sighted her and shot when she tried to run. Hadn't shot to kill; his aim had been off.

Same thing they said when they shot runaway slaves.

The hole expanded, and her hopes clung she would elude him. Her stomach knotted. She'd devoured the loaf which, though stale, had fueled her. Now she wished she'd rationed it over the hours. What if she crumpled like the dainty towel she'd used to wipe her hands and had tossed away filthy?

She dug alone; the girls did not come back. She discovered a method: scrape with the stick's blunt end until a crevice opened in the mortar, then pry at this with the sharper end, hewing fragments. Twice chunks the size of her fist thudded satisfyingly to the floor. Sand gritted her fingers and forearms. Every couple minutes, panting from the exertion, she paused to listen for Hock.

What if he'd turned his lustful intentions to the girls? Forced himself upon them. The thought sickened her.

Her endurance surprised her—she hadn't thought she had the physical strength or the will to labor so relentlessly. Her arms, though they ached, did not fail. She feared that her determination would, and she'd despair and do nothing.

Balancing on the wicker basket's rim, she inserted her head into the cavity. The strange sensation evoked no equivalent in her life's experience. Must be how miners tunneled underground, and an unpleasant feeling it was, the surface rough against her skin. The grit clung to her hair, and the mortar pressed so close she could flutter her eyelash against.

How must she look? She be very embarrassed, were Holland to see her like this. Of course he wouldn't see her—for all she knew he didn't even think about her, though she thought about him constantly.

Hock, when he returned, could not fail to observe her covered with dirt. Preferable that she look awful and thus less appealing to him? Or would her dirt-smeared face, matted hair, and soiled dress strip away the last vestiges of her Southern-woman's stature and render her less formidable? Never had she contemplated such alternatives. Despite her sympathy for the slaves, and her poems condemning slavery, and her role helping her father with the Underground Railroad, she had not come close to thinking as the slaves must think, how they must perceive the whites who had power over them. To be a slave was to be powerless every minute, and she, a white woman, could accept this as a fact yet not apprehend its true terror. How could she know, she who had not waited helplessly for a master to pass through a doorway to rape her, or beat her, or sell her, or enact none of these atrocities, simply hold the power against which there was no appeal?

She thought of Sarah, whose master Fournier had taken away her children and sold them. And not solely *her* children—they were Jerome's too.

How could Jerome not have held it against whites ever after?

How could she not have thought of this before?

The answer was obvious. She'd been part of the society whose citizens were comfortable around blacks only when the latter were under their authority. She'd not considered them as equals, not even

Bookman, who though she'd often thought of him as her brother had been a servant, someone she'd told what to do. *Soon as blacks intrude on their comfort, they forget about equality.*

She bashed at the mortar. Gravel trickled. The pile rose and the hole expanded grains at a time. With each minute, the stick's length diminished. Her arms, shoulders, and neck ached. How big must the hole be before she could squeeze through? What were the widest parts of her body? If she could wiggle her shoulders through, could she fit the rest of herself? If only the girls would come back, they could tug her—without them, she doubted she could make her way before Hock showed up.

The light dimmed. No longer could she discern the fissures to attack with the stick's sharp end. Could she feel for them? Touching the scraped spot, she discovered that her fingertips had gone numb. In the dark, she could not sustain the pace she'd achieved thus far. She must dig harder while she could see anything! She struck the wall with force. Again. On the third strike, her hands in full motion collided against the mortar, and the stick fell. She yipped, sucked her breath, and strained in the obscurity to inspect her knuckles she could not make out except for a shading that must be blood. It widened and dripped.

Through the fissure splashed rain.

- 17 -

The rain's crescendo smothered other sounds. Rain made sentinels forlorn, and cavalry scouts rode easier knowing that their enemies weren't too watchful. Downpours dulled the riders too—they couldn't smell the campfires or hear the clinks that signaled men's presence. So mused Holland as the drops splattered. Because his center torso would stay dry longer, to protect his gunpowder, he removed the five-chambered revolver from the holster and tucked it under his tunic. Left the reload powder in the sealed cigar box in the saddlebag. His breeches were soaked. Slate in his kindness had tied a blanket behind the saddle, and Holland draped it across his lap. Angled his hat's brim to deflect the drops. Drew into himself in the way of riders who stayed in the saddle in foul weather: chin tucked, elbows tight, hands at the belly, preserving warmth between man and horse, separating the part of his mind that needed to think from the part that wanted to feel miserable and sorry for himself. He knew he could ride like this for a while, although if the temperature plunged he'd have to seek shelter.

The raindrops diffused light, outlining the creek's doodling patterns. He heard dings on metal. Noticed a banded wagon wheel that had come to rest weirdly upright in the shallows. The metal glinted, not much rust—the wheel hadn't been here long. He recalled the great storm. When Henry Van Meer and Bookman had returned from helping Hock rescue his house, they'd recounted pulling themselves along a rope stretched over a bloated creek. This must be the one.

The horse plodded over the rocks and silt. The current frothed around his hooves.

*   *   *

Pounding at the mortar, she scraped her knuckles again. Her hands throbbed. She lifted her skirt, bit at the hem, and ripped away a two-inch strip she tore in half and laced around her palms and fingers.

Did miners bundle their hands? She tapped them against the wall; the wraps cushioned somewhat. Rested her head on the hard surface and drifted at once toward slumber. Even in this hideous cellar and uncomfortable stance, effortless to sleep for a few minutes. She declined the luxury. Now was her chance to save herself. Surely Hock would come back liquored to force his way on her. She would not submit—she would fight him and make him kill her.

Preferable to escape.

Half its original size and blunted on both ends, her stick had lost all credibility as a tool. Wouldn't serve much as a weapon either. Her forearms ached, and every time she hammered at the hole's edge, the pain bit, dully at first, and in the last two or three blows, acutely. She'd not heretofore undergone this degree of pain. What did it signify? She hefted the stick and smacked the tip on the mortar. Might as well have slammed her forearms against the tips of knives.

The stick thumped to the ground. She did not pick it up. Squeezed her fists and immediately sensed the tissue ballooning. Soon she wouldn't be able to close them.

How big was the hole? Toeing the wicker basket's rim, she inserted her right arm through, then her head. Grass tickled her forehead. She wiggled her right shoulder into the cavity. No farther. The hole formed an oval from whose left curve protruded mortar that jabbed against her shoulder bone, denying passage.

When she twisted back, the basket tipped. She pitched rearward and collapsed to the floor. The dampness bled into her dress, and the musty smell assaulted her nostrils. Instinctively she brought up her hands, stopped before her grimy fingers touched her face. She began to cry. Time leaked like water from a cracked jug, yet she couldn't move, her misery was too thick. Sought refuge in her mind. Scanned her life to faces and events that raced past like blown clouds. Found herself in the courtyard where Dr. Slate had just clipped a rotten sliver from a leg, and in the blinding sunlight she caught Holland's placid expression, his spirit unbroken. Here was her beacon.

Wearily she pushed up and brushed off her dress. Re-tightened the wraps and tucked in the ends. Worked her feeble grip around the protrusion, sensing for a crack. For minutes she yanked, to no effect. Wasn't this stump like a rotten tooth she'd once witnessed her father extract from a slave's mouth? She remembered the fellow's terror as her father had manipulated the pliers. "Hold him tight with the strap," he'd told Jerome, and to her, "Press on the towel, dear. If you ever have to do this, pull straight on the tooth, not sideways."

She'd been tugging perpendicularly. Pull *straight!* She gripped the protrusion, dug her fingers in, and wrenched and yanked in line with the wall. Succeeded only in scratching her fingers.

She searched the corner for the filthy towel she'd tossed away. Swaddled the fabric around the stump. Gripping, the strength in her grip failing, she tugged. Sensed movement. The towel seemed to give her leverage. She tried again, and the protrusion popped loose in her palms, a chunk the size of a melon! The release unbalanced her, and under her shifting feet, the basket collapsed, tipping her to the floor.

Rising unsteadily, she thought, by the time Hock showed up to kill her, she would have done most of the deed herself.

* * *

The creek gurgled. At spots the water deepened. If the horse plunged into a hole and snapped a leg, Holland would be stranded in the cold with no way to build a fire. If he dismounted to lead the horse through, he risked not being able to remount. Barely could he walk, and certainly not far.

Now the animal froze. Holland flicked the reins, to no effect. "You have borne me well," he said. "Do you have the heart to press on?"

The horse did not move.

"You are no cavalry horse. You've been ridden on fair fields and roads, stabled and fed generously. Cavalry horses would scoff at you and bite your flanks. Would you let them think so contemptuously of you? Shall we not prove something to them by pushing through?"

As if yearning for respect in the society of cavalry horses, Slate's ventured forward and sank to the belly. Holland thought the animal would seize up, but he splashed ahead cautiously, until the water reached only to his forelocks.

Five minutes along, through the branches, he spotted the lanterns again. Certainly a checkpoint. Probably sited where the creek crossed the road, to make riding around difficult.

"Let us wait," he told the horse.

Would the checkpoint remain all night, or soon displace?

He sat and watched.

* * *

Outside the rain had stopped. She listened at the cavity, hearing only cricket chirps. Sat on the floor, undid the knuckle strips, and used them to tie her shoes to her feet, looping the fabric under the heel notches, between the leather straps, and around her ankles. Leaned the wicker basket's crumpled rim against the wall, and gripping the mortar's lip, stepped on the rim and bounded, thrusting her arm and head through the gap, pulling her other shoulder past the bite where the piece had broken away. Wiggled until her face touched the grass. Forward she crept. Her extended right arm had no strength, so she inched like a worm, plying every part of her in touch with the ground—side, elbow, chin—to grip. Her legs hung in space, and if not for the oval's tightness, their weight would have pulled her back inside. The rough mortar crushed against her ribs, and she writhed, abrading her dress. Her left elbow wedged immobile. She couldn't budge. When she inhaled, the pressure increased, and the pain soared.

Now she discovered that when she blew out her air, the pressure on her chest slackened, and she repeated in threes—exhale; squirm; suck breaths through the wet grass. Soon she worked her left elbow out. Both arms extended, she wormed until her chest gained purchase. Twisted her hips through the compress, then her legs.

She was free.

Face in the grass, wheezing for air, tasting the dirt's freshness, she slumped until her mind relinquished the struggle through the cavity and turned toward the one that awaited. She lay on a slope. The road wasn't far. She'd head there, run north to her house, and obtain fresh clothes. Sarah would help and warn her if Hock showed up.

* * *

The lanterns hovered. He heard no voices. To ride ahead would make noise those manning the checkpoint might hear. His attention lagged. Much as he struggled to stay vigilant, the darkness rendered the urge to sleep overwhelming. He'd reached a deep fatigue where he could fall asleep unawares and dream with eyes ajar; he might see phenomena not real and miss those that were, even hold conversations with people not present. In times past, he'd glimpsed wispy purple phantoms cavorting in the night trees. Which was why you posted sentinels in pairs after dark, so a man would not open fire at his hallucinations.

He pushed his fist against his thigh. The searing pain delivered an alert interval. The fatigue relapsed like the surf. "I think I have taken us an unlucky way," he told the horse, and his words came slurred. "I would have done better when I was fit. Not tonight, friend."

The horse seemed to be asleep. Again Holland poked his thigh to rouse himself. This time alertness did not take root, and his eyelids lowered, and the raindrops against his hat brim and the horse's breathing lulled him. He no longer saw the lanterns, though perhaps he did so in his dreams.

*   *   *

She flattened her palms on the grass to push herself up, and something hard rammed against the back of her neck.

"I was tempted to pull you in. Got curious to see how far you'd get."

Hock's double-barreled shotgun pressed her face to the grass. She couldn't move.

He hissed, "I been watchin' the whole time since I caught the little niggers at the wall. They paid, you can be sure."

"What did you do to them?"

He gripped her hair savagely. "You're gonna find out. Oh yeah."

He dragged her across the grass, and she scraped over roots and stones. He held her hair in his right hand, the shotgun in his left. She reached to break his hold. Her fingers had no strength, and she dug her heels into the ground, and all she accomplished was to pop off her left shoe—she could feel the fabric tie trailing for a few yards to fall away. Enraged, she screamed.

Undeterred, he yanked her over a board onto the barn's floor, released her hair, and stomped his boot on her back. The weight puffed the air out of her lungs. A flint sparked, a lantern wick ignited. He seized her right wrist, looped a hemp rope. The bristles abraded, and she screeched and managed to swipe the crown of her head against his cheekbone. Ignoring this, he set to work on her other wrist, tightening the rope until the pressure made her shriek. Hitched the trailing lines to a wagon wheel's crescent. With a violent jerk, he hoisted her chest to the spokes. He was going to truss her to the wheel and rape her.

In the lantern's flicker by where her wrists were tied, she noticed dried daubs of blood—somebody else's. She shouted, "Help! Help!"

He cuffed the back of her head, and her nose collided with the wheel's rim. Blood dripped on her forearms. "Shut up! Nobody hears you."

"You'll get hung for this—Southern men do not treat their women this way!"

She braced for another hit.

"You're an escaped spy, they'll *hang you*, and nothin' you say'll be believed. They'll probably reward me for how I treat you."

"They will not."

"No matter, they ain't gonna find you."

"The girls know about me."

"You mean the ones who can't talk?"

He pulled her dress skirt over her back. Grasped the slip and ripped, and her feet went out from under her, her knees smacked the ground, and she decided to stay that way, knees down, so he couldn't get at her. He tried to lift her by seizing the waist fabric; couldn't keep the grip. She pressed her torso against the wagon wheel to which he'd lashed her forearms.

"You're makin' me work, you sure are," he said, out of breath yet not audibly frustrated. The absence puzzled her. She realized he'd expected her to resist and resolved himself to overcome her. Whatever fight she put up, she'd merely delay him. Furiously she tugged on the wagon wheel, hoping to tip the rig and kill herself in the process. Her struggle hardly jiggled the wheel. She hung, panting, hoping he would lay his hand within reach of her mouth, so she might bite off one of his fingers.

The barn went silent. Through the open doors, the rain's dripping had diminished. She bit her lip so as not to cry, not sure why it mattered, only that she needed to have something within her power, and this was all she had.

From behind, a hollow sound, and over her shoulder she saw him rolling a side-turned rain barrel, water trickling from the open end. He pushed the barrel next to her, no doubt with the idea to drape her belly over and, with her arms lashed to the wheel, prop her rear end, posing her so she couldn't resist. Now he looped a rope around her waist, and she was able, with the shoe still on her right foot, to kick him in the shin. The blow didn't deter him. She thrashed and butted her head. Her unruliness accomplished nothing. He doubled the rope around her middle. Clasped her ankle to fetter, and as much as she kicked she could not stop him. He yanked on the waist piece, robbing her of balance. Finished her ankle and went for the other one, and all she could do was flail at him, ineffectually, for with the other two ropes he'd turned her into a rag puppet he could jerk this way and that. Her remaining shoe went flying, and he snatched her ankle and commenced to cinch the hemp.

In rage and frustration, she screamed.

To no effect, for he lifted her legs and hips the way men did to roped calves, and she was about as light as one. Squeezing the ropes together in his one hand, he slid the barrel under, and she threw herself side to side, only to end up in the same place.

He let go of the ropes. Her legs thumped to the ground.

Over her shoulder, beyond the open doors, a horseman's silhouette.

"Help me!" she screamed.

Again Hock cuffed her on the head. Grabbed his double-barreled shotgun from the floor a toss away. "Whaddya want?"

No answer.

"You're trespassing," said Hock. "Here's private property and business between man and wife!"

"Help me, please!" she screeched. "I am *not* his wife! He is a rapist!"

Hock said, "Shut up!" He stepped to the door, the shotgun at port. "Never mind her. She's drunk. What a man does with his wife is nobody's business 'cept his own, and you're intrudin' on my privacy!"

"I'm not his wife! He's got me tied up. Help!"

Now Hock stomped to within a pace of the horseman and pointed the shotgun. "She's drunk and a liar. She's my wife. So get *off* my land!"

No reply.

Hock cocked the shotgun's hammers. "I said ride off!"

*　*　*

When he awakened, he sat on Slate's horse in the middle of a road.

The rain had stopped. Around him, the trees dripped. No lanterns. The horse, given no command from his rider, had stopped contentedly where the stream met the roadway. The animal must have waited until the lantern men, whoever they were, had departed.

An intelligent horse, or luck?

He was wet. Not terribly cold. Opposite the stream and marshy woods, a dense mist.   How long had he slept? How many hours before dawn? No way of calculating.

He might have slept longer, had a noise not disturbed him. Seemed that he'd heard a woman scream. Or he'd dreamed so. At the height of his skills, he might have distinguished between sounds dreamt and those heard in reality. No longer so attuned, he pulled off his hat and listened. Drips and rustles, scuffs of the horse's hooves, his slow breath.

Probably just a whistle in the branches.

Where was Hock's farm?

He turned east. The mist shrouded the landscape. Vaguely he heard squeaks, clinks, and hoof beats. A wagon he couldn't see. He steered the horse a few lengths off the road and waited until the rattletrap passed. Regained the road. Visibility stretched less than twenty feet. No lights. Hock's farmhouse might be forty feet from the road, and he wouldn't have noticed.

To the right opened a trail. Should he spend time following? How could he tell which way it took him?

In the distance, a woman shouted.

Seemed to come from the trail.

Rode in. The mist became impenetrable, and he thought soon he wouldn't be able to distinguish the path. He paused. An odd noise, like splashing water. The river? He strained to listen and caught a hollow echo like an empty barrel rolling on its side.

A closed gate. He eased around the post, tree branches scraping his shoulder. Advanced and heard strange yips.

An outline slipped into view. A barn.

Within, a woman screeched.

He reached under his coat for the revolver. Slipped the gun into his holster. Tucked back the flap.

*   *   *

"I said ride off!"

The man leveled the shotgun at Holland's chest, a deadly posture evocative of the moment when he'd been shot. Lightly rubbing his left hand on the horse's neck, he glanced at the barn door, and the man did likewise. The shotgun's barrel swung wayward.

In a blur Holland's right hand moved from his lap to the holster and to the level, half a second, and he shot the man point blank in the face. The fellow staggered; the shotgun dangled crazily. The small-caliber bullet had struck him in the cheek below the eye, and as with others thus wounded and not killed outright, he was in death's grip and didn't know. A face-shot man gushing blood presents a terrible visage to those who witness for the first time. Which was why green units, rendered numb with horror, generally did not do well in their first fight.

Holland tracked him for another shot. None was needed, for the shotgun went off, barrels to the ground, and abandoning the man's grip performed a somersault to carom in the dirt. The flash illuminated his tongue's obscene protrusion, as if he tasted the blood the bullet hole spurted, and legs cocked he meandered until he toppled in the river whose dark surface flattened over.

Through all this the horse stayed as calm as a board. Holland tugged the reins around, surveying the surroundings. Ropes angled from trees into the mist. On the hillside, a small building. No sounds or movement.

Rode into the barn.

Here was Anna in the strangest posture imaginable, forearms tied to a wagon wheel, ropes around her ankles and waist, bent halfway over a rain barrel. Her dress was muddied. She stared at him over her shoulder in the dim lantern glow, and on the horse he guessed he must blend into the upper barn's obscurity.

This would be difficult; he'd not dismounted in hours, and his leg had lost all sensation. Leaning forward, he wrapped his arms around the horse's neck and rolled, clinging to balance his descent. Managed this so well his hat stayed on. Slate's horse, who seemed to take everything as normal, calmly nudged Anna with his muzzle.

"I am grateful to you, sir," she said, her voice strained but steady. "I am no relative of that man. My name is Mary, and I was visiting from Carolina…"

One hand clutching the horse's mane, with the other he commenced to untie the rope that lashed her forearms to the wagon wheel.

"…and I happened upon this wicked man, who captured me and forced me in here, and kept me prisoner."

He freed her left wrist, and at once she began on the other.

"And so I am quite grateful for your happening along. Perhaps you were riding by and heard my shouts."

Having nearly been raped, here she was concocting a tale, her voice free of hysterics. *She's always thinking, isn't she?*

She wiggled free her right arm and spun to unfetter her ankles. He saw the blood running from her nose. Bruises on her face and forearms. Knuckles scraped and bloodied, nails broken. Legs dirty and bruised and flecked with grass and straw. The cord from the cocoon necklace looped her neck, absent the cocoon.

"I am sorry, sir—I must ask you to undo these other ropes, for my fingers are numb. I think my relatives are looking for me, and I shall be on my way."

"Anna, you can stop talking like that."

Her head lifted, eyes locked on his face, and for the first time he saw profound shock in her expression. She reeled against the barrel, brought her hands raw and red to her face.

"John?" Her voice broke.

"Shift your legs so I can untie your ankles," he said.

"How can this be?"

"Did you think I would not do all in my power to help you?"

Her eyes were full of tears. "The army would not let you do so."

"I did not consult with the army. Please, if I am to untie you."

She repositioned her legs, and he pulled at the tight knots. She kicked loose.

"I rode from Richmond last night," he explained. "I left the hospital without permission, and they'll surely be after me just as they are after you. What matters is to get you to safety."

"How did you find me here?"

"There are slaves who know things."

"The slaves!" She rolled, pushed to her feet, and staggered. He reached to help her, but already she was halfway to the door. She seized the lantern. "That bastard Hock locked them up somewhere. Can you help me search?"

He held to the horse. "Sorry, I don't think I can."

"John, your *leg!*"

"Not very cooperative at the moment."

"Stay and rest. I will look for them." In the doorway she stopped, peered into the dark. "Where is Hock?"

"I shot him. His body is borne away on the current."

Her mouth twisted. "Good."

*   *   *

Lantern outstretched, she scoured the grounds until she found the slave girls. Hock had crammed them in a closet whose door a bent nail held shut; she worked it loose. They gaped at the lantern, then at her beyond, expressions half of puzzlement and half of wonder, two girls so skinny they might be corpses, and with them, a white-haired old man. She hugged the girls. Examined their scraped knuckles, her tears falling on the abrasions. They did not appear further harmed, though she dreaded to think what Hock had done to them. "Thank you for helping me," she said through her sobs. "I owe you my life."

She brought them to the barn. Holland had pulled off his wet tunic. Noticing him, the girls and the old man froze.

She said, "He is a friend come to help me. You can trust him."

The slaves didn't move.

Holland said, "Hock is gone. You don't have to worry about him."

They didn't react.

He picked up his pistol he'd set on the rain barrel. "I shot him dead. He floated away on the river. He will not bother you henceforth."

The old man said, "They'll be blamin' me."

"No they won't," said Anna. "Tell them Hock hid me here, and they will not question your innocence. They will blame me. I am Anna Van Meer, the mistress of Sarah and Bookman."

"I know who you are," he said.

"Is there food?"

"In the house," said the old man. His stare lingered on Holland—the one who shot men dead and tossed 'em in the river.

The barn had an iron stove. "Please make a fire," she told him. "Girls, lead me." Holding their hands, she reached the house kitchen. One of the girls held the lantern while Anna and the other uncovered bread loaves and strips of salted jerky. She chewed bread and rummaged through the shelves, pushing aside the meager parcels of dried spices and beans. On the floor, a half-full jug she opened and sniffed—hard cider, the scent recalling Hock's breath. Longing for coffee, she checked the shadows, hoping he'd hoarded some coffee beans. Found none. Were these sparse supplies all he'd kept? She asked the girls, who simply pointed at the threadbare shelves she'd already searched.

It occurred to her that she was going through the belongings of a man who'd been dead barely minutes, yet she felt neither remorse nor repulsion, only the anticipation of what lay ahead. A strange giddiness flowed over her.

Decided to avoid the sensation.

With scraps of wax paper, she commenced to wrap the jerky. Couldn't grip the meat to place on the paper. "I am sorry, can you help me?" she said. The girls set to wrapping the food.

By the time she returned to the barn, the old slave had accustomed himself to Holland. He'd helped him pull off his trousers, tied them by the lit woodstove to dry, and given him a blanket. Stoked with hickory wood, the stove heated quickly. "Did your master keep coffee or tea?" she asked. "I'd be so obliged for a cup." The old slave brought a kettle of water he set atop the stove. Poured the steaming water into a metal cup, stirred in green leaves. She sniffed mint. Heat from the metal shot along her forearms. For the first time in hours, she was not afraid. She felt as if she were asleep and dreaming of improbable things.

Suddenly she felt exhausted.

The girls delivered the food bundle.

"We need to be away soon," cautioned Holland.

Was there no time to rest? She longed to lay her head on his shoulder and descend into slumber. Even as she imagined the comfort, she knew she couldn't—she must concentrate on practical demands. For instance, how could they possibly travel, she with her gripless hands, he with his damaged leg? "Your leg isn't healed," she said, in the same tone she'd have used had he still been a patient in her house.

"You're right, too early for me to ride. The bone is nonetheless intact, and I shall continue until I can get you well away from here."

She stared at him. He seemed to have thought this through. Good, for she hadn't.

He asked the old slave, "Is there another horse she can take?"

"He got a mule for pullin' the wagon. Ain't no good for ridin.'"

"The wagon is roadbound and slow," said Holland. He studied Slate's horse. The animal must weigh about eleven hundred pounds. For riding over long distances, a horse should carry no more than a quarter of his weight. The burden would equal Holland and Anna together, plus the saddle, blankets, and food. The saddle, though heavy, lacked the cavalryman's standard attachments—saber, rifle, rifle boot, and bag bulging with ammunition and gear. He estimated they would be overweight, not by much. "We can ride together on mine."

She turned to the old man. "Can you feed and water the horse?"

The old man led the horse out. The girls accompanied, leaving Anna and Holland alone. She said, "Perhaps we can head to my house and take my father's horses."

"Nothing is left at your house."

"You were there?"

"Yesterday at dawn. The first place I stopped. They tore it apart."

What did he mean, *tore it apart?* Why would anyone do such a thing? She asked, "How did you know to come for me?"

"Swan interrogated me. He said you were in his custody. Yet he was too insistent in his questions about you, and I realized he was lying and did not have you."

"What about my father?"

"I don't know."

"And the Negroes?" She caught the droop in his expression, and immediately she pressed her hand against his chest. "Do not answer. Not yet. I do not trust myself to hear."

They culled through the pile of clothes she'd brought from the house. Against the stove his trousers had dried, and he tugged them on. Picked out a wool shirt and a coat of tan leather and donned these, shedding his cavalry tunic. She evaluated dresses that had belonged to the late Mrs. Hock. In the barn's shadows, she tried on the smallest that hung on her like a sack. Selected a man's nightshirt she wore beneath like underwear. Retrieved her shoes, one in the barn, the other on the slope, and retied the cloth strips to secure them to her feet.

The wind rattled the planks, signaling the dawn's nearness. The old slave returned with Slate's horse watered and fed, and Holland supported himself on the neck and limped to where the slave girls stood. "You do not speak?" he said to them.

"They talk in their way, and just to each other," remarked the old man. "Nobody else can understand 'em, not even me."

"Can you say your names?" asked Anna.

They didn't. The old man answered, "Sheila and Genise."

"Those are pretty names," said Holland.

"They all the family each other has."

Anna, who'd wondered what the girls knew about families, asked herself what *she* knew.

He asked the old slave, "What is your name?"

"I'm Jonas. And you?"

"Best I don't say. Don't think I'm not grateful for your help tonight, and for what you did for this woman. If soldiers ask you why you aided us, tell them I forced you at gunpoint. Otherwise, tell the truth. I hope one day to come back here, and I will look for you, to repay your kindness."

"Good of you, sir."

"May I ask you a last favor, to help us to mount the horse? I cannot do so without an assist, and she cannot hold on. Please help us tie ourselves together with this rope."

Everyone clustered around the horse that posed unperturbed. Once Holland was in the saddle, Anna positioned herself behind, her legs resting on a draped blanket. Another blanket she wrapped around her shoulders, tucking the edges under the rope.

Through the trees, dawn glowed.

Was she afraid? She could not tell. And if not, it must meant she wasn't. But how long could she tolerate the unfamiliar seat? And how much did they burden the horse—the two of them, the saddle, blankets, and tied-on pouch of food and two corked bottles filled from another rain barrel awash to the brim?

Surely Holland knew.

- 18 -

No sign of Hock's body on the river surface. She hoped his corpse would float far, to roll naked on a bank for someone to find and shroud until flies darkened the mound.

They crossed the road into fields. In the work season, slaves already would be out. Now, past harvest, they encountered no one. She told him about the land and the roads she knew. Fortunately the mist still cottoned the ground, and they crossed the open fields and roads directly.

"How far?" she asked.

"Seventy miles to Fredericksburg. I can get you there by tomorrow night. Beyond the Rappahannock, you'll be safe."

"Will you come with me?"

He was silent for a minute. "I will take you as far as you need to go. I haven't decided what I'll do after."

She said, "I don't think I can stay awake for very long."

"Sleep if you can. Lean into my back. Tuck your arms under the rope to hold you."

"You've ridden before with someone tied on?"

"Yes, wounded men, and cavalrymen whose horses had been shot from under them."

To skirt the Van Meer property, he stayed eastward of the creek he'd followed last night. He could see Anna's battered hands hooked under the rope. Conscious of the immense responsibility to deliver her to safety, he picked his way forward, watchful for patrols. They passed the deserted earthworks.

Northward they encountered the Varina Road and the New Market Road, threading the remnants of fence lines with no fences— the armies must have stripped the wood. The mist dissipated. Wary of being noticed, he tacked along treelines or narrow trails. The trails abounded, widening into roads or abruptly ending. No way to know where a checkpoint might arise. At the forest's edge, he trotted to a canvas tarp draped over a taut rope. A dog leapt out and barked, the horse startled, and a woman with nearly white skin emerged from the tent. She brandished a stick at the dog, which quieted.

"Hello," said Holland. "We're just riding through. Is this your land?"

The woman stared at him.

"Can you tell us what's beyond?"

"Ways on you find a mill."

"A mill?"

"Saws wood."

From the tent stepped a man, skin as pale as hers, his muscles bulging under the threadbare shirt he buttoned. Anna, who'd awakened at the dog's barking, thought his physique similar to Jerome's. His salt-and-pepper hair did not hide rouge fissures on his scalp someone apparently had gouged with a sharp object.

Holland asked, "Whose land is this?"

"Don't know," said the man. "We work different tracts. We move time to time. Stayed on here since the harvest's done, till they chases us off."

These mulattos wandered from place to place like gypsies, thought Holland. "So nobody will mind if we ride through?"

"Don't 'spect they'll mind *you*. Where you goin'?"

"Northward a ways."

The fellow aimed his arm. "Head toward that woodline. Soon you be crossin' the Darbytown Road. The sawmill's by there."

"Told 'em already," said the woman.

"After's the Charlestown Road, and the Williamsburg Stage Road, then the railroad, runs east to Fair Oaks Station, west to Richmond."

"Soldiers hereabouts?"

"Yesterday a party rode through askin' if we seen a gray rider. Offered twenty dollar if we spots 'em."

"Twenty dollars? What'd they say this gray rider looked like? Maybe we'll keep an eye out for him."

"Said he favors his left leg 'cause the right one's hurt, and he's got a horse the color of cinnamon, white stripe on the nose." The man's gaze settled on Slate's horse, precisely the shade, with a white stripe to match. He scratched his head between the scars, perhaps thinking that nobody had mentioned *two* people on the horse.

"Anybody in the field yonder?"

"No sir, not a soul, far as I know."

When they trotted over the field, he felt the mulattos' scrutiny. "I'll bet Swan's men have alerted everyone to watch for a lone rider on a cinnamon horse. This horse is too distinctive, I should have rubbed him with soot in Hock's barn."

"Just stay off the roads," she said.

Easier said than done. Well before they reached the mill, they smelled the sawdust that frosted the ground, rocks, and branches the shade of an autumn gourd. The horse snorted in protest. Above the trees jutted a smokestack spewing a tawny plume, and they heard grinding saw teeth and other clangor of industry. A road ahead. Wagons and people. Holland receded. The road hooked, and after two hundred yards they abutted it again. He detoured. Soon the sawdust dissipated and no longer stung their nostrils, and the woods resumed their natural browns and grays.

Mounted three hours since the dawn, and all yesterday, his leg ached terribly. Ahead loomed a field, and on its far side, horses and men. He halted within the woodline to watch wagons trundle by. "That's a military checkpoint," he said.

"For us?"

"Fair chance."

"Can we go around?"

"We'll have to pass closer by Richmond. I know trails we used last spring riding against McClellan."

He backed into the trees.

*   *   *

They neared places where the Seven Days campaign had wrought destruction: cannonball-shorn trees; stretches of scorched land; the remnants of tents, uniforms, crates, and wagon wheels. Marching in columns thousands long, the two armies had raced south, colliding here and there to fight battles. He couldn't tell whose scraps these were, Confederate or Union, and he detected neither sight nor smell of death except at a stone building tilting at an angle from a hillside. The foundation had crumbled, and a cavity opened in the lower stone wall where a nailed burlap curtain did not smother the odor of decomposition. Holland veered around the place.

Toward Richmond, more homesteads and travelers. He followed woodlines and streambeds, avoiding the hillcrests where people might discern them from afar. Trees rimmed a shallow creek, and he weaved its serpentine course for a mile and branched. Sun over his right shoulder, he took the left tributary until the brambles obstructed. Impossible not to breach open spaces, but he sought the narrowest divides between concealing patches. Where the brush thickened, and the horse no longer could press through, he reversed and sought another way. At the Williamsburg Stage Road, he halted to look around, and by the Richmond & York railroad tracks he listened for voices and other human sounds, scanning cautiously before he crested the embankment and trotted into the forest opposite.

Past noon, they neared the flooded swamplands fringing the Chickahominy River. He sought a crossing away from the main fords where people congregated and traders erected their folding tables to peddle wares. The marsh seemed to stretch endlessly, no landmarks obvious to her, yet he had patrolled these lands and recollected the paths through. Following one they observed ahead a stream where women washed clothes. He back-stepped out of their view. Further west he found a less-congested way, and they dodged branches and broke through spider filaments while the horse in shallows to his forelocks wended among the trees. Ahead rose dry ground beyond a seething current. "Tuck up your feet or take your shoes off," he said over his shoulder. "I can't say how deep we'll go."

Easing into the river, the horse submerged to its belly. Anna undid her shoes and let the water flow through her toes. They reached the bank and bounded up, and a few lengths restored the wind in their faces and the scent of lemongrass. She noticed figures in the distance. Soon they encountered families bearing buckets or wash bundles toward the water. No soldiers. Beyond, through the trees, the silhouettes of buildings. The closest gave a curious aspect, the boards alternately limewashed or bare.

He halted at a fence.

They'd been in the saddle for five hours. "My legs are cramped," she said. "I'd like to get down soon."

"I think this is the east side of Mechanicsville."

"Where you were shot?"

"Close by."

"Looks strange."

"Just a small town—a post office, store, church, and blacksmith shops."

The breeze shook the trees. No animals, birds, or smoke—people were saving their firewood for the cold hours. His mind seemed to rove over their situation. She asked, "What do you think?"

"We could bear knowing what's ahead toward Fredericksburg, so we don't blunder into the army lines."

"Perhaps we can ride into town."

"Better you walked in. People will be less suspect of a woman on foot than of a rider. I'll stay mounted here in case of trouble."

She unfitted the rope and climbed down, holding to his belt to steady herself. Leaning against the fence, she redid her shoes, leaving off the cloth strips she tucked into her dress pockets. "What should I say?"

"If you can, find out if the army is positioned in Fredericksburg, or in the fifty miles between here and there. Soldiers may have ridden into town for supplies. Be wary whom you approach. People will be curious about you, and you don't want to become the subject for their questions. Children speak plainly and often are alert to what's around."

"Maybe I can say I have a brother in the army and I think he's in Fredericksburg, and hear what they reply."

Inventive, he thought. *Was she a spy?* "There's money in the saddle pouch."

From the pouch she took the remaining money, two and one-half dollars, and set off. Legged over a fence and soon came to a trail. The movement felt luxurious—the pumping blood warmed her legs and eased her stiffness. She had to pee, and she watched for a place that afforded privacy. Arced a mound and leapt ruts. Closer to the buildings, raised flatstones made a walkway above the mud. She passed a church where a path ran to an outhouse. Grateful no one was around, she entered, latched the door, and hiked her dress. Kept her bottom from touching the cold seat. The fluid stirred a faint odor, the chill having suppressed the foul stench. How easy to imagine she was in their outhouse at home, and when she emerged she'd awaken from a dream, her life restored.

She came out behind the Mechanicsville church. Smoothed her dress. *Keep fancies out of your head!*

Her abraded hands would provoke people's curiosity, and she hid them in her sleeves that unfortunately were not very long—the late

Mrs. Hock must have had short arms. Folded them at her belly under the excess folds.

The town seemed well tended. The main street stretched toward a lovely ochre building, perhaps a hospital, on a rise beyond. Folks gawked at her. Always did at a woman they didn't know, so the stares meant nothing. She reached an elevated boardwalk laid with new planks. Her heels rapped sharply. A sign marked the post office, and she toed up the steps, opened the door, and joined the line. No soldiers. No children either. Thought of how might she might frame a question.

Above the postal window, the *U.S.* in U.S. Post Office had been painted out and *C.S.A.* substituted. Her voice accustomed to speaking to Holland on the moving horse sounded like she boomed to an audience in a theater. "My name's Jenna Johnson. Mail for me?"

The postmaster's bald pate evinced a burn mark. How had he managed to burn the *top* of his head? Had a flaming house fallen on him? He checked the J box. "No mail in the name."

"I'm expecting a letter from my brother, Galen Johnson. He's a soldier. I think he's in Fredericksburg, or wherever the army is these days."

"Lee's army? I don't think they're at Fredericksburg. Are you stayin' hereabouts?"

"I'm with my sister-in-law outside town."

"Who's your sister-in-law?"

"Emma Johnson. Married to Galen."

"Emma Johnson?" His face crunched. "Ain't come across her. I thought I knew everybody in these parts. Well, I'll hold your mail what comes. Nice to meet you."

"Same."

She sensed stares from the people in line behind. *Ask no more questions.* Anyway, she'd already found out what Holland needed to know—that Lee's army wasn't in Fredericksburg.

Further along, her impressions of a well-tended town vanished. The walkway ended—somebody had torn up the planks—and she treaded on mudded gravel between stumpy posts. The buildings presented the odd aspect she'd caught before of painted and unpainted sideboards, like a checkerboard of random rectangles. At the street's end, a store. Inside she selected six apples, took them to the counter for the storekeeper to weigh.

"A dollar fifty," he said.

"Why so expensive?"

"They're past season and still pristine. I don't expect I'll have 'em for long before they sell out."

She doubted this but pushed the money across. Noticed a jar of sweet candies twisted in wax paper. "How much are these?"

"Oh, you'll like 'em," said the storekeeper. "Dear they are, four for a dollar, but you get one for free." He opened the jar and fished out five.

She had one dollar left. "All right."

"Should I call you miss, or misses?"

"Miss. Why are the house boards painted so?"

"Last June the Yankee army occupied the town. There were skirmishes, and the residents all skedaddled. The Yankees just tore the place up—they stripped off the boards to use for their camps. After Bobby Lee chased 'em out, the people came home and fetched back some of their boards. Nobody could tell which went where, and they're all mixed up."

"Oh my."

"You should have seen us out at night haulin' boards and wavin' torches all around."

She guessed how the postmaster had burned his head.

He said, "You're not from the vicinity?"

"No, I'm…" She picked up the candies and noticed the poster behind him, the same print the slave girls had pushed through the root-cellar hole, her likeness sketched prominent:

WANTED BY THE AUTHORITIES!
ANNA VAN MEER

She dropped the candies that scattered on the floorboards by her feet.

Squatting, she flipped her shawl to hide her hair. Fetched up the fallen sweets. The proprietor, his straw-yellow hair not pairing with the age lines on his face, circled from behind the counter to help.

He stared at her hands. "Looks like you hurt yourself, miss."

"Horse stepped on my hand a couple of days ago."

"Horse stepped on *both* hands?"

"Yep," she croaked.

"Well, sorry for your trouble. What's your name?"

"Jenna Johnson."

"I'm Earl Starkey. I own this store straight out. No borrowed money."

"I see."

The candies collected, he resumed his place behind the counter. "Did you bring a bag, miss?"

"No. My dress pockets will suffice." Deposited the apples and candies. Gripped her shawl under her chin. He seemed to focus on her battered hands.

She strode toward the path where she'd entered town. Mind racing, clutching the shawl, she thought, he hadn't looked much at her face, merely at her hands.

The postmaster had glared at her straight on.

A scrape behind. Against a wagon leaned a man observing her. *People will be curious about you.* Just nosiness at a new woman in town, she told herself.

Swan must have distributed the poster to the localities around Richmond. In the post office, a tack board had hung to the side. What if her sketch displayed? She hadn't covered her hair, and one of the customers might have divined the likeness. Yet how much did she resemble the image that showed her posed and coiffed, against how she appeared today, in rumpled clothes and wind-mussed hair?

Holland had said he'd stay in the saddle in case of trouble. She'd heard the statement as hyperbole. Now she scampered in alarm up the hooking path, and when she reached the fence hurried over, kicking her legs high, checking behind to be make certain nobody was following. Lifting her dress, she dashed toward where she'd left him by the treeline.

He wasn't there. Instead, leaning against the fence, two soldiers.

The gasp erupted from her mouth like kettle steam.

"Hi," said the one. In his gingham trousers and curling amber beard, he resembled a maple tree in autumn's splendor.

"Hello," she managed. She felt woozy, as if she'd stood up too fast.

They straightened, holding their rifles by the snouts, the stocks resting in the dirt between their feet. "Don't be alarmed," said the maple. "Just us is all."

The other fellow wore a black beard and boots that flanged over his knees. He said, "You're lookin' a bit addled, miss."

"I'm fine."

"Don't take offense at me sayin,' seems like we gave you a hellacious fright."

"Don't cuss," said the maple.

The black beard scratched. "You live out this way?"

"A ways yonder. I didn't know the army was here."

"Hanover County Home Guard," he corrected. "We're usually hereabouts."

"Why?"

The black beard's face flattened in wrinkles. "Yankee cavalry, for one thing."

"Could be more reasons too," added the other.

They guffawed. Must think her stupid—a cast perhaps advantageous to her, though she could easily betray herself. "I'll be on my way."

"Surely." The duo touched their hats.

She stepped off.

"Hey, you sure you're goin' right?"

"I think so."

"Just the river's thataway."

"I know. Bye."

Their laughter trailed. Downhill she treaded, lurching when her feet slid into ruts beneath the leaf carpet. Holland must have sighted the two guardsmen and ridden off. Which way? Beyond their view, she cut over a meadow through thorn bushes that snagged at her dress. The brush thickened, and she realized she should have stayed on higher ground, where Holland surely would be. Why? Because he knew now was not the time for poor choices, and the best place for him was where he could survey the land around. Should have crossed her mind earlier.

She pushed uphill, keeping the meadow between her and the soldiers, hoping their duties did not compel them to scout the woods. Could she reach Holland before he rode into town to search for her? Unaware she'd used a false name and her true one and face showed on a poster, he'd ask folks if they'd seen her. Worse—maybe having spotted her on her return, he'd assume the two guardsmen had impeded her, confront them, and kill them as readily as he'd done to Hock. There would be shots, stirring up the whole town.

Faster she stepped. The thorn bushes blocked and she pressed through. *Please be patient, John. Do not think I'm in trouble.* Short of breath, she reached the crest. A road ahead. She scanned for the guardsmen who might be making their rounds. Sank to her knees behind a tree.

What if he did not reappear?

Traffic passed. A hay wagon trundled behind a mule, the loose hay dribbling golden against the spokes. Next paraded three white women, their laughter skipping like bird calls. Trailing, two black women who bore baskets, perhaps for the wares the white trio would buy in town. Then two riders, a father and son, dressed identically in black coats and hats, going-to-town clothes or mourning clothes, hard to tell since men tended to wear black on every occasion.

Her stomach tightened. No sign of Holland. She leaned her shoulder against the tree. Remembered the cloth strips in her pocket and retied them to preserve her shoes in case she had to run. In the same pocket were the candies she'd bought, and she proceeded to unwrap and eat them. In summer they'd have been soft; today they resisted her teeth, and she had to bite hard. Took a while to chew to swallowing. She ate four in nervous succession. With her finger she pushed the waxed papers into the soft ground and tapped the dirt over. Preserved the last piece for him.

A sound behind. There he sat, silhouetted on the horse against the faded sky. Rising, suppressing tears, she kicked through the leaves. He eased the horse forward, and when she came alongside he stretched his left arm and pulled her up.

Got herself seated, the rope tied.

Not a word spoken.

* * *

Northward the land opened. People and houses, and to avoid them he shifted west to the strip between the Virginia Central railroad and the Chickahominy River. The streams ran east-west, and he crossed, staying above the marsh. At dusk, in a brush-screened meadow, they dismounted to rest for the night. "Lee's army is not at Fredericksburg," she told him, after she'd told him everything else, about the soldiers, and the poster with her face's sketch, and the mismatched boards. Unable to speak for a long time, fearful she'd gush into tears, now she couldn't stop talking.

The meadow bordered a stream. She helped him remove the tackle and extend the lariat so the horse might drink and graze. They rested. Leaning against a pine, he rubbed his leg and drew air through his teeth. She picked through the parcel. Bit into an apple and shifted the pulp around in her mouth. Her forearms smelled like Hock's root cellar. Beside the man who had killed him, her knee against his hip, the scent and the idea tumbled in complexity she could not unravel.

He said, "You noticed no soldiers in town?"

"Only the two guardsmen by the road."

"The army marched from Sharpsburg many weeks ago. The winter's coming, and I doubt they'd head north again."

"Who cares where they are, as long as they're someplace else."

He reloaded the single shot he'd fired to kill Hock. Tucked the pistol in the holster. All the while he scanned the woods. "This spot is good. Even so, I feel helpless on the ground."

"Rest. I will watch until dark." She remembered her panic waiting for him, the restoration she felt on seeing him. She wished for him to feel as safe in her presence as she felt in his.

He said, "You must wake me at once if you see or hear anyone."

"Of course."

He shut his eyes. She studied his profile. She wanted to lay down and press her head against his shoulder. If she did, she couldn't watch, and he'd not be able to rest, so she took in the woods and the horse eating grass paces away. The breeze skittered over the pine needles. The branches swayed, and the grass bent to an angle where the color darkened. A gust hit the horse, who twitched his ears forward. For the first time since she'd left home, a poem stirred.

Horse and Praetorian

Wind on the grass
Horse calm and fine
My captain at rest under a pine
I am at watch, awake
Lest danger us overtake.

A day of tumult
Separated, reunited
Scuffed and bruised and abraded

Upon our mount, travelers
We eat bread and apples.

Across flooded marshes
Rivers and woods aplenty
I spent all our money
My face on a poster
Maybe yours too, sir.

Looms the morrow
A dire iteration
Risk our lives toward a free location
So relish the present serene
And sleep, my good Praetorian.

She repeated the words to herself. Spoken verses were elusive. Sometimes they'd sound in her ear, yet her hand, as if empowered to reject what her mind produced, wouldn't write them, and she wouldn't be certain she had a poem until she saw the lines on paper. No way to write this one. She hoped her memory would preserve it for a time beyond.

She surveyed the woods. Wondered what had happened to her notebook and poems. She wanted to ask him. Other questions too.

Chin on his chest, he was fast asleep.

*   *   *

In the morning they ate two apples. He smiled sleepily, and they were content with only murmurs between them. He saddled the horse and got on after three tries, a tree stump making a step-stool for his good leg. The Chickahominy fell away westward, and they edged the railroad line that at times appeared to the east. The ground descended. "I think the South Anna River is ahead. Easily crossable in dry seasons. In this weather we must seek a bridge or ford."

They'd been on the horse for barely an hour, and already her legs screamed. Soon they spotted posters tacked on trees. He pulled one off. She leaned to read the letters on paper limp with dew:

ARREST WARRANT!

The Army authorizes any soldier or citizen to arrest deserter, betrayer of his country, and murderer John Holland, and his companion, the spy Anna Van Meer. They have treasoned against the nation. They are riding together, it is witnessed, on a horse cinnamon brown, white stripe at the nose, of fifteen and one-half hands and richly saddled. If they resist arrest, they may be stopped by any means. A reward of five hundred dollars for each, and one thousand for both, will be paid upon their presentment to authorities, alive or dead.

John Holland, if you might read this, you have tarnished your honor. You might restore it by surrendering yourself and the woman. Rest assured you will be treated fairly under the law.

"Swan wrote this." He gritted the syllables. "I am not a murderer. And I am *not* a betrayer of my country."

She wondered if Hock's body had washed up. More likely, Swan had questioned Hock's slaves, who'd divulged John's declaration: *I shot him dead.* She squeezed his arm. "Do not let his words trouble you—they are insidious guile."

"How did he know we would pass this way?" He stepped the horse forward; every third or fourth tree sported a poster. "Someone must have seen us and reported our direction. Perhaps the gypsy mulattos, or the clothes-washers by the Chickahominy. The news reached Swan, and he will have spread the alert all the way to Fredericksburg and the Rappahannock."

She said, "We can cross at a deserted ford."

"At the other rivers. Not the Rappahannock. By Fredericksburg it is deep, and the crossings are few. Men will be watching for us at the fords and bridges. I had not thought of this until now."

The poster bore no sketch, yet the warrant would make folks vigilant. It empowered them to kill. For an instant she pictured her lifeless body alongside his in a wagon bed, their faces marble in death, while money changed hands for the delivery.

"We must go another way," he said.

"I swam in the Rapidan River years ago, below Culpeper Courthouse." With Bookman. She remembered him wading in the stream, splashing her, his eyes squeezed in delight.

"Yes, the Rapidan's fordable in places below Culpeper. Heading there will detour us miles to the west."

She thought of her aching legs. "How much longer?"

"A day more."

"Can you find the way?"

"Yes."

"Then take us."

They descended to the South Anna River and forded easily. Cut northwest and soon arced the Richmond-Fredericksburg-Potomac railroad line. Skirted fields and places where they sighted people. In an hour they forded a lesser river and immediately encountered the Central Virginia railroad tracks running northwest. Receding from the Hanover Junction, he steered westward for thirty minutes before he crossed.

The distance increased, and she grew confident they'd left behind the posters and anyone who'd be searching for two riders on a cinnamon horse. With every mile, the area Swan had to cover expanded geometrically. At the Augusta Female Seminary, she'd so excelled in her geometry studies that students who found the subject vexatious had come to her for assistance. She tried to remember the relationship between distance and the area inscribed. Yes, a circle's area equaled the number pi multiplied by the radius squared. Halve this result—Swan must know they were headed northward—and thirty miles from their point of origin meant he had to rummage over fourteen hundred square miles. At forty miles, the area would increase to twenty-five hundred. If they'd been spotted en route, the measure would shift, by how much she couldn't say. Nonetheless, the farther they traveled, the safer they were.

She did not share her calculations with Holland. Surely he understood the principle, which was why he did not halt to rest or water the horse. He asked her to watch to the rear. This she attempted, twisting this way and that, and the swiveling strained her neck. After awhile, seeing no one, she rested against his back, trusting the rope to hold her.

At the North Anna River they crossed an unguarded bridge. No people about. Beyond they entered Spotsylvania County. Where the river turned westward, they diverged along a stream, rounding bramble fields. This region lay between the contested counties of northern Virginia and the Richmond Peninsula, and was similarly aloof from the Shenandoah Valley. Military engineers had not gouged battlements or encampments here; soldiers had not stripped the farmhouses and fields. In the mist she could not see the Blue Ridge Mountains, yet they must be close by. From the eastern slopes sprang the Rapidan River that sluiced down the rocky corridors to race across the Virginia piedmont. Almost in reach.

Colonel Schilling resumed buttressing his unit.

Fifty yards behind the line, his quartermaster sergeant posted water buckets, three per company, and a ladle from which men drank or filled their canteens. The water came from the Rappahannock one hundred yards forward. Twice a day, men carried the buckets to refill, and they returned with them less than half full, the rest having sloshed out over the uneven path. Proper water buckets should have lids.

"Do you know of a carpenter among the men?" he asked Major Turgess, the executive officer.

"No sir. In three hundred, we must have one."

"Ask around. If you find an experienced fellow, send him to me."

In an hour he had his man, a Vermonter named Muxon who'd raised barns and houses and in winter fashioned cabinets. Hands were the surest proof of a carpenter, and Muxon's were like an old cutting board that nicks crisscrossed. One of his fingers made a stub at the first knuckle.

In the barn, Schilling sat on a stool behind the flat boards he'd rigged as a writing surface. He said, "For wood you may tear out the planks on the back. The quartermaster sergeant has tools. There must be nails and wire to be found. Can you devise lids for the buckets?"

"Readily, sir. And if you like, I can fix your table. Can't be serving you proper."

No doubt the line's tedium grated on a craftsman like Muxon. "First look for what you might accomplish to make life easier for the soldiers. Perhaps pot stands for the cooks."

Muxon went about pounding and ripping.

Schilling had supplemented his assets with two—a sharpshooter and a carpenter. He needed another. A runner.

During active campaigns, military messages usually proceeded by fast horseman, the favored method up to the hour when a unit entered an infantry battle. For a variety of reasons, horses did not fare well in this hellish setting, and commanders prized the option to use foot runners. To find a good one was difficult. A runner must be fit to dash by roads, fields, and woods. He must not stop for shortness of breath, nap when exhausted, pick wild berries, or bathe in a stream— diversions that common soldiers would take once out of their officers' sight. He must be brave enough to slip past enemy pickets, and day or night to make his way to places he'd never been. Trustworthy to carry sealed documents, to risk his life to deliver, and to destroy if capture threatened. Over time, an officer would discern men with such qualities. Schilling did not know his men so well, having served with them only on the march from Maryland, at the Warrenton camp, and here. Nonetheless he must choose a runner. The army had established an outlying telegraph post on the main road by the Hamet house, and at least daily he must send his reports and collect the dispatches.

To exercise the companies, he brought them from the line to the same field where he'd held marksmanship practice. Here he staged a two-part competition by squads: to run wood blocks in fifty-yard relays, and to race around the field's perimeter measuring approximately a quarter mile. Eventually the winning squads would compete across companies, but for now he could not pull more than one company off the line at a time. During the competitions a soldier caught his eye. Private Lansdale's natural speed would have borne his squad to his company's championship, had several of his fellows not been fat and slow. Younger than most, Lansdale held his rifle straight, kept his pack neat, and buttoned his uniform fastidiously at the pockets and collar.

Schilling summoned him to the barn and extended the paper with its waxed seal. "If I asked you to run this document to the telegraph post three miles away, how long to get there?"

The boy brought the paper to his face, as if he intended to sniff. "Three miles, sir?"

"Approximately."

"Flat road?"

"In parts uphill."

"Pack and rifle, or without?"

"No pack. You must keep your rifle and cartridge belt and stay in uniform."

"Twenty and one-half minutes, sir."

"One-half? Are you serious?"

"Yes sir. My mother timed me for speed."

"Your mother?"

"With a pocket watch. She says quickness is God's gift. I'm the fastest boy in my county. I'd reckon twenty minutes, sir, but I think my rifle and belt and the hilly parts would slow me down."

Schilling heretofore hadn't noticed that Lansdale's eyes were the shade of a robin's egg and gracefully shaped. His mother's softness in them.

He purged the thought. As he had done with so many young men at Antietam, he might have to lead this one to his death.

"The military telegraph post reportedly is by the main road. A house is near. You'll see the wires and sentries when you get close. Other than that, I cannot tell you how they're set up, for I haven't been there. If they have dispatches for us, bring them."

Private Lansdale tucked the document in his tunic.

"Don't tarry to eat. Run all the way if possible. If you cannot find the post or someone to direct you, return at once. Watch for Rebel cavalry—there are folds in the terrain that might conceal them in small bands. If you see they'll capture you, do what you can to destroy the dispatch."

He studied Lansdale's face for signs of puzzlement or anxiety. Neither stirred. Confidence, or lack of imagination?

"Questions?"

"No sir."

The young soldier trotted up the road. Dirt kicked from his heels, and from time to time he changed his rifle from one hand to the other. He angled around puddles, otherwise he did not swerve.

Schilling noted the time on his pocket watch. If Lansdale did well on this first try, he'd send him next at night.

The true test would come when the bullets flew.

* * *

The daylight fled. They could stumble upon pickets. She recalled how Hock had appeared with a shotgun in front of her. "Find us a place," she said.

Hooves threshed in fallen leaves. They reached a clearing, and she gazed through hardwoods that climbed from thick branches to small and made an infinite weave. Traversed a slope, zigzagging around logs. Followed a creek's bank to a bent funnel in the terrain, the wide end opening to the creek, the narrower tip hooking uphill. In the lower bend, the horse could stand and be seen only from close by. In the spout, a person could recline and scan the woods in every direction and not be spotted.

Anna dismounted, and her knee immediately buckled. She collapsed on her side in the leaves. "Oh, my leg fell asleep."

He laughed.

"I shall laugh at you too, who can barely stand except holding to the horse's neck!"

He laughed again. The sound of self-depreciation and humanity ringing like a poem in her ears.

"Cold tonight, I think." His breath plumed against the dark matte.

She remembered her night in the creek bed, the terrible shivering. Four nights ago. She looked at his face that wore the sliver of a smile. His calmness was as firm as the ground on which she sat, and her tension ebbed. She pushed to her feet, and together they unsaddled the horse and spread the blankets, the diminished food parcel on top. Using the horse as a crutch, he led him to the creek for water, and when he returned he settled down beside her.

She was gaining the feel for how the ground could work to their advantage. "This is a choice place," she said.

"Still we cannot risk a fire. The smoke would travel, and a patrol might happen along curious to see who's here."

She picked through their meager food. "Nothing to cook anyway." They finished the bread, stale, from the same batch Hock had given her in the cellar. Each ate an apple, and she set aside the two remaining for tomorrow morning. Studied her hands, their scrapes having scabbed, and she couldn't close them to fists or fully open her fingers.

He'd refilled the bottles in the creek and sipped from one. "Hand me the cork," he said.

Extending the cork, she fumbled it in the leaves, and again he laughed.

Never had she envisioned that the man she'd love would find humor in her difficulty. Why should she wish otherwise? His mind did not hold to society's ruts but took its own course, and she was happy for this.

Dusk bled the loam and dispelled the shapes around them. No longer could she make out his face. He draped the second blanket over her shoulders, and she pressed against him and arranged the fabric over them both. She pulled the edge to his far shoulder, felt the stubble of his beard on her cheek, and tucked in her legs.

Close to her ear, his breathing slowed.

"John?"

"Yes."

She wanted to ask him about his promise to the slaves. *I hope one day to come back here, and I will look for you, to repay your kindness.* She had no doubt he intended to help them, yet what had he meant by *one day?* Had he meant soon, or a day in the murky future?

Would he stay with her after they'd crossed to the North?

She could not ask him, so desperately did she want him to stay.

There was another question she could and must ask. She spoke with the reluctance of thrusting her hands into thorns. "What happened to Bookman?"

"I think you know."

"Please tell me anyway."

"He's dead. They hanged him and Jerome together." He paused, and the night woods bristled, as if the pronouncement offended all of nature. "I lowered them from the tree where they'd been left. The sentry perceived the injustice done, and he helped me. We covered them with one of the curtains."

She could not speak for the tears that flooded out.

"A sergeant grew angry, the sentry said, because the Negroes weren't doing as they'd been told. To kill them was an impulsive act, and a foolish one—no sense in executing men who might possess important information."

"They lay there and no one buried them?"

"Some one will."

She blubbered, "I will never know the place of their graves."

"The slaves will keep the memory of them." As soon as the words came out, he recalled Bookman's: *And how does a black man, whose life leaves no imprint, and no one will remember him, or his family, or any other black person he ever knew, not think of himself the same way?*

She asked, "What happened to Sarah and her daughter?"

"I don't know."

"My God, she has no one to help her. All she might do is to sell herself into slavery, so she might feed Carola. The world is unjust, there is no doubt." She sobbed, peering into the night woods that gave no reflection near or afar.

Minutes passed before he spoke. "Anna, may I ask you something?"

"Yes."

"Are you a spy?"

"I am not, though I think my father was. He would not tell me what he was doing. If he had asked for my help, I would have agreed without hesitation, but he did not ask. He did not have the confidence in me."

"That I have trouble believing."

"It was so. He thought me too full of passion and not enough of deliberateness. Much was at stake." Her voice cracked in sobs. She told him of the Underground Railroad, of the slaves they'd hidden in the old well, of the night journeys to the river landing, the secret messages prepared and received. In the telling, her voice rose and her hands gesticulated. He touched her forearm in caution, and she adopted a whisper that filled the space between them like oratory. She said, "When you mentioned the digging you'd heard, I thought perhaps the Railroad had been resurrected, and our station was open again, and I implored my father to explain. He denied the Railroad was active; no more would he reveal. By the house one evening, I happened on a soft spot in the soil, and I dug up a paper with a code written. I copied the letters, trying to unravel their meaning, but I couldn't."

"Swan's men discovered your notebook. In the hospital he showed me the code, which he said they had solved. It bore a spy's message."

For a while their breathing made the only sounds. The vapor puffs entwined.

"He showed me something else," he said. "A poem."

"Oh?"

"Making me think you were the poet, Anna, and Gibraltar Nash was your invention."

"Were you angry with me, when you realized?"

"No. But I concluded you were versatile at deception."

"How could I reveal my true self to you, a Confederate officer in our house?"

"It was so."

"Which poem?"

"'To My Provocateur.' I think that was the title."

"And what did you hear?"

"Your voice."

"I wrote it the night before you left. The next day I was angry I had not given it to you. How strange, of all my verses, for Swan to show you that one."

"He was trying to trick me to confide what I knew, and inadvertently he displayed what was in your heart, and it matched what was in mine."

She traced her fingers over his eyebrows. He took her hand with its scrapes and scabs, applied a gentle kiss, and returned the hand to her.

She had not slept except for her interrupted dozing on the horse, and the exhaustion of the past four days fell on her like a boulder through the trees. She pressed against him for warmth.

"Shall I keep watch again?" she mumbled, already adrift.

"No. We are safe tonight. Go to sleep."

In the woods' silence, before she lost consciousness, her thoughts tumbled. She remembered Bookman guarding her in the wagon, though his diligence had reaped him a cuffing and humiliation. He'd kept protecting her for the rest of his life. And her father had done the same, though he'd left her terribly unprepared.

Where was her father? He must be in Swan's custody. Would they mistreat him?

Suddenly Hock's image leapt at her, and with a shudder she wondered if his evil visage would haunt her dreams. The week had opened with humanity's worst. Now she journeyed with a good man. During his convalescence, she had grown to like him, even to admire him. Today she knew him for what he was, a person of integrity expressed in action, who kept his word and would always keep it. She owed the depth of her conviction to her experience with Hock.

As she fell asleep, her father's voice sounded in the rustling leaves: *For the contrast shows us what is good. Bravery can be known only in its distinction to cowardice, truth in juxtaposition to falsehood, and honor as it shines above dishonor.*

* * *

She jolted awake, lifted her head from his shoulder, and sat up into dawn. The air was frigid, the woods hazy. Frost crisped the blanket.

She had dreamt of death, and the pieces plunged from her memory like berries rattled off a bush. A few clung, of gunshots and blood. She concentrated on the waking forest, the greening pines. In a minute, the dream's last traces dissolved.

Another damp day awaited them. She wanted to reach a place where they could build a fire without worrying about army patrols. How far must they go, to be certain they had outdistanced Swan and his posters? She shook and rolled the blankets. While he watered the horse, she descended to the stream, knelt, and pressed her lips to the icy flow to drink. Promised herself that when they arrived in the North, they would drink coffee. She conjured a steaming cup she would wrap her hands around.

They rode within the woodline for a mile northwest. Beyond, the ground descended to a crossroads and buildings. He said, "I have passed through here before. They call the place Andrew's Tavern. The Rapidan River is about a dozen miles away."

The ground lay open, and again the mist helped. At any distance, no one could discern they were two people on the horse. They skirted Andrews Tavern, traversing roads and fields. An hour brought them to a smelly swamp where he veered eastward. They encountered tangled woods that slowed their pace, and he backed out to circumvent. Saw no one. At a place where the trees thinned, he cut to the left. Skirted another road and creek, nosing north on a field where the mist and drizzle hid them.

Against his back, she dozed.

When she awoke, her arms were numb within the rope that bound her to him. The horse stood among trees. Grimacing, she withdrew her arms and gave them a shake.

"Shhhh," whispered Holland.

Past his shoulder, she saw soldiers standing by a road seventy yards away. He kept the horse immobile until a breeze stirred and the leaves rustled, and slowly he pivoted and retreated into the woods.

Her legs and bottom ached. They had been on horseback for hours. "John, I must get down for a while."

"All right. The horse must drink and eat too."

In the dense woods they dismounted at a grassy patch by a stream. "Before you awoke, a line of wagons went by on the road. They looked like military wagons. The army may be close by."

"Let us hope not." The inside of her thighs were fiery red, the skin rubbed near to bleeding. Could she bear another full day on the horse?

They rested for half an hour and remounted. Trotted to a wood's edge. The ground opened beyond. The tufting mist obscured her view. Her attention on the white tendrils, she did not notice the soldiers at first, merely wondered why he'd veered away. He turned again, and now she spotted them, hundreds marching along a road, wagons and wheeled cannons interspersed. "That's a division's column," he said.

"Howdy!"

Five yards ahead, a soldier emerged from behind a tree and lifted his rifle to the ready. "Halt ye there."

Holland halted.

The sentry's tawny beard cracked to show yellow teeth in a faint line, as if a sliver of eggshell had snagged in the bristles. His hat brim occulted his eyes. Impossible to say whether he was young or old, friendly or mean, until he spoke: "You look all rode out."

"Quite so," said Holland, voice raspy, his Virginia accent nonetheless distinct. Tightened the reins, poised to dash away.

"State yer business, if you please."

"We're…"

"We're looking for my brother, Galen Johnson," Anna cut in. "He's in the army."

"What's his regiment?"

She stared, unsure what he was asking.

"Infantry, wasn't it?" said Holland.

"Yes, infantry, I think," she said.

"You don't know his regiment?" said the sentry.

"No."

"Well, who commands his brigade?" In the Confederate army, brigades were called by their commander's name.

"I don't know."

The sentry raised an eyebrow. Civilians, even women, commonly could say the unit their close relative belonged to. These two appeared to comprehend as much about military organizations as he did about Byzant-shum. "Is he with Longstreet?"

She hesitated. "I think so."

"Well, there he marches." The sentry nosed his rifle at the column. "McLaws's division, anyway. Keep askin,' somebody's gotta know him."

Holland touched his hat. "We'll ride through, if it's all right."

"Surely. Good luck."

"Thank you kindly."

A blink of teeth.

Along the woodline he maneuvered at a slow trot until they reached a vantage point overlooking the column; it appeared to stretch endlessly. He said, "They are marching fast. Something is happening."

"That soldier wasn't wary of us at all."

"He would have been, if we had asked questions. He said these are Longstreet's men. We need to know where they crossed the Rapidan—we may be able to go westward around them. Yet we have no way of finding out without calling attention to ourselves."

"John, I cannot ride for much longer. And we have no food."

"Swan didn't expect us to head westward or into Longstreet's corps. With reason—for us to be here is madness. Cavalry will patrol the flanks. If they ride up on us, they'll question us."

"We shall invent a story."

"They do not trick very easily. And they may recognize me. Too risky. I cannot gamble with your life."

"If you'd like, I will go ahead on my own, to try to get across, and you can go back." The words pained her to say.

"That is not what I meant. Only that I will never forgive myself if you are hurt under my charge."

"John, listen to me. I am *not* under your charge. I am under no one's charge, and I would not levy the responsibility on you. I would not risk your life any sooner than you would risk mine. I wish to go on, even at the cost of my life. I cannot ask you to pay the same price."

"I do so of my own free will," he said. "In the weeks with you, I changed, and the change was so big, my mind is in upheaval. I see Bookman and Jerome hanging from a tree, killed at a man's arrogant lark, and I feel rage at the injustice. I see Swan's poster declaring me a traitor, and the words cut. I am no traitor, yet I cannot ignore the wrongs I have witnessed. These are my thoughts."

"Commendable to hear."

"You must understand, the marching column makes this place precarious for us, and you or I or the both of us might be killed or arrested."

"All right, we are quite clear on that point."

"Good," he said.

"The more time that passes, the more for Swan to nail his posters everywhere. They sketched a likeness of me from a photograph. They may have done one of you too. You recall the newspaper photographer?"

"I do indeed."

* * *

On the road clacked four supply wagons. Piloting each, a civilian driver under a coat and water-stained hat tipped against the rain. The wagons lumbered between files of marching infantry.

"Hold on," he said. Picking up a trot, he emerged from the woods, spanning a field until he came alongside the fourth wagon.

She said, "Aren't we going the wrong way?"

"We cannot ride against the column—every soldier and officer would stare at us. Someone surely would recognize me."

Now he advanced to the driver. "Excuse me. May she sit in the bed? The horseback is uncomfortable and wears on her."

The driver, a black maybe forty years old, appraised them from under his hat brim. He halted the wagon, and she dismounted and climbed in the bed amid wooden crates. Holland handed her a blanket she flipped over her hair to form a makeshift hood. The driver resumed.

Whereas to linger close by the column was dangerous, to all appearances Anna and Holland now blended in. They hardly stood out to the casual onlooker. The danger was they'd encounter an alert officer who would interrogate them.

They traveled a wide pike. Planks paved the right side that seemed to her like an interminable bridge built above the ground, and the surface preserved the soldiers' feet from the puddles and ruts. The marchers' shoes thudded on the planks whose tops had gone slick in the rain; soldiers slipped and occasionally fell.

The woods by the road reminded Anna of a hairbrush used too much without cleaning the bristles. The column drudged slowly. Rain or traffic had damaged the planks in spots; where boards were missing or broken, the wagons slowed to clump over, and the soldiers leapt the gaps. In places army engineers had substituted rough logs. One repair underway featured a detour where a control officer waved his arms to redirect the wagons. He flicked the briefest glance at Holland and Anna. The wheels galumphed over the logs. Parallel ran a telegraph wire on poles. She didn't doubt that Swan had sent out a warning, yet the best place to have watched for them would have been at the detour, and the officer had paid them no heed.

They rattled past soldiers who squatted by the roadside to rest. The men looked weary and footsore, though she saw none barefoot. Every eye followed her. But weren't soldiers always starved of news and the understanding of what awaited them, whether to march, fight a battle, make bivouac, dig entrenchments, or tarry interminably? The men's faces revealed no suspicion, merely curiosity: Who are you? Where is this place? What is happening here?

Leaving behind the turned heads, they went a hundred yards, and the wagon jerked to a halt. An officer stepped to the first wagon.

A checkpoint.

"John, I'm afraid."

"To him were are simply two people on a normal journey. Try to appear unconcerned. Most dangerous would be to run."

The officer proceeded along the file of halted wagons. When he came to Holland, he stared up. "Who are you?"

"I'm escorting this woman bearing a message for her brother in the army."

"What's the unit?" The officer seemed more astute than the bearded sentry.

"Infantry," she said.

He peered at Anna.

"I'm sorry I don't know further. I can say he's with Longstreet. Yes, I'm certain of it."

What nonsense, thought the officer—Longstreet commanded half of Lee's army. Here were two civilians on a personal mission. He had encountered many such. They fretted over their husbands, pampered their brothers, or lingered too long after conveying family news. Invariably they wasted his time. "In Fredericksburg, seek out an adjutant. He may be able to help you. Move on."

The wagon rumbled. Soon they encountered another delay while they eased through a rain-washed gulch. In the wait, the driver stepped off to urinate. She noticed a farmhouse shack on the right. Climbed down from the bed, ran around to the building's rear, and peed out of the men's sight. When she returned, a unit of infantry marched by, the ranks having nothing better to do than to stare at her.

The driver seemed to take a liking to her. Handed her a dry square of white muslin. "My wife gave me this kerchief I don't nary use. Help keep your head dry."

His dialect was thick, and she strained to understand him. "Thank you," she said.

"You're welcome."

She tied on the kerchief. "What do they call this road?"

"Call it the Plank Road. Why not just say the *long* road? Or the *bumpy* road?"

Had she heard him right? Sounded like sarcasm.

He twisted in the seat. "Where'd you begin your journey?"

"Richmond. And you?"

"Been movin' so often, can't tell where I started. Left Culpeper yesterday."

"Where are you headed?"

"Can't say that neither. Someplace to put a line 'gainst McClellan, or whoever took McClellan's place. Heard they swapped him with another fella."

She wanted to ask him whether he was a slave or a freedman, and how he'd come to work for the Confederate army. Instead, because Holland wished to know, she asked, "Where did you cross the Rapidan River?"

"At the Raccoon Ford. Or so they say—all these places look the same to me." He went on about his home in southwest Virginia below the Shenandoah. Big Lick, the name. Featured infinite hills, ridges, and wildlife. She struggled to comprehend his words. Interpreted that the war had taken away Big Lick's men but had yet to despoil the land. "Beautiful spot," he said wistfully.

Now a poem came to her:

Short of the Rapidan

We speak in different voices
You whose scarf I wear
And I, passenger
Your words reach my ear
As if through a wall
Without a door
Dare I hope for other

Than misinterpretation?

Helplessly I am borne
The wagon drawn by nags
Along the road of planks
And soldiers in ranks
Marching in the rain
On a gray November day
Headed the wrong way
With Longstreet's army.

My friend alongside
His convalescence broken
In clothes sodden
Upon our horse hard ridden
Changed, his mind in upheaval...

The wagon bumped hard in a washout. The unfinished poem fled.
The soldiers had to push the wagon through. She tried to balance atop the sliding crates. On the planks, the ride steadied. More rain. Damp wool might keep a person warm; sopped wool did not, and her shawl and blanket were. Her hair too, despite the kerchief; dripping strands pasted her forehead. She hugged her arms around her knees, and her forearm rubbed against something in her dress pocket—the last piece of candy she'd kept for John. Immediately she ate it.

Left side hulked a grand mansion, two and one-half stories, seven chimneys poking from the roof. On the pillared porch, white and black women watched the column go by. Beyond opened a wide crossroads where signs pronged. One read, 'Ely's Ford.' A painted burlap swatch warned, 'High water, ford closed!'

A second sign angled the same way read, 'United States Ford.' Odd name during a war of succession, she thought. No marker the ford was closed.

A third sign announced, 'Fredericksburg, 10 miles.'

The plank road stabbed ahead.

"Swan will have tacked his posters throughout the town," she told Holland.

He bit his lip. Every mile brought them closer to being recognized and arrested.

She said, "What about the United States Ford? Is it open?"

He seemed to ruminate, balancing the perils. No safe choices availed. Finally he said, "Let us find out."

"Driver, please stop so I can get on the horse."

The wagon halted, and she mounted from the bed. The two of them had blended with the column's details. Now scores of soldiers trained their eyes on the man and woman together on the horse.

She went to untie the kerchief. The driver waved his hand. "You keep it," he said.

For a hundred yards they trotted against the column before hooking northward at the intersection, abandoning the plank highway. Ahead stretched a muddy trough, half pond, half road, ribboned between the thickest woods she'd ever seen, the branches as disheveled as Hock's brows. If they spotted trouble, they couldn't simply dart into these gnarled woodlands to get away.

They reached a road fork and more signs. The left pointed to Ely's Ford, the right to the United States Ford. She asked, "How far?"

"Four miles."

The horse's hooves sprayed clay, muddying her lower legs and dress. The road curled eastward. Gaps opened, and she discerned a gray shimmer in the far distance.

She pointed. "What is that?"

He peered. "The confluence where the Rapidan joins the Rappahannock, I think."

The road dropped into the river valley. A large structure ahead—she guessed a mill or mine—on a field that descended toward the water. Riding closer, she noticed tents and soldiers. The soldiers had piled stones into parapets, and behind them they walked stooped over, their backs and knees bent.

He stopped.

She asked, "Why do they stoop so?"

"They must be within rifle range of the enemy."

Vaguely visible on the Rappahannock's opposite bank, another parapet, and men in blue uniforms.

The Federal army is across the river!

Over his shoulder he said, "This place is guarded. I do not think we can cross here."

"What should we do?"

"What *can* we do, except to watch for another ford?"

"What if we don't find one?" She did not think they would.

"If we reach no crossing short of Fredericksburg, we can linger until night, then look for a way."

The hopefulness she'd heard heretofore in his tone had fled.

A side road angled eastward toward Fredericksburg, and they followed. Late afternoon, the day fading, and the low overcast afforded scant distinction between sky and land. The trees ran sparse by the Rappahannock, and she caught the ripples on the swollen surface. How maddening, to veer so close and be unable to cross. She recalled Bookman in the shallows of the Rapidan, whose waters mixed here.

If I go, will you go with me?

You'll have to ask me closer to the time.

Now was the time. She could not ask him, for he was gone, her brother in life, murdered because he'd talked back to Confederates. Jerome too, whom she'd treated scornfully. Her head drooped at the memory.

Minutes along, they sighted activity. A long canvas tent nudged to the road, the flaps rolled up. One side was full of fodder bales, the other of crates. Cooking smells. Horses hitched to trees. By the crates gathered soldiers, perhaps to get food or coffee. Voices and laughter. The place seemed to portend no danger. He said, "A provender's tent. We'll ride past. Pretend we know where we're going."

They gaited forward. Men who loitered by a field stove turned to look. They wore spurs and carried metal cups of coffee or soup. The horses must belong to them. A fellow balanced a tin plate. His gaze focused on Holland and Anna. He said something, and the rest of them froze and went silent. On their faces, lines of puzzlement.

One with his back to the road now turned around.

Captain Swan held a cup. His eyes locked with hers.

Anna gasped.

The cup fell from Swan's grip and clanged on the ground.

Holland pivoted, flicked the reins. Cut sharp right and raced toward the United States Ford.

A pistol fired.

They galloped, threading the sparse trees. Ahead, two sentries who'd heard the shot stepped in front and tipped their rifles.

Revolver drawn, Holland aimed back and forth at their foreheads. "Discharge your rifles into the ground! Quickly!"

The soldiers depressed their barrels to the ground and pulled the triggers. A crescendo and dirt flew. "Drop them and step away!"

They did. He spun the horse around. And around again. Through the woods a hundred yards back, she saw men mounting horses. The other way, Confederate pickets stirred, having heard the shots, not sure what they signified.

She said, "How did Swan anticipate we'd come here?"

"Just our bad luck. That man is pernicious." He twisted to see her face. "If we are to try, we must go now. I don't know if we will make it. If we do, we will be very lucky."

"Take me across," she told him.

He tightened the reins. "Lean forward, grip to my belt and hold close against me." A shudder flowed from the horse, who, sensing an impetus in the rider, tensed his muscles.

You are a cavalry horse at last!

Holland pressed his heels and flicked the reins.

The horse shot forward like a bullet, hooves churning orange dirt. In ten seconds they'd gone past the mine building and between soldiers who stared at them dumbfounded. Men pointed. Others held their rifles ready, but not having been ordered to shoot, did not.

The horse leapt a stone wall. Wind coursed through Anna's hair. The kerchief she'd tied over her head blew away. Never had she ridden so fast.

Behind them, pistol shots.

He leaned over the horse's neck, and she pressed against his back. Glanced behind at four riders trailing at a desperate pace. The hat blew off Swan's distinctive red hair. He raised his pistol and fired, and she heard the bullet's strange hiss sailing past. At full gallop, and with a single rider on each horse, the pursuers were gaining. In a few seconds, long before they reached the river's far side, the riders behind would be in deadly range.

I've gotten the both of us killed.

- 20 -

_____

Onset of grainy twilight. Shilling had repositioned his desk and chair outside on a plateau behind a rock mound from where he could observe the line. The carpenter Muxon had crafted the desk to be portable, the legs and top foldable, drawers to hold papers. In the dusk, the colonel barely could make out his own writing. He had forbidden lanterns within sight of the line, so he must take his paperwork inside the barn—the rules he levied on the men applied equally to him. For the same reason, he'd left behind the gilt-framed photograph of his wife and daughter. He cherished the picture so fondly his heart ached. He might have indulged himself; he didn't. His men did not did not have room in their packs for mementos.

Shots from across the river.

A shrill whistle.

Lifting his head from the report he'd been squinting at, he relinquished the pen. Strode toward the line, tightening his pistol belt, pressing on his hat.

Captain Bedford, the line officer, crouched at the parapet and waved his arm to bring riflemen to their positions. Into Schilling's view came the terrain beyond, and immediately he spotted riders racing toward him. He shouted, "Send me Grunwald!"

Grunwald, the regiment's best marksman and posted with the sharpshooter's squad, scampered, his assistant trailing with the second rifle. "Sight on the lead rider," Schilling told him. To the officer of the line, "Rifles ready! Do not fire until you hear Grunwald's shot. On that, ranks fire."

"Aim, hold all fire until the first shot, from here!" Bedford shouted the command, and the lieutenants echoed.

Murmurs from the line. What was happening? The lead rider charged at full pace, and behind galloped four horsemen in a cluster. The pursuers fired pistols at the rider in front.

Schilling trained his spyglass on the lead rider. Not rider—_riders_! A man and a woman together.

They are escaping across the river!

"Grunwald, shift aim to the riders in pursuit. Bedford, pass the command!"

"Yes sir."

Along the Union line, the soldiers, seeing what was happening, began to yell for the lead rider. The chasers' shots resounded. A soldier yelled, "Come on!"

"Keep low there!" Schilling shouted. Even as he did, he rose and waved his hat in an arc, bellowing, "*Ride to me!*"

The lead horse splashed into the river, tacking against the current. One hundred yards, seventy, fifty. The animal strained forward, ascending in the shallows, picking up speed. But the chasers had closed the distance. They fired, and the lead horse crumpled and pitched, sending the two riders tumbling, the fabric of the woman's skirt momentarily blooming. The four pursuers came on, and the one with red hair pointed his pistol and shot the man. He fired again. And he rode over to the woman and took aim.

"Shoot that son of a bitch!" growled Schilling.

Grunwald's rifle barked, and the red-haired head exploded.

An instant later, the Federal line erupted, and the river around the Confederate horsemen spouted a hundred founts. The three riders and four horses collapsed in the maelstrom. The current curled the bodies downstream.

The enemy pickets opened fire. Bullets peppered the Federal line.

"Party of volunteers!" Schilling dashed down the slope, with Bedford and Grunwald and several other men close at his heels. Bullets whizzed past. He splashed into the shallows that reached to his calves. "Grab them!" he shouted. They gripped the shot lead rider and the woman by the arms and legs and half-dragged, half-carried them back, as the bullets whipcracked and exploded mud. "Hurry, hurry!"

The rescue party scrambled upward. His regiment's concentrated volleys suppressed the Confederates. Behind the parapet, none of his soldiers injured, thank God, Schilling ordered them to bear the man and woman to the barn. He called for the medics, who quickly converged.

The woman was bruised and stunned, not seriously hurt.

The man was in grievous condition. Shot twice, he lay with his right thigh at an ugly angle, the bone shattered.

Schilling put the two under guard. Headed again to the line and imposed one-hundred percent vigilance in case the Rebels planned to follow this bizarre escapade with another. Nearly dark. He verified his soldiers were loaded and ready. Ordered a signal flagged to Captain Oulette's cavalrymen, who, having heard the shots, had charged to the flanks. By the time he'd retraced his steps, the semaphores waved, and he made out the acknowledging strokes.

Captain Bedford appeared. "Sir, the woman wishes to speak with the commanding officer."

Through his spyglass, Colonel Schilling gleaned stillness across the field. An ominous feeling.

"I shall be there in a minute."

* * *

He finished penning Anna Van Meer's tale. Folded the report and applied a dispatch seal. Now he summoned Private Lansdale. "You've been to the telegraph post in daylight. Can you get there in the dark?"

"Yes sir," said Lansdale.

"I do not mean to offend—I realize you are a religious man—yet I must ask you to run like you have escaped from the gates of hell. Deliver this to the telegraph operator to send at once. Then wait for a reply—maybe hours—and run it back. Understand?"

"Yes sir."

"Your rifle will slow you down." He unholstered his Colt. "Do you know how to use this?"

"Yes sir."

"Leave your rifle here." He presented the sidearm. "Go."

Revolver in hand, Lansdale commenced his run. Wagon wheels had gouged the road, and he lurched and stumbled in the ruts he couldn't see. His eyes adapting, he distinguished gradations showing the ruts and the spaces between, and he accelerated. Arched his back. *Run like you have escaped from the gates of hell.* He pictured the devil and his evil hounds chasing, the silver tracery of heaven afar. He pumped his arms. His legs flew. The air ballooned his cheeks and rushed into his lungs.

The incident's first account, telegraphed to brigade headquarters and forwarded to General Burnside's staff, attracted little notice. The general's junior staff did not judge the information of merit to call to their commander's attention. Not until an hour later did an astute colonel read the message, grasp its significance, and notify Burnside. The headquarters thereupon relayed the report to Washington. A tapping key in the War Department annex clacked. A clerk copied the words to paper for messengers to carry to General-in-Chief Henry Halleck and to Secretary of War Stanton.

Thirty minutes later, another messenger ran a copy to the White House.

The response came at midnight. Lansdale sprinted it back to the regiment. The priority was urgent. The Southerners—the woman Anna Van Meer and the wounded Captain John Holland—were to be escorted without delay to Falmouth, Virginia, then eastward to the boat landing at Aquia Creek on the Potomac, where a riverboat would wait to bear them to Washington. The telegram added that a senior officer and medic must accompany them on the journey. An official party would meet them at the destination.

Reading the telegraph, Schilling exclaimed, "A senior officer? How many senior officers do they think we have?"

Major Turgess studied the telegram. "Sir, the order comes from the army staff. You *must* go."

Schilling reflected on Anna Van Meer's story. An extraordinary account. Even so, the instructions astonished him. "We shall take the medical wagon. Get everyone loaded. I'll ride with the wagon. Is the cavalry lieutenant close by?"

After the incident, Captain Oulette had assigned the lieutenant to serve as liaison through the night. Schilling now coordinated with him for a cavalry escort.

They left at two A.M.. The ride to Falmouth lasted an hour and a half. At a sentry post, a lantern illuminated an officer who said, "Where is Colonel Schilling?"

"Right here."

"Sir, I'm Highsmith, Captain of Engineers. Is your party complete?"

"As you can see."

"You may relinquish your cavalry escort—we are within the army lines. I shall lead you to the Potomac. Please follow me."

Captain Highsmith mounted his horse, and the wagon trailed him into Falmouth town. A severed rail bridge groped toward the far shore where Fredericksburg's rooftops carved leaden silhouettes. The party veered the opposite way alongside the tracks of the Richmond,

Fredericksburg, and Potomac line, threading woods and crossing hills that flattened to marshes. In the chill darkness, hard not to doze. Schilling struggled for alertness, for they were quite isolated, though Captain Highsmith proceeded with no apparent worries for their safety. Ahead, syncopated hammering resounded ever louder. They reached the bank of a wide stream where lanterns dappled a hundred shirtless men laboring to repair a rail bridge, ripping away the burned timbers and nailing on the fresh. Other figures rimmed a bonfire amid the smells of sweat and coffee.

Highsmith dismounted. "This is the Potomac Creek bridge the Rebels burned. Soon we will restore the bridge and the rail line from the Potomac River to Falmouth. A massive enterprise we pursue around the clock. I suggest that everyone save for the driver and wounded man descend to walk."

Two inventions had reshaped warfare. One was the telegraph, whose instantaneous communication had produced tonight's journey. The second was the railroad. For an army approximating one hundred fifty thousand men, supplies relied upon the tracks. The cross-laid planks rattled under their footsteps, Highsmith treading first and leading his horse, followed by the wagon bearing Captain Holland. Last came the woman, Schilling, and the medic.

Beyond the Potomac Creek they rolled to a second rail bridge and further repairs underway. They crossed, and into view opened the Aquia Creek estuary. Lanterns and fire barrels spread an orange effluence over a panorama of tents and crates. On the rails reposed a locomotive, its stack smoking.

Schilling had harbored doubts the boat would be held for them as promised, yet here waited a steamer 100 feet in length, the paddle wheels arcing in the glow. The medic and driver stretchered Holland aboard to a windowed cabin. The boat's crew had stoked an iron coal stove that radiated heat.

The ship's master arrived. He appeared to be a mulatto, and for the occasion he had donned a blue uniform jacket over a grease-streaked shirt, lending the impression he readily plied his sinews to the labor. "Colonel, welcome aboard. You and the lady can ride in the passenger space above."

"I'm staying," said Anna. In the same muddy dress she'd worn when the horse was shot from under her, her face, hands, and forearms scraped and bruised, she nonetheless emanated a certain authority. Nobody argued.

"I'll remain with them," said Schilling. "Let's get underway quickly, please."

Most of the crewmen were black. The pilot shouted instructions; the sailors unmoored the ropes, leapt aboard, and dashed to their stations. An aspect of pandemonium prevailed until the paddle wheels churned briny water and the ship nosed into the Potomac. Anna held Holland's hand, and every few minutes, she leaned to feel his faint breath. The two bullets had passed through him, one at his shoulder, the other his side, and the medics had bandaged the holes. They had cut away his soaked clothes and wrapped him in blankets. Occasionally he stirred, and his eyelids fluttered, but the morphine overcame his restlessness. She was grateful he slept, for she did not wish him to learn about his leg. Not yet.

She recalled the poem she had written late in the night of his fever. Now she whispered to his ear:

"The Peace of the Ages

The peace of the ages be upon you, sir
Let your visions fade
Of meadows shorn from cannonade
Of the wrecks of men in fresh earth laid
Look at me, sir, and let it go.

Find yourself in the still of the eve
In a righteous land
Where black and white work hand in hand
Where folks aren't owned or must abscond
Look at me sir, and let it be."

She drifted in and out of sleep. Colonel Schilling covered her with a blanket, and she leaned against the cabin wall, her legs tucked. Her shoes had stayed on despite her tumble from the poor horse. The medic stoked the coal stove, and she felt the warmest she had in days.

The sun blushed the cabin glass. They pushed north with the incoming tide, and to her eye the shoreline blurred past. A black crewman served her a plate of eggs, fried potatoes, and coffee. She wrapped her fingers around the tin cup. A promise kept.

She asked the crewman, "Where are we?"

"That's the Fairfax County shore. My home town Alexandria port's coming up in about half an hour." His speech evinced little of the black vernacular. He explained he'd been free all his life and worked aboard ships, and he knew the Potomac like the back of his hand. Recently, ex-slaves had joined the crew, and they held the lowest rank, titled 'boy.' He added, "I can't hardly understand what they say."

At Alexandria she stepped to the rail to observe. The port's scale and industry amazed her, far exceeding what she'd witnessed in Richmond. Crowding the piers, ships of all varieties, their decks piled with supplies. A steamboat shoved a barge bearing two entire boxcars. Vast railroad stocks—ties, rails, train wheels, and engine parts—mounded the docks. Thousands of crates, some open and full of produce—*apples!*—and massive burlap sacks stamped 'COFFEE' that must weigh a hundred pounds. On flatcars, countless forage bales. Men by the piers noticed her and waved. All her life she had waved to men on boats. Today, she waved to the shore.

The helpful tide abated, and the rain-glutted Potomac bashed against the ship's bow and flecked the windows. She could not preserve her balance without holding on. The medic helped keep Holland from sliding on the floor.

Late morning by the time the boatmen flung their mooring ropes to catchers at Washington D.C.'s 6th Street wharf. She spotted a hospital coach, green trimmed in red, copper-framed lanterns pendant, the sides lettered *The Douglas Hospital, Washington D.C.*. They disembarked and loaded the stretcher aboard. She climbed in with the medic. The colonel rode atop.

The coach windows framed the city bleak. Up from the wharf ambled soldiers whose shouldered rifles swung everywhere. A pedestrian woman caught an errant rifle barrel against her cheek; her knees buckled and she slumped to the ground. Shouts, and at once gathered a crowd so numerous they blocked the coach. Uninterrupted, a music grinder played while his partner in harlequin gamboled and juggled wooden balls. Pennies plinked in a hat. Soldiers lined up in front of sutler wagons that dispensed pan-cooked pastries, their bottoms burned as black as the coal smoke in which Washington's roofs appeared to float. Fire barrels issued distorted waves, the sparks spewing skyward into the obscurity. Surrounding the barrels, men with soot-smudged faces—she could not tell if they were blacks or whites—rubbed hands over the vermilion flames. Where 6th Street grafted onto Maryland Avenue, the wagon veered. Seemed impossible that only nine weeks had passed since another hospital coach had delivered Captain John Holland to her house. Never had she imagined that all the foundations of her life would crumble and her emotions shift to the coach's patient.

Broad mud tongues licked over the cobblestones, and the coach slowed to grind over. They skirted the U.S. Capitol Building. Through breaks in the haze she viewed the capitol's unfinished top—meant to be a dome, she guessed—a confluence of open girders and a jutting object resembling a giant pump handle. Northward the ride smoothed, and the surroundings altered to sparse buildings amid empty spaces with flooded ponds or camps with aisled canvas tents too numerous to count. On I Street, they paralleled a brick wall until they reached a four-story building she perceived was three grand townhouses joined. The ambulance stopped.

A young-looking man, straight blond hair groomed, gold-rimmed spectacles magnifying pallid eyes, stepped forward. When he spoke, the impression of youth vanished, his authority eminent. "I am Dr. Bell, Chief Surgeon of the Douglas Hospital."

"I'm Colonel William Schilling. This is Anna Van Meer. I must inform you, Doctor, that these two people are under military escort, and my orders are to watch them at all times."

"And I inform *you*, Colonel, that this hospital falls under the exclusive authority of the Surgeon General, and your orders have no authority here. The patient will come with me to the operating chamber, without your escort."

Anna asked, "May I accompany the patient, Doctor Bell?"

"The regulations prohibit. This is a professional clinic, the best in the country, and visitors may not attend surgery. We apply these strict practices for the patients' benefit."

Bearers from the ambulance and two from the hospital took the stretcher's corners. Alongside, Dr. Bell lifted the blanket and studied the leg. To Anna, "I must tell you this is grave."

"Do you have a Banderton box?" she asked.

"What is that?"

"An apparatus to mend broken legs, such as they use at the Chimborazo Army Hospital in Richmond."

Dr. Bell blinked. "I regret we have no such device."

"Then I doubt this is the best clinic in the country, doctor."

* * *

Anna and Colonel Schilling sat in the waiting parlor. She could not relax for fear of what was happening with John. Nonetheless she noticed the parlor's elegance: the wallpaper, embroidered curtains, and fine furniture. On the wall hung an oil painting depicting a strikingly beautiful woman, her white dress resplendent. There were nuns about—they seemed to administer the hospital—cloaked in whispering habits and scarves over their hair. When one of them brought tea, Anna asked, "Who is she in the painting?"

"That's Adele Cutts Douglas," said the nun. "The widow of Senator Douglas. This is her home she donated to the army."

In the mid-afternoon, Dr. Bell descended into the nearby chair. He seemed to evaluate her to gauge how candidly he might speak. "We treated the bullet wounds, which are serious but by themselves manageable."

"By themselves?"

"With multiple injuries, adversity plays in concert. The leg, as I feared, shall have to be amputated, and weakened as he is from the gunshot wounds, I cannot assure you he shall survive. His fate will be in God's hands for a time."

"Why can't you mend his leg?"

"I have examined carefully. The evidence disallows. The bone is fractured in two places. Moreover, there are prior breaks—healed perhaps by benefit of the Banderton apparatus you mentioned. The original breakage probably was clean; the fresh is not, and no healed bone is the same as the original."

"Might you not at least wait, so he is stronger before you amputate?" The last word tasted like poison in her mouth.

"I will not mislead you. His life hangs like a wisp in the air, and if we wait, he shall drift away and be lost."

"And your skills, sir? Are you competent to accomplish this?"

"I assure you I am, and I shall do all within my power. Have no fear of that."

"How soon may I see him?"

"Hours, at a minimum. He will be under the influence of the ether anesthetic, which we are fortunate to have in ample supply. And we must let his shock recede."

When he left, Anna sobbed. Tears streamed down her face. "I asked him to bring me across. I am responsible for what happened."

Schilling gave her his handkerchief. "I think the men who chased you are the ones responsible."

"Colonel, thank you for your kindness. For me there is no denying. All my life I will remember. I *must*."

He perused her bruises, scrapes, and scabs, and he realized he understood little of what had happened to her.

She daubed her eyes, lowered the handkerchief. "I have a favor to ask. I wish to be outside for a while. I would like to walk."

"I must stay with you. My orders do not permit otherwise."

"Very well. If you can leave me the illusion of privacy, I would be grateful."

"I'll try."

They reached the gravel street beyond the clinic. The coal smoke drifted, a somber shroud. The puddles bore films of coal dust. The chill air bit, and Schilling pulled off his coat to drape over her shoulders. She regarded the Union-blue wool, the colonel's epaulets, deliberating, then said, "All right Colonel. But you shall be cold."

He stayed thirty paces behind as she strode southwest, clutching the coat's edges. Following I Street, she crossed New Jersey Avenue toward buildings two blocks away. At Massachusetts Avenue she veered toward the North K Street market. He noticed her startle at the stalls and wares stacked high, the heaps of coal people bought in bucketfuls. He hoped she would stroll through the market, to take her mind off her troubles. She continued past.

Blocks along Massachusetts rose a church, and she paused and stared at the facade before ascending the stairs and passing inside. Losing sight of her, he broke into a run, took the stairs quickly to the thick oak door left ajar, and pushed in. Dim candle light, no heat, the atmosphere damp. For a minute he thought he'd lost her. Soon his vision adjusted, and he spotted her in the front row. Carpenters had laid boards across the pew tops, and sawdust had replaced incense as the pervasive smell. He'd heard that Washington churches had donated their worship spaces to be improvised for hospitals, and he guessed such a conversion was underway here. In the rearmost pew, arms folded for warmth, he gazed over the boards to her outline in the candle glow. As far as he could tell, they were the only ones present.

*   *   *

In the pew, Anna sobbed. She could not stem the tears that patted onto the colonel's overcoat. From somewhere he watched, yet true to his word he'd left her this separation mimicking solitude. The church's quietness availed, and she cried freely, for Holland, for her father, for Bookman and Jerome and Sarah. For her life as it had been.

"John, I will never abandon you," she promised, her fists clenched. "Please do not abandon me. Stay on this earth."

She sat on a tarp spread to cover the pew, apparently to protect it from the construction. A scaffold framed the alter space where hung the statue of Jesus crucified, and she wondered whether religion, so long ignored, would reinstate with her. "I do not believe in you," she said, "but if you do exist, I thank you for bringing us across. Please use your power to help good men, and lead them through the struggle to the end of slavery and suffering."

She sat for what seemed a long time, until her tears no longer flowed, and she wiped her face with Schilling's handkerchief. She looked again at Jesus on the cross the candle flame weakly illuminated. Her breathing slowed, and without intending to she fell asleep, and the dimness of the church settled on her like a blanket, and dreams arose, of her house, of the faces of the people who had lived there, the peaceful murmur of the James River going by. But her dream had no grip in happiness and shifted to a darker place she could not identify, and she discerned tenuous shapes: the tracery of a ship's masts drifting in a storm; the silhouettes of men on horses, guns raised; of a severed leg, or seemingly severed, until she saw the leg was attached to a person, not a whole person, rather one wretched and deformed. She stared at the head, the neck writhing in agony, and thought at first the man was John. No, the face was not his, rather Captain Swan's, ashen and contorted, and she backed away. She perceived another form, not John either, instead, twisted upward in despair, Hock's face. Dread filled her, and she understood that the ground on which these grotesque figures lay was the floor of hell. In the dimness she saw no one else, and she ran, and she was grateful for the good shoes that saved the skin of her feet from touching the rotten soil. She panicked because she could not see John, and a light appeared ahead, and she wondered if she should flee toward the light without finding him, and she realized she needn't fear for him, for if indeed this were hell, he would not be here. No, he would not be here.

*　*　*

She awoke, and the light she'd seen in her dream was the church's feeble candle. The cold had stiffened her. In the patina, the statue of Christ.

How long had she slept?

She stood, scanned around. Shouldn't Schilling be in a corner or pew? Not seeing him, she hurried outside to the failing daylight sifting through the coal smoke. Must already be evening.

She thought, John might have died while she dozed.

Furious at herself, she set off toward the Douglas Hospital, past the market no longer busy, the coal mounds diminished from before. She strode as briskly as she could, her heels clicking. The hospital's rectangular silhouette rose in the distance.

Over her shoulder, no sign of Schilling. Two men in dark clothes, one on either side of the street, walked fifty paces behind. Strangely, they seemed to focus entirely on her.

How odd she must look in the army overcoat, she thought.

She pressed her steps along I Street to the brick wall, and opposite she spied another man, similarly in dark garb and a bowler hat, his gaze meeting hers. She tapped faster. Now, from behind a tree, a fourth mysterious sentinel emerged.

What was happening? Had these men come to arrest her?

By the clinic stood soldiers who had not been there before. They appeared alert. Warily she approached, expecting them to advance. They remained still; no one spoke. She passed the parked ambulance and through the gate. Toed up the Douglas mansion's steps and across the ochre foyer tiles to the waiting room. Here she came to several men, among them Colonel Schilling in his officer's tunic. He stepped toward her.

She slipped off the coat and passed it to him, her hands shaking. "Colonel, please tell me John is not dead."

"They shall inform you inside." He nodded toward the hallway.

She asked, "Who are these men?"

"Go in. He's waiting for you."

"He's… *waiting?*"

Unable to comprehend what Schilling meant, sensing something odd in his tone, she entered the hallway, her knees trembling, and ventured cautiously along. A doorway. The curtains had been drawn from the windows, no doubt so sunlight could enter, though at this hour the luminance seeped from gas lamps in whose cast she saw a bed paces away, and John's face, uncovered and sedate. And *alive!* On the bed's far side stood Dr. Bell, watching her.

And on the near side, a tall man alone.

He turned. "You must be Anna," he said softly.

The furrows of Abraham Lincoln's face seemed etched in charcoal. Dark, slightly wavy hair topped his wide forehead, and his eyes rested compassionate and wise. She felt her fears recede, and without thinking, she gave a slight curtsy.

"How is he?" She took a step toward John.

"Grave but stable," said Dr. Bell from across the bed.

Anna breathed, and the air was full of smells, of camphor and gas and astringents. She was in a city she hadn't visited before, among people she'd not imagined to meet, except for John, and she knew that what had been normal for her in her life had fallen irretrievably into the past, and that every turn led toward things unknown. In this strange place, Lincoln seemed almost familiar to her—his face from newspaper sketches had been in her memory the longest. She said, "Those must be your guards outside."

"They are not for me, but for you. And they shall protect you for as long as need be."

"I don't understand."

"I am, and this nation is, deeply grateful for your father's sacrifice. He saved our army with the information he sent, at enormous risk to himself. The danger may follow you."

"There were others who helped him."

"And I hope you too will help us carry on their work."

She felt she should ask her father's permission, yet he was not here, only the President, who sought her help. "Of course, sir."

Lincoln smiled.

She said, "Do you know what happened to him?"

"He is in the custody of the Rebels. We've heard nothing more."

Her eyes wanted to swell in tears, but she had cried all she could. She summoned another breath and felt herself slump. The President stepped forward and gently laid his broad palm on her shoulder, bought her against him where she settled her head against his wool coat.

"My poor dear," said Lincoln.

In the bed, Holland stirred. His eyelids fluttered, and now they opened to what seemed at first incomprehensible, then altogether implausible. He stared for a minute, looked up, and here was a youthful doctor in gold-rimmed spectacles. In the doctor's expression, the same astonishment that Holland felt.

Holland flicked his gaze. Could this be what it appeared?

"You must rest," the doctor said softly.

Cognizant of immense pain, Holland kept it at bay. Thoughts of his own condition he fended away too, for they were full of fear, and he didn't wish to be afraid, not yet, for just one thing mattered—Anna was safe.

In the gaslight he beheld her. His perusal was momentary, for a weight seemed to tug at his eyelids, drawing him into sleep.

Before he drifted, a smile crimped the corners of his mouth.

The End

About the author:

Jeff Wallace lives with his family in southwest Virginia. His prior novel, *The Man Who Walked Out of the Jungle*, is an historical thriller set in 1970 Saigon.

www.ingramcontent.com/pod-product-compliance
Lightning Source LLC
Chambersburg PA
CBHW020239180626
46810CB00006B/2267